ALL WOUNDS

Published by Mundania Press
Also by Dina James

*Light in a Dark World**

*Time Heals: A Stranger Things Novel**

(*Forthcoming)

All Wounds

Dina James

All Wounds Copyright © 2011 by Dina James

All rights reserved under the International and Pan-American Copyright Conventions. No part of this book may be reproduced or transmitted in any form or by any means, electronic or mechanical including photocopying, recording, or by any information storage and retrieval system, without permission in writing from the publisher.

The scanning, uploading and distribution of this book via the Internet or via any other means without the permission of the publisher is illegal, and punishable by law. Please purchase only authorized electronic editions, and do not participate in or encourage the electronic piracy of copyrighted materials. Your support of the author's rights is appreciated.

Warning: The unauthorized reproduction or distribution of this copyrighted work is illegal. Criminal copyright infringement, including infringement without monetary gain, is investigated by the FBI and is punishable by up to 5 years in federal prison and a fine of $250,000.

This is a work of fiction. Names, characters, places and incidents either are the product of the author's imagination or are used fictitiously, and any resemblance to any actual persons, living or dead, events, or locales is entirely coincidental.

A Mundania Press Production
Mundania Press LLC
6457 Glenway Avenue, #109
Cincinnati, Ohio 45211-5222

To order additional copies of this book, contact:
books@mundania.com
www.mundania.com

Cover Art © 2011 by Niki Browning
Healer's Mark © 2011 by Becky Hitchin
Edited by Skyla Dawn Cameron

Trade Paperback ISBN: 978-1-60659-276-2
eBook ISBN: 978-1-60659-275-5

First Edition • October 2011

Production by Mundania Press LLC
Printed in the United States of America

10   9   8   7   6   5   4   3   2   1

DEDICATION

For Warren

You read even my most fanciful tale with the utmost seriousness.

I miss you, Daddy.

ACKNOWLEDGEMENTS

This book wouldn't have been possible without so many people. If I forget anyone, I apologize now. I should probably thank my mother first thing. Hi, Mom! Thank you for um...stuff.

Next, thank you to the namesakes of this novel—the real Becky, Robin, and Amy for the encouragement, tea and inspiration. I threatened to name the characters of this novel after you, and so I have.

Thank you to Lilahel, Sherrilyn Kenyon, Jacqueline Carey, Jean Auel for the same. Thank you to Lili, Skye, Audry and David, and Ilona and Gordon for things they probably don't even know they've done.

Thank you to Valtinen for too many things to list.

A huge thank you to the Windsor House of Tea and her staff. Though you are no more, you are deeply missed, and this novel is in part in existence because of you. Thank you for the time, the atmosphere, the quiet, and of course, the tea. I couldn't have done this at all without vast amounts of your tea, both at the shop and here at the house.

Thank you to the long defunct Wannabes and Wish-They-Hads (AKA "Waiting For Bill Honl"). I keep my promises.

Thank you to Trisha, who is solely responsible for me even attempting a young adult story, let alone a novel, and for giving me a shot. Thanks also to Froggies in the Timber-Batts for the chips and the fire.

A HUGE thank you to my editor of awesome, Skyla Dawn Cameron. Thanks for the week-long slumber party. We'll make it two next time. Thank you to Mundania Press for this opportunity and for being awesome. Thank you to Niki Browning for the awesome cover, and Becky Hitchin for the Healer's mark design used on the cover. It's awesome and I loved it so much I had it tattooed on my left arm. No, really.

And finally, my eternal gratitude to my husband, Rob. You've supported me through everything. Thank you for this as well. Thanks for the understanding, late night food, enduring my weird hours and facing the Dalek.

CHAPTER ONE

The only thing in the room that made any sort of noise was the clicking keys of the old computer keyboard, pushed—no, more like jabbed—by a very annoyed secretary.

Rebecca shivered and bit her bottom lip to keep it from giving her chill away. Was it always this cold in here, or did she just feel cold because she was sitting in the principal's office? She almost envied the black leather jacket of the smirking dark-haired boy sitting in the corner with his hands clasped behind his head. He caught her looking at him and leaned his plastic chair as far back as it would go against the wall.

Ryan Dugan. Of all the people to be in here when she was. Of course, when *wasn't* Ryan in the principal's office?

Rebecca dared a sideways glance at the girl with carefully styled-to-look-messy thick, blonde hair sitting beside her and risked a whisper. "Sorry."

The tapping of the computer keys stopped abruptly. Behind her metal desk the secretary leaned around the old yellowed computer monitor to glare at them with narrowed eyes. When she did the same to Ryan, the boy doubled over in a fit of totally fake—and very loud—coughing.

"Sorry," Ryan said after he sat back up. He slapped his chest a few times and cleared his throat as he smiled at the secretary. "Must be coming down with something."

Rebecca could tell the woman was convinced that Ryan's apology was about as sincere as his coughing had been.

"That's enough out of you, Mr. Dugan," the secretary said in a clipped, exasperated voice.

Ryan grinned at her and clasped his hands behind his head again as he kicked his chair backward to lean against the wall once more. He winked at Rebecca.

Rebecca hoped her cheeks weren't as red as they felt, and bit her top lip this time—hard—to keep from smiling. It had been pretty funny,

8 • DINA JAMES

the way the evil toad-faced woman had given Ryan a look that would have made Rebecca cringe, and Ryan just smiled back at her. Rebecca bowed her head, hiding her blue eyes—and her amusement—behind her straight, mouse-brown hair.

The principal's office door opening kept Rebecca from risking another illicit whisper to her friend.

"Miss MacDonnell? Miss Turnbull?"

The principal shook his head after gesturing to his doorway. "I have to say, girls—yours are two names I never thought I'd call until your commencement ceremony."

"Hey, I was here before they was!" Ryan spoke out as he got to his feet.

The scowl on his face made Rebecca wince. It was much darker than the one the annoyed secretary had given her.

"'Were'," the principal corrected as Rebecca and Robin got to their feet. "Which you'd know if you spend any kind of time in your English class, Mr. Dugan. And while you might have been here before these two ladies were, and you're likely to be here for most of the day, not to mention the day after that, as well as the following day, so I don't see any reason why I should make these nice girls wait out here any longer than they have to, especially with the likes of you. I'll deal with you later, so you just sit down and keep quiet. You're already in enough trouble as it is."

Ryan flopped back down in his chair, muttering curses only Rebecca was near enough to hear him say. She thought for a second he was going to start turning chairs over or ripping the bulletin boards off the wall, but he sat back down and assumed what seemed to be his careless pose, leaning back in his chair, his hands behind his neck, cradling his head. This time he closed his eyes and looked like he was going to sleep.

"Come on, girls," said Mr. Harris as he ushered them into his office. He looked almost sympathetic that they'd had to endure Ryan's company for as long as they had. In fact, he even apologized for it...before he sat them both down and gave them each a detention.

◆━━ ━◆━

"I'm so sorry, Ro, really," Rebecca apologized in a rush the moment she and Robin were out of the principal's office and on their way back to their respective classes.

"Rebecca, stop worrying so much," Robin replied, shaking her head. "So we got sent to the office. It could have been worse. One max detention? It could have been a week's worth, or mopping the cafeteria floor, or—Rebecca? Are you even listening to me?"

"What?" Rebecca asked, distracted. "Sorry I thought I..."

"Thought what?"

She could have sworn she'd seen some little brown dude in rags—like one of those goblin things from *Labyrinth*—peeking into the girl's bathroom. She'd been seeing a lot of weird stuff lately and was starting to wonder if she wasn't starting to lose her mind like her nana. As far as she knew, what Nana suffered from wasn't catching, but the doctors weren't even really certain what form of mental disorder Nana had, so maybe it was or ran in the family or something. It would explain a whole lot if it did.

Rebecca shook her head. "Never mind. It's nothing. I'm just tired. Algebra is getting to me."

"Obviously," Robin said, rolling her eyes. "You've got to find a way to get more sleep. Maybe you should call—"

"No!" Rebecca interrupted, almost shouting before she remembered to keep her voice down. "I mean...sorry. No. I'm not going to call anyone for anything. It's okay, really. Just...just a bad patch."

"But what if it isn't?" Robin asked. She put a hand on her friend's shoulder. "What if...what if this is what it's going to be like, from now on?"

"Well." Rebecca's voice cracked over the word. She swallowed hard. "Well, then I guess I'll be getting to know Ryan Dugan pretty well."

"Everything in the universe forbid," Robin muttered. "That's the last thing you need."

"Thanks for being there, Ro," Rebecca said, changing the subject. "You didn't have to stick up for me in Wilson's class this morning. If you'd treat me like everyone else has the sense to, you wouldn't have gotten into trouble with me. First grade was a long time ago."

"And I'll never stop being your friend, so forget about it." Robin gave Rebecca a big smile and a hug. "You were there for me when I needed you. I'm just glad I can return the favor...sort of. Dad's going to have a fit, and let's not even talk about Mom."

"Just blame me," Rebecca said as she gave a little shrug. "They'll pity me enough to hopefully spare you the lecture."

"As if." Robin sighed. "They'll probably be grateful they finally have something to actually lecture me about that they don't have to make up."

Rebecca laughed as she knew Robin wanted her to, said goodbye to her only sort-of friend, and went down the hall to her history class, already dreading the stares of her classmates as she interrupted the lecture she was seriously late for.

In addition to Rebecca's own detention, Mr. Harris had made her promise to apologize to Mrs. Wilson first thing tomorrow morning for mouthing off. Rebecca blushed again at the memory of snapping at her Spanish teacher. Maybe she really was crazy. Nana would have been mortified if she knew—

Rebecca stopped her thoughts cold. There was no way Nana was going to know about this. Ever, if Rebecca could help it. The one saving grace about Nana losing her mind was that she rarely noticed anything anymore, and didn't care about what she did.

Rebecca pushed the door open to her classroom, ignoring the stares of her classmates. She murmured an apology to Mrs. Iverson for her tardiness, handed the teacher her hall pass and took her seat, keeping her gaze focused on the floor as she tried hard not to hear the whispers around the room.

Mrs. Iverson called for everyone's attention. "Welcome back, Rebecca."

"Thank you, Mrs. Iverson," Rebecca replied without looking up from her desk.

"We're on page 212."

Rebecca took her history book out of her backpack and opened it.

"You're such a loser, Spot," a girl whispered behind her.

No need to look around or even guess who said that. Marla Thompson hadn't come up with a different insulting nickname for her since she thought of "Spot" back in fifth grade.

As usual, Rebecca ignored her and pretended to pay attention to the lecture she'd obviously interrupted as Mrs. Iverson continued.

<hr>

With a powdery crunch, the tip of the pencil lead snapped and slid out of the wood beneath her fingertips. It rolled across Rebecca's paper, leaving a gray smudge across the question she'd been attempting to answer.

She threw down her pencil in disgust.

"Now what?" Robin asked in a hushed whisper. She glanced around, looking for Mr. Nairhoft.

"My pencil is being stupid again. Besides that, I really don't think writing an essay about the Inquisition is going to help Nana remember where her bedroom is, or not to turn on the stove." Rebecca sighed, glaring at the offending question on her assignment. "I need to get home."

"Well, you should have thought of that before you went and mouthed off to Mrs. Wilson. At least make it look like you're working," Robin replied with another fast glance around for the detention room monitor.

"Shh!"

"Is there a problem here, ladies?" Mr. Nairhoft said in a smooth, arrogant voice. "Rebecca MacDonnell?"

"Sorry, Mr. Nairhoft," Rebecca apologized with a sweet smile. She really, really hated it when people used her name as though she'd done something wrong—to single her out. She had enough singling-out by her classmates every day. She didn't need teachers doing it.

"This is the third time today my pencil's broken," she went on. "And I got frustrated with it. I'm sorry to have caused a disruption. May I go sharpen it again? That might help it, at least through the end of detention, anyway."

Rebecca gazed up at the tall, rail-thin Mr. Nairhoft, hoping her repentant smile would earn her his permission. She had to fight not to giggle as she noticed the toupee he wore was listing to the left, threatening to slide off. She was already in enough trouble as it was without being disrespectful to another teacher.

"Does anyone have an extra pencil Miss MacDonnell can borrow?" Mr. Nairhoft asked loudly, turning around to view the detention hall, which was really just the cafeteria with the tables moved around. He'd glanced around so fast that he couldn't have even bothered to see if anyone had an answer to his question. "No?"

Mr. Nairhoft turned back to Rebecca with that stupid fake smile he always had plastered on his face.

A surprising flicker of anger surged through Rebecca and she had the overwhelming desire to slap that smarmy grin right off the detention monitor's face and send his cheap hairpiece flying. The thought was quickly followed by a sharp stab of hot pain from her middle, gone almost as quickly as it had come.

"Well—" Nairhoft began.

"Here," said a voice from the far table in the corner.

Rebecca turned around to see who had spoken, as did Robin and Mr. Nairhoft. Actually, everyone in detention swiveled their heads to see who was denying Mr. Nairhoft the occasion to be his usual unpleasant self.

Alone at a table in the corner, a boy wearing a familiar black leather jacket, faded jeans that were more gray than black and a t-shirt in the same condition waved a yellow pencil in the air.

"She can use this one." He said it almost defiantly, like he was daring Mr. Nairhoft to come over and take it himself.

"Mr. Dugan, surely you haven't completed *all* of your *long overdue* assignments," Mr. Nairhoft said, folding his arms.

"I've completed all I'm going to," Ryan replied, matching Mr. Nairhoft's tone exactly. He looked at Rebecca. "Want this?"

Rebecca nodded and stood up, her frustration with her own pencil, assignment, Mr. Nairhoft and detention forgotten as all the attention shifted from her onto Ryan.

"Rebecca, no," Robin hissed.

The boy's eyes went back to Mr. Nairhoft's as he held the pencil out for Rebecca to take.

Ryan Dugan wasn't just a bad boy, he was *the* bad boy. Everyone knew it. Always in trouble, always getting sent to the principal's office, always in detention. There was even a rumor that last summer he wasn't in summer school like he usually was, but in Mariposa Juvenile Detention Center three towns over for all sorts of different crimes.

The school rumor mill might not be right about much, but it was about the fact that Ryan never, ever gave anyone anything without expecting something in return.

Rebecca wondered why she was doing this. Why Ryan was even offering to help her. Whatever the reason, it felt good doing something Mr. Nairhoft couldn't really complain about, even though she was technically breaking the "don't leave your seat without permission" rule. Really she just wanted to see the look on Mr. Nairhoft's face as she took the pencil from Ryan with a quiet "thank you."

"Don't worry about it," Ryan said with a big grin. He winked—actually *winked*—at Mr. Nairhoft as he held onto the pencil before letting Rebecca take it. "Wouldn't want you to get in any more trouble, now would we?"

Rebecca shook her head, stunned, and hurried back to her seat where she sat down and bent her head over her assignment. She wondered if he knew what had landed her in detention. He *sounded* like he knew. Like he knew, and approved.

Her hair hid her eyes enough that it kept Mr. Nairhoft from seeing that she was secretly glancing at Ryan while she pretended to work. She felt immensely better. Ryan hadn't really been winking at her in the principal's office. Not *at* her, not like that. It was just one of his...*things* he did. To mess with people. He'd just winked at Mr. Nairhoft. It didn't mean anything.

The last thing in the world she wanted was the rumor going around that she had anything to do with Ryan Dugan. She had enough to deal with.

Rebecca's eyes went to the clock on the wall. Twenty minutes of detention left, then she could get home to Nana.

Ryan sat back, clasping his hands behind his head as he leaned against the wall while Mr. Nairhoft berated the boy. The detention monitor railed until he was blue in the face, said something about "another week's worth of detention!" and stalked away to harass another student he didn't think looked busy enough.

Ryan just grinned and caught Rebecca looking at him. He winked at her again.

She blushed and bent her head back over her paper, trying not to think about how much time she had left to sit there.

Or that Nana might be setting the house on fire.

Everyone else had someone to pick them up when detention was finally over. Even Robin, whose dad looked unhappy as she got in the car, even though he smiled at Rebecca.

Although Rebecca would have been perfectly happy taking the bus, Nana used to drive her to school and pick her up afterward, when Nana could still be trusted to drive. She hadn't driven in about three years. They'd taken away her license when Rebecca was thirteen. Not that Nana was old. There were plenty of drivers on the road older than her, but they could remember which house was theirs and which gear made the car reverse, and *where* they were going.

Nana couldn't.

The doctors called it "early onset senile dementia," but everyone knew that was just a polite way of saying that Nana was really too young to have Alzheimer's, even though it was obvious she did.

The school busses only ran before detention, not after, so that meant someone had to pick you up, or you had to walk home. Rebecca offered Robin and Mr. Turnbull a little wave of apology—after all, Robin wouldn't have gotten into trouble if it hadn't been for her—then shouldered her backpack and turned away to begin the long walk home before Mr. Turnbull could offer her a ride. There was just no way she wanted to be in the car with that much tension, or face any questions Mr. Turnbull was sure to ask, and she really needed to clear her head before getting to her house. Who knew what disaster would be waiting for her today. Whatever it was, it could wait just another few minutes. She needed to think, to get her head on straight so she would have the brains and strength to deal with the evening ahead.

The last thing Rebecca wanted was for Nana to catch on that she'd been in detention, and if she saw Mr. Turnbull dropping her off, Nana would possibly notice how late Rebecca was getting home.

That is, if Nana even noticed.

Rebecca didn't see any smoke coming from the general vicinity of her—well, *Nana's*—house, or hear fire engines, so it seemed safe to take a little time to breathe on the way home. With any luck, Nana was sitting in front of the television, brushing that evil white furball she called a cat.

Rebecca lost herself in her thoughts as she walked, remembering all the little "funny" things she and her nana used to laugh about, like Nana putting her keys in the fridge, or putting toilet paper on the paper towel rack. Then things had started to get scarier, like Nana leaving the gas stove on, or forgetting to turn off the water she was running in the stoppered sink for the dishes and flooding the kitchen.

I don't suppose I should complain too much to Robin about how much I have to do for Nana, Rebecca thought as she pulled her jacket tighter around her. *Because she could have given me up for adoption or something after mom and dad died, and she didn't.* Rebecca took a deep breath and let it out in a long sigh. *She looked after me all these years, so it's only fair I look after her now.*

A gust of wind swirled brittle leaves around her ankles, and Rebecca picked up her pace. October was cold, and it wasn't even Halloween yet. It was getting dark earlier and earlier these days, and when it got dark, it got colder. It was getting close to dinnertime and Nana needed to eat, and if Nana got hungry when Rebecca wasn't there, she'd try to cook for herself. Rebecca really didn't want to spend another night in the emergency room explaining to the doctors how Nana burned herself again.

"First time, huh?"

Rebecca stopped in her tracks. She knew that voice. It was the same one she'd heard earlier, in the principal's office and detention. So much for not being noticed.

Ryan Dugan stepped out from behind a tree that bordered the sidewalk she was on. He leaned against the trunk, brought a little box out of the pocket of his leather jacket and flipped open a small, silver—

"Is that a lighter?" Rebecca asked, scowling.

"Yeah," Ryan said, bringing a cigarette to his lips. "You got a problem with smokers?"

"Way to add to the bad-boy stereotype there," she said, raising an eyebrow at his tone. "How did you get ahead of me anyway?"

"Back alley," Ryan said, lighting his cigarette. "You know...the stereotypical bad-boy escape route." He pointed back over her shoulder. "If you cut through the gym and across the football field you can hop the fence and skip most of the block." He exhaled a cloud of smoke.

Rebecca fanned the cloud away with her hand and wrinkled her nose.

"Where do you get the money for those anyway?" she asked.

"What is this, the Spanish Inquisition?" Ryan countered. He put a hand to his chest at her look of surprise that he'd mentioned precisely what had been on her detention assignment. "Wow, how about that? I actually *do* learn in school. Hair-off loves Spanish history and gives all the first-timers that assignment, so unless you want to learn more about the Conquistadors and the Inquisition, I'd keep out of trouble."

She wanted to laugh at his use of the name everyone called the toupee-wearing Mr. Nairhoft behind his back, but thought it would only encourage him.

"What are you doing here, anyway?" She shifted her backpack to try to cover up her nervousness.

"You have my lucky pencil." Ryan held out his hand.

"Right." She rolled her eyes as she slung her pack off her shoulder, pulled out the pencil in question and offered it to him. "Good to know you cut through the gym, across the football field and jumped the fence just to rescue your pencil."

"Hey, this is my *lucky* pencil!" he defended, though Rebecca knew he wasn't being serious. He reached for it, and smiled a little as she held onto it for just a moment as he'd done to her when he'd loaned it to her in detention. "For this, I would even have rifled Hair-off's office...which is where I got the cigs."

Rebecca looked horrified. "You didn't!"

Ryan grinned. "These things will kill you, you know. I did him a favor." He was quiet for a long moment, seeming to debate something with himself before he went on. "So what'd you do?"

"What?" Rebecca asked stupidly. He'd gotten what he came for. Why didn't he just leave now? Then she remembered how Ryan always got something in return for whatever he'd given, and figured this must be the price she had to pay. Besides, it wasn't like the whole school didn't know what she'd done, and she told him so.

"I know what the rumor is," he said, curling his lip in disgust. "I want to know what you *really* did."

"I just...lost it," she admitted. "It had been a crappy morning and Mrs. Wilson's snarky comment just hit me wrong."

"I hear you told her to shut the hell up and mind her own fuckin' business." He took a long drag off the cigarette, stabbed it out against the trunk of the tree and put the remaining half back in the box. He tucked the box away in his pocket along with his silver lighter. "You really cuss out a prof?"

Rebecca shrugged. "Yeah. I'm not proud of it. It was just...my last nerve, you know?"

He shook his head and laughed. "Well, you looked like you were in a hurry, so..." Ryan gestured down the block as if to excuse her. "Stay out of trouble, huh? You got more than a smart mouth on you and don't belong in detention with Hair-off and the rest of us delinquents."

"How do you know? Maybe I'm just starting out on delinquency," she said before she could stop herself. "I hear all the cool kids are doing it."

Ryan laughed. "Yeah, and you're just being cool, aren't you? I've seen you around school, in class. You're about as cool as a jalapeño. See you around, Hot Stuff," he said, and turned to go.

She blushed. Yeah, one of the "cool kids", she wasn't. She was surprised he even knew who she was.

"I'm really sorry that whole pencil thing cost you another week with Mr. Nair...I mean Hair-off," she blurted as she shouldered her bag again.

He waved a hand. "Don't worry about it," he said, walking away. "He won't make it stick. Besides, some things are worth putting up with a little punishment."

Funny, that sounds just like what I was just thinking about Nana.

Rebecca hesitated for a moment as she watched him go, and then turned back toward home, hurrying even more now. She thought about Ryan, and what he'd said. He'd seen her around? Sure, they had a couple of classes together, but she wasn't the kind of girl anyone noticed. Just the opposite, really. The only reason anyone noticed her was because of Robin. Robin was the pretty one. The popular one. Robin getting busted was the talk of the school, as was the fact that it had been Rebecca's fault. Robin had only been trying to help.

That might explain how Ryan had known about her, but how had he known which way she was headed home afterward? She could have gone in any direction...unless he knew where she lived.

Rebecca shook her head, laughing at herself. He'd just guessed lucky or something. He didn't know where she lived.

Did he?

Rebecca forgot about Ryan, Mr. Hair-off, detention and Robin the moment she walked through the front door of her house. It looked like Nana was having one of her "good days." Rebecca was utterly relieved that everything seemed normal. Nana was sitting in her favorite chair, listening to some boring wildlife program on television, with Mishka on her lap. Mishka was a grouchy old cat—a big white fluffy thing that needed lots of brushing. If Nana remembered nothing else, she remembered to brush Mishka.

Not that Mishka minded if she was brushed three or four times a day. That cat loved attention, and would happily sit all day in Nana's lap being groomed. Only Nana's lap. Mishka hated Rebecca and the feeling was mutual. Mishka was *Nana's* cat.

Rebecca stowed her backpack in the foyer, and made sure the doors were locked and the stove off and everything else was safe before greeting her grandmother.

"Hi, Nana!" Rebecca said as she entered the living room.

"Oh, Rebecca, you're home," Nana said, smiling even though Rebecca knew she was confused. "Did you have a good day at school?"

Rebecca nodded as she always did. Even though today had been a horrible day at school, she still told her nana that everything was fine.

"Do you have a lot of homework?" Nana asked, earning a glare from Mishka as she stood up, emptying her lap of the cat.

"No, I got most of it done at school," Rebecca answered honestly. You could get a lot done in two hours of detention. "And I'm really hungry. How about some dinner? It's my turn to cook tonight."

Nana's brow furrowed. "I thought you cooked last night." She didn't sound at all sure.

Rebecca really didn't want to lie, but Nana in the kitchen was dangerous. Rebecca cooked every night now, but let Nana think that she only cooked sometimes.

"I was really craving some spaghetti at school," Rebecca hedged, steering the conversation away from who was going to do the cooking. "I thought that would be good for dinner. It's easy to make—I know how. Your show isn't over either, and I know the ones about wolves are your favorite. You can finish it while I go start dinner. I can do it, I promise."

"All right," Nana said with an absent nod and sat back down. Mishka jumped back up in her lap and Nana went back to brushing her. The cat glowered at Rebecca as if to say "Well? Go on, then. You're not needed here." Rebecca stuck her tongue out at the evil cat and went into the kitchen to start supper.

Half the dishes on the draining board had been wiped and put away when she heard an insistent pounding at the front door, like someone kicking it. Hard.

Rebecca scowled as she looked at the clock. It was nearly nine o'clock, and they never had visitors anymore. Nana's friends used to come by, when she could still remember who they were and what they'd been talking about. Rebecca never had friends over. Not that she had any besides Robin, but even if she did, she wouldn't have them over anyway. Other people just upset Nana now.

The noise came again, and Rebecca looked over her shoulder toward the bathroom door. Nana was in there getting ready for bed. Rebecca hoped she couldn't hear the racket.

Rebecca frowned and looked out the peep hole at the dark figure on the porch. She snapped on the porch light, and a blond head cringed away from the brightness with a grimace, but remained still. He kicked at the door again, and Rebecca could see why. The bloody, unconscious body of the dark-haired boy who had just that afternoon come to get his "lucky pencil" from her filled his arms.

CHAPTER TWO

"Turn off that light! Do you want the entire neighborhood to see us?" the boy out on the porch spat. "I don't know about you, but that's something I'd like to avoid!"

Rebecca had to agree. She flicked the porch light off before opening the door.

"That's better," the tall, skinny blond boy said. He waited a moment, standing there, looking at Rebecca and the interior of the house past her. When she just stared at him, he spoke again. "Well? Come on, Healer...I can't stand around here all night!"

"What—" Rebecca began.

"If friend ye are and healing ye seek, enter this place and my blessing keep!"

Rebecca whirled around at the sound of her nana's voice, stronger and clearer than it had been in years.

Nana was clad in her pink bathrobe and matching slippers. Her wet hair clung to her neck and shoulders.

The blond boy made a relieved noise of obvious gratitude and gave Rebecca an irritated glare as he shouldered his way past her. He strode into the living room with Ryan, muttering under his breath.

"My apologies, Lady Healer," the blond boy said as he reached Nana. "You were closest. The entrance was sealed or I would have used it—"

Nana's raised hand cut him off and she reached for a long-disused candle lantern sitting on the mantelpiece above the hearth.

Why would she grab that thing? It's just an old decoration. Something of Grandpop's?

"Take him up," Nana ordered, and followed the boy up the staircase. Nana didn't falter on the stairs as she usually did, leaving Rebecca standing dumbstruck in the open doorway.

Remembering herself, Rebecca closed and locked the front door before she ran up the stairs after her nana.

She just caught a glimpse of the hem of Nana's pink robe disappearing through the door at the end of the upstairs hall. That was a linen closet. What...?

Reaching the door, Rebecca found that the shelves of the linen closet weren't shelves at all. They were like those spooky fake bookcases in movies with haunted houses, now pushed aside to reveal a hidden passage.

Wow. She'd known this house was old and creepy—it had been in the family for generations—but a secret passageway? Really? That was just like something out of *Nancy Drew*! She hesitated only a moment before going through after her nana.

"My apologies, Martha," the blond boy said, his voice faint as it carried from within the hidden passage. His tone was almost reverent. Rebecca had never heard anyone speak that way, to her nana or anyone else. "I thought...her mark...she looked so surprised. Isn't she trained?"

Martha. The boy had called Nana "Martha." No one did that... except Nana's old friends, and that boy didn't look like he was even old enough to be out of school. He didn't go to *her* school though. That was for certain. She'd remember a guy that hot.

"She's not of age," she heard Nana reply. "Set him down so I can have a look. Do something about the bed, would you? It's been a long time since I've been up here."

Was that her *nana* talking like that? Like she'd suddenly...gotten better? Nana hadn't sounded that sure of herself in a long time, and certainly hadn't used that many words in that normal a way for more than three years.

"She's here, listening to us," the blond boy said. "Come on out, Acolyte. You may as well see what's going on firsthand."

Rebecca stepped out from the secret passage and into the light of the candle lamp that had somehow become lit. Funny, Rebecca couldn't remember if that thing had even had a candle in it.

Her nana barely looked at her as Nana bent to examine Ryan, peering into his eyes and glancing at his clothed body.

"His clothes," Nana ordered.

The blond boy's hand moved and Ryan's clothes vanished instantly, except his underwear. Rebecca's eyes widened and she flattened herself against the wall. The clothes just—what was going on?

Nana glanced at the blond boy, arching an eyebrow.

"Afford the boy *some* modesty, Martha," he said smoothly. "None of his injuries are around his middle."

"And you bit him as well!" Nana exclaimed with a gasp as she turned

Ryan's head toward her, revealing two small punctures on the boy's neck. She reached to touch them. "Sydney! Why would you...it *was* you...! Oh!"

Rebecca watched, fascinated, as Nana's eyes lingered on the second wound on Ryan's bleeding thigh, below the band of his briefs. Her fingers prodded the injury, and the unconscious Ryan cried out in protest.

"Rebecca, go into my room," Nana said in a voice that broached no argument. "In the closet, on the top shelf, you'll see a leather suitcase. The one I always told you was full of old pictures? Bring that here, and fast. Go!"

Too stunned to do anything but follow orders, Rebecca nodded and ran back to the passageway and down the stairs, returning quickly with the case Nana wanted. The whole time questions ran through Rebecca's mind. What had the blond boy—Sydney—meant when he said Nana was closest? Closest to what? And he would have used the entrance but it was sealed? What entrance? How was Nana acting like her old self, *and* as though this kind of thing happened every day? Entering the hidden room again, Rebecca passed the case to her nana.

"Thank you," Nana said in that same, calm voice. She reached for the case and opened it, pulling out various things out as she spoke again to Rebecca.

"Go downstairs and bring me the two big pots, filled with water. The temperature doesn't matter. Sydney will help. Won't you, Syd? And Sydney? See to the portal seal and raise the boundary? That's a good boy. Just in case anything followed. We may need additional help."

Sydney looked like he'd been about to protest, but nodded with a wry smile.

"As long as this doesn't take too long," Sydney said, standing up. "After all, I left things in disarray. They'll need me back soon."

Nana waved her hand, dismissing Syd's words. "This is more important than hand-holding your scared little clan. Now, tell me, what's this? Who broke the truce?"

"There really isn't time, Martha," Syd said. He looked to Rebecca. "Shouldn't you be getting that water?"

"Look, I don't know who you are—" Rebecca began, irritated and tired of being ordered around like a lap-dog. She might do whatever her nana wanted, but there was no way some guy she didn't even know—

"Rebecca," Nana interrupted. "Quickly now or this boy is going to die."

A glimpse of yellow caught Rebecca's eye. Ryan's lucky pencil was sticking out of the back pocket of the jeans that lay in a discarded heap at the foot of the bed. Rebecca's head spun as she tried to take in being in this strange hidden room with this strange, unfamiliar woman that looked like her nana who was somehow working to save Ryan's life.

Why couldn't they have just gone to the hospital? Rebecca thought as she ran downstairs again, her brow furrowing. *Why did they come here? Why is Nana acting like...like normal? Well, not normal, but like she does this sort of thing all the time?*

The questions came faster than Rebecca could fathom as she filled a large stockpot with water. She was filling the other when suddenly Sydney was standing beside her.

"Holy crap!" Rebecca flinched away from the boy and stared at him, wide-eyed. "How the heck did you do that?"

Sydney lifted the full pot into Rebecca's arms. She took it automatically, wrapping her arms around the bottom. Wow, it was heavy.

"The same as always," he said, sounding confused by her question. "You need help getting this stuff back upstairs, and your way takes forever."

He didn't wait for Rebecca to ask him anything else. Instead he shut off the water filling the second pot and put a hand on her shoulder. He put the other on the second pot and suddenly they were back in the dark room with Ryan and Nana.

Rebecca's stomach lurched and she set the pot of water next to Nana, just in time to be sick in the corner.

Sydney's eyebrows rose. "Don't worry, that happens to a lot of humans when they shift for the first time," he said.

"A lot of *humans?* What? I mean...Nana? What's going on?" Rebecca asked, her stomach tightening more at the disturbing suggestion in Syd's words.

"I don't have time to explain now, little dove," Nana said distractedly as she soaked strips of cloth into the water they'd brought up which was suddenly steaming hot, though it had been only lukewarm moments ago. "Give me a few minutes to see to this boy. What's his name, Syd? Names help, as you know."

"Ryan," Syd replied in a whisper. "Ryan Dugan."

"'Ryan'," Nana repeated before turning back to Rebecca. "Give me a few minutes to see to Ryan, little dove. He's been bitten by a hellhound. *And* a vampire." Nana muttered those last words under her breath in disapproval. "Really, Syd. Did you have to bite him?"

"It was either turn him or watch him die. He's been good to us," Syd replied. "You know I wouldn't have done so this way unless there was no other choice, Martha."

Nana nodded. "I know. It's just...well...he won't die of the hellhound bite, that's for sure. If he survives the turning...well...we'll deal with that part when it comes. *If* it comes."

Sydney nodded and sat on a chair beside the bed as Rebecca watched Nana work.

Hellhounds? Vampire bite? *What?*

It finally seemed quiet enough for Rebecca to ask a question, but she didn't want to bother her nana. Instead, she looked to Syd.

"Because this is the place wounded Ethereals are supposed to come," Sydney said before she could form the question in her mind. He glared at her deliberately, his eyes flashing in the light like Mishka's sometimes did. Hadn't they been a shade of dark blue in the kitchen? "This is neutral ground, a haven, where the wounded can come for healing."

"Wounded?" Rebecca asked. Wow, what was with his eyes? "I don't understand." Was that her voice sounding all dreamy like that?

"Rebecca, don't look a Master vampire in the eye. It's not only rude, it's dangerous. Sydney, stop it," she heard Nana order in that firm-yet-soft voice Rebecca had never heard her use before. "Leave it lie. She doesn't know any of it. I...I never trained her. I didn't want her involved."

Leave it lie? Rebecca thought as she shook her head to clear it of the fuzziness she hadn't even noticed was there. *Who talks like that anymore? Master vampire? Oh, please. I've finally watched one too many late-night horror movies.*

Sydney looked at Martha, incredulous. "You mean to say that she doesn't know you're a Healer?" He sounded surprised and a little angry. "*The* Healer, if it were told true? *Lady* Healer. Or that she's one of your line?"

"After losing my daughter, do you think for one moment I would want Rebecca exposed to this?!" Nana snapped, pointing to Ryan's limp body. "We're mortal, and maybe you don't know just how short a time that is, but to we humans, it's too short! I'll not lose my granddaughter as I did my daughter!"

"But...Mom died in a car accident," Rebecca spoke out. "You told me a drunk driver killed her and Daddy."

Nana looked pained and guilty. She didn't say anything more as she kept her eyes on Ryan's deep wound, cleansing it with a concoction she'd made from the contents of a jar taken from the suitcase.

Sydney stood up and reached for Rebecca's shoulders. She flinched as he touched her, but he held her firm and guided her to a long mirror mounted on the wall of the room.

With a gesture of his hand, the unlit candles in the wall lanterns all blazed bright, bringing much more light into the room, illuminating the mirror.

"Thank you," she heard Nana say.

Rebecca gasped as she looked into the mirror and saw only herself reflected back. She knew Syd was right there, behind her. She could feel him touching her. She looked to her shoulder and saw Syd's longish blond hair mingling with her own, but there was no trace of it in the mirror.

His lips twitched in a little smile as he looked down at her and nodded at the mirror again.

Rebecca looked back, and though she couldn't see him do it, she saw her hair being moved aside. She felt him tilt her chin so she could see the huge mark on the right side of her neck she hated so much. It was a dark, tea-colored stain that covered half her neck, shaped like a funny asterisk.

Ever since she'd started school, kids had teased her without mercy about her birthmark, and Rebecca tried to cover it as much as possible. Everyone still made fun of it, except Robin. Robin only teased her for keeping it hidden with her hair. Robin thought it was cool—almost like a tattoo of an eight-pointed star.

"Be proud of it! Show it off! You have this great piece of body art you didn't even have to pay for, that no one will yell at you for getting! How cool is that?" Robin always said in that over-enthusiastic way that made her such a great friend. Rebecca didn't mind it when Robin mentioned her birthmark. Robin never made her feel horrible about it. Robin never made her feel different, or that there was something wrong with her.

That didn't make her feel any better about that horrid thing on her neck. It looked like someone drew a little *t* on her neck, then changed their mind and drew an *X* over it. Rebecca was going to see about having it removed as soon as she was out on her own and had the money.

She felt Syd's fingers touch her neck and she glanced at it in the mirror, scowling at her reflection. Her brow furrowed as she realized that she could see the pulse that beat below the skin there.

She looked up at him, confused. Rebecca could see two small white points poorly hidden behind a suppressed smile.

Were those *fangs*?

"If you're really a vampire, shouldn't I be staking you through the heart or something?" Rebecca asked with a bravado she didn't feel. "I mean, you know...like in *Buffy*?"

A soft laugh escaped Syd as he released her.

His laughter almost annoyed her. People laughed at her all the time and it always made her feel stupid and hurt. She didn't need yet another gorgeous guy making fun of her—certainly not when *he* was the one who had shown up at her house totally uninvited. Yet somehow Syd's

laughter didn't hurt like it did when the kids at school did it. His was...
Rebecca didn't have a word for it, other than "warm." Gentle, maybe. Not
meant to hurt. He was amused by her, not trying to make her feel stupid.

"Do you really think you could?" He smiled so that his fangs could
be seen. Rebecca gasped and took a step back at the sight of them. "Tell
me, Acolyte—ever kill a spider?"

Rebecca nodded, wide-eyed. How did he know about—?

"It hurts, doesn't it, just a little bit?" Syd continued.

Rebecca nodded again, biting her bottom lip. She always tried to
catch them instead, and take them outside because it *did* hurt. Physically.
Not just because she felt sorry for them when she accidentally killed one,
which was probably dumb, but it didn't stop her feeling it.

"Or when you want to hurt someone, like today in detention, when
you wanted to slap—"

"Shhh! Please!" Rebecca glanced over at her grandmother, but Nana
was focused on Ryan and hadn't seemed to notice her talking to Syd.

"Did Ryan tell you about detention?" she whispered to the boy.
Well, he wasn't really a "boy," was he, if he was a...a...

Syd smiled again and gave that soft laugh that both annoyed and
captivated Rebecca. "'Vampire,'" he said. "You can say it. I'm not as
sensitive about the term as some."

"Sydney," Nana called suddenly. "I can't slow it. It's too late. He's
turning."

Sydney instantly crossed to the bed where Ryan lay and knelt beside
it. He took Ryan's hand as the bed shook. Ryan seemed to be having
some kind of seizure, and looked all but dead to Rebecca.

"It's all right, buddy," Syd soothed. "I've got you the best Healer
here, and we're going to take care of you. Don't fight it. I know, it's earlier
than we planned, but take it in stride. Come on..."

Rebecca just stood and watched as Sydney stroked a damp cloth
over Ryan's forehead, which came away stained with pink and red. Ryan
seemed to be literally sweating blood.

Nana stood and sighed, shaking her head. Rebecca moved to her
grandmother, and when Nana held her hand out, Rebecca, like a child of
seven instead of a girl of nearly seventeen, took her grandmother's hand
and clung to her side as she watched the wounded boy on the bed thrash.

"Come on, let's get some tea," Nana said in that weird, gentle voice.
"Syd will stay with him. There's nothing really to be done now but wait
until it runs its course."

"This wouldn't have happened if the entrance hadn't been sealed!"
Syd snapped, glaring at Nana. "Why was that done? You wasted my time,

making me come ask for entry like a common human!"

Nana didn't seem at all offended by Sydney's outburst or his accusations. "Who broke the truce?" she countered. "That entry has been sealed for nearly fifteen years, which you well know, Sydney Alexander. After the last battle, you know what precautions were taken."

"Precautions that apparently included keeping your own granddaughter, the last of your line, ignorant of her own power!" Sydney growled darkly. "You didn't tell the Council *that* part of your plan to close the Eastern Enclave. She doesn't even know...how could you not warn her, Martha Althea? If the flames of war have again been fanned, what makes you think her ignorance keeps her safe? She is a valuable asset to any side, and keeping her unaware can only lead her unknowingly astray!"

Nana and Syd continued to glare at one another for a long moment before Rebecca felt a tug at her hand.

"Come," Nana said again. "This isn't something you need to see."

Rebecca pulled her hand free. "No, wait, Nana," she said, looking toward the now-still form of Ryan on the bed. "He...I know him. I mean, not very well, but... He goes to my school. He won't know where he is, and he'll be scared when he wakes up."

"Sydney will stay with him, Rebecca," Nana replied. "Let's wait down in the kitchen. It's not a good idea to be so close, even with the protections we have. A fledgling vampire is not easily controlled. It's fortunate we have a Master here with us to watch over him as Ryan turns."

"'Turns?'" Rebecca echoed, looking back to her nana. "You mean..."

"Into a vampire, yes," Nana said. "And though turning a human is never easy or done lightly, Sydney had to do it to save Ryan's life. Ryan is fortunate that he was brought to me in time to wrest the dark magic from the bite of the hellhound or he wouldn't have even survived long enough to turn. I'm sorry, Sydney. I wish I could do more."

"There is no cure for the final bite," Syd said. "Nothing can stop a turning."

Rebecca could all but feel his acceptance...and regret.

Syd kept his eyes from Martha's as he wrung out the blood-soaked cloth with fresh water. "I know that." He brought the damp cloth back to Ryan's face and continued wiping it. "I couldn't let him die, Martha."

"I know, Syd," Nana said with a gentle smile. "I know."

They left the two boys in the hidden room. Rebecca marveled at the linen cupboard shelves that swung shut behind them as Nana led the way down to the kitchen. Rebecca put the kettle on and made a pot of tea. She felt very, very strange and needed to do something that made her feel somewhat normal again. Nana sat quietly in a kitchen chair, but without the usual, vacant look on her face that Rebecca was accustomed to seeing.

As Rebecca sat a mug of tea in front of her, Nana—Martha—spoke.

CHAPTER THREE

"I never wanted you to know, but I see now I shall have to tell you, before Sydney leaves with Ryan," Nana said in pained resignation. "Once he leaves, he'll take his power with him and I'll forget myself again. I'm sorry, Rebecca. I'm sorry for what's become of me, what you have to endure day after day."

"Nana—" Rebecca began to protest.

Nana held up a hand. "Please. Let me talk and don't interrupt." She took a sip of tea and swallowed hard.

Rebecca sat down in her own chair, cradling her hands around her mug in a futile effort to warm them.

"I should have told you all these things long ago, but after Helene died—" Nana closed her eyes for a moment, then smiled at Rebecca.

"No matter what I might not want you to know about things, *I* still know about them. I just can't quite remember everything. This happens, when Healers reach the age of sixty. While Syd's here I'm able to use his power to clear my mind, but he won't be here long enough for me to tell you all I need to," Nana said. "I'm sorry for not telling you these things before. Syd's right. I've likely done more harm than good trying to protect you from your birthright with ignorance. I should have expected the war to start again, but the peace has held for so long... I forget that mortal time means so little to Ethereals. I suppose I was hoping you'd be grown and gone before—"

Nana stopped herself and shook her head before going on. "But, you're not, so now we must deal with that."

"Before...what?" Rebecca asked. She bit her bottom lip.

Nana reached across the table and took one of Rebecca's hands in hers. "Rebecca...you're a Healer."

Well...that didn't sound so bad, Rebecca thought. In fact, something inside her leapt at the word, and a kind of heat spread through her limbs. Her cold hands were suddenly warm, and she smiled. Still—

"A Healer? Like...a doctor?" Rebecca asked.

"In a manner of speaking," Nana replied and released Rebecca's hand. "You were born with the gift to channel power to your own use... that is, to share your life's force with those who are in need, and to heal those beings thought to be immortal. 'Immortal' does not mean 'invulnerable', little dove. Your friend was bitten, very nearly lethally, by a hellhound, who no doubt attacked Syd's clan. Vampires are a delicacy to hellhounds because they have no soul. It was only Syd's bite, the final bite of a vampire, that saved Ryan. I don't agree with it, but it saved your friend's life."

Rebecca tried to process everything her nana was saying. It was like talking to someone else, someone completely different than the grandmother she had grown up with.

Nana was a...a what? A healer of vampires? And I'm supposedly one, too?

"So..." Rebecca said slowly. "We're a family of...vampire healers?"

Nana laughed and took another sip of her tea. "More or less," she said after a moment. "Sometimes more, sometimes less. It's not just vampires. We help the hellhounds, too. Goblins, ghosts, specters, shades, werewolves—demons are really the only ones who shun us and refuse to ask a mortal for help."

Goblins? The word brought a flash of something to Rebecca's mind, and she recognized it as what she'd seen that afternoon peeking in the door to the girl's bathroom at school. Those...were real? All the things she'd been seeing...those had been real things? She thought back over the past few...how long had she been seeing things? Months? A long time, anyway. First little weird things in the garden that she dismissed as birds, then spiders behaving strangely—looking like they were waving at her and so on, then stuff with huge eyes peeking out behind shelves and bushes and even people's pet doors. What were they?

"We observe neutrality," Nana went on. "We don't take sides. We have the gift of healing those who cannot heal themselves—those who need power and the force of life that comes from a living soul like ours. Unfortunately, by using our life force in this way, it's depleted quickly. It gets used up by the time we reach sixty. *If* we reach sixty. A lot of us don't."

"You keep saying 'us'," Rebecca said. "Are there more of 'us', then?"

"There are a few, in various parts of the world, or the 'mortal realm' as the Ethereals call it," Nana replied. "A great number were killed in the last war by the very beings we try to heal. As far as I know, less than a hundred of us remain. Here, in a place of healing, the ground is neutral—wars and battles stop here. Had the hellhound who bit Ryan tonight been in need himself, we would not have denied him assistance.

He would have been treated and sheltered just the same, right at the side of the one he harmed, with no further hostility between them. Once they leave here, however...that's another matter. You are safe here as well, and your Healer's mark grants you certain clemencies both inside and outside the boundary, but you, like the Immortals, are not invulnerable."

"So...now what?" Rebecca shrugged. "You're not better, and you're not going to get better. The only reason you're okay right now is because that...vampire boy is here, right? And there's someone from my school upstairs who's turning into a vampire himself. Are more... *people* like them going to show up? What did Syd mean when he said the 'entry was closed'?"

"The mirror up there serves...*served*...as an entryway," Nana said. "It was sealed after your mo—after the last truce was declared. To put it in terms you can understand, I went out of business, so to speak. It seems now, however, I need to reopen. But I'm too old. Not only do I no longer have any power of my own to share, I'm too slow. I can't remember much. Sydney is a powerful Master vampire, the leader of a vampire clan, and he's the only reason I'm able to manage at the moment. When he leaves...you'll be...burdened with me again. An old woman who has lost her mind. I'm so sorry, Rebecca. You shouldn't be wasting your youth like this. Maybe you should look into a home for me."

"This is your home!" Rebecca protested, leaping up from her chair. She went around the table to hug her nana tight. "You're not going anywhere. You're not a burden." She hated herself for crying but forced the words out from her tight throat, not caring that her voice was thick with tears. "You wouldn't let them put me into a foster home when mom died, did you? I'm not going to let anyone do that to you either! If anything, I'll...I'll chain Syd to the wall so he can never leave! You'll be okay again. I won't let anything happen to you, I promise."

Nana gave Rebecca a squeeze. "You know that can't happen. Syd has responsibilities just like we do, and if you really want to look after me, Rebecca..."

Rebecca pulled away a little to look at her nana. "Yes? What?" she prompted when Nana didn't continue.

"I never wanted you to know," Nana said again. "But I wouldn't let them take you away, so I guess that means you're going to be involved whether I want it or not. If you really want to look after me, Rebecca, you're going to have to look after those I once did. If war has once again come to the Ethereal planes, and it looks like it has, then Sydney and Ryan are just the first of those who will need our...*your* help."

Rebecca's eyes widened. "*My* help?" she squeaked. "Why my help?

What good would I be? I'm not trained! *You* said! And you said you can't help anymore...and once Syd leaves you won't even..."

"We'll ask him to start your apprenticeship early," Nana said. "Once a Healer comes of age—at seventeen—they train for a year with a representative of one of the great Ethereal clans, and then a different clan each year until the age of twenty-two. It's usually begun with vampires because they're the closest to mortals, and it eases a Healer into her training if she has something more like herself to accustom herself to. Now, you're not going to have the luxury of accustoming yourself to your training. In truth you should have been learning about what you are since you were five. As it is, you're just going to have to learn on your own, or from Syd. He can't exactly object to training you early if I insist on it. It *is* his job." Nana's brow furrowed. "Ryan's bite is...unfortunate... for him, but strangely fortunate for us. For you, rather. I could almost think...but Syd is a Master..."

Rebecca looked at her grandmother as if Nana had started speaking a foreign language. None of what Nana was saying made any sense, but Rebecca felt like she should understand it. She reached to touch her grandmother's shoulder, recalling her attention.

"You said that...before. Up there," Rebecca said, lifting her eyes to the ceiling for a moment before looking back at her grandmother. "That we're fortunate to have a Master here. Syd is a Master...? What's that mean?"

"A Master vampire leads and sees to the affairs of a vampire clan. Sydney is the Master of a great, well-respected, powerful vampire clan—Cardoza. He was your mother's mentor when she apprenticed the vampires."

Rebecca didn't know much about her mother, but she certainly hadn't thought anything about her being a veterinarian to the undead. How was she going to...?

"Oh, don't look so dismayed, Rebecca!" Nana said. She smiled at her granddaughter. "Healing is easy once you get the hang of it. It's inside you—a part of you. It comes as naturally as breathing after awhile, and Syd will be here to at least get you started. We'll convince him to stay until you're ready to work by yourself. I'm afraid I won't be all that much help. I drain too much energy now, and can't focus my efforts the way I used to. However, I have some books with my notes and things, and I'll show you where I've kept all my herbs and special equipment. It will be a lot of work and you'll have to learn fast, but this is in your blood, and what you were born to do."

"Is this why I always wanted to be a doctor?" Rebecca asked,

32 • DINA JAMES

smiling a little.

Nana smirked. "Very probably so," she answered. "Now, let's go check on Ryan. He should be over the worst by now."

Rebecca nodded and rose to follow Nana upstairs.

They neared the linen cupboard that hid the entrance to the healing enclave. Nana reached in and pressed a large knot in the wood. It gave way at her gentle push and the shelves swung back and to the side.

They entered quietly, though Rebecca collided with Nana when the older woman stopped short.

"Rebecca," Nana said in a calm voice. "Back slowly out of this room."

When Nana used that tone, Rebecca didn't argue. Even though she had only heard it once or twice, she knew it was meant to be obeyed right then, without question or hesitation, and took a step back.

"I would not deny the Healer, nor her apprentice, access to her own enclave, my lady," came a deep, rumbling voice that shook the floorboards beneath Rebecca's sneakers.

"My apprentice is untrained, my lord, and I would wish no offense to thee," Nana replied in that same calm voice, though Rebecca could hear the tremor in it. Whatever was in there had Nana scared to the bone.

"No offense will be taken," the dark voice replied. "Upon my word. I have come only to see about the boy."

"Yes, my lord," Nana said to the voice. "Rebecca, follow me and do exactly as I do. Bow your head and keep your eyes on the floor until I tell you it's all right to look up. Ask no questions now. They will be answered later."

Nana must have known there were about a billion questions running around in Rebecca's head and a hundred more on her tongue just begging to be asked, to tell her to keep quiet. Rebecca took a deep breath and whispered "'Kay," ready to face whatever Nana was afraid of.

Here there be monsters, Rebecca thought, remembering a line from a pirate movie she liked. But what kind of monster was it? Even if Nana hadn't been blocking her way, she'd been told not to look, except at the floor. She noticed that Nana had bowed her own head, and remembered quickly to do the same.

Rebecca felt Nana grasp her hand tight and took a step into the room. Once they were both out of the enclave entrance, Nana went to her knees, tugging Rebecca's hand to follow.

She knelt beside her nana, careful to keep her eyes downcast and her head bowed.

Nana let go of her hand and put both of her own flat on the floor in front of her. Rebecca copied her.

"Bow low slowly, then don't move," Nana whispered before doing so herself.

Rebecca did as she was told and held the position. Breathing hard and trembling, she felt like throwing up.

"Easy, Acolyte," she heard Sydney say. "Your own enclave, remember."

A low growl met these words, but Sydney didn't apologize for speaking.

Rebecca felt her hair being moved and heard a long sniff. Then another.

"Raise your eyes to me, Acolyte," the rumbling voice commanded.

"My lord—" Nana began, and Rebecca noticed Nana's hands weren't beside hers anymore.

"Hush," the voice commanded, and Nana immediately fell silent.

What kind of thing could talk to Nana like that in her own house, and have Nana obey, just like that? Rebecca thought.

Rebecca did as she was told and slowly looked up from the floor. Her mind went blank with shock as her eyes took in the form of a very, very large black... Dog? Wolf?

She remembered that it had spoken to her. Neither dogs nor wolves could talk. She didn't know what he was, but he was familiar, somehow...

"Hellhound," the creature replied to her thoughts in that rumbling voice.

She scrambled away from the huge black monster-dog, pressing her back against the wall with a frightened squeak, shaking from head to toe.

The hellhound seemed to enjoy her fearful reaction as they studied one another. Dark, rippling fur covered its entire form, save for a shiny black nose and a mouth full of serrated teeth that reminded Rebecca of a shark. Its eyes were crimson and danced like a candle was inside them. Gentle red-orange flames, mixed with the occasional flash of blue, flickered at the tips of its ears, the end of its tail, and it seemed at the end of every hair on it. Even around its feet, but the floor wasn't scorching for some reason. The flames clung to the creature, but they didn't seem to help lighten the terrible darkness emanating from it.

"Fire burns within you, Acolyte," the hellhound said, approval in his words, though they sounded just as dangerous as any of the others he'd spoken.

"Rebecca, get back to your knees," Nana said in a sharp whisper. "This is Lord Notharion, chief of the Hellguards."

It was all Rebecca could do to peel herself away from the hard,

34 • DINA JAMES

safe wood of the wall behind her, gather her knees back under her and bow her head. She remembered what her nana had said and hoped she was about to do something right. She looked back up at the hellhound and met his eyes, though it took all her willpower to make herself do it.

"Forgive me...my lord," she managed, though it was hard to unglue her tongue from the roof of her very dry mouth enough to speak. "I meant no offense. This is the first time I've seen a...a...hellhound."

"Well spoken, apprentice," he said, approving. "She will serve, Martha Althea."

Nana inclined her head in a nod. "My gratitude, my lord."

Notharion raised an eyebrow at that, and Rebecca thought it was extremely odd that a dog raised its eyebrow.

"I am not a *dog*, and you will cease comparing me to such mortal creatures," the hellhound said, turning its candle-eyes on Rebecca. "Rebecca Charlotte...you and I will have an interesting relationship."

"You said you were here to see 'the boy'. I'm guessing you mean Ryan," Nana said. "But you weren't the one that bit him, were you, my lord?"

"No," Notharion replied. "I am here to see what damage one of my young has wrought."

"One of your young! My lord! You are a father?" Nana asked, smiling.

The hellhound turned his large head to regard her.

"Maelia whelped," he affirmed with a single nod.

"My congratulations to you upon the—"

Notharion looked away before Nana finished her sentence, apparently uninterested in congratulations, and took a step toward the bed.

"Stand aside, soulless one," the hellhound ordered Sydney.

"I will not," Sydney replied with a dark scowl. "If you've come merely to gawk—"

Notharion glared at the vampire and the floor vibrated with his deep growl. "You dare accuse me of coming to take pride in this? It was *you* who baited *us*."

Sydney had no reply for that and, after a tense moment, moved aside to let Notharion see Ryan's injury.

Notharion inspected the wound and took a deep sniff at it before he turned to go.

"My lord," Nana called before Notharion could reach the mirror-portal. "Can you offer no advice on how to heal such a wound?"

Notharion looked back over his shoulder, then to the bed. "Appeal to the Light, for the Dark will offer no aid," Notharion intoned formally.

He hesitated a moment before adding, so quietly that Rebecca wasn't sure if it was meant to be heard by anyone in the room, "Nor any hindrance."

With that, Notharion walked through the full-length mirror at the end of the room and vanished.

Rebecca cocked her head and considered the now-still mirror Notharion had disappeared into. "I think he just told us to pray," she said. "Big help there."

"Rebecca," Nana scolded in a whisper. "You're lucky he didn't maim you, despite his assurance he wouldn't take offense. Hellhounds aren't the...nicest...of creatures, no matter how much deference you show them."

Man, how did Nana manage to be that calm and quiet, when people...things...*creatures* were so offensive?

Then Rebecca thought about everything she put up with from Marla Thompson and decided it must be something like that. Marla wasn't nice to Rebecca no matter how often Rebecca tried to be nice to her, or stay out of Marla's way. The thought of Marla being like a hellhound made Rebecca smile inside.

"Is that what that was? That bowing we did?" Rebecca asked, trying to mimic Nana's soft voice. "We were showing him deference?"

Nana nodded. "With hellhounds, you have to show a great deal of respect, even—" Nana glared again at Sydney as she led Rebecca to the bed where Ryan lay. "—in your own enclave. Otherworlders have different rules and customs about a lot of things. Respect will get you more places and help you a lot more than rudeness, so when in doubt, always be polite, even if you know you're right and they're wrong. You can't let their attitude affect yours—they're a lot older and smarter than you, and many of them wield powers we'll never have. That's why they're called 'supernatural'. What we just did with Lord Notharion was a combination between old courtly behavior and mortal wolf manners. They're related in a lot of ways, and watching a few nature specials on how animals behave wouldn't hurt you."

Nana looked Ryan's still, quiet form, then to Syd. "How is he?"

Syd returned to kneel by the bed. "He's shed his mortal coil," he replied.

Rebecca's heart broke at the grief and anguish in his voice.

"I'm sorry," Nana said. "Even if the entry had been unsealed—"

"I know," Syd interrupted. "And I offer my apologies. I spoke out of fear. He's like a brother to me, Martha. It wasn't supposed to be like this."

"But it is. Now we must both accept and endure, not lament what should have been," Martha replied in that same wise tone Rebecca had never heard her use before that night. "I need you to remove the rest of the seals. I don't know if you've realized, but I'm not fit for much anymore, let alone the time and effort it would take for me to do it myself."

Sydney didn't acknowledge her comment, but gestured a hand at the mirror. It glinted seven times in the candlelight then returned to normal.

"He's going to need..." Sydney shook his head and looked helplessly up at Martha as he stood.

"I can't," Nana said with sympathy. "I'm not enough. I don't have enough to help him and sustain us both."

Sydney nodded and looked back at the still form on the bed.

"But she does."

Both Rebecca and Syd looked up at Nana's words.

"I...do what?" Rebecca asked. She didn't like the way they were looking at her.

"Oh please, Martha. For this kind of healing, it has to be her choice. She's not even trained." Sydney curled his lip. "You know that."

"We can help her. If she's willing. Rebecca...remember what we talked about downstairs? Well, now's the time. If you want to help your friend, and help me do what needs to be done, that is."

"What needs to be done?" Rebecca asked, wary. She had a bad feeling she already knew what they were going to ask, and she didn't want to be right. She was not about to shove a stake through Ryan's heart!

"You'll have to feed Ryan."

Rebecca blanched. Let Ryan suck her blood? That was disgusting!

"Oh, no," she said, taking a step back and holding up her hands. "No way."

Sydney swore under his breath. Nana chastised him.

"Listen, young Healer," Sydney began, speaking with exaggerated patience. "He can't kill you here. He can't take too much from you, either, as he could from your grandmother at her age. That's why you're a rare and valuable commodity among Ethereals. You have mortal years of use, of life in you. You more than others. He can't drain you of your life's force. Of blood...possibly, but that's rare, and nigh on impossible when a Healer is in her own enclave. That's right—Healers are always and only female. Healing comes from the life force created by a living soul, and it is the female who creates and bears life. Now, Ryan needs life restored to him and the only life strong enough for that in his condition is yours. So will you, young, untutored Healer, restore my fledgling?"

His pleading. His hurt and regret and helplessness. Rebecca could feel them all, and her heart broke with them.

"Promise me I will not regret it."

Where did that come from? Rebecca had spoken the phrase as though she'd known exactly what to say when asked such a question.

Sydney smiled with relief and looked to Nana. "Untrained she might be, but a Healer nonetheless," he said in approval. He looked to Rebecca.

Her insides tightened as he smiled at her. Her mouth went dry and she bit her bottom lip. *What? Why is he looking at me like that?*

"Promising," he went on as he turned to Nana. "She'll learn quickly, if such knowledge is that easy to tap." He turned back to Rebecca. "Upon my honor, my lady," he said and offered her a slight bow. "I promise that you will not regret your actions."

Rebecca nodded, still unsure, but knew something had been done correctly. Then, without thinking about what she was doing, she rolled up her sleeve and went to the bed. Her earlier nervousness—what had there been to be nervous about?—vanished. Her pulse beat beneath the skin of her wrist, warm against the cool air of the enclave.

Ryan's eyes opened and fluttered. He mumbled incoherently.

"Hey, Stereotype," Rebecca called. "I hear you didn't eat lunch. Did you get banned from the cafeteria, so that now I have to feed your sorry butt?"

Ryan didn't reply, but the confusion in his dark eyes seemed to lessen as they found her face.

She smiled down at him as she pressed her wrist against Ryan's mouth. She looked away, over her shoulder and waited.

I can't believe I'm doing this, she thought.

Believe it, she heard Syd's voice in her mind.

Rebecca looked up at him, startled. Syd couldn't help but grin back at her.

"You have much to learn, Acolyte."

"Ouch!" Rebecca gasped as Ryan's fangs pierced her wrist.

Then the pain faded, and she felt nothing. She really expected to feel *something*...but there wasn't anything at all. She didn't feel weak or dizzy, or like something was being taken away from her. On the contrary, she felt...really, really good. Helpful and...and...

"Nurturing?" Sydney said out loud.

Rebecca blushed and nodded. "I guess that's as good a word for it as any."

She closed her eyes, but there wasn't the usual darkness behind them. Instead there was...something. Darkness, yes, but...things...moving in the dark. Shapes and fire and flame and—

Rebecca gasped and her eyes flew open. Nana came to rest her hands on Rebecca's shoulders.

"You're strong," Nana said. "Stronger even than I was, I think. It's all right. He won't take much, this first time, but he'll need more over the next couple of days."

"Days?" Rebecca echoed. "Doesn't this take—I don't know—just a few minutes?"

"This isn't Hollywood," Sydney said with a roll of his dark blue eyes. "You don't get bitten by a vampire then change in moments to bite your friends."

"Well...no offense, but isn't that kind of what just happened?" Rebecca countered. She pointed to the wrist Ryan had pressed to his mouth.

"Point taken," Sydney replied. "However, he won't remember himself for a couple of days." Sydney glanced up at Nana. "Though something tells me you're accustomed to people not remembering themselves."

Rebecca felt Nana's hands on her shoulders tighten slightly before Ryan dropped her wrist and began to tremble.

"That's enough," she heard Nana say. "Move away now."

Rebecca did as she was told, and Sydney reached for the damp cloth as Ryan's trembling once again escalated into convulsions.

"Is it going to be like this until he's...um...converted, or whatever?" Rebecca asked in a whisper.

Nana nodded and pressed a cloth to Rebecca's bleeding wrist. "Mmm hmm. But don't worry. He's with us now, and safe. Comfortable. But it's also very late, and you have school tomorrow."

Rebecca looked horrified.

"Nana," she reasoned. "You can't possibly—"

Nana held up a hand, an old familiar gesture that said she was through talking about a subject.

"I *can*," Nana said, firm. "Your wrist will be healed by morning, and Syd will stay and help me set up a privacy partition for Ryan. Rebecca, you can help in the evenings, *after* your chores and schoolwork are done, *not* before. It will be a lot of hard work, but you'll likely be trained enough in a year or so of hard study that we can tell the Council you're ready to be mentored. That's not too long for you to help out here, is it, Syd?"

"A *year?*" Rebecca squeaked.

Syd voiced the same protest.

Nana folded her arms and looked stern. "Sydney Alexander, you came seeking a Healer, and you've found one untrained. Rebecca Charlotte, you have a great deal to learn and a vast amount of power to harness. You'll be lucky if a year is all it takes. And that's just the bare minimum! Remember, you should have been studying the basics with me for at least a dozen years by now. Most Healers begin at age five.

I'm sorry this is late, but if it's what you both want, it's all or nothing."

Syd looked mutinous.

Rebecca was just as unhappy as he looked, but asked, "Will you be more like your old self, Nana? I mean...with him around?" She jerked her head in Syd's direction.

Nana nodded. Syd looked skyward.

"Then that's worth a year of...Blondie...and 'hard work' to me." Rebecca glared at Syd out of the corner of her eye.

The vampire groaned. "And I suppose, Martha, since I owe you my own existence and those of my various clan members more than once over, a mortal year isn't so long a time, especially if it is given to train the granddaughter of Martha Althea in the art of Healing. Provided, that is, she works hard and doesn't waste my valuable time."

Oh, that was it. She was done trying to be nice to this guy. He sounded just like one of those jerks at school. She knew now what she'd seen behind her eyes when Ryan had bitten her, and it wasn't like this guy didn't have anything to do with Ryan being hurt. All Rebecca's patience left.

"Valuable time? How about provided you don't go around getting anyone else I know bitten by hellhounds!" Rebecca retorted.

Sydney stiffened and found a corner of the room very interesting all of a sudden.

Nana glared at him.

"So that's what Lord Notharion meant. You were *provoking* hellhounds?" Nana asked in a brittle voice.

"Wonderful," Sydney mumbled. "She's a Seer as well."

Nana looked at Rebecca and smiled. She didn't seem a bit surprised at her granddaughter's talent.

"It's an uncommon gift among Healers, Sydney," Nana replied. "But not unheard of. It had been three generations since there's been a Seer in our line. Rebecca's great-great grandmother, Agnes, was one. I always knew Rebecca was special."

Then Nana seemed to remember what Rebecca had been subject to seeing with that special power and glared at Syd.

"You show up here, with a wounded boy—" Nana began.

It had always made Rebecca cringe when Nana took that tone.

Sydney held up a hand. Rebecca was starting to wonder if that wasn't some kind meaningful gesture instead of what it normally meant to her. Both Nana and Syd had used the motion more than once.

"Can we please not talk about that?" he asked. "I know, this is my fault. However, the truce hasn't been broken. That is, it hasn't been broken *yet*. There have been reports of demons massing near the southern border of their realm. Nothing has been said to the clans—no declaration of open war has been issued to or by the Council, and though there hasn't been any encroachment on or breach of the borders, I've been around long enough and through enough Ethereal wars to know what this means. I, for one, will acknowledge the threat even if the Council won't, and I assure you, as sure as I'm standing here before you, war will break among the planes before the mortal week is out. We're going to need all the Healers—all the enclaves—we have at our disposal just to have a chance at holding a demon raid off long enough to get any females and young away. Without the Eastern enclave, there's no Healer or boundary in this part of the mortal plane, and shifting through the planes is dangerous with those who are wounded..."

Sydney caught Nana's disgusted glare and trailed off, looking completely ashamed.

"*Two* years. For your serious lack of judgment," Nana said imperiously. "Then she can begin her apprenticeships in earnest. Late, but there's nothing to be done about that."

"Yes, Ma'am." Syd hung his head. "Two years indebted to your service. To train your replacement, at least until she's suitable for mentoring. I believe Kyle has the honor next."

"Good," Nana said with a frustrated sigh. "At least Kyle has a modicum of sense, which is more than I can say for you at the moment. Rebecca? Bedtime. It's well past midnight, and a school night."

Rebecca didn't have to be told twice as she hurried out of the hidden healing "enclave," as Sydney had called it, and down to her own bedroom.

Two years. Two years of Nana being herself again. *Wow*. And Blondie was kind of cute. Okay...more than "kind of." He was totally cute.

She couldn't wait to tell Robin all about him.

CHAPTER FOUR

"...on this fine Wednesday morning! Bundle up today, it's going to be a cold one...!"

Morning radio hosts should be forced to wake up to other perky morning radio hosts, Rebecca thought before she opened her eyes and smacked her alarm clock into silence. Just once she'd like to wake up to actual music instead of some annoyingly cheerful voice telling her about the day's weather. Of course, unless she changed the time she got up, and she couldn't do that now with all she did in preparation for the day in the mornings, she was stuck with irritating energetic radio personalities. They seemed to be on every station in the morning—even the Spanish one.

She sat up and stretched with a yawn, groaning inwardly as she remembered she had an algebra test that afternoon she hadn't had time to study for. A smell reached her nose, cutting off her deep morning inhalation.

Oh, no. Nana. Rebecca leapt out of bed and sprinted down the hall to the kitchen, where she stopped dead in her tracks at the doorway. Her mouth fell open as her eyes widened.

Nana was standing next to the stove, scrambling eggs. In another skillet on the stovetop was the source of the smell that had awakened Rebecca...bacon frying. The table was set with two plates, forks, knives, napkins and glasses. Juice was poured. Nothing was on fire.

The gorgeous blond boy she'd met the previous evening was sitting at the table. Dark, wraparound sunglasses covered his eyes, and Rebecca noticed the kitchen windows had been covered over with thick blankets from the linen closet upstairs, making the room dark. The only light came from the bulb in the vent hood over the stove, illuminating the food Nana was cooking.

Toast popped up, making Rebecca jump.

Syd raised an eyebrow at her over his glasses. "A fair morning to you, Acolyte."

"Oh, Rebecca, you're up!" Nana said over her shoulder before Rebecca had a chance to return Syd's greeting. "I hope I didn't wake you with the noise. I tried to be quiet."

Rebecca shook her head, still staring. Nana was...making breakfast... like normal...

"Oh, good," Nana said as she reached for the butter dish and a butter-knife. She slathered each slice of toasted bread with a creamy yellow pat and set them on a plate. "Sit down. The eggs are almost ready. I was going to make biscuits, but I couldn't find the flour."

"We don't have any," Rebecca replied, still struck by the sheer weirdness of the scene. "I don't know how to use it and so I haven't bought any since I cleaned out the pantry last."

Nana nodded absently as she brought the eggs over to the table.

"Well, we'll have to get some more," she said, scraping eggs from the skillet onto the plates. "I can't make any kind of bread without it. I'll need baking powder, too. And more butter. I saw baking soda in the back of the fridge, and though that's probably still good for baking, I'll need a fresh box of that too."

Rebecca just stared at her grandmother. Nana looked back at her with eyes that saw her clearly...like it used to be. Was it going to be like this every morning now while Syd was around? She hoped so.

"Come on, Rebecca. Eggs are getting cold. Come and eat," Nana urged, beckoning to her granddaughter with a gesture.

"I promise I won't bite," Syd said.

Rebecca scowled at him as she crossed the kitchen to one of the chairs and looked down at the plate Nana pointed to. The eggs looked and smelled normal. Nana obviously remembered she was an awesome cook. Rebecca glanced at Syd and sat down. "Uh...morning, Blondie."

"So it is," he replied. "Morning for you, rather. This time is my night, past my usual time to retire. One of my kind should be well into rest by mortal sunrise. However, *you* are mortal, and we are not at the lair."

"I don't get it," Rebecca said. "If you should be in bed, why are you still here? Oh. Ryan, right? How is he?"

"Rebecca," Nana said. "Syd is still here because you need to start your training right away. I told you last night, I can't help you. Now, get some breakfast in you. As for Ryan, he made it through the night and will need to be fed before you go to school. Syd was going to give you a quick lesson before you leave the prote—the house."

Nana met and held Rebecca's eyes for a moment, then went to the stove and put the crispy strips of bacon on a plate with paper toweling before bringing it to the table. Then she brought the plate of toast over as well. "Would you like some jam for your toast?"

"Just buttered is fine," Rebecca replied without thinking. She refused to think about how both weird and awesome this was. She glanced at Syd as she picked up her fork. "I feel really weird, eating in front of you."

"Would you like me to leave?" Syd asked.

Rebecca shook her head and reached for her orange juice. "No, it's just...it seems rude. Hey...what are you doing?"

Nana hesitated as she lifted her plate of untouched food from the table. "You and Syd have a lot to talk about, and there isn't much time. I'd only be in the way. I thought I'd go and eat in the den. I've missed so much...I wanted to see the news. Besides, you have lessons to learn, and Syd is already sacrificing his well-being by staying up later than he should."

Rebecca wanted to protest. She wanted to say something about how much she'd missed something as normal as a regular breakfast with her grandmother, but Nana looked so happy at the idea of doing something as normal as catching up on the news. Rebecca didn't have the heart to say anything against her nana's wishes.

"Thanks, Nana."

Nana smiled and continued on her way out of the kitchen with her breakfast.

Syd watched the older woman leave the room and waited until she was gone before he turned back to the table.

"My name is 'Sydney', Acolyte. Not 'Blondie'. Sydney Alexander Cardoza, to be exact. Names have tremendous power. Do try to remember that."

Rebecca felt chastised, but couldn't help wanting to ask a question. She swallowed her bite of toast, but before she could speak, Syd answered it.

"I've known your grandmother for forty years," he replied. "She is a very old and very dear friend."

How was it that he was wearing dark sunglasses that hid his eyes, but she could still feel them? Almost see them? His gaze seemed to bore into her, and she remembered what Nana had said about not looking a Master vampire in the eye.

Rebecca nodded and went back to her eggs. She couldn't remember the last time she'd had a real breakfast. Usually it was just a glass of juice and a piece of toast on the way out the door. She'd taken to bringing change to school to grab a Coke out of the vending machine before the first bell and chugging as much of it as she could before homeroom.

Thinking about school made Rebecca wonder what story Robin had told her parents about what had earned her detention. They'd believe some lame excuse about talking on her phone too long in the morning or being in the bathroom fixing her makeup and not hearing the bell because she was listening to music, but Rebecca knew the truth.

Robin was strange like that. She was pretty, popular, and gave everyone the impression she was a self-absorbed, superficial ditz, but really she was super-smart, got straight A's, and had a heart of gold. What's more, you could trust her to be there when you needed help, and Rebecca was grateful she had at least one person to talk to about what it was *really* like living with Nana. Robin was a great friend. Why she still hung around with Rebecca when everyone else had moved on from grade-school friendships was beyond her. What happened to her brother Pete was a long time ago, and it seemed like Robin was never going to forget how Rebecca had stood up for her against a group of older boys teasing her about Pete's death.

Of course, that presented a problem. She wanted to tell Robin all about Syd, and Nana being normal again, and Ryan, and...and...well *everything*. But...

"But of course, you cannot, and who would believe you anyway, if you did?" Syd said, echoing Rebecca's thoughts. "Few humans can perceive our world, even when and where it spills into their own."

"Then how come I can?" She dabbed at her mouth with her napkin.

"You're one of those 'few' who can. While you are *of* this world—mortal, human—you are not truly a part of it. Not like...normal people. 'Regulars', they're called."

"That makes them sound like coffee," Rebecca said, arching an eyebrow. "So if everyone else is 'regular', I must be 'decaf', right?"

Syd smiled indulgently and shook his head. "You are a Stranger," he replied. "Not from here, but not from the Otherworlds, like I am. A *Stranger*. That is what Healers are."

"So you're basically telling me that I don't belong here," Rebecca said with a snort. She rolled her eyes and stabbed a bite of egg with her fork. "*I* could have told you that. I've known that since kindergarten."

"Ah, but you did not know why," Sydney countered. "Further, most humans feel they don't belong from time to time. It's just that in your case, it's true."

Syd leaned down to look at her, trying to get her attention. When she looked up from her plate, he smiled, allowing the tips of his fangs to show against his bottom lip.

"Can you honestly tell me that you aren't relieved to finally know what you are? Why nothing here has ever felt right to you, or made sense to you?" he asked. "And does it now?"

ALL WOUNDS • 45

"I felt...something...last night, when Nana was telling me about... things," Rebecca replied. She took another swallow of her juice, hoping it would moisten her dry throat. "But you make me sound all special and everything. I'm not special. I'm nothing. Nobody. I seriously don't think I'm...whatever you think I am. I'm just me. If you knew anything about me at all, you'd know I can barely handle a pop quiz, and now I'm supposed to handle...feeding vampires and who knows what else?"

"If you can care for your grandmother all these years, you can certainly manage a fledgling vampire, ghost, ghoul," Syd assured her. "Or anything else that comes through that portal needing help. Believe me, you're going to see some things that you'll truly wish you hadn't. You wished to study medicine, yes? Become a doctor, and perhaps help your grandmother or those like her? Well, this will be no worse than what you'd see on any given night in any mortal emergency room. Regulars do some of the most horrific things to each other, and for the most ridiculous reasons—if they even have a reason. At least with Ethereals it's usually either an accident or a war injury, and there's always a war go-ing on between one faction and another, and some are mortal enemies. Vampires and werewolves, werewolves and ghouls, ghouls and shades—"

"Godzilla and King Kong," Rebecca interjected. "Bad guys like fighting with each other." She took another bite of her toast. "So...you're going to help me learn to be a witch, right?"

Syd scowled. His entire being seemed to change, and the room suddenly felt a whole lot colder. Even darker. "I know some wonderful witches, and you're nothing like a witch."

Rebecca's eyes widened. Oh, wow, she totally hadn't meant to offend him. What had she said? They were just talking, and—

"I...I didn't mean—" she began to apologize.

"I know you didn't." He stood.

She dropped her fork and pressed herself back hard against her chair.

He shook his head and placed a hand on her shoulder. She was surprised that it was warm, not cold. Wasn't he a walking corpse? Shouldn't he be cold?

"Hush. I will never harm you. However, you must be careful with your words now. A Healer has certain immunity and clemencies to things, but her conduct is an important part of that."

Rebecca looked up at him and bit her bottom lip. He thought she'd thought...was she afraid of him? Why? He wasn't scary.

Well, yeah, he was. Very, but...warm and safe, too. She knew he wouldn't hurt her. She *knew* it. She felt guilty for flinching, and making him feel like he scared her.

When he didn't. He really didn't.

Does he?

She remembered he could hear her thoughts, and shook her head as she spoke again. "Meaning I can't be an idiot and expect people to take it just because I'm...me."

"Precisely," Syd said. The room seemed to warm, matching his tone as he went on. "You have a lot to learn. You'll have to do a lot of training *out* of Regular ways. We can start with names and titles. First, you're a Healer, born of the line of Panacea, goddess of healing—the first Healer. That means something, as you'll learn soon enough. Second, you must never identify as anything else. For example, you're not a witch. They practice a very special kind of earth magic and are loving and tolerant, but most witches wouldn't heal a vampire like me. Healers like you observe complete neutrality. You respect and attempt to help whatever asks or presents itself for healing, to the best of your ability."

"Wait—if witches practice magic, doesn't that make them...like me?" Rebecca asked.

"No," Syd replied. "They use the magic around them, the magic of this realm, this world, not of the Otherworlds. Oh, there are some mortals who try to use the magic of the Otherworlds, and who succeed with heavy assistance from a demon or other Sinister, but I wouldn't deign to insult the witches by associating them with dark magic users. There's a vast difference, Acolyte, between the occult and the Dark. Remember that."

Rebecca nodded, though she wasn't sure she understood.

"Seventeen is when a Healer's power manifests in its entirety," he said. "And for you...well...let's hope I can train you enough before you come of age that you'll be able to manage that when it happens."

The way he said it made the idea of her upcoming birthday sound... ominous.

"Manage *what?*"

"The manifestation of your power."

"You make it sound like I've got some terminal illness and only have until my birthday to live," she retorted with a scowl.

The vampire didn't reply. Even with the glasses covering his eyes, the look on his face spoke for him.

He looked...worried. Or maybe mad. She hoped she hadn't offended him again. She was always saying stuff without thinking, and it always came out so wrong. When would she learn?

"I...um...I was kidding," Rebecca said, contrite. "It was a joke.

This...this 'manifestation' thing isn't going to kill me, right?" A nervous laugh escaped her.

Sydney didn't reply right away. It was a long moment before he spoke, and when he did, the answer wasn't what Rebecca wanted to hear.

"Possibly."

"Wait," she said, shaking her head as she held up a hand. She took a deep breath and looked at Syd. "What do you mean, 'possibly'?"

"I'm not attempting to frighten you," he replied in a calm voice. "But you must be aware of the dangers, and I will not keep the truth from you out of fear of how you might be affected by it. I am not your 'Nana'."

"That's pretty obvious," she said with a wry frown. "I suppose I should be grateful that you're not going to baby me."

"You've been coddled long enough, and exposure to the Otherworlds isn't for the weak. The manifestation of your Healing ability is almost as dangerous as a Turning. Though I don't believe it *likely*—"

Rebecca couldn't believe what she was hearing, but she tried to pay attention to every word.

"—that you will be harmed...or killed, there is a very slim *possibility* that the manifestation of your power could...overwhelm you. However, you're a strong girl, and you'll learn fast. You think on your feet and adapt quickly. There's no reason that anything should go awry. Had your grandmother trained you from the time you were a child as she should have, this wouldn't be as large a concern."

That didn't help. Not one bit. Rebecca was just getting used to the idea of vampires and demons, and now this...this guy was telling her that she might not live past her seventeenth birthday?

She looked up at Syd and shook her head.

"Is there a way out? I mean, Nana tried to keep this from happening, right? If there's a way out let's hear it, because I don't think I can do this."

Syd lowered himself to a crouch and looked up at her. He waved a hand at the range and the light above it blinked out. A dim glow from the morning light around the edges of the blankets covering the windows bathed the kitchen in a dark gray Rebecca could just see in. Though it must have been very bright for him, she watched Syd reach up and lower the dark glasses covering his eyes.

Rebecca immediately turned her face away and looked at the floor, remembering again what her nana had said about looking into his eyes being rude. Besides, her stomach did weird things when she looked at Syd.

"Please," she heard him said in a gentle voice. "Look at me. Just... not directly into my eyes. But at least look to me."

Rebecca hesitated for a moment before she obeyed.

"Martha shielded you from what you are for so long, Acolyte, for this very reason. So you would not feel this fear. This weakness. That you would not see yourself as you do now—as not strong enough to be what it is you were born to be. She was hoping that, through her neglect, your power would simply fade and you would not have to endure the weight of the responsibility of it, but that has not happened. Quite the opposite. It's only grown stronger despite the neglect. Acceptance of yourself and your abilities is the only way you are going to make it safely through your coming of age. The Otherworlds, and those in it, are no more dangerous than this realm is, and it serves no purpose to keep you ignorant. Just as it serves no purpose to fear something because you don't understand it. I am here to help you to understand it."

Help me understand. Understand weird things?

Rebecca bit her bottom lip as she remembered something that had happened in algebra during her last exam.

There had been a problem she was trying hard to solve and wasn't getting anywhere. She'd been thinking on it so hard, staring at the numbers on the paper, knowing she knew how to solve it, but unable to remember the formula she had to use. She had been concentrating so hard, the answer startled her when she heard it.

Heard it. In her head. In someone else's voice. She'd glanced around the room as much as she dared. It had sounded like someone was standing right beside her, telling her what she wanted to know.

Rebecca looked at him, wide-eyed, and told him about it. "Does that have anything to do with...um...this stuff?"

Syd nodded. "Somewhat. However, that was minor. A trifle. Wait until your power manifests when you come of age. You will be able to hear much more than thoughts, *without* such concentration or against your will. You'll be able to use the emotions of other beings for your own purposes. Each of your mortal senses will sharpen, and though your abilities will be nowhere near 'supernatural', as you say, they will be 'superhuman'. That is, they will far exceed those of a Regular. Just wait. Your world will cease to be ordinary and become *extraordinary*. Nothing to fear about that, is there?"

Rebecca smiled and hid her face in her hands, laughing. What had just seemed so terrifying and dangerous was now fascinating and wonderful. He'd taken her fear and her dread and turned them into anticipation and hope.

"However, just as you can hear the thoughts of others, others can hear yours," Syd went on. "Others like me. Ethereals. Teaching you to shield your thoughts and feelings will be of paramount importance. For now, though, there's a fledgling vampire upstairs in desperate need of healing."

Syd stood and put his dark glasses back on as he gestured to the range again. The light came back on and he held his hand out to her. He nodded at the kitchen door. "Come. Unless of course you still don't think you can do this."

Rebecca hesitated a moment, then reached for his hand. She pushed her chair back as he helped her to her feet, then released her hand with a smile. She took a deep breath, then followed him out of the kitchen.

"There's something you must remember...one of many things, actually, but this is something you should know right away," he said as they climbed the stairs. "As a Healer, you need to embody quiet and calm. Move as quietly as you can, speak softly and gently. Most of those you're going to heal have senses beyond yours, and it's more than just polite to try and respect that. Sometimes something as usual to you as a normal speaking voice can do serious harm, and your enclave is a place of comfort."

Wait. My enclave? Hers?

"Think of it as a cross between a library and a critical care unit in a hospital," Syd went on. "No loud noises, sudden movements or excess stimulation. Calm and comfort. Remember that."

Rebecca nodded but kept silent as she followed Syd. Wow. He had a nice...back. She expected vampires to be dressed like Dracula in the movies—a tuxedo under a cape or something. Syd was wearing blue jeans, a white t-shirt with some saying printed on it and a windbreaker, just like any guy at school. Really nice jeans that fit just—

She remembered he could hear her thoughts and tried to concentrate on what he was saying and not on what was in front of her as they climbed the stairs.

"A fledgling vampire can be difficult to manage. Turning is never easy, and usually done in the privacy of the clan's lair, but Ryan is injured, which doesn't help. Turning someone—more times than not, truth be told—doesn't always go well for the human. He's going to need you to feed him at least twice if not three times a day for the next week or so until his change is complete and he can hunt for himself. Possibly longer."

Rebecca stopped just before she reached the top step and looked toward the closed linen closet door.

There was a vampire in there just waiting to suck her blood. *Unreal.*

What was even more unreal was that she felt more like herself than she had in a long time. She had a purpose and knew what to do for the first time...ever.

This felt right, no matter how strange it sounded.

Strange. *Stranger.*

She remembered what it was like when Ryan took her blood. The things she saw. The images and the feelings and the—

"Wait."

Syd stopped and turned to regard her.

"You—you and Ryan. It was on purpose, wasn't it? You planned for him to get hurt. To get bitten by a hellhound."

The words tumbled out in a rush, and she didn't think she could stop talking even if she'd wanted to. Images and feelings flooded her mind and they flowed out of her mouth. She stumbled and leaned against the wall, clutching at the staircase railing for support.

"You and Ryan both decided. He would be the bait. You knew the demons were massing, where to find them. You took Ryan and lured the hellhound away and then—oh! Oh, no! No—run! OW! Oh, god, that hurts! Oh please—oh no—!"

"Stop!" she heard Syd's voice order. She felt herself being shaken, hard. Strong hands gripped her upper arms, hurting her. "Pull it back, now! Don't let it overwhelm you!"

Her eyes went to his face and she shivered. It was so cold in there. So frightening and—

"Remember what I said about strength," Syd said. "You're apparently a Seer as well, and after Martha mentioned it last night, we talked a little about it. Such an ability has its advantages...and disadvantages. One of the drawbacks is that you're going to see more than you want to. More than you *need* to. But you *can* control it. You must, or you'll go mad. Hush now."

"You did this," Rebecca accused in a weak voice. She shook her head at him. "He was bitten, badly. Worse than...than what you wanted. You wanted him to get bit! And he did and almost died, so you bit him... just so you could bring him here! Why?! Why did you do that?!"

Syd dropped his hands, releasing her, though Rebecca felt it more as a shove.

"It wasn't like that, despite what you think you see," he said. "Yes, it was planned, and yes he was bitten worse than intended, but not for any reason you'd understand. Sometimes what you see and what actually happened are two different things. All you need to know is that your world has changed and will never go back to the way it used to be for you, no matter what you want."

"What? What does that—" Rebecca began.

"Don't interrupt!" Syd took her shoulder and guided her ahead of him. "This is the only way. You'll understand soon enough. I'm the only hope you have of coming of age at all. Your seventeenth birthday is in a few days—"

Rebecca jerked out of his grasp. "So! I—"

"I said 'don't interrupt'!" Syd snapped. He removed his dark glasses again and looked down at her. "As Martha has no doubt told you, this isn't the way things are usually done. I do apologize that I don't have time to ease you into things, but there really isn't time. *You* don't have the time, understand? If you don't learn—" Syd cut himself off, shaking his head.

And Rebecca understood.

"You...you did this...on purpose, so that I'd...have something to heal?"

"No," Syd replied. "So that your power, which shines like a beacon even now to Otherworldly beings, could manifest—as it is going to with or without your training—under your control. So that Martha—and you—would realize your importance. In short, Acolyte, I'm—we're—here to save your life. As I said, Ryan wasn't supposed to get seriously hurt. Besides, what you saw and what happened are two different things. Demons are massing near the border of the Hell realm, and certain information was necessary. Ryan...attracted more attention than he was supposed to."

They neared the linen cupboard that hid the entrance to the healing enclave. Syd gestured to it and showed Rebecca the large knot in the wood. The knot gave under at her gentle push and the shelves swung back and to the side.

Syd held his arm out to stop Rebecca entering the enclave.

"What I told you and Martha was true," he said in a low voice. "Historically, war has always been formally declared after the demons have encroached on some other territory. They're forever doing the most stupid things, thinking themselves clever and strong enough to get away with whatever it is they end up doing. They don't limit such to any one realm—they attack the Otherworlds just as they do the mortal realm—burning cities, destroying resources, plundering kingdoms. They are an idiotic, violent, aggressive race of beings. For all that they love to destroy, nothing gives them greater pleasure than to take that which is not theirs...especially other beings. Especially those useful to their enemies."

"You mean...kidnapping?" Rebecca asked, incredulous.

Syd nodded. "They have not done so as of yet, but demons love war. They love conquest. They also know that nothing will get them a war faster than the kidnapping of a Healer. Nothing enrages all other Ethereals—no cause is greater—than that offense. The last Healer taken was Helene MacDonnell. Your mother."

My mother? My mother is dead...

Rebecca swallowed hard. "You're saying..."

"Yes," Syd said in a whisper. "They'll be coming for you."

CHAPTER FIVE

Rebecca stared at Syd for a long moment before she made a noise of disbelief.

"Yeah, right," she replied. "If Nana were worried about something bad happening to me, she would have...have..."

"Have done everything she could to protect you?" Syd finished for her. "That's what she's tried to do the whole of your life. After losing her daughter..."

Rebecca shook her head. "No. You're wrong. I don't believe you! Why would they want anything to do with me? I'm no one!"

"You're a Healer," Syd replied in a firm voice. "Whether you want to be or not. Whether you believe that or not. And you have a patient to attend to, so if you please." He motioned her into the entrance before them. "Martha, of course, knows none of this, and it should be kept that way. There's no need to upset her, and such news would likely cause her to panic. She draws enough of my power as it is. Frightening her would only increase her need."

Rebecca's head was swimming, but she nodded like she understood. Something inside her pulled at her and settled into some kind of happy relief as she entered the room of healing. She raised her eyebrows at the curtained frame that had been erected around the bed Ryan was on, just like in an old hospital movie. Why would that be here? It wasn't like there was anyone else to keep him out of sight from. Maybe it had some special purpose she didn't know about. She went around it and squinted into the darkness behind it.

Syd gestured into the dark and the candle by Ryan's bed flared to life. Syd took off his dark glasses.

"Now, I will not allow Ryan to get out of hand, but he's ravenous. Can you feel his hunger?"

Though the boy from her school hadn't moved an inch, and for all intents and purposes looked like he was dead or sleeping very, very deeply, Rebecca felt her insides turn and twist like she hadn't eaten in weeks, even though she'd just had breakfast.

She nodded. "I think so. I mean...I feel...something..."

Then she was watching herself push her long nightgown sleeve back from her wrist. It felt like she knew what to do automatically, and wanted to do it.

"Careful," Syd cautioned, though the warning wasn't necessary. "They're often...difficult...when awakened, but your nearness should have awakened him by now. His hunger should have."

Rebecca heard the worry in Syd's voice as she sat down on the bed beside Ryan and, as she had done the night before, pressed her wrist to his mouth.

Nothing happened.

"Oh, now, come on, Stereotype," Rebecca said, careful to keep her voice quiet. "You said you didn't want me to get in anymore trouble, remember, and I'm going to if you make me late for school. You know what happened the last time I came in late. Come on, the bus is going to be along soon and I need to get ready..."

Rebecca moved around and slid her free arm behind Ryan's head, cradling it. She lifted his head gently and pressed her wrist harder into his mouth. She winced and grimaced as she felt his pointed teeth—*fangs*, she reminded herself, though it sounded completely silly to call them that—pierce the skin of her wrist.

Ryan's eyes flew open, his back arching as his shoulders pressed hard into the bed beneath him. He grabbed Rebecca's wrist and arm with both hands and bit down hard.

She yelped and pulled back, trying to get away.

"Ease," she heard Sydney's voice in her ear. She felt his hands on her shoulders, pushing her back toward Ryan. "Close your eyes. Don't watch. Don't think. Don't feel."

Rebecca did as he said and felt herself relax. Her breathing slowed, and her heart stopped pounding wildly against her ribcage.

Wow, Sydney's hands on her shoulders were very warm...nice...

She felt Ryan release her arm and her wrist fall away from his mouth. The hands on her shoulders fell away also and Ryan once again lay still. His eyes were open, but they weren't looking at anything. It was just a blank stare.

Blood trickled from the left corner of his mouth. Syd reached past Rebecca with the edge of a cloth and wiped it away.

"Move away now," Syd ordered though his voice was gentle.

Rebecca did as she was told and moved from the bedside back

ALL WOUNDS • 55

around the curtained frame. Maybe that's what it was there for. Some kind of...power shield. Sydney followed, looking back over his shoulder at Ryan. He looked so worried. Maybe she'd done something wrong. "Sorry. I screwed that up, didn't I?"

Syd shook his head. "I said I would help teach you, and that much uncontrolled power could harm him," he replied. He smiled at her. "I merely assisted. The gift is yours, and you've quite the gift, Acolyte. All you lack now is control and a broader education."

"Uh, thanks, I think," Rebecca said, confused. *Is he being serious? Or sarcastic?* She looked down at her hands and gasped at the deep puncture wounds on her wrist. Blood continued to flow from them, staining her nightgown. She covered it with her other hand and noticed the cloth Syd held in his. "Could I borrow that? He uh...it's not healing over as fast like it did last night. I think this is a lot deeper. This *hurts*."

"Allow me," Syd replied, and reached for Rebecca's arm.

"What—?"

He turned her hand over so gently it was more of a caress and brought her wrist to his lips. Closing his dark blue eyes, Sydney licked the wound, then again, sealing the punctures.

What the—? What was he—? Oh, wow, this is nice. The pain in her wrist faded and Rebecca couldn't help close her eyes at the rush of...something... tingling through her. It was warm, but cold, like shivers, but nice ones. Why hadn't he done this last night after she'd fed Ryan?

"Because Martha wouldn't have thought it...appropriate," Syd replied to her thoughts.

Rebecca opened her eyes and blushed. She could see why, if Nana knew what it felt like to have...um...

What had he been doing?

"It's not that she would have objected to such for knowing how it felt," Syd said aloud, again answering her thoughts. "But because she knows that such things can lead to...the relationship between mentor and apprentice. Such things can get out of hand."

Rebecca looked at him, confused. "Out of hand? What do you mean? You just...helped me, that's all. Helped me heal, right? Sped things up?"

Syd nodded. "Well, that and such gathers up any remaining trace of power your blood might have left on your skin. However, young Healers often...confuse such things. Mistake them for other than their true intent."

Yeah, she could see how things could feel a whole lot different than they were intended, if the way he made her feel when she just *looked* at him was any indication. Never mind how it felt when he *touched* her.

"I am your mentor, your teacher—nothing more. It would do you a service if you'd remember that," Syd said.

"Wait, you're worried I'm going to...what? Fall in love with you or something?" Rebecca asked. A bitter laugh escaped her. "Hey, look, you're cute and all, and I know you think I'm stupid, but I'm not stupid enough to think a guy as gorgeous as you would be the slightest bit interested in someone like me, let alone interested in me like *that*, so I wouldn't waste my time dreaming about something that's never going to happen like a bunch of those airhead cheerleaders at my school do. I'm *not* delusional!"

Syd shook his head.

"What?" Rebecca asked, confused. "Am I missing the point? I just told you that you don't have to worry about me falling in love with you. What's the problem?"

"I'm four hundred and twenty years old, Acolyte. A Master," Syd said.

"Wow."

"Indeed. You are but sixteen—"

"Almost seventeen."

Syd raised an eyebrow at her.

"Indeed," he said again. "Almost seventeen mortal years. I was just a year older than you when I was turned, and while I still look a mere mortal eighteen years, I am centuries old. What you just experienced was a whisper of what you're going to under my tutelage. The mentor-apprentice relationship—especially your first—is a close, emotional, intense one. You are just learning your abilities, discovering and harnessing your power. You'll be tempted to misuse it, or use it to excess. It will be as exciting as it is dangerous, and you'll desperately want to share that excitement. Apprentices have been known—often, I might stress—to...develop strong feelings...a deep attachment...to their mentors. It's not uncommon, especially with a Master vampire. I am warning you now—guard against this. Experience the things you feel as they come, but always remember to put them in perspective. No matter my age, I do remember what it felt like to be as young as you. It is not an age of rationality. Heed my warning, I beg of you."

Rebecca knew her assurance that she wouldn't fall in love with him was something important to him. She could feel it, somehow. She could sense that he'd been through it before, and didn't want to have to break another girl's heart. Or something. He'd probably had to break more than a few, and he probably already had someone waiting at home for him. A mate or a bride or whatever vampires called their significant others. He didn't need—well, want—some little girl falling all over him, making him uncomfortable when all he was there to do was teach her.

Not a problem. A professional relationship. Besides, all she had to do was keep reminding herself that he wasn't even human, no matter what he looked like. And that he was *four hundred and twenty*! FOUR HUNDRED AND TWENTY!

Talk about an age gap. Oh, yeah. No problem there.

"I will," Rebecca said, hoping she sounded normal though she knew her face was aflame with the aftereffects of...whatever that had been. She looked at her unblemished, pain-free wrist. "Thanks, Blondie. I mean 'Syd'." She forced a happy, teasing smile. "The last thing I need is the school counselor calling me into her office to talk to me about teen suicide rates."

Rebecca felt a twinge below her breastbone and went around the curtained frame to look at the once-again motionless form of Ryan. He was lying just as he had been before, his eyes still open.

"Is that...normal?" Rebecca asked Syd as he peeked around the curtained frame after her.

Syd smiled and nodded. "At least, normal for a vampire. We 'sleep' with our eyes open."

Rebecca reached to brush a lock of Ryan's dark hair back from his face. She felt his forehead, then inspected her hand. It came away clean. No blood.

Syd made a noise of approval. "Well, he's stopped shedding. That's a good sign."

"'Shedding'?" Rebecca repeated. "Like Nana's cat does on the furniture?"

"Surely you're not implying we're animals," he said, smiling in a way that showed his fangs.

Rebecca gave him an innocent look. "I wouldn't insult animals with the comparison," she replied with a sweet smile.

Syd laughed.

That strange, warm tingle went through her again at the sound of it. Wow, he had a nice laugh.

Stop it, Rebecca. What did he just say about keeping things in perspective?

"Shedding blood," he continued. "Sort of like your sweat. A fledgling vampire sheds his mortality, and part of that is purging his form of the dead blood that ran in his veins. That Ryan has both stopped shedding and is resting with his eyes open says that he's over the worst and most dangerous part of his transformation. It's a good thing, Acolyte."

"It's a bit creepy," Rebecca said, glancing sideways at Ryan's now dark blue open eyes. She looked at Sydney. "No offense."

58 • DINA JAMES

"None taken," the Master vampire said with a mocking bow. "I can hear your thoughts, and I understand. Time, however, is beyond my ability to control, and it passes while you stand here talking."

"The bus!" Rebecca cried. She was going to miss the bus if she didn't get going! "Oh my God, bye!"

Rebecca dashed downstairs. She was dressed and ready for school in record time, and was in the foyer about to put on her jacket when a hand on her arm stopped her from shrugging into it.

Syd stood there, his dark glasses once again hiding his metallic blue eyes, careful to stand out of the way of the pale morning sunlight coming in the frosted glass of the foyer windows around the door.

"Be vigilant," he warned. "The portal has just been recently opened, and as I said, your light shines like a beacon, even now. Also, remember what I told you."

He nodded toward the living room and released her.

Rebecca remembered what he'd said about not worrying Nana. But...

"I...I don't suppose I need to lock the door today, do I? For Nana? She'll be fine now, won't she?"

"She'll be fine," Syd assured her. "It's not her welfare that concerns me. You know, you should really consider finding a helper. Is there anyone you trust—a friend from school, perhaps—who could lend you a hand...?"

"A what?"

"A helper," he said again. "Someone who isn't a part of the Otherworlds, but helps you in the mortal realm. For instance, there will be times when you aren't going to be able to make it to school, and so on. When I first met Martha, she had a helper called Loughman."

"I remember Mr. Loughman. He used to live next door," Rebecca said.

"He was her helper for many years," Syd replied. "Until he died. Helpers are hard to find because it has to be someone you can trust implicitly, as they'll have to keep your secrets, but who also has the strength of spirit to be able to participate in your world. For instance, they may have to assist in holding down a werewolf while you administer medicine, or feed a healing herb to a goblin. You should at least begin to think about someone you could ask."

"Well, there is...someone. She'd be perfect. She can definitely keep a secret," Rebecca said. "She's been helping me...um...keep the secret about Nana for more than a year now. Sometimes when I have to stay home because...something's happened...Robin hands in notes to the principal's office excusing me. She's gotten really good at forging Nana's signature."

"So Ryan has said," Syd replied. "And speaking of missing school, you're going to if you don't hurry."

With that, Syd gave Rebecca a little push toward the door and disappeared from the foyer.

Rebecca didn't have time to think as she sprinted to the bus stop half a block away and just barely made it. She found a seat near the middle and flopped down in it with a deep sigh.

Robin was waiting at the school door—her bus always seemed to get there before Rebecca's, even though it had farther to go and more people to pick up.

Before Rebecca was even off the bus, Robin was shaking her head.

"Look at your hair! And is that the same pair of pants you wore yesterday?" Robin clucked her tongue. "Another bad morning, huh? You want a soda or something?"

It had been a morning all right. Rebecca wasn't quite sure if it she'd consider it "bad." All Rebecca could do was nod, and reached for her backpack to get out change for the vending machine.

Robin didn't bother waiting for Rebecca to give her quarters as she went to the Coke machine and fed it a handful of coins from her purse.

"Thanks," Rebecca mumbled as Robin opened the bottle and handed to her. Rebecca took a deep drink of the soda before offering it back to Robin. "Will it ruin your diet to share it with me?"

Robin rolled her eyes and took the bottle. "Off the diet," Robin replied before taking a long sip. "Bryan broke up with me."

"Oh, Ro, I'm so sorry!" Rebecca said. "I know you really liked him. What a jerk, breaking up with you! Why?"

"Marla Thompson," Robin said with a grimace. "I really hate that skinny blonde bitch. Just because she has big—"

The warning bell cut off what Robin was about to say. She looked at Rebecca and smiled.

"So a few sugar calories won't kill me," she went on. "Neither will the caffeine." .

Rebecca held up a finger and dug into her bag, coming up quick with a bag of small candies. She offered them to Robin with a smile. "Chocolate cures all wounds."

"Oh, Beck, you're the best!" Robin squealed, hugging Rebecca hard. "This is truly the noblest sacrifice a girl can make! Giving up her chocolate!"

"It's a worthy cause," Rebecca said. "Though I suppose if we want to risk detention again we could toilet paper Bryan's car between classes.

I could get to like this 'delinquent' rep we seem to be working on." She eyed the group of popular girls heading toward entering the school. "Your adoring fans have arrived. Thanks for the Coke."

Robin halted her with a hand on her arm and looked at her seriously. "I know it seems stupid to be upset about a guy dumping me when you have...bigger issues than I do, but thanks for understanding and letting me whine," Robin said, also glancing at the flock of girls heading her way. "Not one of them would do anything like that for me, or even understand why I care that Bryan dumped me—leaves me free for someone better, you know?—and that's why you're a better friend than that entire herd. And you can bet not one of them would give up their chocolate either, no matter who'd dumped me!"

As if those skeletons even ate chocolate, Rebecca thought. She smiled and nodded as though Robin had asked to borrow her biology notes or something. She didn't want to cause Robin any more grief than she already did. Those girls always gave Robin a hard enough time just for talking to Rebecca, saying it was bad for her image. Now with word of their mutual detention circulating, it was just going to get worse.

As Mr. Bradley called roll in her homeroom, Rebecca thought about how Ryan wouldn't answer when his teacher called his name. His teacher would probably just figure that he'd cut class again. It's not like the school wasn't used to Ryan's absences.

The day seemed to drag on longer than usual, and Rebecca couldn't help glancing at the clock on the wall far too often. She couldn't believe how grateful she was when lunch came and she headed into the cafeteria with everybody else. For some reason she was hungrier than she usually was. Famished, in fact. Even the cafeteria's macaroni and cheese that looked more like yellow paste than anything edible sounded wonderful, and she couldn't wait to at least attempt to eat it.

She was even more grateful to find an empty table near the back wall of the cafeteria and smiled as she remembered it had been the one Ryan had been sitting at yesterday in detention. She set her tray down, slid onto the bench seat and picked up her fork.

"No wonder you have skin problems, Spot," came a familiar mocking voice as Rebecca sat down. "With what you eat, it's a miracle that huge zit on your neck hasn't taken over the rest of your face."

Gah. Marla Thompson and her gaggle of brainless bimbos were sitting at the table in front of her. How could she have not noticed them?

Her stomach growled in reply. That's why she didn't notice them. She was more focused on her food than anything else.

Why was she so hungry today?

ALL WOUNDS • 61

"I swear, Spot. If I had that gross thing attached to me, I'd get three jobs and save every penny I could just to have it removed. At least a scar might make you interesting enough to get you a date."

She ignored Marla and the giggles of the other girls at that table. What was Marla doing in the cafeteria anyway? She usually went out somewhere.

Marla's next overly loud comment answered that. "It will be nice when my car is fixed and I can actually eat somewhere I don't have to look at things that kill my appetite."

As if you have an appetite to kill, Rebecca thought. She wished she were brave enough to say it to Marla's face.

"No sack lunch today, Spot?" Marla asked. "Grandma too busy playing Bingo to pack one for you?"

Rebecca concentrated on her food, though she'd lost her own appetite. Instead of trying to take another bite of her macaroni paste, she opened her milk and took a sip.

"Did you and Robin have a good time in detention with the rest of the lowlifes?" Marla continued.

Rebecca picked up her fork, deliberately ignoring Marla.

"As far as I'm concerned, you and Robin both deserve—"

"Why are you bugging me and not hanging out with your new *boyfriend?*" Rebecca interrupted Marla's next question. Marla could pick on her all she wanted, but she was not about to say anything bad about Robin! "You know...the one you had to steal from *Robin.*"

Marla's eyes narrowed. The skinny girl stood up.

Rebecca instantly regretted her smart mouth. Why oh why hadn't she just ignored her like she'd been doing? Now Marla was mad.

She walked to Rebecca's table. "Not that it's any of your business, but Bryan is at the dentist."

Must have gotten a cavity from how sweet you are, Rebecca thought with disdain as she stabbed her fork into what passed for macaroni and cheese.

"And I didn't *steal* him from anyone," Marla hissed as she put both hands on the table, leaning down so that only Rebecca could hear her. "Bryan has his own mind and Robin is a self-centered bitch. She only hangs out with you to make herself look good, which is hilarious since *you're* the one who made her look like a dork in front of the whole school, getting her in trouble yesterday! Bryan dumped her because of that. Because of *you!* Way to go, charity case, screwing over the only person you could remotely consider a friend. I hope whatever you did was worth it."

Rebecca stood up and shoved her tray away. She ran from the table as fast as she could, biting her bottom lip to keep from crying.

62 • DINA JAMES

"When will you realize that all you ever do is mess stuff up? Stay out of other people's lives, Spot!" Marla called after her.

Rebecca heard loud giggling behind her as she made it to the cafeteria doors and out into the hallway.

She choked back a sob. It wasn't true! She wasn't the reason Bryan dumped Robin!

Was she?

The bathroom she raced to was blessedly empty. Rebecca ran to the last stall and locked herself in it. She sat down on the toilet and pulled up her feet so no one would notice her in there. She took breaths as deep as she could, trying to make as little noise as possible, swallowing hard in an attempt to keep the lump in her throat from forcing her tears out in an uncontrollable flood. Marla was *not* going to make her cry!

It wasn't true. It wasn't! Robin would have said something...wouldn't she have? Not just...asked about her morning and bought her a soda and... Robin wouldn't lie to her! She said Marla Thompson was the reason Bryan broke up with her, and that's what Rebecca would believe.

She'd never hurt Robin. Marla was right in that Robin was the only person Rebecca could call a friend, even if they had a strange relationship only they understood. She trusted Robin...Robin would have said something, or been angry with her, or...or something if Rebecca had hurt her, even if not on purpose!

Right?

Unless Robin was lying to her, and Rebecca refused to believe that.

She heard the bathroom door open. Rebecca held her breath and stayed very still, hoping someone was just in the bathroom to fix their hair.

"Rebecca?" she heard Robin's worried voice call. "Rebecca, come on. I know you're in here, and I know you're upset. Come out here."

Rebecca didn't want to. She didn't want to see anyone right now. She should just go home. Make up another excuse note or just take the heat when the school called her nana about her missing classes. She didn't care. She just didn't want to be here.

A few moments passed. Rebecca watched Robin's shoes come closer, stall by stall, until they stopped at hers. The handle rattled and Rebecca heard a sigh.

"I know you're in there," Robin said. "Come on out or I'll come in there and get you."

"Go away! I'll just mess up your life more!" Rebecca protested. Ugh, her voice gave her away. It was thick with tears.

"Don't be stupid," Robin said. "I'm going to count to three then I'm going to crawl under this door."

Rebecca sighed. She knew Robin wouldn't give up or leave until she at least saw her, so Rebecca stood up and opened the stall door.

Robin smiled at her. "Come with me. We'll go somewhere and you'll feel a lot better."

"Are you crazy?" Rebecca said, shaking her head with a wry smile. "You can't leave school. Haven't I gotten you in enough trouble this week? Marla's right. Just leave me alone, Ro. You shouldn't be hanging around me."

Robin just smiled and held an arm out.

Rebecca shook her head and went to her friend, giving her a warm hug.

Robin didn't hug her back. In fact, she flinched and pulled away. Rebecca leaned back a little, then dropped her embrace in complete horror.

What she saw wasn't anything like the pretty friend she'd just hugged.

It was a...a thing.

CHAPTER SIX

A *big* thing that seemed to grow taller by the second.

Huge gray-green wings rose over its head and shoulders matched the color of its face. Glowing green eyes, like the color of the toxic waste always shown on TV—*radioactive green*, Rebecca thought insanely—raked over her, making her shiver again. Pointed ears stretched up into long black hair that was neatly separated by two short, curved, shiny black horns growing from the top of its head, making it look even taller. Gray fangs rested upon its gray lips.

Rebecca had never seen anything so disgustingly ugly, yet strangely beautiful. It wasn't slimy or grotesque...just...ugly.

"Even immature, your power bleeds from you," said the creature. It clamped a gray-skinned, black-clawed hand around her wrist.

Something inside her moved and leapt, infusing her limbs with warmth, and she knew what the creature was.

A demon. Syd had said demons kidnapped Healers.

Just as the thought entered her mind, the demon tugged her toward the row of mirrors above the sinks lining the opposite wall. "Come."

Rebecca tried to pull away and couldn't extract herself from the being's tight hold.

"No! Let me go!" she screamed.

"Go?" said the creature. "Where? Are you not unwelcome here? Unwanted? I have come to take you to a place where you will be more than appreciated, just like you want. You do want that, do you not?"

"What? No!" She fought to free her wrist. "Leave me alone!"

The demon looked down at her with a sneer. "You are alone, are you not? And you wish me to leave you here, like this, when there are so many waiting for you?"

Rebecca felt whatever was inside her leap again and crash into her ribcage. She closed her eyes and gasped as images behind them filled her mind.

They wanted her. The demons. Unlike anyone here. How nice, to be wanted somewhere by someone for a change. Yes...there were many waiting for her. Waiting to—

She screamed and her eyes flew open. She didn't want to be a queen of demons! Her free hand pried at the demon's fingers around her wrist. "No!"

The menacing being glared down at her and released her wrist, only to clamp the same hand around her throat and lift her from the floor without effort.

"You will come whether or not I must force your consent," said the demon. "You will come away from here, where you'll be celebrated. Among us, you will be appreciated beyond imagination. Not like here. We will lay worlds at your feet, but you must part from this one."

She shook her head and managed to force words out. "Get off!"

The demon released her and she fell hard to the floor.

Rebecca didn't waste a second in screaming. "HELP!"

The demon laughed. It grasped her upper arm and jerked her to her feet, its black claws digging deep into her skin. Rebecca screamed again, this time from pain.

"No mortal can hear you now," it said as it leaned down to lick her face. Rebecca tried to cringe away from its foul breath. "No one can help you. No one *will* help you."

It let go of her arm. Rebecca pressed her hand tight against the wound then looked at her hand. She was bleeding, badly. She cupped the injury again and looked up at the demon.

Unconcerned, it clasped a hand around her other wrist. "The pain you feel now is nothing compared to what you will endure if I must force your consent to return with me. Now come. Come, and you will be a queen. A goddess. You will be worshiped."

Yeah, before you kill me! Rebecca thought as it dragged her to the row of sinks.

"Death for a mortal is inevitable," the demon replied, and Rebecca knew it had heard her thinking. "Why do you fight against it so? Let us give yours meaning and purpose."

It leapt with a cat's grace into the mirror above one of the sinks. Then the demon turned and grasped Rebecca's arm with its other hand.

Her hand smacked the glass. The demon's hand tightened on her wrist and tugged her forward a fraction of an inch.

Pain unlike anything she'd ever felt ripped through her. Rebecca's legs went out from under her as her fingers were forced through the glass of the mirror. She screamed and fought to pull away.

"There will be more, and much worse than this if you do not give your consent," said the creature in the mirror.

"You've...got the wrong...girl!" Rebecca panted as she braced her foot against the sink that always trickled a stream of cold water no matter how many times the maintenance man fiddled with it.

Water.

The hands on her arm.

That warm flush went through her, and she knew water didn't have to be "holy" to hurt a demon.

Her eyes found the trickle of running water and she shoved her free hand under it. She flung the small palmful at the demon in the mirror and put her wet hand over the demon's hand on her arm.

It howled and released her. Rebecca fell back, landing hard on her butt. The demon growled and climbed back out of the mirror.

This time it didn't look like it was going to ask her to come with it. Her eyes widened and she shrieked as she got to her feet.

"I have no wish to fatigue your abilities in your attempt to flee. Fighting means you will only exhaust yourself, Acolyte," the demon growled.

"Is that like 'if you run, you'll only die tired'?" came a dark voice with a heavy Southern drawl from the doorway. "You guys gotta get better TV down there, I tell ya. Bad movies lines ain't scary." The voice's owner looked at Rebecca. "Y'okay?"

Rebecca just nodded, staring at him. He was huge. Bigger than even the largest football player on her school's team, and he didn't look any older than seventeen. Well, if he combed his shaggy brown hair a little better and changed his clothes from jeans and a t-shirt to something more...mature, he could probably pass for twenty, but certainly not any older. But that wasn't why she was staring.

Not only was he good-looking on the level of Syd's gorgeousness, this guy's muscles literally bulged and rippled beneath his t-shirt as he breathed. His dark eyes sparkled with what one could only call impishness, and he looked like he was about to start tearing the sinks off the wall before he set the place on fire.

"Who are you?" Rebecca asked stupidly. This guy was just...standing in a girl's bathroom grinning at a demon like it was *normal*! What...?

"Name's Billy. Now how 'bout you get behind me while I deal with old Armaros here?"

"Armaros?" Rebecca echoed.

The demon growled and Rebecca took a step back, inching in Billy's direction. She didn't know who the big guy was or where he'd come from, but she'd take any help she could get about now.

"Oh my God, you see it too," she babbled. "This is real. This is really real..."

Before she could take another step, the demon had her by the arm again.

The demon closed his eyes in seeming relief and relaxation. "Can you not feel it, anubi? Think of the purpose such power could be put to—"

Billy growled, and Armaros opened his fluorescent green eyes.

"Or do not," the demon continued with a contemptuous glare down at Billy. "I forget your kind is incapable of rational thought."

"I'm about to rationalize you, buddy," Billy warned. "Back in your hole, before I really get mad. And leave that little bit of nothin' you got your dirty mitts on. She ain't worth the hurt I'll put on you."

Armaros laughed and shook his head. "Anubi," he said with a wry smile. "Forever looking at what is in front of them, never what is behind. Foolish creatures, the lot of them."

The demon nodded and the door to each of the bathroom stalls opened to reveal a demon, each holding a thick chain leash attached to metal collars of large black dog-like creatures.

Hellhounds.

One of the hounds snarled, black drool glistening at the corners of its mouth. Some of the creature's drool dripped in gold-colored threads to the floor where it hissed and smoked like acid.

Rebecca's eyes widened.

Billy laughed and shook his head. "If that's the way you boys want to play..."

Coarse, shaggy brown fur grew from his skin. The hair on Billy's head lengthened to meet the identical hair on his back while his ears lengthened into furred points and moved up and closer to the top of his face.

He simply...all Rebecca could think of was that he *melted*—clothes and all—into a very large...beast.

She did her very best not to scream. Not only did this new creature—what had just called himself "Billy"—tower above her, he stood on two legs. The fur that now covered his chest didn't hide obvious scars. If the fur along them wasn't missing entirely, it grew in all-opposite directions, unlike the smoothness of the undamaged parts of him.

Anubi, the demon had called him, and Rebecca knew that she was staring a werewolf in the face.

The face. That was perhaps the most frightening thing of all.

68 • DINA JAMES

The left side looked like it had been torn away then put back together again with glue that never dried. His left ear drooped much further down than the right one, and his left cheek did the same.

Large, sharp canine teeth protruded from the top and bottom of Billy's long, pointed muzzle. The undamaged right side of his wolf's face curled in a sneer at the five other demons that had shown themselves. Rebecca was shocked to hear him speak again.

"So, we gonna do this or what?" came Billy's voice faintly through the darker, deeper growling that the beast was using to talk.

Armaros laughed. "A lone anubi and an untrained Healer against us and our guardians? I believe you are greatly overestimating your chances."

Billy was *on her side!* Rebecca hadn't been sure.

"There ain't enough of you," the anubi scoffed. "Pups and all, you wouldn't make a mouthful. I thought you knew better, Armaros. But I forgot, you can't count. Six against one makes for poor odds...on *your* side."

"One does not need an entire force if one does not intend to fight," Armaros replied. He smiled, though it emanated nothing but cruelty, and gestured at Rebecca. "We wouldn't want to damage—"

"Touch her and it will take you a month to find all your parts," Billy cut Armaros off with a deep growl. "You can't have her."

"And why not?" Armaros replied, raising an eyebrow.

"'Cause she ain't yours to have," Billy replied.

He jerked his head in the direction of the bathroom door behind him without taking his eyes off the six demons in front of him.

"Bit, these boys want to dance, I'll be glad to show them the steps. Move your butt and get out of here."

Rebecca took another step back. Strong hands clamped around her upper arms. She screamed.

Armaros laughed and shook his head. "You can't hide her now, and no anubi lapdog is going to interfere in our business."

"And you just done what I told you not to," Billy said with a grin. "Eat it, demon boy."

Billy snarled, his warped face contorting into an even more fearsome shape. He reached with one of his clawed hands for the demon holding Rebecca and tore her from its grasp with the other.

"Get out of here!" Billy yelled.

Rebecca screamed again as Billy hurled her through the air by her arm, over his head and away from him and the demons. She landed hard against the floor, but was somehow unhurt. She looked up to see Billy leap with a vicious growl upon Armaros, his dangerous wolf's jaws snapping shut on the neck of the demon.

All the lights in the bathroom exploded, drowning the room in instant darkness. Rebecca broke into a sweat as she scrambled to her feet. She'd seen the door next to her somewhere! She didn't have time to think as she let out a frightened squeak.

Darkness wreathed in flames was bearing toward her. Eerie candle-flame eyes grew ever larger as the hellhound moved with frightening speed, chain flying behind it illuminated by the fire-tipped ridge of hair along its back. Rebecca did the only thing she could think of and ducked as the hound leapt toward her. The hound crashed hard into the wall behind her, vibrating it and shaking the door loose from the top hinge. The door folded in on itself, blocking the exit. Even though she could see light from the hallway now, there was no way she could get out of that!

A yelp and a low howl reached her ears.

"Billy!" Rebecca screamed.

She heard another snarl, but couldn't see if it was Billy. It was so dark!

Or, at least it had been for a moment. The hellhound against the wall started to get up, glaring at her with scarlet eyes as its flames burned brighter.

"He is dead," the hound snarled as it rose. "As you are soon to be."

"No!" Rebecca managed as she took a step back, shaking her head.

The hellhound laughed, showing its teeth. Rebecca was again reminded of a shark's mouth, only in the darkness she could see the fire burning in the back of the thing's throat, making the serrated teeth glow white-hot. She remembered looking up at Lord Notharion and something inside her told her what she needed to do. She looked the hellhound directly in its' candle-flame eyes and made herself keep at it, though it was hard.

"You won't hurt me," she ordered as firm as she could. "Try it and...and you'll answer to Lord Notharion."

A yelp echoed through the small tiled room again, recalling the hellhound's attention. It left Rebecca and bounded in a smooth leap back toward the fray. The lights flickered and Rebecca glimpsed a patch of dark brown fur in the middle of a writhing mass of gray and black and flames before the entire room once again went black.

Silence fell with an abruptness unlike anything Rebecca had ever experienced. She listened hard for any kind of noise and didn't hear a sound. She remembered what the hellhound had said about Billy being dead, and what Billy had said about six against one. Was he...?

"Billy!" Rebecca screamed again.

Silence answered.

"BILLY!" she yelled again, as loud as she could. Her bottom lip trembled and she caught it between her teeth, biting it hard as her eyes started to burn with tears. "ANYONE?!"

"Not so loud, Bit," came a weak voice in the dark near her. "I ain't got nothin' left to fight another bunch, and demons come out in droves. Really lucky it was just Armaros and his little gang of wimps, though you know he probably called for backup the second he got jumped. C'mon, before there's more or they get their act together."

Strong furry arms wrapped around her. Rebecca hugged the form hard and choked back a sob. She was such a baby. Maybe she wasn't brave enough to be a Healer. The lights flickered as though in agreement and tried valiantly to stay on.

"Hush up now," Billy said. "You know how to ride piggyback, don't you? Do that while we get out of here. They're already starting to figure themselves out, see?"

Billy pointed to a dismembered gray-green arm near their feet, dragging itself along the tile floor by its black claws back toward the center of the darkened bathroom.

"C'mon." Billy shoved her on his back and Rebecca dug her hands into the loose fur at his shoulders, gasping as they met something wet and cold.

"You're hurt, Billy," Rebecca said, hating herself for crying when he was the one who was torn up. "You're bleeding."

"So're you. Ain't nothin'," Billy said, though Rebecca knew...could *feel*...different. "Now watch your head. We gotta get out of here quick."

"Um..." Rebecca stammered. She took a deep breath as they crashed through the broken door. Billy landed on all-fours in the middle of the hallway and moved into an easy lope, rushing down the corridor at a frightening speed.

"Wait! Stop!"

Billy skidded to a halt and growled as he pulled her off his back. He stood her in front of him and clasped her upper arms in his huge, clawed hands.

"What?" he demanded.

"Who...I mean what...I mean...?" Rebecca couldn't think of what she wanted to ask and just buried her face in her hands with a sob.

Billy grumbled and took a deep breath. Rebecca heard a grunt and felt his hands on her arms move. She lifted her head to look at him.

Before her stood the young man she'd seen earlier in the bathroom.

"Listen, I know you're scared," he said. "But there ain't no time to explain, so stop your crying. Can stand most anything but a female crying! Now let's go!"

Rebecca jerked her arm out of his hands. "Go where? Who are you?!"

"Your bodyguard, Little Bit, now move!"

Without waiting for her to ask any more questions, Billy clamped a hand around her wrist and dragged her along behind him as they ran down the hallway.

"Hey, you can't just take me out of school! Hey!"

Why wasn't anyone seeing this? Hearing her? There were kids and teachers milling around the halls, getting ready for their next classes.

"Hey! Help!"

"They can't hear you, Bit," Billy said as he tugged her hard around a corner and out the main doors. "Can't see us neither, but them demons can, so knock off the yellin'."

He thrust her in the passenger seat of an old blue Mustang before she could utter another word and half an instant later was behind the wheel. In seconds they were backed out of the parking space and out of the school parking lot, barreling down the street at a highly illegal speed.

She looked over at Billy. He had a silly grin on his face as he rolled down his window.

He'd just been in a fight to the death with demons and he was smiling about it.

Rebecca couldn't help but laugh, then put her head in her hands and started sobbing.

"Aw, Bit," Billy said. "Don't do that. We're all right. You ain't hurt too bad." Billy turned the car sharply to the right. "I'll have you home in no time."

Rebecca cried harder. "What...those things...! They just...and you...!" she managed between gulping sobs.

"Demons ain't nothin' to get upset over," Billy said. "They're complete wimps."

Rebecca just looked at him. Nothing? Wimps? *Those things*?!

Billy grinned at her. Human-looking or not, he was covered in blood and...demon goo.

She choked on a half-sob, half-giggle and sniffed hard. She wiped her eyes and tried to smile for him.

"There you go," Billy said. "No crying. I can't stand a woman crying. Makes me feel all funny. Let's get you home, you can patch up—I'll even get you some dinner. I don't know about you, but fighting makes me hungry."

Rebecca was about to ask how he could think about food at a time like this when he growled and glared at the rearview mirror.

"Uh oh," Billy said.

Her stomach tightened at his tone. "What?"

"Company," was all he managed to get out before the car's roof crumpled between them.

Rebecca shrieked and pressed herself hard against the passenger door.

They were in the middle of town—people were everywhere on the street, in other cars. Wasn't anyone seeing this? It didn't look like they were. Why not? Why weren't the cops all over Billy for his insane speeding and dodging in and out of traffic? She'd give anything for red-and-blue lights and sirens right about now!

"Damn it!" Billy yelled as he punched the roof hard above his head. "DUCK!"

Rebecca just managed to comprehend and slide down in her seat before was showered with glass from the window. She screamed again as a black-clawed hand entered the car, followed by a gray-skinned arm.

A loud bang deafened her and she clamped her hands over her ears as she looked up. Billy's arm was extended across the seats above her. Rebecca barely had time to realize there was a gun in his hand before Billy fired again.

There was another thud from the roof followed by an outraged howl.

Billy tossed the gun in his hand into Rebecca's lap and punched the roof again. "Stop beating up my car, you horror-movie reject! Bit, hang on!"

Hang on to what? Rebecca thought as she grabbed the door handle next to her.

Billy jammed on the brakes, bringing the Mustang to an abrupt halt. Rebecca slid from the passenger seat and barely caught herself against the dash, or she would have ended up on the floor like the gun that had just been in her lap. She braced herself against the dashboard and looked out the windshield.

The demon on the roof hit the ground in front of them. Before it could get to its feet, Billy hit the gas and the car leapt forward. Rebecca heard a crunch as they ran over the demon and cringed before she realized something.

She hadn't felt anything when Billy had ripped the demons apart like she did when she hurt a spider. Like now, she could feel Billy's wounds hurting and bleeding. Why not demons? She was sure there was a simple answer and didn't have time to think about it as she pushed herself back into her seat and grabbed for her seatbelt.

It wouldn't give. She tugged and tugged at it, but Billy's insane driving had locked it tight. She gave up, let it go, and looked back behind them. She didn't see anything and took a deep breath.

Billy looked in the rearview again. "Damn. Hellspawn just don't know when to give up. Hang on! I'll have to jump this thing."

That didn't sound good. Jump what? Ten cars, like some dude on the Extreme Sports Network?

"Oh, cripes," Rebecca moaned, and shrank down in her seat again, this time sliding into the small space on the floor between her seat and the dash.

There was a feeling of weightlessness before there was a hard thump beneath her. Rebecca was knocked from her crouch onto her behind, and she yelped as a bolt of pain shot up her spine.

"You okay?" Billy asked. He leaned down and hauled her up into the passenger seat, and she'd just managed to nod when she noticed it was dark outside.

Hadn't it...it had just been afternoon! Why was it dark? Where were they?

She didn't have time to ask as the car was again hit from behind.

"Damn demonic jerks," Billy growled.

Another loud bang from the back of the car tore the wheel from Billy's hands. He grabbed at it and pulled the careening car out of the near spin it had gone into.

"KNOCK THAT OFF!" Billy yelled over his shoulder. "DO YOU HAVE ANY IDEA HOW HARD IT IS TO FIND STOCK PARTS FOR A '65?"

The insane thought that she didn't think they'd care flashed through Rebecca's mind.

She glanced out the windshield.

Long, sharp spikes covered the hood of the car, stuck between rows of what looked like chain on fire. The blue hood of the car was now black, but Rebecca wasn't sure if that was just the darkness around them or if it had actually changed color along with...growing spikes and fire-chains.

The rear window shattered into tiny pieces.

Billy swore again and grabbed hold of what looked like some kind of gearshift. "All right, Rox, don't let me down, girl."

"Who's Rox—" Rebecca managed to get out before she felt a strange sense of being squeezed and that weird feeling of weightlessness enveloped her. Another hard crash—this time from beneath them— rocked the car, and it was once again daylight. An overpass was directly in front of them, and Rebecca recognized it as the highway intersection that led out of town.

The car spun onto the ramp and cut off three cars as Billy accelerated once again to a speed that was far beyond legal.

Rebecca watched the cars they swept by as Billy dodged in and out of the lanes like a maniac.

No one seemed to notice.

"Why can't they see us?" Rebecca shouted over the noise of the wind whistling through the broken windows.

"Humans are the blindest race in history," Billy replied with a laugh. "They never see anything, not even when it's right in front of their face!"

Billy took an off-ramp and made three left turns. He turned the wheel hard to the right and cut through a field.

"Ha, ha! Crop circles!"

Rebecca put her face in her hands.

"Here we are! Told you I'd get you home in no time!"

She looked up and sure enough they were on a street that paralleled her own.

No time? It had seemed like hours passed before Billy turned onto her street and even longer before he reached her driveway.

As they passed the fence marking the property, Rebecca felt her fear ease. She looked back over her shoulder at the rear window. Billy found the gun he'd tossed in Rebecca's lap on the floor of the passenger side and got out of the car to look behind them before the car even stopped rolling.

She heard a howl and a shriek of outrage and got out of the car just in time to see a gray-winged thing look like it hit a pane of glass in thin air and fly off into the dark past the orange light of the streetlamps.

Streetlamps? But...they'd just left the school, hadn't they?

Billy's laugh brought her attention back to the moment.

"Ha! Suckers! Good thing the boundary's back up, hey Bit? I'd say we stirred up them up like a nest of hornets." Billy tucked his pistol back into the band of his jeans. He turned to look at his car and his mouth fell open in horror. "Aw, look what they did to Rox!"

Rebecca turned and saw that the car looked like a beer can someone had crushed. She was amazed that they weren't mashed inside like sardines. It looked like it was back to being a shade of blue, though Rebecca couldn't tell if the spikes and chains had been smashed into the car body or were just gone.

"*That's* 'Rox'? Your *car*?"

"Yeah," Billy said, looking a little embarrassed for a moment. "Short for 'Roxanne'. She's gotten me out of more trouble than I can remember."

"Is she...uh...alive?"

Billy laughed and shook his head. "Nah. Well, I say all cars have attitude of their own, but she ain't any more alive than any other mortal car. Good thing, too. She took one hell of a beating."

He leaned down and kissed the hood of the car. "Don't you worry, girl. Billy'll get you back in top shape in no time. Thanks for saving our butts. What about you?" he asked as he straightened and leaned against the mangled hood of the Mustang. "You hurt?"

"I don't think so," Rebecca said. "I mean, my arm, but I don't think anything is broken. I think I might have cracked my head against your dash, but since you probably saved my life, I won't hold it against you."

"You probably did more damage to Rox than she did to you anyway," Billy muttered.

"What about you?" she asked. "You look...um..."

"Ain't nothin'," Billy said again. "I'll heal up. Just glad I got to you in time. Syd sent me. Demons are nasty."

"Yeah, I kind of got that," she said with a tearful sniff. She laughed a little. It was either laugh or cry. She looked toward the street. "They're gone now, right?"

"Yep," he replied. "For now, anyway. The boundary'll hold 'em off. They'll figure out a way past it, though. They always do. Stupid they might be, but demons got patience like you wouldn't believe. Persistent, too. Don't give up."

"I noticed that," she said, looking at Billy's car again. "What's...I mean...where's the boundary?" she asked, trying not to seem *too* ignorant.

Billy looked at her sidelong for a split-second before running his fingers over a large dent in his car hood. "It's where the worlds meet. Otherworlds and this one. Where Ethereal power has more of an effect," he explained. "It's kind of like a border between states. You cross it and you're in your own territory, not in anyone else's."

"And where is it?" she asked, still confused, but hoping the answer to the *where* would answer the *what*.

"See the fence, around your house?" He continued at her nod. "That's not just there to define a property line. It's a boundary line. Your house is old, and built on an even more particular line called a ley line. It's where the veil between worlds is thin, and more easily negotiated. The boundary holds that power in, and keeps other influences out."

"'Other influences'?" she asked, confused.

"Okay, let's put this in easier terms," Billy said. "You ever see *Star Trek*?"

She nodded. "Yeah. Robin's dad is a nut about it."

"Okay, so you known what a force field is," he said with a grin.

"Yeah," she said again. "Something that holds whatever in or keeps something out, like a jail cell."

"That's kind of like the boundary," Billy said. He gave the front tire of his car a soft kick and nodded. "It's where the force field is, and just like in *Star Trek*, if you've got the key or know the way, you can go in and out of it. Some things it keeps out, other things it keeps in, and still other things can cross it as they want. Make sense?"

"A little," she said, her brow furrowing. "When...I mean...Nana asked Syd to 'see to the boundary'. What did she mean?"

"Few years back Martha closed off the portal to her enclave and brought the boundary around her place down," Billy answered. "It basically was like putting up a 'no vacancy' sign at a hotel. No room at the inn, so to speak. No welcome there, no help available, closed to business, however you want to phrase it. For things needing to get back across the boundary, or back into one of the Otherworlds, it was a real pain in the—"

Billy reached under the wheel well and tried to push out a dent above it. He cursed and growled and it finally gave under his insistence. He leaned back with a grin.

Rebecca gaped. Wow. He had to be seriously strong to bend molded steel back into shape with his bare hands.

"Need tools to smooth that," he muttered. His satisfied smile disappeared and he straightened a little as he noticed her still standing in front of him. He cleared his throat and went on. "So that meant they had to find another place, and believe me, there aren't many. When Martha told Syd to 'see to the boundary', she was telling him to put her shingle back out—raise the force field—and make the place safe again for those needing a haven. Kind of like a stop on a train line that had been closed, and now the train goes there again. It will be slow at first for things to get back to normal, because everyone knows the train doesn't run to that stop anymore and they've had to find other ways and means to get around and get help, but eventually word will spread that the Eastern Enclave is back in business, and things will go back to normal."

"'Normal'?" Rebecca echoed. "Normal for who?"

"For us," Billy said as he stood up and went to the open driver's side door. He shoved it closed with his foot. The handle fell off and clattered to the cement of the driveway. He cursed again.

"'Us'?" she repeated, still confused.

"Yeah, us," Billy replied with a scowl. "But don't you worry none. Got you across the boundary. Nothin' gonna touch you here. Well, nothin' smart anyway. It would have to really be worth something's while to take on the vamps, werewolves, ghouls, ghosts, shades, goblins, zombies—"

"Zombies?!" Rebecca interrupted, her eyes wide. "There are zombies running around?!"

"Well, they don't really run too good, and only sometimes stumble into the Regular realm, but yeah, there are 'zombies running around'," Billy said. "You're safe now, so why don't you run inside and assure Syd I didn't have you for a snack on the way home? He knows I ain't much for the 'damsel in distress' thing."

He bent down to pick up the fallen door handle, scowling at it in disgust as he tried to fit it back where it belonged.

Rebecca thanked Billy again—she felt totally weird thanking a werewolf who almost killed her as he drove like a psycho for saving her life—and ran to the house, surprised to find the front door locked.

Why would Nana lock the door?

Rebecca fumbled for her key, turned the lock, and pushed the door open wide.

"Nana, I'm home!"

A loud, insistent beep coming from the kitchen answered. A thin white haze dimmed the light in the foyer, making Rebecca's stomach clench tight. The all-too-familiar feeling of dread rushed through her, making her skin tingle. She glanced into the living room to see her grandmother's chair empty.

"Nana?"

CHAPTER SEVEN

The incessant high-pitched wail from the kitchen penetrated her shock. The smoke detector! Rebecca ran into the kitchen, glad that it was so close to the foyer.

Smoke billowed from around the oven door in clouds. A pot on the stovetop was also smoking, whatever had been in it reduced to brown scorching gloop at the bottom.

Rebecca tore the pot from the stove and dumped it in the sink before turning the faucet's cold water on full-blast then dashed back to the stove. She turned off both the burner and the oven then grabbed a dishtowel from a drawer. She opened the oven door, slow and careful.

She coughed and squinted against the heat as a dark cloud of soot assaulted her. The smoke detector continued to screech, earsplitting and ceaseless. Rebecca flapped the dishcloth at the cloud to disperse it and see what was burning. There was a blackened casserole dish on the middle oven rack, its contents burned to a cinder though continuing to cook. Whatever liquid it had contained had spilled over onto the heating element below it, causing the smoke that now filled the kitchen.

Flames leapt to life along the element as fresh air entered the oven, reaching for the pan above. Rebecca shrieked and dropped the dishcloth as she leapt back. Hesitating only a moment, she sprinted to the pantry and grabbed the fire extinguisher she had learned to keep at the ready there. She yanked the pin and depressed the lever as she got back to the oven, aiming the flame-suppressing spray at the base of the blaze.

The small fire was out in moments. Rebecca breathed a sigh of relief as she looked around the kitchen. Nothing seemed to be seriously damaged by the fire, kept mercifully contained by the oven, though smoke did enough by itself.

The burner on the top of the range continued to smoke angrily as if in protest. Rebecca scowled and squirted it with a short blast from the fire extinguisher in annoyance. The burner sputtered and hissed a reply, then quieted.

Rebecca looked up and glared at the smoke alarm. She was appreciative of its warning, but it could get extremely annoying once the danger was over.

She went to the kitchen window and opened it wide in spite of the cold October day, shutting off the cold water tap on her way to open the screened kitchen door that led to the back yard. Rebecca grabbed the dishcloth off the floor again and flapped it up and down, helping the smoke all but clear before she found the broom and used the handle to press the "hush" button on the alarm mounted on the kitchen ceiling.

The smoke detector was silenced immediately, letting out a sharp *CHIRP*. It would continue to chirp vigilantly every thirty seconds for the next seven minutes, reminding everyone that it was there and on guard.

Rebecca was grateful she had the calendar carefully marked to include regular changing of the batteries in the smoke detectors, and that she'd visited the local fire station and had them teach her how to properly use a fire extinguisher. The first time Nana had set the kitchen on fire had been enough to prompt her to learn all she could about fire prevention and safety.

Beep! Beep! Beep! The smoke detector in the kitchen was now silent, but the one in the hallway was still going off, as was the one upstairs.

Were there more fires? Where was Nana?

Rebecca dropped the broom and the dishcloth and grabbed the fire extinguisher before she ran from the kitchen.

"Nana!"

No reply came.

Sprinting down the hall, she searched Nana's bedroom, the bathrooms, and the other rooms. The door to the garage was locked when Rebecca checked it.

Ignoring the other alarms still going off—they'd shut up eventually now that there was no more smoke—she dashed upstairs.

"Damn noisy in here!" she heard Billy yell from downstairs.

Rebecca didn't answer. Slumped on the floor next to the linen closet at the end of the hall was her nana, still clad in her pink bathrobe.

"Nana!"

She set the extinguisher down and tried hard to swallow the lump in her throat. She ran to her grandmother's side and knelt beside her. Nana's hair was disheveled and her eyes were closed.

Rebecca's heart all but ceased to beat. *Oh, please...*

"Nana?!"

Rebecca gathered her grandmother in her arms and felt for a pulse like she'd learned in first aid class and was relieved when she found one. Nana's skin was warm, and Rebecca saw her chest rise in a breath. "Nana!"

"What you yellin' about, Bit?"

Rebecca looked up to see Billy standing over her. The big guy shook his head at Rebecca holding her grandmother.

"Oh, that ain't good. What—?"

Billy stopped mid-sentence and sniffed the air. A deep, inhuman growl issued from his throat.

"You stay up here, and don't come down 'til I yell you can, got it?" He didn't wait for Rebecca to reply before he leapt over the railing down to the ground floor.

Nana's eyes fluttered open and she blinked several times.

"Nana!" Rebecca called again as she patted her grandmother's cheek. Was she hurt? Burned? Just scared? Why had she fainted?

"Nana, can you hear me? Are you all right?" Rebecca asked, careful to keep her voice calm. Nana was easily upset when she couldn't remember something, and it only made it worse if she saw Rebecca was upset too. Rebecca had learned that a long time ago.

Nana didn't reply. She looked at Rebecca as though she knew she was supposed to say something, but didn't remember what it was.

Rebecca inspected Nana's arms and sleeves, checking for burns. She didn't see any, but that didn't mean anything.

"Are you hurt?" Rebecca asked. "Did you fall? Should I call an ambulance?"

Nana shook her head and looked at the linen closet door. The older woman reached toward it slowly and laid a wrinkled, trembling hand against it. She glanced back to Rebecca.

"What?" Rebecca asked, taking Nana's other hand.

"Couldn't stop them," Nana whispered, looking at the door again.

"Who?" Rebecca asked. "Come on. We'll find you a chair, and I'll call an ambulance."

"No," Nana replied, a little louder, though she sounded unsure. "I'll be all right. Just...give me a minute."

"Nana, you need help! I'm trying—"

"No!" the older woman interrupted, insistent. "They *took* him! He needs help!"

She wasn't confused, Rebecca realized.

Nana was afraid.

"He's dying," Nana managed, grasping for Rebecca's hands. Nana squeezed them hard and tugged at them, urgent. "He'll die without help! Demons came through, and I couldn't stop them taking...I wasn't strong enough. I didn't have enough to hold them off... They took him!"

"Enough? Enough of what?" Rebecca asked, still not understanding. "Oh, cripes, Nana! I'm useless! What do I do?"

"Help me up."

Rebecca put an arm around her grandmother's back and helped the older woman stand. When Nana was steady, Rebecca opened the linen closet door.

"P...push," Nana insisted, looking at Rebecca.

This wasn't confusion. This was helplessness, as though Nana didn't have the strength to do for herself instead of not having the mind.

Rebecca's fingers found the knot and pushed it. The closet shelves swung inward and back, revealing the entrance to the enclave.

Nana tried to take a step forward and swayed on her feet unsteadily. Rebecca kept her arm around Nana's back, holding her upright. Reaching for her grandmother's left hand, Rebecca secured her nana's arm around her neck and together they stepped into the enclave.

The bed Ryan had been in that morning was empty, the room a mess. The privacy curtains and their frame were ripped to pieces. The chest of drawers that had stood in the corner was overturned, its contents strewn about the room. Books that hadn't been there when Rebecca left that morning were scattered across the floor, many with their spines broken and pages ripped out. The bedclothes were in disarray, with the mattress hanging half off the bed as though it had been dragged along with whomever had been on it.

Nana shook her head and lifted a weak hand. Rebecca heard her sniff, and even though Rebecca couldn't see very well in the low light, she knew her nana was trying hard not to start crying.

"I couldn't stop them," her grandmother whispered again. "That boy is going to die because of me. I'm so sorry, Rebecca."

"I'll call an ambulance," Rebecca said. "You don't look good."

Nana shook her head and swallowed hard. "I'll be fine. Billy's here. He's Ethereal, and will help—"

Ethereal. Syd.

"Where's Syd?" Rebecca asked suddenly. "Is he all right? Did they take him too?"

Nana shook her head and looked as though she didn't have the strength to explain.

Rebecca thought about asking after him again—*where is he?*—but her nana looked too tired, and she'd said Syd wasn't...that they hadn't... Rebecca wasn't sure if she were more relived or angry. Syd had said he'd be here! If he'd been here—

"Come on," Rebecca said, shaking her head. "You need rest. Let's get you downstairs."

Nana looked toward the bed where Ryan had been and then back at her granddaughter and sniffed again. Rebecca's heart broke at the helplessness on her nana's face.

"There's nothing we can do right now," Rebecca said, her voice gentle but firm. "Let's go downstairs and figure this out." She put her grandmother's arm around her neck again. "Have you brushed Mishka today?"

Nana frowned at Rebecca. "I'm not a child."

That sounded more like Nana.

Rebecca smiled. "I know. But with all that's apparently gone on, I wouldn't be surprised if you forgot her, and you know how she is about being forgotten. You sound a little better. You're sure you don't need that ambulance?"

"Yes," Nana breathed, nodding. "I'll be fine soon enough. It was so sudden..."

Rebecca willed herself not to cry. The danger was over now. There wasn't a need to cry. She'd kept herself from panicking and freaking out in front of Nana like a baby. Everything was safe.

Well, safe enough. What *could* have happened—that was what scared her now.

Rebecca helped her grandmother out of the enclave and was about to head down the stairs before she remembered what Billy had said about staying where she was.

She also remembered what he'd said about thinking of him as her bodyguard, and decided it was best to listen to him. The house felt weird—scary and cold and dangerous—like it wasn't hers. Not like the home she knew. She felt like a stranger in her own house...like she didn't belong here...and knew it wasn't right. This was *her* house!

She shook the feeling off and called for Billy.

No answer.

"Billy?" she yelled, louder. Her voice cracked over the name, and she ignored the way her nana looked at her. Rebecca hated herself for being scared and didn't want her nana to know she was, but...

"Billy! Come on!" Rebecca shouted, willing strength into her voice. She could at least sound like she wasn't afraid. "Where's my bodyguard when I need him?"

"I'm comin'! Damn, Bit—you got a set of lungs on you! Ain't like I'm deaf you know!"

Nana gave a tired smile and a quiet chuckle. "Anubi have excellent hearing."

"Hey, Martha!" Billy greeted from the top stair. "You look like—"

"She needs to sit down," Rebecca interrupted the werewolf. "Help me get her downstairs, huh?"

"Downstairs ain't no better than up here, Bit," Billy said, shaking his head.

"Why?" Nana asked, looking from Rebecca to Billy. "What's happened downstairs?"

Billy rubbed the back of his neck with one of his large hands and looked at Rebecca. He gave her a shrug.

"Just a little bit of a mess, that's all," Rebecca said. "Come on. I'll make you a cup of tea. It might take me a few minutes. I have some cleaning up to do first."

"Let me," Billy said, and took Nana into his arms like a doll before Nana could protest. "Hey, Martha! How you doin'?"

"I can walk, you big brute!" Nana said, though she blushed and Rebecca could tell she was pleased.

"Yeah, but that ain't no fun for me, is it? Besides, I got this whole hero thing going on with Bit here. Don't ruin my rep, huh?"

Nana blushed again and Billy carried her downstairs.

"Living room, the big chair," Rebecca called as she followed them. Nana sure didn't need to see the kitchen anytime soon. "I'll bring her tea in there."

"Good idea."

Settling Nana in her favorite chair, Rebecca thanked Billy and smiled down at her grandmother. Nana's big white cat appeared out of wherever the smoke alarms had driven her and leaped into Nana's lap, glaring at everyone as though she had been tortured in all manner of unspeakable ways.

"It's all right, Mi-mi," Nana soothed, stroking the cat. Nana reached for the brush that was always kept on the table at the chair's side and began to run it through Mishka's fur.

"Want some help cleaning up, Bit?" Billy asked.

"I got it, thanks," Rebecca said. She smiled at her nana. "Will you be okay here for a bit while I make you a cup of tea?"

"What was that Billy said about helping clean up?" Nana asked, her brush hesitating in mid-stroke.

Rebecca looked pained, not wanting to tell her nana what had happened. The smoke alarms were all quiet now, and though the smell of the burnt *whatever* in the kitchen lingered, it wasn't too heavy in the air. Something else did, and Rebecca wasn't sure what, but she didn't think it was whatever had been in the oven.

"My casserole," Nana whispered. "The cheese sauce."

"It's okay," Rebecca said quickly. "Well...not edible 'okay'. House-intact 'okay'. Nothing seriously damaged...I don't think. I really didn't have time to do much other than put the fire out and—"

"Fire?!" Nana interrupted, wide-eyed.

Rebecca nodded. "It's okay, though. It's out, and the kitchen is clearing of the smoke, and—"

"The house could have burned down!" Nana exclaimed, shaking her head.

"Nana, it's okay," Rebecca said again, kneeling by the side of the chair. She looked up at her grandmother. "Really, it is. It probably won't make you feel any better, but I'm kind of used to it. You used to try and cook all the time, and forget. I've put out more than one fire. I'm just glad you didn't have any oil on the stove this time."

Nana looked unsure. Rebecca smiled at her.

"I know how to use the fire extinguisher and everything," Rebecca assured her.

"You always were a smart girl who liked to be prepared. I think that's the Healer in you," Nana said. "Always trying to keep people safe, making sure everything was all right."

"Speaking of 'everything being all right', what about you? You really okay?" Rebecca asked past the lump in her throat. "You scared me, Nana. Fires I can handle, but if anything happens to you..."

Nana patted Rebecca's back soothingly. "I'm fine. I'll be all right. That boy, though...Ryan. Syd's thrall..."

Rebecca pulled away from her nana, her stomach turning a funny flip at the mention of Syd.

"Where was he during this demon thing?" she asked. "He wasn't here, was he?"

Nana shook her head. "He had responsibilities to see to."

Rebecca stood up fast and turned her back to her nana to hide the scowl on her face. Her hands clenched into fists, her nails digging into her palms. If the Master vampire had been here like he said he would be—

She turned back to her nana and crossed her arms over her chest. "So that thing about being here for two years? What was that? He can just go off whenever he wants to, regardless of what he said? Is he even going to come back?"

"Hey, now. Don't go knocking off Syd," Billy said. "If he wasn't here, it's 'cause he had somewhere more important to be. No offense, Martha."

"None taken," Nana replied. "And I understood. I told him I would be fine here with Ryan until he returned. Syd needs rest, too. He hasn't been getting all that much around here, and has been using his power a great deal."

Rebecca unclenched, threw up her hands and shook her head as she left the living room for the kitchen. Syd had assured her that morning that Nana would be all right, and Rebecca had believed him.

She mumbled to herself as she filled a mug with water and set it in the microwave. She jabbed at the buttons, setting it for two minutes so that her nana could have a hot cup of tea. "Demons nearly eat my grandma while they kidnap his friend, but that's all right because there was something more important going on! Well, I'd like to know what!"

Movement out of the corner of her eye caught her attention, and she ignored the big werewolf who entered the kitchen.

"Aw, Bit, don't be mad," Billy said in what had to have been his best pleading tone. "I could hear you in there, you know, moanin' about Syd not bein' here. Don't be mad at him. Nothing happened."

"Nothing—" Rebecca began, ready to scream at someone—anyone—about how she didn't think this could be called "nothing." Her nana had nearly been killed and Ryan and Syd were both *gone*!

"Nothin'! 'S good. Syd'll be—"

"'Syd will be' what?" came a familiar voice from the darkest corner of kitchen.

Rebecca glared at the tall vampire who slid from the shadows. Sydney bowed to them.

Her temper snapped. She'd had enough of everything jumping out at her today.

"Dude, don't even," she said, her voice cold. "You're lucky I'm not very violent, 'cause I have half a mind to beat the living crap out of you before I shove Ryan's lucky pencil through your heart!"

Sydney straightened, his brow furrowed in confusion. He took in the deplorable condition of the kitchen and looked to Billy. The werewolf just shrugged.

"I told her everything was fine!"

"Fine?! I get attacked by demons at school who try to drag me through a mirror, who only didn't succeed only because a werewolf showed up to save me, and once we get away he drives me home—if you can call what he does behind the wheel 'driving'—"

"Hey!" Billy protested.

Rebecca ignored him and went on.

"—chased by demons the whole way, am nearly crushed to bits

inside the car, have had a gun go off just inches above my head, and barely get away from them only to find the house nearly on fire, my nana upstairs looking like she's dead, the guy turning into a vampire gone and possibly dying while who-knows-what ran through the house despite the fact that you told me before you left this morning that everything would be fine! If this is your idea of 'fine', I'd sure like to see your idea of a problem!"

She turned and tried to run from the kitchen. There was no way on earth she was going to let Syd see her cry.

Syd had her by the upper arm before she could move two steps. She glared at him, only to see an astonished look on his handsome face. He turned his metallic blue gaze back to Billy and again surveyed the utter disaster that was just that morning a perfectly ordered kitchen.

"Billy, what's happened?" he demanded. "Where is my thrall?"

Billy growled. "Take your hands off her. Then I talk."

Syd released Rebecca and she glared at both Billy and Syd. The microwave beeped and Rebecca got the hot mug out of it, took a tea bag from a drawer and left the kitchen.

Rebecca sniffed and plunged a rag hard into a bucket of warm water, sloshing some over the sides onto the floor at her knees. She wrung it out as though she wished it were someone's neck instead and went back to cleaning the oven of the fire extinguisher residue. She had to work fast or it would harden even more and be almost impossible to get out, and she didn't want to be here all night scrubbing.

Not that I'm not going to be scrubbing all night anyway, she thought, remembering the gray sticky deposit the smoke had left on the cabinets and walls. She sighed and attacked a corner of the heating element in the bottom of the oven.

She felt Syd's eyes on her before he took a step into the kitchen. She looked over her shoulder at him, unsure of what to say. She didn't think she could speak to him right now without screaming at him or saying something completely mean.

He didn't say anything. She watched as he closed his eyes and brought his hands up to his chest. He touched the tips of his middle fingers together for a moment before sliding one hand down toward his middle and the other one up to his chin. Then he flipped them both out to face the kitchen.

Rebecca felt a light breeze brush her skin and flutter through her hair. She knelt back to look at the vampire standing in the doorway and hated the way her stomach crinkled and her mouth went dry at seeing him.

Damn it all, she was mad at him, she told herself. How could he have left Nana?!

Sydney lowered his hands and opened his eyes. He glanced around the kitchen.

Rebecca followed his gaze and gasped. No trace of any fire, current or previous, remained. Even the smell of smoke was gone. The walls were again white instead of the pale, smudged gray that never seemed to lighten no matter how hard or how often Rebecca scrubbed them.

Syd lifted his left hand in a careless gesture toward the sink, and the ruined pot and casserole dish were at once clean and mended.

Rebecca was dumbfounded. She looked back at the element she'd been scrubbing. The oven was clean, the burner unblemished, like nothing had happened. The rag in her hand and the bucket of warm water on the floor seemed completely silly now.

She noticed that his eyes were dark, when only a few minutes ago they'd been bright and pulsing.

"I'm sorry," Sydney said, his voice soft. "My apologies, Acolyte, for all you've endured today."

She wanted to tell him it was all right. She wanted to forgive him—to accept his apology. Really, she did. She hated fighting and did her best to get along with everyone, no matter how horrible they were or what they'd done to her. Even Marla Thompson.

But Rebecca had left that morning assured by both Syd that everything would be all right. For the first time in years she hadn't worried herself sick the whole day about her nana being alone and had come home to...to...

Rebecca found she just couldn't nod and say she understood like she usually would have. She wished she could speak past the lump in her throat and tell him it was okay, but the words wouldn't come.

It *wasn't* okay, and she couldn't pretend that it was. Syd had made her feel so safe and so sure, and nothing was.

Rebecca felt like he'd betrayed and lied to her. She stood and glared at him.

"You can't leave like that, do you hear?" Rebecca said, trying hard not to scream at him, though it felt really good. He *deserved* to be screamed at. "You said you'd be here for two years! Which two years did you mean? A day at a time? You just show up whenever you feel like it? Whenever you've got time to bother with being here? If that's the case, can I get you to call me whenever you don't feel like being around so I can be? I know you don't care about what happened to Nana or me today, but what about Ryan? He could be dying! You sure made it look like you cared about him when you brought him here! Was that just pretend? Do you only care about yourself?"

"Do not accuse me of being uncaring, Acolyte!" Syd shouted, advancing on her. "Ryan would understand my necessary departure!"

Rebecca flinched and took a step back. Maybe she'd gone just a little too far. Syd wasn't just some good-looking guy. He was a Master vampire and she knew that he could hurt her if he wanted to. Rebecca was suddenly afraid of him for a moment, but the look on his face made her forget her fear.

Sydney collapsed into a chair at the table, all the fight leaving him. He brought a hand to his forehead.

"All you can see is how this has affected you," the vampire continued. He looked up at her. "Though your concern for your loved ones is admirable, there *are* others involved. I had to leave. I believed Martha would be all right here with Ryan. You make it sound as though I abandoned you both on a selfish whim. I assure you, this was not so."

He sounded so tired. Rebecca blushed and stood, emptying her bucket in the sink and rinsing out her cloth. *Now* she felt horrible about yelling at him and making him feel bad.

"I'm...I'm sorry," she said in guilty contrition, looking back at him. "It's just...been a hard day, you know? I don't mean to take it out on you, Syd. Really I don't."

He smiled a little. "Apology accepted. Now, let us use these unfortunate circumstances in some kind of positive manner. There are many lessons to be learned from this by both of us. You no doubt have many questions, not the least of which is why I sent a werewolf to aid you when you've been told his kind and mine are mortal enemies."

"That's really creepy," Rebecca said, though she smiled a little. "Even if the thought did cross my mind, please stay out of my brain."

"I try to as much as possible," Sydney replied, teasing. "I have no interest in the thoughts of a teenage human girl. However, there are times when what you think can't help but be overheard. That's another lesson you're going to have to learn—to shield your thoughts and emotions, lest they be used against you." He ran a hand through his hair.

This time she could feel his fatigue and helplessness. Hopelessness. He didn't just *seem* tired, he *was* tired. Drained. How could a vampire be tired?

"Are you okay?" she asked.

Syd hesitated a moment. "I feel extremely uncomfortable telling you things that you should, theoretically, already know," he confessed.

"However, I agreed to assist in your training, and this is as good a lesson to begin with as any. To answer your question, look at my eyes, Acolyte, and tell me what you see."

She did so, cocking her head a little. "They're dark, when just a minute ago they were bright, almost pulsing," she replied. "I'm guessing that your little clean-up stunt used a bunch of your power and now you're weak."

He nodded. "That's essentially correct, though I wouldn't have phrased it quite that way. But my efforts—" He gestured around the restored kitchen and up at the ceiling, indicating the enclave he'd also restored to order. "—did indeed consume a great deal of my power. In addition to Martha's need increasing with her upset..."

Rebecca looked at him a moment then at her wrist. Without thinking more about it, she began to roll up her sleeve.

Sydney looked at her. "I did not ask for replenishment." He sounded almost defensive.

"Do you have to ask? I'm offering. You look horrible."

"I do not require your assistance," he replied, defiant and sullen.

Rebecca sighed. "What? You're going to punish yourself because you went and left Nana alone and Ryan—er—your thrall's gone missing? Who does that help? You're just going to make things worse if you don't take care of yourself. You're starving, and you're in the house of a Healer. I can't let you hurt yourself here. Don't ask me how I know that. I just do. Besides...maybe it's my way of saying 'thanks for the help and I'm sorry for yelling at you'. Now, are you going to let me...help...or not?"

Sydney nodded and refused to look at her. Rebecca knelt down beside his chair and looked up at him anyway.

"I thought you guys were...you know...immortal," she said. "Nana is so worried about Ryan dying. You are, too...I can feel it. Don't worry. I don't know how, but we'll find him, okay?"

"We live, and we die, just as you do," Syd replied in a murmur. "Just...not as often, from the same things, or as in so short a time. Our children are our thralls—those we nurture and take into our lives, under our wing, just as mortal parents do with their children. We're born into this life, we live it, and yes, we can—and do—die. We honor our fallen and mourn our dead, just as you do. Just because we are not human does not mean we are not humane."

Rebecca reached up to touch Syd's cheek, encouraging him to look at her. "You eat too," she reminded him with a smile. "Just like real people."

Sydney smiled at her teasing and brought his hand to cover hers.

He turned his head and kissed the inside of her wrist, nipping it playfully with his fangs as he looked into her eyes.

"You're doing that...that hypnotic thing to me again," she murmured.

"Remember what it means to look into the eyes of a Master vampire. Not only is it extremely rude, you should never do so unless you're prepared to surrender control of yourself. However, this is just simple entrancement, not allure."

"Why is it rude?" Rebecca asked in a dreamy voice. "Eyes are a big deal in your world, huh? Earlier I had a staring contest with a hellhound. Was that rude too? It didn't seem like it..."

"Hellhounds are different," Syd replied. "To them, eye contact establishes rank and dominance—says who is in charge and who has the right to speak first. It isn't rude to stare down a hellhound. It's rude to meet a vampire's gaze—especially that of a Master—because such a thing involves...let us say...a level of intimacy. And yes...eyes are a 'big deal' to Ethereals because eyes are, as you humans say, the window to the soul. Looking a vampire in the eye is like saying you wish to see their soul, and they have none to see. The immortal soul was sacrificed so that the body and consciousness might take on that immortality. Now do you understand why it's rude?"

"Mmm," Rebecca said with a compliant nod. "I think so...I don't know. You're making it hard for me to think."

Syd gave a soft laugh. "Shall I cease?" he asked as he got to his feet. He urged her up with him, tugging her arm lightly.

"No, after everything scary today, this feels lovely," Rebecca replied with a silly smile, rising with his help. "All warm, and happy, and makes me forget that I'm supposed to be mad at you..."

"Don't be angry with me, Acolyte," he said in a soothing whisper as he brushed her hair back from her neck, exposing her Healer's mark. "Anger taints the blood, and I'm not much for spicy food."

His fangs pierced her throat.

Rebecca gasped at the swiftness of it. Her arms went around his neck and she closed her eyes, giving herself completely over to him and hating herself for it.

Don't hate yourself, she heard him say in her mind. *And don't hate me.*

I don't, she replied. *I was just scared. Nana—*

Hush.

Sorry.

It seemed to last a lot longer than when Ryan had done it, but Rebecca couldn't be sure. Still, it was warmer, more intense, and she wasn't sure, but she thought she heard Syd moan as he lifted his mouth from her throat.

"Mmm," Rebecca murmured again, blinking her eyes as she tried to force the cobwebs from them. "I don't feel like this after Ryan takes my blood."

Sydney laughed again.

"Ryan doesn't use entrancement, or any of the other niceties available to us," he replied. "Yet." He pulled back a little to see her face. "Think of it as the difference between a gentleman and a brute."

"He's been the gentleman?" Rebecca replied, teasing.

Sydney smiled so wide she could see his fangs. His eyes had returned to a bright, metallic blue. "Oh, Acolyte, I'm afraid you know exactly which one I am," he said. "Feeling better?"

She nodded, still trying to clear her brain of fuzziness.

"My apologies again for all you've endured today," he said as he released her. "And my gratitude for your restoration. You've provided me with much more than replenishment."

"I have?" Rebecca said. "I don't understand."

"Through your blood I've made sense of what has happened here today, both to you and in this house, and your feelings about it," Syd replied. "And I assure you, I will put everything right."

Then he was out the kitchen door, yelling for Billy.

CHAPTER EIGHT

The anubi was nowhere to be found.

Rebecca made herself a cup of tea and sat down at the kitchen table and tried hard not to think as she sipped at it. Her brow furrowed when she heard the front door open and heavy thuds in the foyer, like a very large person wiping their shoes on the inside mat.

Instantly Syd was by her side, looking highly annoyed.

"Where have you been?" he demanded when Billy finally entered the kitchen.

"Out," Billy replied. "Some of us need real food, not like you blood-suckers."

He grinned at Rebecca, and she couldn't help but smile back at him.

"I told you, fighting makes me hungry!" Billy said as he set four family-size pizza boxes down on the table. "And didn't I say I'd get you dinner?"

He opened the top box and held it out to Rebecca.

She shook her head. "No thanks. Not hungry." She surprised herself. She'd been ravenous all day, until...until the demons...

"More for me," Billy mumbled around an obscene bite of what looked like three slices of pizza folded into a taco-shape.

Rebecca looked to Syd, wrapping her hands around her own warm mug of tea. She took a sip and studied the vampire sitting across from her. All she really wanted to do was go to sleep and take care of her nana and go to school in the morning and deal with Marla Thompson like normal. Instead she was sitting at a table with a werewolf and a vampire, listening to them discuss how best to raid a demon lair.

She forced her thoughts back to what Syd was saying.

"Now, Billy we need to know which clan they're from. Can you scent them?"

"Sure I can," Billy said with a shrug. "Their stink is all over the house."

"Whose stink?" Rebecca asked.

Syd turned on her, his blue eyes fierce. "The demons that came looking for you! Do pay attention, Acolyte!"

Rebecca shook her head. "I don't get it. I mean...why now? Everything's been...I don't know...*normal* forever. Now suddenly, in the last twenty-four hours..."

"It's in your blood now," Syd replied. "Now that you've been exposed to the Otherworlds, and your birthday is so close, more will follow. More demons. And they will do so at a pace I only hope you can keep up with, lest they consume you. Your power, that is. It's far too strong. As...as Armaros said, I can't hope to hide you. They already know where to look."

Rebecca glanced toward the ceiling, imagining the mirror-portal upstairs just waiting to unleash an army of demons the second she turned seventeen. She swallowed hard and looked at Syd.

He nodded as though confirming her thoughts.

"If they can get to a Healer before she comes into her power, they can harness its manifestation for their own purposes," Syd replied. "You're turning seventeen in two days."

"Can't we...I don't know...close the portal? To keep them from coming through until then?" Rebecca asked.

Syd leveled her with a piercing stare. She was careful not to look directly into his eyes, dark or no. "You could close the portal, yes, but to do so now would be turning your back on all that you are and everything you could become. You have that choice. It's something mortals have that most Ethereals do not."

"What?" she asked, confused.

"Free will," Syd replied. "The portal hasn't been opened long enough for most beings to realize it, and though war is on the horizon, all-out battle hasn't begun yet. Believe me, it will begin, and casualties—all manner of creatures in dire need of your assistance—will come through it soon enough. That is, unless you close it again. Martha made that choice for you once, and now the choice is yours. Is it what you truly want, Acolyte? Could you now go back to your old life—for that is how you must look upon it now—knowing that you made this choice when it was presented to you? That you—forgive my melodrama—turned your back on both who and what you were destined to become?"

Rebecca didn't hesitate. Not for a second. When she thought about her life as it had been—macaroni and cheese in the cafeteria, Marla Thompson, not having a date for the winter formal—it all seemed so completely idiotic compared to what she had the chance to be. She was needed. Wanted. For the first time ever in her life, she mattered, and the thought of losing that twisted her insides until they hurt.

She shook her head. "I can't. I won't. No matter what...things... might um...try to hurt me. So if we can't close the portal, what else can we do?"

"We know you're a definite target," Syd replied. "At first, it was just an educated guess that you would be, and I wasn't even sure they knew about your existence, but apparently they do. How, I'm not sure. Demons are a lot of things, and one of the things you can do to protect yourself is control your emotions. Demons deliberately provoke stress and anxiety because those are the things they can sense most. Those emotions make you vulnerable to attack. You have to become strong and decisive—"

"Quit cryin'," Billy interrupted, his mouth full.

Syd glared at the werewolf and went on. "If you do not, they will not only be able to find you easily, they will be able to access your mind and thoughts without much effort. Once they have control of that, it's only a matter of time before they force full possession. You don't want that, do you?"

"It's just...this is hard, and new for me, and—"

"And you're worried and anxious," Syd interrupted her. "Time to get tough, Acolyte. Another thing you can do is put the things that worry you away somewhere safe."

His eyes went to the kitchen entry, and Rebecca understood what he meant before he looked back at her.

Nana.

"You're in danger, Acolyte, and Martha even more so," he continued. "They will kidnap her and use her to make you surrender to them. She doesn't have enough power to be any use to them besides that, and they will not hesitate to use her to get to you. While Martha is in this house and the portal is open, both of you are in terrible danger."

"Then we have to get her somewhere safe," Rebecca said. "But... but she said...she's only herself again because you're here. If we send her somewhere...won't she...slip back to being confused again?"

"I'll give her a talisman and see that it contains enough of my power to sustain her in her absence," Syd replied. "So she'll be safe and you won't have to worry about her. Remember what I said. You must not worry. You mustn't. You're just making yourself a larger target when you worry."

"I can't help it! She's my nana!"

"Then where can she go that you won't worry about her?" Syd asked.

"Can't she go somewhere with you?" Rebecca asked. "I wouldn't worry if she were with you."

Syd shook his head. "The demons know I'm here now and it won't take much for them to deduce that I'm protecting you. They'd come for Martha first thing if I tried to conceal her at my clan's lair or one of the Otherworlds. And while I fear for her safety, you're more important." He held up a hand to stop Rebecca's protest before he continued. "I'm sorry, but you are. You're the concern, the priority. Now stop worrying and *think*."

Rebecca swallowed hard and thought for a long moment. "Nana used to have this really good friend. She lives two towns away and they haven't talked in a long time. Once Nana stopped driving... Anyway, I'm sure Gretchen would be glad to...um...have the company for...for awhile. But Nana will worry and want to be here, and—"

Syd held up his hand again. "Stop worrying about her comfort. This is for her safety *and* comfort. Make the call. I'll talk to her and explain."

Rebecca nodded as Syd left the kitchen. She tried to convince herself that this was the right thing to do. The safe thing. She had to get her nana out of there. The demons could have killed her nana today, or taken her hostage, or something horrible. All because of her.

Call! she heard Syd order in her mind.

Rebecca stopped worrying and picked up the phone.

⊰——⊱ ⊰——⊱

Less than an hour later, Martha waved goodbye to her grand-daughter from the passenger seat of a, "classic" according to Billy, 1981 Imperial. Gretchen had been overjoyed to hear from her old friend's granddaughter and was more than happy to host Martha for a week or so. "More than happy" was an understatement. Gretchen had detailed the remodel of her guest bedroom for Rebecca and raved about how nice it was that Martha would be the first to stay in it. Gretchen insisted that Rebecca not worry at all about her grandmother—she was going to have such a great time! They'd play Scrabble and Nana's old favorite, gin rummy, and maybe even bridge if their other two friends that made up their old foursome were available.

Rebecca smiled and waved back, assuring her nana she'd be safe. After all, what was she going to do? Throw wild parties with all her friends?

When the car had disappeared from the driveway with her nana and the evil white menace Mishka inside it, Rebecca went back into the kitchen. Syd and Billy were upstairs trying to figure out what clan the demons had come from. Rebecca poked what little remained of Billy's three pizzas around inside their boxes and thought about cleaning up when the werewolf entered the kitchen carrying the fourth box with him, still scarfing now-cold pizza. He offered her the box again, and again she waved him off. Ew.

Rebecca made a pot of coffee, glad for once that her nana wasn't there. Nana never let her make herself a coffee. She believed it would stunt her growth. At the very least it would keep her awake all night, which is exactly what Rebecca was hoping it would do.

It's not like she was tired anyway. Like she could think about sleep after today! Besides, with everything that had happened over the last day or so, she was going to need the caffeine just to keep up with all she had to learn!

Billy tossed his pizza box on top of the others on the table and went to rummage through the fridge. "Got anything to drink?"

"I'm making some coffee," Rebecca offered. "Want some?"

"You humans don't know how to make coffee." Billy scowled at the fridge and slammed the door shut, causing the condiments in the door to rattle. He took a deep sniff before he stood up went to the pantry. He reached above the door, his brow furrowing before he smiled. In his hand was a brown unlabeled bottle. "Ha! Wasn't sure Martha had any left. Not like this stuff goes bad."

Billy pried the brown leathery-looking cap off with his teeth and spit it toward the sink where it landed with a thud against the stainless steel. He took a long drink, draining half the bottle.

"Even warm, this stuff is the nectar of the gods!" He took four more bottles down and went to the kitchen table where he flopped in a chair next to his empty pizza boxes.

Rebecca's brow furrowed and she went into the pantry and looked up. There, above the door, was an open cupboard without a handle. She looked at Billy, confused.

"Most Healers have a place to stash stuff outside the enclave that don't belong in it, and don't want company snooping around in your private things," Billy explained the hidden cupboard in the pantry. "And I have a sensitive nose. Can't hide a whole lot from an anubi, especially in this realm!"

"Hey, I'm beginning to realize there's a lot of stuff hidden in this house," she replied, shrugging as she came back to the table. "What is that, anyway?"

"Fae ale," Billy said. "Faerie beer," he clarified when Rebecca gave him a confused look. "Those garden boys know how to make all kinds of stuff from the plants they love so much, and they make a mean drink!"

Rebecca shook her head and made herself a cup of coffee with loads of milk and sugar. She sat back down at the table and smiled at the big guy.

The werewolf winked at her and nodded toward the pizza box. "Eat up. You wouldn't make a mouthful."

When she made a face and shook her head, Billy shoved the top box toward her. "Come on now. You gotta eat. Chow down."

Rebecca sighed and took a single slice of the cold pizza just so he'd stop offering it to her. "I'm not a dog, Billy."

"Neither am I, Bit." He took a swig of his beer. "Since I'm stayin' here tonight, you got anyplace special you want me to den up?"

Rebecca shook her head. "Wherever you like, I guess. I'm not real sure what a guy like you would find comfortable. You can have Nana's bed if you want, I guess. It's not like she'll be using it, and it's the biggest one we have."

"Nah. Beds is for humans. I'll find someplace comfy. Just the night, mind. Any longer and...well...let's just say you ain't the only one with jerks wanting to take a bite out of you. My brother Denis makes old Armaros look sweet."

He eyed the pizza left over in the box in front of Rebecca. With an impish smirk he leaned over and took two slices in one hand. He winked at her stuffed both pieces in his mouth at one time.

"Do you always eat like that?" she asked.

"Like what?"

"Uh..."

"Like a pig?" Billy teased. He grinned at her. "I might look it sometimes, Bit, but I ain't human, and you humans don't eat enough to keep a pup alive, let alone a full-grown anubi."

"Which is right? 'Anubi' or 'werewolf'?" Rebecca asked, propping her chin up on her hand. "'Anubi' sounds like that Egyptian god we learned about his history class—Anubis. He has the body of a man and the head of a jackal."

Billy nodded and grinned. "Egyptians worshiped us as gods once, and named Anubis after us. The real word for my people is 'Anubi', though 'werewolf' is an easier term for humans to understand. I'm an anubi—a *man-wolf*, not some silly wolf-man like in a movie."

"What's the difference?" Rebecca asked. She was serious and interested, not flippant. "Are there...wolf-men?"

Billy shook his head. "Those are just made up, and a way for humans to explain the occasional anubi sighting. I'm a wolf who can look human. I walk on two legs, just like humans, but can and do run on all-fours like you've seen. Just remember, when you see me as a human, it's just in human form. That's not what I am."

"So, you're just looking human?"

"No, I've changed my form to be human at the moment," he clarified. "And if you noticed, it isn't some stupid transformation under a full moon where I snarl and drool and howl and every bone in my body cracks and stretches blah blah blah. This form won't fool anything Ethereal. It's really just for looks. For humans."

"Why don't I see you as a wolf then? I'm supposed to have this power, right?" Rebecca asked. "You look like a normal guy that belongs on my school's football team."

"You're not old enough," Billy replied. "When you turn seventeen, your power will manifest fully and you'll be able to see more things for what they are."

"I still don't know what this power thing really is," Rebecca admitted. "Or what's so special about me turning seventeen. I'm supposed to have a lot of power—so much that Nana and Syd are worrying about it possibly doing something bad to me when my birthday comes. If I'm this big deal, why hasn't anything messed with me before?"

"Because you're not an Ethereal," Billy replied with a matter-of-fact shrug. "You have power, yeah, and a lot of it. Even I can feel it and anubi ain't no kind of sensitive to those things like the vamps, but it's...mortal. It comes from you, your life-force, here, not from another realm. Mortals can't share their life-force with anyone, not even among themselves, except a few like you. Ethereals can, and do, share their power with one another, and with those who can be receptive."

"Like...?" Rebecca prompted.

"I'll try to explain in a way you'll get, but I ain't no good at stuff like this like Syd is," Billy replied, sighing a little. "Let me think."

His eyes went to the pizza still in the box before them. He pointed to the missing slices.

"Say this pizza, when it still had all the pieces, is the power an Ethereal has," Billy said. "Let's say...a vamp, like Syd."

"Syd is a pizza, got it," Rebecca said with an impish grin.

I am not a pizza, Acolyte.

Syd? Aren't you supposed to be finding out which demon clan took Ryan? Stay out of my brain!

Aren't you supposed to be working on shielding your thoughts?

Oops.

"Hey, Bit, pay attention," Billy chastised, though he was smiling. "I'm lessoning you here."

"Sorry, Billy," Rebecca said, but without sincerity. She enjoyed the thought of Syd being a pizza too much to really be sorry.

Billy rolled his human eyes at her and continued. "Now, we've eaten some of the pizza, and it's filled us up, right? We're not hungry anymore."

"Well I'm not," Rebecca teased. "Can't say you're not, because you're probably thinking about waffles."

"Good places, waffle joints, especially the ones that are open all day and night. Sometimes a guy just needs a waffle, no matter what human time it might be. But you're missing the point. You ain't hungry no more, are you?"

Rebecca shook her head.

"So Syd gives—let's say Ryan, who has a hard time keeping hold on his and making his own, or your Nana, since she ain't got much of her own no more—a slice of pizza...his power...so they ain't hungry," said Billy. "He's sharing his own with them. Get it?"

Rebecca's brow furrowed. "I think so. It kind of makes sense. So...Nana...can't remember things because she needs...a slice of pizza?"

Billy nodded. "When she was younger, like you, she had her own pizza to keep her fed. Like you, she could make more pizza to replace what she shared with others, unlike now. She could, and did, share it with those who needed it, like you do with Ryan."

"I'm a pizza too," Rebecca said, looking at the boxes.

"Right," Billy said. "But where Syd is an extra-large supreme pizza with everything on it, you're just a small cheese pizza. Well, that's not really true. Nobody's sure yet exactly what size or kind of pizza you're going to be, or...or even if a pizza is what you're going to be."

That didn't sound good.

"What do you mean?" Rebecca asked, her heart pounding in an uncomfortable rhythm against her chest.

"You're still being made," Billy said. "And since Martha didn't do nothin' with your dough when you was growing up—she just let you sit there—you might not come out a pizza like you're supposed to. Whatever you end up being, you gotta be baked first. But that doesn't mean that parts of you ain't okay to eat now. It's just your dough that isn't ready to eat."

"And my birthday is baking day?" Rebecca asked. "The day we find out? And if I'm a good...whatever...or a bad one?"

Billy nodded and snagged the last slices of pizza before he closed the lid of the box.

"Syd is like the baker," Billy went on. "And with luck, maybe you'll be a good pizza. The size you're going to turn out and toppings you'll have nobody's sure about yet, but even if they're wrong, a cheese pizza is still a good pizza if you bake it right, and don't pull it out too soon or too late. Burnt pizza ain't good no matter how fast you choke it down."

"And that's the part everyone is worried about, right?" Rebecca asked. "That it might be too late to make me a good pizza?"

"It's more 'how you're going to turn out' now. You know those guys you see tossing the pizza dough in the air and catching it?" Billy asked.

Rebecca nodded.

"Well, you been dropped a few times," Billy said. He looked at Rebecca and smiled before he stuffed the pizza in his hand in his mouth and shrugged. "Didn't seem to make no difference, though. You're still good."

"Gee, thanks," Rebecca muttered, feeling less assured and more confused than before.

"Hey, you asked," Billy said. "Told you I wasn't any good at this stuff."

"So after my birthday...will things stop...messing with me?"

"Things are always hungry, Bit, and you're about to open an all-night waffle joint."

CHAPTER NINE

"Ready?" Syd asked as he returned to the kitchen.

"When you are," Billy replied. "Ain't gonna sit around here. Bit'll be safe enough."

"Ready...for what?" Rebecca asked. "You're not leaving me here alone!"

"And what do you propose I do, Acolyte?" Syd asked. "*You* tell the anubi to sit out the search for one of his clan—especially Ryan."

"Don't do that! I gotta go, Bit," Billy said, giving Rebecca puppy-dog eyes. "I ain't hurt half as bad as that kid, and he's gonna die if he don't get help soon. Those Hell-goons...they ain't nothin'...once you find them. Really they ain't. They're good at hiding, though, so Syd needs me to sniff them out. Vamps ain't got no sense of smell. Well, not like anubi do. I gotta go! Don't tell me I can't, please!"

Rebecca just looked at Billy. Why was he begging her? What did Syd mean, one of Billy's clan? Was Billy related to Ryan somehow? She made a mental note to ask about that later when she wasn't about to be left alone in a house that had just been ransacked by demons.

"Because the word of a Healer is to be obeyed as ultimate law," Syd replied to her unspoken question. "Tell him to stay, he'll stay."

"But...I'm...I'm not..." Rebecca began, swallowing hard. Wow. She had no idea she had that kind of power. That kind of authority.

That kind of responsibility for lives. Existences. Whatever. Suddenly she wished that the only responsibility she had to worry about was studying for her algebra test. She remembered thinking something like that about taking care of Nana. That seemed so silly now—a tiny little thing in comparison. If she screwed this up, she couldn't just erase the answer and try again, or retake the test. If she screwed up now, lives would be lost.

How did real doctors deal with that? How was *she* supposed to deal with that? She could barely deal with an exam she'd studied for!

102 • DINA JAMES

Suddenly she wanted to talk to Robin, but what would she tell her?

Rebecca shook her head and put something of her thoughts into words, more for Billy than Syd, as she knew Syd had likely heard her thinking.

"So if he goes and he gets hurt even more, or worse, he gets killed because I didn't tell him to stay here, that would be my fault, wouldn't it? And then his clan or family or someone would come after me for letting their...whatever...die?" Rebecca asked.

Syd shook his head. "You are a Healer. Your decisions will never be questioned. Resented, perhaps, and disagreed with, but never called into question. Remember what Martha said about Healers having certain clemencies? That is one."

"Bit, please," Billy said. No puppy eyes this time. Just deadly earnestness. "I gotta find that kid. I'm...I'm the one that busted the little punk, and—"

"—and he's like a brother to you, right?" Rebecca said. She smiled and heaved a sigh.

Billy grinned.

Rebecca shook her head and sighed.

"So what are we going to do?" Rebecca asked as she looked at Syd.

"'We'?" both Syd and Billy echoed.

Rebecca rolled her eyes at both of them. "You don't honestly think I'm going to sit around here alone while you two go off and do who-knows-what chasing after these demons, do you? I have to go, too. Ryan will need help right away, and...and..."

She looked at Billy. "I might not have senses like an anubi or eyes like a vampire, but I have something. I can't explain it. Maybe I'll be able to...I don't know...feel him, or something. I've been feeding him, and I felt it today when Billy was hurt so maybe...maybe I can feel Ryan, too."

"That's an awful lot of 'maybes', Bit," Billy said. He rubbed the back of his human neck with one of his large hands and looked at her from under his shaggy brown bangs.

Syd shook his head. "I'll not risk a Healer, Acolyte or no."

Rebecca scowled and crossed her arms over her chest. "So, it's all right if demons come in my house, mess stuff up, hurt my nana, take someone I'm looking out for and, according to both you guys, probably kidnap me too, but it's not all right if I try and take back what it is they stole? How is that fair?"

"Everyone deserves their vengeance, Syd," Billy said in a low voice. "You don't let them take it, it just sits inside and gets so big eventually it comes out in ways you never meant it to. Let her come. She should see, anyway."

"I think she's seen enough for one day, don't you?" Syd asked. He met the anubi's eyes.

This time, Billy didn't flinch or look away. "That shit don't work on me, fang-boy, so back the hell off. I'm in your clan, but that don't make me your bitch."

So Billy was in Syd's clan. *How does that work?* she wondered. A were-wolf in a vampire clan? Didn't Syd say the vampires and werewolves were at perpetual war? Whatever they were to one another, they weren't going to get anywhere arguing. Something else Syd said prodded her memory and she decided to put this supposed authority she had to the test.

"Guys, knock it off," Rebecca said. She pinched the bridge of her nose between her thumb and forefinger. She was getting a serious headache, and her stomach rumbled. She hadn't touched the slice of pizza Billy had brought her. Her stomach might be empty, but she just couldn't think about food right now. She looked at Syd. "So you're going after Ryan? You know where he is?"

Syd nodded. "I know which group took him, and where they generally make their lair. We can start there. That is, Billy and I can start there. You're staying here."

"Not with that portal thing I'm not!" Rebecca said, shaking her head as she pointed at the ceiling. "What makes you think they're not just waiting until no one is here before they come back? What if they took Ryan so there'd be nothing in the house that has any kind of power so they could...I don't know...read me or something when I got back? Pick me up on their power radar or whatever? I'm not any safer here alone than I am with you!"

Syd began to pace the room.

"You can't take her to the clan lair, Syd," Billy said. "They'll look there. They'll know from Ryan who his Master is. Matter of fact, you should—"

"I've already linked with the others and apprised them of the situation," Syd interrupted. "They know not to expect my return and to fall back to the haven."

"What about—" Billy began.

Syd cut him off with a sharp look. "She'll be all right."

Rebecca couldn't be sure, but she didn't think Syd was talking about her.

"So like Bit said," Billy went on as though Syd hadn't said anything. "What are we going to do?"

"Can you jump the car?" Syd asked.

104 • DINA JAMES

"With your help, yeah," Billy replied, though he didn't sound happy.

"Then let's go," Syd said.

"Go...where?" Rebecca asked, suddenly hesitant.

"Into the lair of a demon."

Rebecca swallowed hard and made herself remember that she'd pitched a fit about being told she couldn't go and followed him and Billy out the door.

Rebecca slid into the mangled passenger seat of Billy's Mustang. Syd got in the back as Billy got behind the wheel.

"You know—" said Billy.

"Not now, anubi," Syd interrupted.

"Just sayin'," Billy muttered. "Bit ain't had nothin' to eat. Some of us actually need to eat. Also easier to fight with food in me, and if I'm gonna die, I want to do it on a full stomach! Besides, the gate's just past a burger joint next to the interstate. We could—"

Rebecca looked at Billy in open-mouthed horror. "You just ate four whole pizzas! Extra-large ones! How can you still be hungry?"

"Them? Barely a snack. 'Sides, we're about to go into a demon lair—"

"Fine," Syd interrupted again. "Let's just get going."

Billy again drove like a maniac, and Rebecca realized that doing that was probably normal for him. Once they got to the fast food place, he ordered a huge amount of food before asking Rebecca what she wanted, then shook his head at her when she stammered that just one cheeseburger would do for her.

"I'll share my fries with you," Billy said, giving her his lady-killer grin before he ordered drinks.

Rebecca glanced at Syd and made a deliberate effort to speak to him in her head.

He can't possibly eat all that before we get there..., can he?

Syd smiled, but he hid it fast. *Just watch. I suggest if you want any of those fries he said he'd share that you take them immediately, for they won't last long.*

Uh...thanks. This is weird. I mean, talking like this. Not just...ordering fast food with a werewolf.

Syd didn't reply as Billy started filling up the space between the seats and Rebecca's lap with bags. He shoved a drink carrier full of soda at her, then balanced another full of milkshakes on his own lap.

"There we go!" Billy said as he pulled out of the drive-thru. "A nice snack before I munch on some demons. They're chewy and not at all filling, so we might have to stop back by here after we find the punk."

"This is a snack?" Rebecca looked at the bags scattered all around her, filling up her lap, the floor at her feet, and the space between her and Billy.

"Mmmhmm," Billy said as he turned one of the bags in his lap upside down. Burger wrappers went everywhere as he drove toward the interstate, and Rebecca just watched in fascination as each burger Billy ordered was devoured in a single bite.

He was indeed finished with fifteen burgers, ten orders of fries, three colas and four milkshakes in the less than five minutes it took them to reach their destination.

Rebecca hadn't touched her own burger, or the fries in the box resting against her thigh, or the soda held between her knees.

"Eat, Bit," Billy said as he parked the car beneath an on-ramp at the highway. "I'm gonna prep Rox for the jump."

Rebecca didn't ask what that meant as Billy got out of the car. Syd sat in the back seat, silent, though Rebecca could feel his anticipation, worry and urgency. She opened her burger wrapper and took a bite. She nearly spit it back out. It tasted awful and she couldn't bring herself to swallow it. She found a napkin and spit the bite into it before stuffing it into one of the empty bags.

"It would have done no good to tell him you can't eat," Syd said. "Take a drink instead."

Rebecca reached for the soda between her legs and took a long sip. Now *that* was rapturous. She took the lid off and drank directly from the cup, gulping the cold drink down.

"I don't get it," Rebecca said when she finished the soda. She wrapped up the rest of her cheeseburger and set it on the dashboard. "What's the deal?"

"To put it in easy words, you need to replace your fluid loss," Syd said. "A side effect of having your blood taken. It will wear off in an hour or so. Then you'll be ravenous."

That explained why she'd been so hungry at school that morning. No wonder the macaroni-and-cheese paste had sounded wonderful.

"Syd, move your butt," she heard Billy call. "Almost done here."

Rebecca wondered what they were doing. Billy had said something about "prep," and said he could...jump the car with Syd's help. Rebecca knew what jumping a car meant, but she didn't see...

She got out of the car to see what was going on.

Billy and Syd were staring at thin air under the overpass and talking in low voices, gesturing at the incline that led up to the ramp.

Rebecca sure didn't see any jumper cables.

She looked back at the car.

The crumpled blue Mustang wasn't blue anymore. Now it was black, and again it had spikes and chains covering it. She shook her head and walked toward the two Ethereals.

"Tricking out your ride is your idea of jumping a car?" Rebecca asked.

Billy laughed. "Taking her through the realms is rough—poor Rox's gotta have protection." He looked at Syd. "We ready?"

Syd looked back at the car and then at thin air again. "I think so."

"Ready to do what?" Rebecca asked.

"Jump the car through realms," Syd replied. He pointed to the overpass. "Just between the ground and the mortal construct there is a gate. We're going to take the car through it to the demon lair. With any luck, we'll land right on top of them."

"Why didn't we just...I don't know...poof from the enclave, like you did with the kitchen and the water?"

"Because this is a much bigger jump over a much greater distance, and we're doing it with an anubi and a mortal," Syd explained.

Rebecca just looked even more confused. "But Billy and I... jumped...earlier and didn't have to stop and do anything special. We weren't even close to here, either."

Syd looked at Billy and raised an eyebrow.

"That weren't a jump. Just a quick slip between the realms to shake the goons after us," Billy defended. "Ain't like what we're doing here."

"To put it simply, a big job needs big tools. This is a big tool," Syd said.

"I still don't see anything," Rebecca said. "But I'll take your word for it."

"When your own power manifests in its entirety, you'll be able to," Syd said. "At least, you should be able to. For now—let's go."

"What if someone sees us?" Rebecca asked as they all got back in the car.

Billy snorted. "Humans never see anything. Bunch of the blindest—uh—I mean...well..." He put his hands on the wheel and took a deep breath. "All right, Rox. Don't let me down, girl." He looked in the rearview mirror at Syd and gave him a nod.

Syd closed his eyes and tilted his head back. Rebecca saw his hands clench into fists, and looked back just in time to see Billy doing the same, except his head was bowed.

Rebecca felt what she could only call a "pop" and suddenly the overpass in front of them was gone, replaced with an empty field. The stars shown bright outside the window in the night sky, unhindered by the glow of the streetlights they'd just left.

It was very dark, and very, very quiet.

It didn't look at all like a demon lair.

"Just what did you expect a demon lair to look like?" Syd asked, amused.

"I don't know," Rebecca replied. "Blood, guts and gore, I guess. Red guys with pitchforks poking people on sticks?"

"You watch far too much television," Syd said. "However, you are correct. This isn't the demon lair. This is just where the gate ends. The lair is farther on."

"Good thing you all have a car or you'd have to walk it," Rebecca muttered and looked back out the window again.

"You didn't eat your sandwich, Bit," Billy said, nodding toward the wrapped burger that had fallen off the dash to land in Billy's lap.

"Uh...there's...mustard on it," Rebecca said, remembering what Syd had said about Billy not understanding she couldn't eat right then. "I forgot to say no mustard."

"I'll remember that next time," Billy said as he unwrapped the burger and polished it off in one bite. "Which way, Syd?"

"Fifteen miles south," Syd replied. "Then four to the west. A warehouse overlooking the river."

River? Warehouse? Where were they?

"Demons prefer the mortal realm," Syd said. "And the leader of this little band of miscreants, favors an outpost in Scotland."

"We're in Scotland?!" Rebecca asked, incredulous.

"I told you it was a great distance," Syd replied as Billy started the car.

"We don't have a lot of time here, either," Syd continued. "The night hours have been considerably shortened by this jump eastward."

"In other words, we gotta hurry," Billy said, and gunned the engine.

Fifteen miles sounded like a nice, leisurely drive to Rebecca. Billy had them there in less than five minutes.

"It's a good thing I didn't eat," Rebecca said as they ground to a halt before the turn to the west. "Or I'd have thrown up. Haven't you ever heard of a speed limit?"

"Stupid mortal rules," Billy muttered. "Limits are for humans."

"Don't you ever get pulled over?"

"What? Cops?" Billy asked with a snort. "They gotta catch me first, Bit, and I ain't met a human yet who can keep up with me behind the

108 • DINA JAMES

wheel. Besides, Rox has an engine in her like you wouldn't believe—"

"Slow this time, Billy," Syd interrupted. "Remember, they don't know we're coming. Let's not give them any warning."

"Let's leave the car here then," Billy said. He looked at Syd in the rearview mirror. "You can get us all the rest of the way, right? You're the one knows where we're going."

Syd nodded. Billy parked the car under a nearby tree. Rebecca got out and noticed they hadn't been driving on a road.

"Don't you ever get a flat tire?"

Billy grinned. "Remember when I said I had to prep Rox? Well, she's prepped. Better than a Humvee, Rox is, especially with Syd's help. I'm gonna leave the keys in her, just in case."

"Just in case...what?" Rebecca asked.

"In case I don't make it out of there alive and you all do," Billy said with a shrug. He looked hard at Rebecca. "Now you listen close, Bit—"

Syd didn't wait for Billy to finish. Instead he took Rebecca's hand and brought her wrist to his mouth. He bit down hard and Rebecca yelped. Billy grabbed her shoulder and closed his eyes.

Rebecca's eyes slid shut of their own accord. Was this what it was like for Syd when he took her blood? So much...she knew so much now. Billy kept another gun under the driver's seat loaded with silver bullets... there was a first aid kit in the trunk and a blanket and pillow...

Directions to the gate and how to use it.

But she was powerless. Didn't she need—

Just get there, Syd ordered.

I don't know how to drive!

Syd dropped his hold and his bite. Billy let go of Rebecca's shoulder.

"You don't know how to drive?" Syd asked aloud.

Rebecca blushed and shook her head. "I never learned. Nana—"

"Then run," Syd growled. "If this goes badly and neither Billy nor I can help you, you get to that gate, do you understand?"

Rebecca swallowed hard and nodded.

"Then let us go."

"Syd?" Rebecca asked, her voice trembling.

"Yes?"

"What if...?"

"Yes?"

"What if...I'm the one who...doesn't make it out of there alive?"

"They won't kill you," Syd assured her. "They'll keep you alive. At least until—"

Syd stopped speaking, but Rebecca knew what he'd been about

to say.

At least until her birthday.

"Let's go," Syd said, and took her hand again. Billy rested his hand on Syd's shoulder this time, and Rebecca felt the familiar sick feeling in the pit of her stomach as they disappeared from one location and appeared in another.

In another dark, smelly, oppressive location. Rebecca would have been a lot more afraid of this place if she weren't all-but-surrounded by a tall, blond vampire now brandishing some kind of sword, and a brown-furred hulk of a wolf on two legs.

Rebecca suddenly wondered what use she was going to be, and fought to think. She was here to find Ryan. She closed her eyes and tried to relax. He was hurt...hungry...she should be able to feel that. After a long moment of feeling nothing at all like she had before, she opened her eyes.

"I can't feel anything," Rebecca whispered.

"Let's move," Syd said. "They wouldn't keep him here in the open. Let's get into the lair proper. This is just outside."

Rebecca felt stupid, but then asked herself how she was supposed to know that.

Syd and Billy kept her close between them. Billy led the way, taking deep sniffs of the air every now and then. The farther they went, the hotter it became, and the harder it was for Rebecca to breathe. She tried to pay attention to something other than her heart pounding against her chest and the sweat dampening her shirt as she followed the werewolf through dark doorways and empty corridors.

They came to a flight of stairs leading down and the corridor split into two different sections, offering them three ways to continue.

Billy froze. "Bit?"

Rebecca closed her eyes and let her mind go blank. There was something...

She nodded, then felt dumb again. It was dark.

He can still see you, as can I, she heard Syd in her mind. *It may appear dark to your eyes, but not to ours.*

She lifted a finger and pointed down the hallway at the end of the stairs. "There's something...I feel like I'm being called...or pulled...down there," she whispered.

"Down we go, then," Syd said, and Billy led them down the dark staircase to another lightless room.

The room wasn't unlit for long. As they moved toward the end of the hall, a torch flared to life and seemed to hang by itself in the middle of the room. Nothing was holding it.

At least, nothing Rebecca could see. She could hear the laugh that echoed through the room perfectly. A shiver ran down her back and, for all the heat in the room, Rebecca felt as though she'd been submerged in ice water.

Billy growled and halted, straightening to his full, considerable height. As wide as the fridge in the kitchen, Billy had no trouble at all hiding Rebecca behind him.

Still, even Billy wasn't a match for the size of the creature that stood before him. It towered so far above the anubi that Rebecca could clearly see its inhuman face in the light of the torch it held. Huge gray-green wings rose over its head and shoulders.

She took an instinctive step back as she recognized the creature as the Bathroom Demon.

Rebecca couldn't help but think that the demon looked like something off one of those horror movie magazine covers or the box of a computer game. Still, computer demon or not, it seemed like one of the really big bosses you fought to win the game, and Rebecca was scared to the bone.

"I got no fight with you, Hellspawn, so back off," Billy spat with a growl, interrupting Rebecca's thoughts. "We just got a bit lost lookin' for somethin' is all."

The demon laughed. Rebecca shivered. It was so...cruel. Malicious. Evil.

"Lost?" the demon replied with an indulgent glare. "Perhaps we should help you find your way. A bit more light should do it. I know your kind has poor eyesight."

Torches flared to life, illuminating the dark around them.

No, not torchlight. Hellhounds.

The demon smiled, though it emanated nothing but cruelty, and gestured at Rebecca.

She felt instantly better. The heat disappeared, and she could breathe easier.

"There, Acolyte, is that not an improvement?" the demon said in a smug voice. "I know the delicacy of your kind. Personally. A pleasure to see you again."

Billy growled, his clawed hands clenching into fists. Rebecca put a gentle hand on his arm, and the anubi relaxed somewhat. Still, the scowl on his scarred face deepened. "So you've come to see us off then, Armaros, or just make sure I leave without marking your door?"

Armaros laughed again. "You have crimes to make restitution for, anubi," the demon replied with an indulgent smile before looking again at Rebecca over Billy's shoulder. "As for the Acolyte...her power will be a valuable asset to—"

"Remember what happened the last time you touched her," Billy cut Armaros off with a deep growl.

Armaros raised a smooth black eyebrow. "She is in our lair, of her own will, is she not? Even shielded, her power bleeds from her. You can drop it, bloodsucker. Don't think we haven't noticed you."

Rebecca heard Syd swear.

Billy snarled. His clawed, furry hand clamped down on her shoulder. "Syd! Get her out of here!"

Chapter Ten

Billy shoved her hard backwards. The heat around Rebecca returned instantly, making it again very hard to breathe. She broke into a sweat as she slowly got to her feet. She tried to move, but it was hard. Like walking through water up to her chest. Why could she barely move? Where were the stairs? She couldn't see! Where was Syd?

A yelp and a low howl reached her ears.

"BILLY!" Rebecca screamed.

She heard another snarl, but couldn't see if it was Billy from this far away. It was so dark!

"BILLY!" she yelled again, as loud as she could. Her bottom lip trembled and she caught it between her teeth, biting it hard as her eyes started to burn with tears. She couldn't cry! Billy told her that demons liked it when she was scared and crying. But... "SYD!"

Strong furry arms wrapped around her and a feeling of instant comfort washed over her. Billy! Rebecca hugged the form hard and choked back a sob.

"Hush up now," Billy said. "I got 'em. You think they'd learn by now not to mess with ol' Billy. Now we gotta find Syd. Those bastards grabbed him."

Billy shoved her on his back as he had earlier that day and Rebecca dug her hands into the loose fur at his shoulders. As they had been that morning, they were bathed in wet and cold, seeming even colder in this deathly hot place.

"Billy, you're bleeding bad."

"Ain't nothin'," Billy said. "Don't worry 'bout me. Think now! What was it you felt? I'll bet it wasn't Ryan, but those demons making like they was him. Do something, Bit. Figure this out! Where'd they take Syd?"

"Um..." Rebecca stammered. She took a deep breath and tried to stop crying long enough to focus. She couldn't.

Billy growled and pulled her off his back. He stood her in front of him and clasped her upper arms in his huge, clawed hands. It was dark, but there was enough light in here that she could see his face and his eyes.

"Listen, I know you're scared," he said. "But you gotta do this. Now hush up and see to what needs doin', all right? We ain't leavin' here without him or somethin' that says he's dead, so stop your crying. Cryin' makes it worse!"

Rebecca wiped her eyes on her sleeve and swallowed hard. Billy was right. She wanted to be here. Had asked to come. She had to do this. Billy had fought demons to get her this far just so she could help like she said she might be able to. The least she could do was be as brave as he had been and do what she'd offered to do.

She put a hand on Billy's arm, felt him near and protective and closed her eyes. She was safe, protected by Billy. Safe. Safe and warm. Syd. Syd always made her feel safe and warm...

Her insides twisted and something below her breastbone tugged at her. She pointed to their right. "I can't see anything there, but—"

Rebecca didn't finish her sentence as Billy picked her up and put her on his back again. They moved down a hallway and at the end of it was a flight of stairs. Billy raced up them.

Pre-dawn light filled the large warehouse that looked more to Rebecca like an airplane hangar. In the grip of a demon was Syd. A limp, unresponsive Syd—his blond head lolling to one side like his neck had been snapped.

Billy growled and crouched low. Rebecca instinctively slid off his back, and Billy was off and charging the demon before both of Rebecca's feet touched the floor. The demon was taken down before it even knew it was being attacked, and Billy ripped it apart, scattering the different body parts across the concrete floor.

Rebecca fought not to vomit at the stench and the gore. She was about to say something about dismembering the body when she saw one of the arms inching its way back toward the torso. She looked around and saw a leg doing the same, and the head struggling to right itself.

"Billy?" she called in a wavering voice.

"I know, Bit," Billy said. "We ain't got a whole lot of time and Syd's been drained. We gotta move."

Billy took Syd under one arm and Rebecca under the other and did just that. Almost before Rebecca could draw another breath they were out of the warehouse. The light that had looked bright inside was actually very faint, but in comparison with the darkness of the basement, it was brilliant.

114 • DINA JAMES

Billy swore as he looked to the horizon and stopped. He set Rebecca down on her feet and laid Syd gently in the tall grass. "We ain't gonna make the car if I carry you both. I'll go on ahead and bring Rox to you all."

Rebecca heard in his tone that he didn't think he'd even make it to the car in time without them, but he was gone at a speed she'd never seen anything move like before she could reply.

She knelt down beside Syd's body and glanced over her shoulder toward the warehouse. She shivered with fear as she remembered the body parts moving back toward each other, and knew that they hadn't killed the demons—only bought themselves time.

Birds chirping around her made Rebecca look to the rising sun. Four miles was a long way to run, even for someone as fast as Billy, and he was hurt. She looked down at Syd. Maybe...maybe...

Awful lot of maybes, she thought.

Rebecca rolled up her sleeve and pressed her wrist to Syd's open mouth.

Nothing happened.

"Come on," Rebecca pleaded in a whisper. "Come on, Blondie."

She glanced up at the horizon and heard an unearthly howl coming from the direction of the warehouse behind her. She closed her eyes and bit back the sob rising in her throat.

"Syd...Syd, please," Rebecca said as she lay down in the tall grass alongside him. If she got lucky, maybe the demons wouldn't see her.

Don't be stupid, she told herself. *They'll sense you. They know you're here and how close you are and they're going to get you.*

Rebecca cradled Syd's head and pressed her wrist hard into his mouth and felt his fangs against her skin, but they didn't puncture hard enough to break it.

Another demonic howl broke the silence of the morning.

It was all Rebecca could do not to run. Running was stupid. It didn't matter where she ran. They'd find her. Besides...she wouldn't leave Syd, and if she wasn't where Billy left her, he'd get killed too trying to find her.

Killed. They were going to kill Syd. They were going to leave him drained and exposed to the daylight.

Rebecca looked at his limp form and back at her arm. She brought her wrist to her own mouth and stifled her yelp against her flesh as she bit down hard. When she tasted blood, she tore her wrist away from her mouth and pressed it hard against Syd's fangs. She squeezed her arm above the wound with her free hand, willing her blood to flow.

Syd's eyes startled open. They were black in the purple of lightening-ing sky.

"Shh!" Rebecca ordered, bringing a finger to her lips. "They're coming."

What—?

No time! Billy's gone to get the car. The sun is rising and you're drained. Take what you need so you can at least have a chance of getting somewhere safe!

Are you all right?

The question shocked Rebecca, but she nodded.

Leave me here, Syd ordered in her mind as he turned his head away from her wrist.

Don't be stupid, Rebecca retorted and shoved her wrist back in his mouth. *There's nowhere I can run they won't find me, and I'm not going anywhere without you!*

Syd just looked at her for what seemed like an eternity before he took her wrist away from his mouth. He turned over on his side and gathered her to him. He looked deep in her eyes for only a moment before his fangs found her neck.

Rebecca gasped and clung to him.

I thought you said it didn't matter where you drank from, she thought.

Faster, was all she heard him reply.

She closed her eyes. Oh, this was warm. She was safe here. She heard a demon howl somewhere in the distance and didn't care. Let them find her. She was safe right here.

"I'm gone for three minutes and you two start making out," she heard Billy say. "Let's move before either the sun makes one of us toast or those Hell-goons get their heads back on straight."

She heard Syd groan as Billy lifted him up and laid him in the trunk of the car. He shut the trunk and knocked on it before he returned and grabbed Rebecca. Before she knew it, she was in the passenger seat and Billy was back behind the wheel, in his human form. They were speeding toward the rising sun, and he looked over and smiled at Rebecca.

She put her head in her hands.

"Aw, Bit," Billy said. "Don't."

His sympathy made it worse and she couldn't hold back her frightened tears anymore.

"How about some pancakes?" Billy said. "No, too late for pancakes at home, unless you want to go to that twenty-four hour waffle place. How about that? How about some waffles?"

Rebecca just looked at him. Billy grinned at her.

"You can't eat waffles looking like that," she said. "They'd throw us out or call the cops or both."

"You ain't cryin' no more, are you?"

Rebecca choked on a half-sob, half-giggle and sniffed hard. She wiped her eyes and shook her head as she smiled for him.

"There you go!" Billy said. "No crying. I can't stand a woman crying. Let's get you home, you can patch me up—I'll even shower if you want me to—and let Syd get some rest. I'll get us some waffles, and we'll figure out where those bastards have the punk hid." Billy looked in the rearview mirror. "Sonofa—"

"Oh, no," Rebecca groaned and slid down in her seat. "Not again."

"Tell me abo—" was all he managed to get out before a thud came from above them, the car's roof crumpling even more between them.

Billy punched the roof hard above his head. "AIN'T YOU DONE ENOUGH TO ROX FOR ONE DAY?!"

Rebecca just managed slide down in her seat before she was showered with glass. The demon on the roof of the car reached through the shattered windshield and clawed at her.

She screamed and looked up to see the gun in Billy's hand just as he fired. There was a thud from the hood followed by an outraged howl.

Billy reached across the seat and hauled Rebecca up. She yelped as he pulled her under the crumpled roof across the seat and into his lap before guiding her hands to the steering wheel.

"Take the wheel!"

"I can't drive!" she protested, though she clung to the hard plastic. She shrieked again as Billy hauled himself out from under her and through the driver's side window. Rebecca saw a gray-winged form fall in front of the tires and heard a sickening crunch.

Billy slid back in the window and shoved Rebecca out from behind the wheel into the passenger seat as he stomped the gas pedal. The car shot forward. The werewolf looked over at her.

"So, waffles?" Billy asked.

Rebecca just looked at him.

Billy looked in the rearview again. "Damn. Those assholes just don't know when to give up."

"Oh, cripes," Rebecca moaned, and slid into the small space between her seat and the dash on the floor.

She saw the gun Billy had used was wedged near the passenger door. She reached toward it just as the car was hit hard from behind.

Rebecca couldn't help but scream again. The gun skittered away from her, back toward the driver's side.

"SYD!" Billy yelled. "Hang on, Bit! Almost there!"

A feeling of weightlessness followed by hard thump beneath her knocked Rebecca onto her behind, and she yelped in pain.

"You okay?" Billy asked. He leaned down and shoved her into the passenger seat, and Rebecca realized it was once again dark outside.

She remembered he'd asked a question and managed a nod before the car was hit again from behind.

"Damn," Billy growled. "Rotten bastards. SYD!"

There was another loud bang from the back of the car and Rebecca turned around to see the trunk burst from its hinges and fall away from the rear of the car. A blond head emerged.

It didn't look like the Syd she knew. This creature looked more than dangerous. Fangs bared in a menacing snarl, the Syd-thing brought up what looked like a rifle. Rebecca didn't realize it was a crossbow until she saw a silver-tipped bolt fly from it and heard a something like a shriek.

"IT TOOK ME SIX MONTHS TO FIND THAT LID!" Billy yelled over his shoulder.

"DRIVE!" Syd shouted back as he reached down and came up with another bolt. He fumbled with it, like he couldn't get his fingers to obey him and dropped it twice before he managed to get it loaded into the crossbow. He put the crossbow to his shoulder and pointed it behind them.

It seemed like hours before Billy turned onto her street and even longer before he reached her driveway.

As they passed the fence marking the property, Rebecca felt as though a weight had been lifted from her chest. Billy got out of the car to look behind them.

She heard a howl and a screech of outrage and got out of the car just in time to see the demon chasing them fly off into the dark.

A moan reached her, and she turned to see Syd's dark eyes roll back as the he dropped the crossbow and swayed forward.

Rebecca ran to the back of the car and peered into the dark hole that had once been Billy's trunk. "Syd!"

She looked to the werewolf. Billy was covered in blood and a slick black goo that looked like oil, but he was standing. She hated to ask him to help her get Syd into the house and up to the enclave, but she knew she couldn't move the vampire herself. Who knew how late...early?...it was. It was still dark, but Rebecca looked to the horizon anyway, searching for the tiniest hint of daybreak.

"I'll get him," Billy said, saving Rebecca from asking. "Should just stake him though. I mean...look what he did to my car!"

Rebecca finally saw what the car looked like. Though it was dark, there was light from the streetlamps and the porch.

The car, besides missing the trunk lid, looked less like a beer can someone had crushed and more like something even a junkyard wouldn't sell as scrap. The tires, however, were all still fully inflated. Rebecca shook her head and couldn't help but laugh.

"That's the spirit, Bit!" Billy said, smiling in approval.

"Thanks," she said. She gestured to the house. "Come on. Let's get you guys patched up."

"What about you?" Billy asked as he pulled the unconscious Syd from the trunk and cradled him in his arms like a rag doll. "You hurt?"

"I don't think so," Rebecca said. "I mean, probably, but I don't think anything is broken. I guess I'll find out later."

"I don't smell a whole lotta blood on you," Billy muttered as they walked up the porch into the house. "Just your arm a bit, but you done that yourself."

"Just because someone isn't bleeding doesn't mean they aren't hurt," Rebecca retorted. "Look at Syd."

Billy went upstairs ahead of her to the enclave, carrying Syd in silence.

As much as Rebecca didn't want to think, there were questions that she really wanted answers to.

Had the demons set a trap for them? Where had they taken Ryan? Were they really after her, not him? Why? How did they know she'd have gone with Syd when he came after Ryan? Or had they planned on taking Syd too? What was going on?

She automatically looked at the clock on the mantle in the living room before she went upstairs. Two in the morning. Wow. No wonder she was tired. They'd left somewhere around six that evening.

Tired and hungry. But was she really hungry? Or was that feeling of starvation coming through from Syd.

Wherever it was from, there wasn't time for sleep or food. There was a vampire that needed restoration and who knew what else. Rebecca had no idea what the demons had done to...what had Billy called it? Drained? Whatever they'd done to take everything from Syd in the blink of an eye. Syd was a powerful Master vampire. How could they have incapacitated him so fast?

Then there was Billy, who acted like nothing hurt him and that fighting was fun and that waffles could cure everything. Or burgers before a fight, or—

Rebecca all but collided with the big guy as she entered the enclave.

"Thought I'd go grab us a bite," he said as he backed into the healing space and let her in.

"Is food all you think about?" she asked, and immediately hated

ALL WOUNDS • 119

herself for sounding grouchy.

Billy didn't seem to notice her grumpiness and shrugged. "We gotta eat, right? How about Chinese? You like Chinese? I know this all-night Chinese joint—"

"Sure, Billy, whatever," Rebecca said with a tired sigh. Then she looked hard at him and shook her head. "Let me have a look at you first."

"I'm all right," Billy said, shaking his head. "You look after Syd. He's out while I just have a couple scratches. I'll patch myself up in the car."

Rebecca started to say something about how someone would definitely notice the condition of the car if not the condition of the driver, but found she just couldn't think about what people might notice anymore. According to Nana, these Ethereal guys had been around a long time, and if no one had noticed them before, they weren't going to notice them now. They probably had their ways of keeping themselves hidden anyway, and Billy had said himself that humans weren't all that great at noticing things right in front of them.

And Chinese did sound really good all of a sudden.

She wondered what her nana had eaten before she went to bed, or even if she had done so. Maybe she and Gretchen had got to catching up and hadn't eaten anything. Just sat there sipping tea or coffee.

Billy looked like he was waiting for her to say something, and she remembered he'd asked if she liked Chinese.

"Oh, uh...broccoli and beef, and General Tso's if they have it," she said, and was rewarded with Billy's lady-killer grin.

She couldn't help but smile back. He just had one of those smiles.

"You got it! Broccoli is the best!"

He was down the stairs and out the door before Rebecca could say anything else.

She shook her head again and went into the dark enclave. She'd just lit a candle and shook out the match when she noticed Syd's dark eyes open and on her.

"Hey, Blondie," she said in her best version of Nana's calm, quiet voice. "You look like crap."

Syd didn't reply.

"Blondie? Syd?"

The dark eyes continued their blank stare.

Rebecca almost panicked before she remembered that vampires slept with their eyes open. She swallowed hard and took a deep breath. He was all right. Just sleeping. If he'd...died...he wouldn't be there. He'd have just disappeared. The knowledge of what happened when a vampire died was just...there. There wouldn't even be a pile of dust to mark his passing. Just empty clothes. Her eyes went to the large signet ring Syd wore on his left hand. It would be left behind, too...if Syd...ceased to exist.

She looked down at her hands. Her left wrist hurt where she'd bit it to get at her blood for Syd. She saw two punctures there and laughed at herself for being surprised. Of course he hadn't had time to heal them before he took her blood from her neck. She reached up and touched her throat, wincing as her fingers found the ragged wound he'd made. Her hand slid up her neck to her head, and sure enough she could feel a lump swelling there. She'd definitely whacked her head against the crumpled roof when Billy had thrown that demon under the tires. She looked more at herself in the light of the single candle.

Her sweatshirt was torn at the shoulder and at the neck—probably from being grabbed by either Billy, Syd or a demon—and her jeans at the knee. She had no idea where the jacket she'd been wearing was. Her ponytail had come loose and strands of her hair hung in her face. She didn't even want to know what that looked like.

She sighed and stood and went to the chest of drawers that held various healing supplies. She found a bandage and a clean cloth and dipped the cloth into the big pot of water left up there.

Rebecca dabbed at her wrist, sponging away the dried blood. She hissed and winced as the movement disturbed the deep wound, and scratched at her neck.

It wasn't until Syd spoke that she realized her patient was awake and in need.

CHAPTER ELEVEN

Let me see that.

Rebecca just looked at Syd, aware he'd spoken to her, even if he hadn't used his voice. She hesitated a moment, unsure what he was asking for, before she held her wrist out to him.

Not that wound. Your neck.

Rebecca turned her head and brushed her hair back from her neck, showing Syd the wound he'd made.

Let me see it, she heard again, more insistent this time.

She made no move to do as he said. This wasn't the Syd she knew. This was a different person—different *creature*—than the warm, comfortable, safe, sometimes ironic and annoying blond guy she'd somehow gotten used to, and she was not only afraid of him, she was alone with him for the first time.

"I'd better go," Rebecca stammered, and made to stand up.

Syd's hand clamped over her wrist. "No."

He said the word aloud, and Rebecca knew how much effort he had to make to voice that single word.

"You're hurting me," she said, and hated the quiver fear gave her tone. She winced and tried to pull away.

You mean I'm scaring you, he said in her head as he released his hold.

Rebecca heard the loathing in his words in her mind. He was disgusted with himself.

She immediately felt sorry for him, and reached to brush his long blond hair back from his face. "I didn't mean it like that," she replied, careful to keep her voice low. "So you're a little scary. So what? Billy is too, and look what a nice guy he is."

Syd laughed, though it was bitter. He turned his face away from her. *I told you to leave me.*

She reached for his chin and turned his face back to her. He resisted, but was too weak to do so for more than a moment. She looked into his eyes and smiled down at him.

"And I told you I wouldn't leave without you, so the least you can do is give me the courtesy of not dying, since we worked so hard to save you. Now come on. Let's get you some kind of fixed so we can figure out what to do next. The sun is due to rise in a few hours and you're already weak."

Are you always this contrary?

Rebecca smiled. "I don't know. I haven't had a whole lot of reason to tell anyone what to do before you showed up, so maybe I am. Eat."

She held her wrist out to him. He turned his face away.

"Hey now. What's the problem?"

Syd looked back at her. *I won't take anything more from you today. You've been drained enough.*

"And you're the one that said I couldn't be drained, especially here in my own enclave, so get to it. It's late and I'm tired."

Syd didn't look at all happy about his words being used against him, and brought the wrist she offered to his mouth. Rebecca closed her eyes.

It wasn't nearly as warm or as nice this time as it had been the previous times Syd had taken her blood, nor was it was painful and harsh as it had been when Ryan had done it. There was no nicety in this either—just pure, simple, unadulterated need. Rebecca suddenly felt exactly like the food Syd had said she was, and it made her stomach clench.

She tried her best not to think about anything but how helpful this was to Syd, and waited for him to finish. It seemed like a very long time before he dropped her wrist and looked back at her with eyes that could see her.

"My gratitude, Acolyte," he managed, though it was barely above a whisper.

His eyes, though not the brilliant, metallic blue they were when he was fully restored, were not as dark as they had been.

Rebecca didn't do more than nod. She knew he needed a great deal more than he would take from her, but that he'd taken all he was going to from her at the moment.

"Don't you dare go out and hunt," she ordered, knowing what he was planning to do without thinking about it. "You're too weak. You stay right here and let me heal you. You're not going anywhere."

Syd started to protest, but instead settled for a scowl and mumbled something rude about the abilities of a Seer being highly inconvenient.

Her stomach growled. Syd smiled a little.

"You should replenish yourself before you consider doing more for me," Syd said.

ALL WOUNDS • 123

"Billy went to get Chinese," Rebecca said. "But I thought you said I couldn't eat after...doing that."

"I didn't take much," Syd replied, looking guilty. "Just enough to... ease things a bit. It will be better for us both if you see to your own needs before you see further to mine."

"So I'll be all right then?"

Syd nodded. "It's only when one of my kind takes beyond a certain quantity that you will avoid nourishment."

"Great. I'm a fuel tank," she muttered.

Syd reached up and brushed her hair back from her mark again, exposing her neck and the wound he'd made.

You're much more.

His hand cupped the back of her neck and he pulled her toward him. Rebecca thought to panic for only a moment before she felt his lips upon her throat, followed by his tongue.

Pain she hadn't even been aware of until it was gone ebbed. She closed her eyes and wasn't aware of tilting her head to give him better access. She thought she heard Syd moan again, and almost asked him if he was in pain, or thought maybe he was taking her pain into himself or something when his hand tightened on her neck. His fingers tangled in the hair at the base of her head and Rebecca's mind went blank.

The only thing she felt was warmth and safety, like the Syd she knew.

When she opened her eyes, her head was pillowed on Syd's shoulder. She realized she was stretched out on the bed beside him. Though she couldn't see his light blue eyes, she knew they were open and staring up at the ceiling.

She was reluctant to move. Syd's hand was still curled at the back of her neck, her hair still wound around his fingers. If she moved, she'd wake him, and something told her he'd just fallen into a restful sleep.

Besides, she was tired too, and it was warm here. Safe. She hesitated a moment, feeling both very awkward about being where she was and really good about it. Before she could think more about what she was doing, she moved her arm, slow and gentle, to rest across his chest.

His fingers curled more in her hair, and Rebecca felt his arm tighten around her shoulder. She closed her eyes and sighed. Wow, this was nice.

This was also wrong, she knew. *Felt.* What was she doing, snuggling up to a vampire?

Syd wasn't just a vampire. He was a Master, and—

And...what? And this felt nice? And he was a boy who actually looked at her? What?

Rebecca felt completely stupid and used the hand she'd draped across Syd's chest to push herself up and away from him. Sure enough, he turned his head toward her as she moved.

"Go back to sleep," she whispered. "I'll be up later to check on you, or you call me if you need me."

Syd looked at her a long moment before he nodded.

Rebecca hurried out of the enclave and tried not to think about what she'd just done, lest Syd hear her freaking out. He really didn't need to know about it.

"Bit?" she heard at the same time the front door slammed shut.

"Shh! Not so loud, Billy! You'll wake Syd!"

"Got your Chinese!" Billy gestured to a stack of white cartons covering the kitchen table.

"Wow," Rebecca said, wide-eyed. "I didn't need a whole Chinese restaurant menu. You didn't have to bring all this."

"This?" Billy snorted. "Ain't but a snack, Bit. Well, a snack for me. Least I could do after everything, and you lettin' me den here tonight. 'Sides, I saw your fridge earlier, and there ain't near enough in it for a decent meal."

"I'll grab some plates," Rebecca said as Billy sat down in a chair with one of the cartons. "Oh, never mind."

Billy made a questioning noise around a mouthful of what appeared to be an entire order of lo mein.

"Nothing," Rebecca said, shaking her head. "You apparently don't need a plate."

"What for?" Billy asked. "Neat thing about take-out—no dishes to dirty."

"Want anything to drink?" Rebecca asked the werewolf already on his third carton. Two bites seemed to be all the guy needed to finish one off.

Billy stood up and went to the pantry. He reached up over the door and brought down another four bottles of fae ale. "Neat thing about this stuff, it gets replenished when you take a bottle. Those garden boys must really like Martha, to have given her so many."

The werewolf returned to the table and set one of the paper cartons in front of her.

Rebecca sighed and found a pair of chopsticks among the mess.

They ate in silence for awhile. Rebecca traded her broccoli beef for the General Tso's chicken about halfway through a carton. Billy tried to get her to take some of the fried rice that came with the dinner, but

Rebecca shook her head and said she was full. Billy, undeterred, shoved a handful of fortune cookies at her and downed the rest of her broccoli beef.

She stretched and yawned. "It's about time for bed. I'll go up and check on Syd before I hit the sack. You find a place to den?"

"Yep," Billy affirmed. "Right there at the bottom of the stairs, between you and anything that might try somethin' stupid. I thought about sleeping under your bedroom window, but figured you might get upset about that."

Rebecca laughed and nodded. "You'd be right. There're more blankets in the linen closet if you need them."

"Nah," Billy said. He waved her off and set about emptying the last of the take-out containers.

Rebecca shook her head as she left the kitchen and took the candle lantern from the mantle in the living room. She lit it as she reached the top of the stairs, then went into the enclave.

"All right, I've eaten now," she said as she entered. "So you can't say anything abo—"

She was talking to an empty room.

Rebecca's insides clenched.

Where was Syd? Had the demons come back and taken him away too, like they did Ryan? She was just about to scream for Billy when she heard her name coming from the other end of the room.

"Syd?" Rebecca called again as she approached the mirror with slow, careful steps. "You're supposed to be in bed, sleeping."

There was no one there.

Rebecca studied the mirror in front of her. Only her reflection was within it.

She turned to leave again, suddenly anxious, alone in the dark room.

Then she heard it again...her name, very faint.

"Ryan? Hello?"

Rebecca's brow furrowed. No answer came.

She shook her head and blew out the candle in the lantern. She set it on the bedside table, confused about what she thought she heard. As soon as she was out the enclave door, she leaned over the banister.

"Billy!"

Rebecca heard something like a growl from below and took a step back. She managed to stifle her scream as she recognized the familiar scarred, lop-sided face of the huge furry beast that made it up the stairs with frightening speed.

"What? Was just bedding down."

"Syd's gone!"

"WHAT?"

Billy growled and swore and swept past Rebecca into the enclave. She ran after him and was just about to enter when Billy came back out again.

"He ain't dead if that's what you was thinkin'," he said. Rebecca could hear the relief in his words. "Wasn't taken neither. No demon stink in there or anything else. Probably he went back to the lair to heal up on his own ground. Better for vamps to do that if they can."

"But you said the demons would find him there!"

Billy snorted. "Not if he's holed up in the lair's haven, they won't."

"What's the 'lair's haven'?" she asked.

"Place where the vamps go to hide. He probably went to check on...stuff," he said. "Anyway, he ain't dead. Dead vamps leave a stink when their body fades, and I don't smell anything like that. Don't you worry none, Bit. 'Sides...you gave him your blood. He'll be all right. His clan will take care of the rest of him. Now you stay here and wait for him to come back if you want, but it's too near sunrise here for him to do that, so it will be awhile. He's probably resting, and I'm gonna go do the same. You should too."

"But I told him to stay here," Rebecca said. "He said that whatever a Healer says is to be obeyed as ultimate law or something!"

Billy snorted again. "That don't work on Masters, so he can do whatever he wants, no matter what you say. I'm goin' back to bed."

"I...I thought I heard..."

"What?" Billy growled.

She shook her head. "Nothing. I...I mean..."

"Spit it out, Bit, I'm tired!"

"I thought I heard the mirror in there calling my name," Rebecca said in a rush. "Okay? I know it sounds idiotic—"

Billy just stared at her for a long moment. "Them stupid, clever bastards..."

"What?" Rebecca asked.

"Nothin," he said. "Just give me an idea is all. None of us would have heard...but you can, Bit..."

"Hear what? It was just my name, that's all," she said.

"Still, good job listenin'," he replied. "Bet they didn't expect you to go back up there, bein' all scared of stuff like you are. Anyway, goin' to bed now. You go too and don't worry none."

"But what did I hear?"

"Dunno!" Billy growled. "Maybe somethin', maybe nothin'! Either way, ain't nothin' to do about it tonight! Sleep!"

Rebecca made a frustrated noise and stepped out of the anubi's way as he lumbered past her. This time Billy didn't bother with the stairs and just leapt over the banister, surprising her by landing on all-fours without a sound on the floor below. She could hear him muttering to himself before the house was once again quiet.

Alone on the second floor, Rebecca shivered. She told herself she was cold—it *was* nighttime in October—and closed the enclave door. She forced herself not to run down the stairs, and almost didn't bother taking off what remained of her clothes before falling into bed.

It was almost too much effort to go into the bathroom, change, wash her very dirty face and brush her teeth before she crawled into her bed.

She was asleep before her head hit the pillow.

━━◆━ ━◆━

Rebecca awoke to bright sunshine streaming in her window. The clock beside her bed read two in the afternoon, and her eyes widened as she threw back the covers. Why hadn't anyone come to wake her up?!

She went into the hallway.

No Billy at the bottom of the stairs, nor was he in the kitchen stuffing his face with whatever he'd brought in to eat.

Rebecca went up to the enclave. Syd hadn't returned. It, too, was empty.

For the first time since she could remember, she was alone in the house.

Not knowing what to do with herself, Rebecca went downstairs and poured herself a glass of orange juice. She gazed out the kitchen window without really seeing. She looked to the driveway and noticed it was empty. Billy's—well, what had been left of it—car was nowhere to be seen, and she wondered where it was, or if it was really still there and just made invisible or something. With everything she didn't know, and given how careless Billy seemed to be about being noticed by humans, she wouldn't bet on it. Then probably get told off by Syd for believing silly human things.

Syd. Syd. Where was he? Where was Ryan? And for that matter, where was Billy?

Rebecca finished her juice and put her glass in the sink. First no Ryan, then no Syd, now no Billy.

Great, Rebecca thought. So much for keeping her protected.

She shrugged and muttered "whatever" as she went back down the hall to the bathroom. She found a bottle of headache medicine, shook two tablets out and gulped them down with a handful of water, thinking about the catch-up work she'd have to do for missing school again today.

That reminded her. Nana said she had books and things. There had been books up in the enclave, and Syd had restored them to order.

Rebecca decided she'd put the rest of the day to good use, and learn more about what it was she was supposed to be.

***

Propped up on her bed, engrossed in a book about healing ectoplasmic beings, Rebecca jumped when a shout interrupted her reading.

"BIT!"

That sounded like...

Rebecca tore open the bedroom door and ran toward the living room. "Billy?!"

"GET UP HERE!" the anubi's voice thundered.

Rebecca took the stairs two at a time and dashed into the enclave.

There on the bed lay Ryan, eyes closed tight, sweating blood and thrashing.

"Found him," Billy stated the obvious in little more than a grunt. Rebecca's eyes widened as she noticed the big werewolf was in his human form and covered from head to toe in red and black. He was breathing hard and holding his side. "Right where you said he was. Had him hidden between realms."

"But—I didn't say—what do you mean—you're hurt!"

Rebecca moved toward Billy, but he flinched back and shook his head at her before she could get a closer look at him. He nodded to Ryan.

"Ain't nothin'. Help the punk. Rox saved my hairy butt again, and his too, but damn...she looks worse than he does."

Rebecca hesitated only a moment before she moved to the bed. She remembered what Syd said about it being faster to take from her throat than her wrist and slid an arm under Ryan's shoulders.

She pulled with her arms as she leaned back, lifting Ryan as best she could to sit most of the way up. Wow, he wasn't as heavy as she thought he would be.

The dark-haired boy groaned and thrashed and tried to struggle out of her embrace, but Rebecca held him tight. Ryan went limp in her arms and Rebecca's stomach tightened in immediate fear. He should have been able to get away from her with hardly any effort at all.

She didn't think about it any longer. Instead she focused on what she was doing.

Ryan's head lolled on her shoulder. He groaned.

"That's it," Rebecca encouraged. "Come on. Wake up."

She placed a hand on the back of Ryan's head and turned it for him. Rebecca held the boy close with her right arm under his, tight around his waist as she reached with her left hand and pulled her hair away from her neck.

She returned her left hand to Ryan's head and turned her own slightly away, exposing her throat.

Ryan didn't move. If anything, he just felt heavier in her arms as he sagged against her.

"Come on," she said again, giving him a little shake. "It's right there. You can do it. You've got to help. We're all working hard here to see that you get better. The least you could do is try."

Ryan groaned again and moved his head a little.

"I'll bet Travis Hoffman could do it, no problem," Rebecca said in a bored voice, bringing up the captain of her school's football team. Ryan hated Travis Hoffman more than Robin hated Marla Thompson. "If you die, maybe Syd will make Travis into a vampire, since you can't seem to manage it."

Ryan groaned again, and she felt his fangs scrape her neck, but not pierce it.

She tightened her hold on him and shook him again, harder.

"Now," she ordered in a firm voice, not bothering to try and speak in that soft tone Nana used. "You can do better. Bite me or I'll bite you, and you won't like it, I promise!"

Ryan's fangs bit deep into her throat. It was all she could do not to yelp in pain and fear. Ryan's bite wasn't at all like Syd's. She wasn't ever afraid when Syd bit her. Syd was warm and gentle, not like this. This was frightening and cold.

Rebecca closed her eyes and forced herself to relax. Peace and calm. She was safe here. Safe. Warm. Safe and warm. She felt Syd's hands on her shoulders, and instantly the uneven panicked beat of her heart slowed to a steady rhythm. The soft pressure of Syd's fingers spread across her back in a gentle massage brought on a deep, cleansing breath, calming her even more.

She brought her other arm around Ryan's back. He was rigid and trembling. Holding the boy close, Rebecca kept her eyes closed until she felt Ryan's body go limp again, only this time in relaxation. Ryan's mouth left her neck and his head rested on her shoulder once more.

She held Ryan against her for a long moment, catching her breath. She looked up, expecting to see Syd standing behind her, but he wasn't there, or anywhere in the room.

He'd been right there, hadn't he? She'd felt him, standing behind her, his hands warm on her shoulders, comforting her.

Had she really just imagined it?

"His eyes," she heard Billy say.

Rebecca was careful not to jostle the boy too much as she laid Ryan back down in the bed and looked at his eyes.

They were open, and completely blue. Not the brilliant, metallic glow of Syd's eyes, but a distinct shade of blue, and not the almost-black they had been.

Rebecca smiled. "Good. Let's see how good."

She reached for a damp cloth and pressed it against Ryan's forehead a few times before doing the same with a dry one.

That one came away still dry and unblemished.

"He seems to have stopped shedding again," Rebecca with a relieved sigh. "Now let's have a look at you."

She crossed the room to Billy. To her surprise, Billy reached for her face and turned her head a little to see her neck.

The anubi shook his head. "Let's hope he comes back to himself soon. That's gotta hurt."

"It's all right," Rebecca said, waving off Billy with a shrug. "He doesn't know any better right now. I don't think he means to hurt me. But speaking of hurt—" She looked at Billy and shook her head.

"What?" the anubi said with a guilty—and pained—look.

Rebecca didn't have the heart to say anything to him about getting himself hurt. She was beginning to realize that Billy's natural state seemed to be either bloody or hungry. Probably both.

"Shower," was all she said.

Chapter Twelve

After making sure Ryan was comfortable and resting in the enclave, Rebecca met Billy in the kitchen.

"Oh, hey Bit," the freshly-showered werewolf in human form said in a small voice. "I, uh—" He nodded toward the floor. "Sorry about the mess. But don't worry—it's Ethereal."

Her brow furrowed. "What is?"

"The blood," he said. "You don't have to clean it up. It'll fade in a bit."

"Maybe so, but that won't stop you from bleeding more," she said as she crossed the room to him. "Let me see."

"Ain't nothin'," he protested, though he lifted his arm up for her to see his wound. "Well...nothin' much. Soon as I get the bleeding stopped it will start to heal up by itself."

"Everything is 'nothing' to you. I'm beginning to wonder what you consider 'something'," she muttered. "And that's really deep. It's not going to stop bleeding with just a rag pressed to it."

She felt the warmth of her Healer's ability tingling in her hands and a picture flashed through her mind. She reached to touch the wound and gasped at the instant change in her vision. It wasn't like what had happened before. This was sharp and focused and she could clearly see Billy reaching out his car window to pull a demon off the roof, Ryan slumped in the passenger seat. She watched as a jagged piece of the damaged car body sliced deep into the underside of Billy's right bicep from elbow to armpit.

The vision stopped as abruptly as it had come and Rebecca took her fingers away. Now she knew, in addition to what had caused the injury, how bad it was and what she needed to do to heal it. She looked up at the wolf in human form.

"That's going to need stitches," she said. "You've been cut clean down to the bone by something mortal. It won't heal up like a demon

132 • DINA JAMES

claw or bite."

"Ain't noth—"

"Sit!" Rebecca ordered, cutting him off as she pointed to a chair. "And get rid of your shirt."

"Thought I already said I ain't no dog," Billy muttered, though he obeyed and flopped down at the kitchen table, bare-chested. "I hate needles!"

Holy...wow he had some muscles on him. Scars, too. Lots of them. Still, Rebecca could see his ribs sticking out and shook her head.

"Good boy," she replied with a wink. "Now don't move while I go get what I need."

Billy grumbled and reached for a bottle of the fae beer he liked so much with his uninjured hand.

Rebecca rushed upstairs and into the enclave.

She barely looked at Syd, refreshed and returned and sitting at Ryan's bedside as though he'd never been hurt or gone. She didn't have time to deal with that now. Syd wasn't hurt or in need. Billy was. Rebecca began rummaging through the chest of drawers at the end of the room.

"What is it?" Syd asked.

"Billy needs stitches," she replied. She swallowed hard. "I've never...I don't even know...I mean I *know*, because I can feel it or something, and see in my head what I need to do, but..." She looked at Syd and shook her head.

"I'll assist you," Syd assured her as he stood up.

Immense relief washed through her.

"Oh, would you? I mean, thanks, really. Just...someone to make sure I'm not screwing up too badly will be a huge help. I hope it won't be too bright for you in there. The windows are still covered up, but I need the light to see Billy's wound."

Syd shook his head and opened his hand. His pair of dark glasses appeared in them and he put them on with a grin. Then he flashed out of the enclave.

Rebecca rolled her eyes. "Show-off."

She found what she needed and went back downstairs.

Syd was leaning against the doorframe, shaking his head and laughing. Billy sat at the table, looking extremely put upon.

"Hey," Rebecca said, giving Syd a poke under his folded arms as she entered the kitchen. "You're here to help, not laugh at poor Billy's misfortune."

"Yeah," Billy said, and looked even more pathetic. How that was possible, she didn't know, but she was sure it had something to do with being a wolf in human form. He could do puppy-dog eyes like no one else. Billy lifted his injured arm and rested it atop his head, exposing his wound.

"Oh, Billy," Rebecca said as she knelt down beside him. "I told you not to move."

"Didn't!" Billy protested as he brought his drink to his mouth. "Well, not much," he said around his mouthful of fae ale.

Rebecca rolled her eyes again. "Want anything for the pain? This has to hurt."

"Nah," Billy replied, shaking his head. "Don't need none."

"Remember you said that." She stood up. "Let me clean this properly and we'll get started."

Billy sighed and reached for another bottle. "Hey, Syd? Be a sport and shove them others over here so Bit don't yell at me for movin'."

Syd uncrossed his arms slightly and twitched two fingers at the bottles Billy indicated.

"Aw, thanks man," Billy said.

"Don't mention it," Syd replied.

Billy continued to drink as Rebecca cleaned his wound. He winced occasionally, and kept offering her sips of his ale.

"You're stalling, Acolyte," Syd said from the doorway. "That wound is clean enough. Get to it."

Rebecca almost protested, but she knew Syd was right. Just...the idea of putting a needle into Billy. *Into anything!*

"What, you ain't scared of me, are you, Bit?" Billy asked as he swallowed a sip of ale. "Ohhhh...you're scared of hurtin' me, or messin' up, ain't you?"

Rebecca bit her bottom lip and nodded.

Billy grinned. "I'm already messed up and you ain't gonna change that by tryin' to help. You can't be scared anymore, remember? You'll only get yourself in trouble that way. 'Sides, how else you gonna learn if you don't do things? I might hate needles, but I ain't gonna hurt you none!"

Rebecca looked at Syd.

He just gestured to the wolf in human form sitting at her kitchen table.

"All right," Rebecca sighed. "Here goes nothing."

She threaded a very large curved needle with some kind of gossamer thread she knew to be specifically made for Ethereals and grasped the two pairs of scissor-like suturing ties. She clamped the needle with one of them, took a deep breath and pierced the undamaged skin of one side of Billy's wound. The anubi didn't flinch. She let out the breath she'd been holding slowly and repeated the same thing on the other side of the wound. With the second instrument in her other hand, Rebecca pulled the needle and suturing thread through.

"Atta girl!" Billy encouraged. "Hardly felt a thing!"

Rebecca smiled and looked over her shoulder at Syd.

He peeled himself away from the doorframe and came to kneel beside her. He took a clean cloth from the table and dabbed at the blood dripping down Billy's arm, clearing the area for Rebecca's next stitch.

"This is what your Helper would be doing for you, if you had one," he said. "Sometimes you need more than two hands, and another pair makes it easier. Otherwise you'd have to put down one of your instruments and do this yourself, which, while possible, would make your task longer."

She nodded her thanks.

"Continue," Syd prompted with a nod at Billy's wound.

"Yeah, I ain't got all day," Billy grumbled as he uncapped another bottle.

Rebecca sighed and shook her head. Syd offered encouragement and instructive comments as she went on, slow and methodical, stitching Billy's long wound. She was nearly finished when Billy yelped and pulled away from her.

"Ow!"

"Hey, you're the one that said you didn't want anything to numb you up!" Rebecca said. "I'm not finished! Almost, but not yet. Now, come on."

"Aw, come on! That's good, ain't it? I ain't bleeding much anymore! Can't you be done now?"

"Just a few more stitches, Billy, honest, then I'll find the ice cream in the deep freezer and you can eat the whole carton. Just let me finish, okay?" Rebecca cajoled.

Billy whimpered and Rebecca felt horrible, but she reached for his elbow and pulled him back toward her.

She pierced the sensitive flesh near his armpit with the needle and Billy yelped again.

"Would you stop it?!" Rebecca cried, exasperated. "That's an awful noise! You didn't even flinch when this happened to you, and I've seen demons almost tear you to bits, and now you're whining about a little needle poking you?"

"That ain't a little needle! 'Sides, that's different!" Billy protested. "Little things like this hurt a lot more than a bite or something!"

Syd tried to suppress a laugh and couldn't. Rebecca scowled at him.

Billy sighed, deep and dramatic, and made a big show of forcing himself to lean back toward Rebecca. "What kind of ice cream?"

Rebecca's reply was cut off by a knock at the door. Everyone froze and glanced toward the noise.

"Cripes," she whispered. "Maybe they'll go away."

The knock came again and Rebecca winced and swore. "I can't leave this right now!"

"Go see who it is and what they want," Syd murmured. "I'll make sure Billy doesn't move, and that we're not seen if it comes to that. It will be all right for that long. Go on."

Rebecca nodded and went to the door. She looked out the peephole and sighed in quiet relief.

"It's okay! It's Robin!" Rebecca called into the kitchen.

Syd looked confused.

"The one I want to ask to be my Helper," Rebecca clarified.

He considered that a moment, then nodded.

"Bring her in if you think she's ready," Syd replied. "If it goes badly...well..."

Rebecca nodded and closed her eyes for a long moment before going back to the front door. She opened it a crack and motioned Robin inside and put a finger to her lips.

"Sorry to come barging in on you like this," Robin apologized in a rush. "But I didn't see you yesterday afternoon and you weren't in school today and I heard what Marla did and—"

Robin stopped short as she saw the blood on Rebecca's hands.

"Oh my god, are you all right?" Robin asked as she seized Rebecca's wrist and brought up her hand to look at it. "What's going on? Are you making steak for dinner or something? Where's your Nana? Is she okay?"

"It's all right, Ro," Rebecca assured her friend. "It seems I've got... another secret for you to keep, unless you're tired of keeping secrets for me."

Robin studied Rebecca for a long moment before she nodded.

The confusion was clear on Robin's face as she followed Rebecca into the kitchen. It gave way to shock as she took in the sight of the huge, muscled Billy sitting with a needle and thread trailing from the nearly-sewn wound in his arm and another guy, blond, wearing sunglasses indoors kneeling by his side.

"What is going on?" Robin managed.

"Have a seat and I'll tell you while I finish up what I'm doing," Rebecca said, and returned to Billy's side where she picked up the needle once more.

Billy took a deep breath and gritted his teeth, his free hand clench-

136 • DINA JAMES

ing into a fist as Rebecca finished stitching his wound.

⊷⊶

"So, you're a werewolf," Robin said, looking across the kitchen table at Billy.

The young man was again fully clothed, sitting at the table with Robin and Rebecca. They shared a pot of tea between them while Billy sat with another bottle of fae ale.

Syd, his assistance with Billy's wound finished and confident that Robin wasn't going to have a complete fit about becoming a Helper, went back upstairs to check on Ryan. Robin had stared after him and, when she was sure Syd couldn't see her, gave Rebecca a smirk, fanning herself while mouthing "gorgeous."

"That's what you humans call us," Billy said, shrugging, heedless of his freshly-sutured injury. "My people are called 'Anubi' by everyone else. Well, mostly. The vampires got some pretty rude names for us, but yeah, I'm a werewolf."

"Prove it," Robin said.

Billy snorted. "What? You want me to change forms right here at the table?"

"Yeah. What? You need a full moon or something?" Robin asked, raising an eyebrow at him.

"No," Rebecca interrupted. "You'll tear your stitches. No changing forms for at least a couple of mortal days, Billy."

"'Need a moon or something'..." Billy muttered as he took a swig from his bottle. "Sorry to disappoint you, girly."

Robin gave him a murderous look.

"He's really a werewolf, Ro," Rebecca said. "I've seen him change, and it's like the blink of an eye, not like those ones you see in the movies. And there are vampires too. That blond guy you just saw? He's one. And I've been taking care of Ry—um—his friend for a couple of days now."

"Which is why you haven't been in school, right? And you're a... what again...?" Robin asked. "Healer? Stranger?"

Rebecca and Billy both nodded.

"And you want me to help out?" Robin asked. "How?"

"By doing just what you already do," Rebecca said, taking a sip of tea. "Like you've seen, I might need to miss school so you'll have to cover for me, just like you've done before with Nana. Questions would be a bad thing. That's what Helpers do. They're kind of a bridge between us and the human realm."

"You make it sound like you aren't human," Robin said with a nervous laugh.

"The way I understand it, I'm mortal," Rebecca replied. "But a different kind of human, with different abilities. I can see and...and do... things most other people can't—"

Billy interrupted. "What Bit's trying to say, girly, is that she's going to need a Helper. A human Helper. You may have to be an extra pair of hands now and then, maybe help hold down a tough customer or ornery patient. Most times you just gotta make sure she eats and stuff. Days in the enclave can get long and busy, especially during wartime, and the way things is lookin', that's comin' up right quick. You'd be spendin' a lot of time here."

"You're so busy though, Ro," Rebecca said. "And there's school to think about, and your friends—"

"Rebecca, I'm not going to let you do this alone! I think this is a bit more important than stupid slumber parties," Robin said, shaking her head. "I'm totally in. You'll have to tell me more about everything, though, starting with what's been going on the last couple days."

"That's kind of a long story," said Rebecca.

"Well, if you gals are going to sit around flapping your lips, I'm going to find somethin' to eat," Billy said, and got up from his chair.

As Billy moved away to rummage through the fridge, Robin moved closer to Rebecca and whispered in her ear.

"I always knew there was something about you, Rebecca. Ever since first grade, when you stood up to those boys for me. You took care of me—wouldn't let me be hurt, and it just makes more sense now. I always knew that mark you hate so much was something special, and have always been just a little bit jealous of how cool it is. Knowing what it really is, what it really means, makes it even cooler."

"Really?" Rebecca managed. *Robin is jealous...of* me? *What? Why?*

Robin nodded. "You're way cooler than I'll ever be, no matter how popular I am or who my boyfriend is."

"Ain't nothin' to eat in this house," Billy growled and slammed the fridge door shut. He turned and was about to head out of the kitchen when Rebecca eyed him.

"And where do you think you're going?"

"Uh, out?" Billy replied in a cautious tone. "Grab a bite to eat, find somewhere to den up for the night—"

"What about right here?" Rebecca said, gesturing around the house. "Syd told me that you don't have a safe place to den, and by the look of you, it's been more than a while since you've had a real home."

Billy scowled. "Seems Syd said more than he oughta. My gratitude for the offer, Bit, really but neutral ground or no, I ain't about to hide behind your skirts like a whelp."

"I'm not offering you a place to hide," Rebecca protested, hurt as she took another sip of her tea. "I wouldn't do that, and I didn't ask because I think you need one. I didn't mean for you to think that, either. It's just...well...go on then. Sorry I offered."

"Aw, Bit, I didn't mean it like that—"

"I'm scared, Billy!" she said. "You and Syd keep telling me not to be, because it just makes things worse, but I can't help it! I need help! I turn seventeen in two days. You would be doing me a huge favor if you'd stay...I mean den here. Not just for tonight, either, or until my birthday. Permanently."

"*Stay* here?" Billy said, incredulous. "Bit, you *live* here! Martha, too! And having me here is just asking for more trouble than I think you're figurin' on."

Rebecca and Robin exchanged a look. Robin looked back at Billy, and Rebecca could see that her friend was totally enamored with the big wolf.

Rebecca shrugged. "I'm already in big trouble, according to Syd. Besides, with you here...what's a little more? Now you said the other day to think of you like my bodyguard, and I'm asking you to please stay and keep being that."

"I don't know, Bit... This ain't no kind of casual offer. You can't just ask an anubi to den—"

"I can so," Rebecca interrupted, smiling him. "Please, big guy? The house is more than big enough, and Nana said I should have been learning this stuff all along, and you know how new I am to all of this. What you explained to me the other night about power made sense, and with you around to explain more of the stuff Syd tries to teach me, I'm sure to learn quick like we all want, especially him. Please?"

Billy rubbed the back of his neck and looked thoughtful for a long minute.

"Well, Syd did say I should look out for you," the anubi said with a deep sigh. "And it is true I ain't got a place. Sure as hell ain't denning at the lair with them bloodsuckers. Sleepin' in Rox gets old real fast and it's hard to get any kind of comfortable...so I guess if you don't mind a hairy roommate—"

"You'll be able to take your true form as often as you like," Rebecca said. "After you're healed, of course, and not have to worry. Syd told me he sealed the windows with illusion, so no one can see anything out of the ordinary from the street."

ALL WOUNDS • 139

"Illusion?" Robin asked.

"You can see why I'm going to need a Helper," Rebecca replied. "But I'll understand if you don't want to."

"Of course I want to, especially if *he's* going to stay here." Robin smiled at Billy. Oblivious that he was the subject of their conversation, she spoke a little louder, addressing him. "You're staying, right?"

Billy turned red and mumbled something before he left the room quick.

Robin and Rebecca giggled together.

"How many people get to meet a werewolf? I mean, without, you know, being eaten or something," Robin asked with a laugh as Rebecca refilled their tea mugs. "Or a vampire? You said you've been taking care of that cute blond one's friend. Can I meet him...or her?"

Rebecca shook her head. "I don't think he should be disturbed just now. He's healing, and it's just now starting to get dark. Let's let him rest. You'll meet him another time. Being a Helper, you'll have plenty of chances to see a vampire up close. You've likely already met one as it is. They're everywhere."

Robin turned around, making sure they were still alone and whispered, "Is the hurt vampire as gorgeous as Billy?"

Rebecca snorted as she tried to hide her giggling. "Hardly. You didn't get to see the blond one's eyes behind those glasses. They glow and pulse, like living liquid metal. They're this absolutely gorgeous blue, too. But you're really not supposed to look a vampire, especially one like him—he's a Master, meaning he's the leader of a clan—in the eye. Just sneak a quick look next time. His name is 'Syd.'"

"Are all vampires totally hot?" Robin asked.

Rebecca couldn't hide her blush as she nodded. "From everything I've been reading, it looks like most male Ethereals are...um...yeah."

"Well Billy sure is!" Robin said with another wicked grin. "I wonder if he's busy for prom."

"Robin!" Rebecca protested, though she couldn't quite hide her grin.

Robin closed her eyes a moment, daydreaming. "How old is he?"

"Eighty-seven!" Billy yelled from the other room. "And stop talking about me!"

Robin looked horrified for a moment before she and Rebecca looked at each other and burst out in a fit of giggles.

"For...forgot to say...! Great hearing...!" Rebecca managed through her laughter.

140 • DINA JAMES

Her Helper set on her first task of cleaning up the carnage in the kitchen—that is to say Billy's bottles—Rebecca went upstairs to check on Ryan.

She went into the enclave. Syd was nowhere to be found, and Rebecca wondered why she felt a twinge of disappointment. She'd been hoping to see him, she realized. To thank him for his help.

Rebecca went to the boy on the bed and sat down beside him. Ryan groaned, making Rebecca jump in surprise. Was he waking up?

She checked his eyes. They were open, but completely blank. Cripes. No such luck.

Rebecca lowered the band of the clean pajama bottoms she had found for him to check his hellhound bite. She was so focused on her work that she didn't hear Robin come in.

"You didn't say the vampire you were helping was Ryan Dugan!" Robin said from around the privacy curtain.

Rebecca jumped again at the sound of her voice and looked at her, embarrassed.

"Oh, hey Ro! Um—you...uh—shouldn't be...um—up here. He's a fledgling vampire—newly turned—and he's hurt and not in control of himself. You could get hurt," Rebecca said, blushing as she reached to pull Ryan's pajama bottoms back up. "He's got a nasty hellhound bite on his thigh. I was just checking on his wound."

"Really? Is that what you're doing? Because from here, it really looks like you're...um..."

"Oh, shut up," Rebecca muttered, blushing again as she felt Ryan's forehead and looked at her hand.

Dry. She smiled.

"He was—he needed—I had to—"

"Uh huh," Robin said, grinning. She held her hands up as though she were defending herself. "If that's what you need to say to get his pants off. It's not like I'd say anything anyway. I mean...he *is* cute. Too bad he's such a phenomenal jerk."

"He's not a jerk!" The words were out before Rebecca could stop them. "I mean...well—he's...um—he's nice—in a way—"

"In the 'he hasn't killed anyone yet' way?" Robin asked. "Look, if you have a thing for him, I wouldn't blame you. I just didn't figure you for the 'bad boy' type."

"I'm not!" Rebecca defended. "I mean...I'm not any 'type'! I don't even...I haven't—"

"Oh, give it up Rebecca," Robin interrupted as she rolled her eyes. "Cripes, I'm just teasing you." Robin eyed Ryan with a smirk. "He *is* cute, though. Or do I say 'was' now?"

"Vampires aren't 'undead'," Rebecca said looked down at the sleeping Ryan. She brushed his hair back from his face and arranged the bedclothes so he'd be comfortable. "They're immortal. They...I don't know how to explain it. Trade their soul for immortality, or something. Their body lives with the consciousness that makes them who they are, but their soul is outside of it or something. He has to take the blood of something with a soul in order to maintain his existence as it is now. He's a body without a soul, not dead. I mean, not 'dead' like when we die. Not like 'die a mortal death' dead. They're not walking corpses. Those are zombies. He's not a zombie, he's a vampire."

"Listen to you," Robin said with a giggle. "Talking about vampires and zombies like you see them every day."

Rebecca thought she detected a bit of an edge in Robin's tone, but why? Robin wasn't jealous, was she? Why would Robin be jealous of *her*? Of *this*? The idea was stupid.

Robin looked at Rebecca seriously. "That's because you do, isn't it? How long...I mean...when...?"

"You want to know if it's been like this for awhile and I haven't told you until now for whatever reason," Rebecca said.

Robin nodded. "I mean, I'd understand and all. And it would explain a lot of stuff you've told me about. Not wanting me to think you're crazy, or thinking I couldn't handle it, or wouldn't want to, or—"

"It's got nothing to do with you, or anything like that," Rebecca interrupted. She got up and went to her friend and hugged her. "I just learned about this a couple days ago. Think, Ro. We just saw Ryan in detention, in broad daylight. Do you think he was a vampire then?"

Robin shook her head and pulled away from Rebecca to look at Ryan's still form.

"You're just mad because you think I'd keep a guy like Billy away from meeting you," Rebecca teased. She elbowed Robin in the ribs. "Come on. Let's get out of here. I'm done for now, and he needs to rest."

Robin blushed and shook her head. Rebecca led the way out of the enclave and shut the door behind her.

"I wouldn't blame you for keeping Billy all to yourself," Robin said. "Talk about gorgeous!"

"That's just what he looks like to everyone else," Rebecca said as they walked downstairs. "He's really a big, hairy wolf-man over seven feet tall."

"I like them tall!" Robin defended. She caught a glimpse of Billy as they reached the bottom of the stairs. "Mmmm...there's my wolfman..."

142 • DINA JAMES

Billy paused and glared at the two girls.

"Jeeze, would you two stop talking about me! Or if you're gonna, get it right! *Man-wolf.* Get that straight. I ain't no 'wolf-man.'"

He had a huge armload of blankets held against his chest he was taking to the den he was making for himself in the garage. He'd found Nana's old car in there and had fallen in love with the musty old workshop. He hadn't wasted a second claiming it as his "room." He glared at Robin. "And I don't need no moon to change either, girly."

"Well, when you're allowed to try and impress me with your bad wolf self, you'll have to show me this big scary *man-wolf* you're supposed to be," Robin replied in a bored voice.

Billy growled and stalked off.

"I think he likes you," Rebecca whispered to Robin.

"I DO NOT!" Billy yelled. "STOP TALKING ABOUT ME!"

Robin and Rebecca giggled again and went into the kitchen. Rebecca reached for the clean tea mugs Robin had washed up and a dishtowel when movement outside caught her eye.

Were those...

"Ro," Rebecca whispered. "Turn off light."

"Why?" Robin asked. She peered out the kitchen window. "What's out there?"

"I don't know! It's dark, but not that dark. I thought I saw something. Turn off the light!"

"Okay, sheesh!" Robin reached over and snapped off the kitchen light. Her eyes widened in horror. "Oh my god! Are those...? Is that what Billy really is? My God, there's...how many are there? Why are they here? What do they want?"

Rebecca shook her head. "I don't know. I do know they can't come in the house unless I say they can if they're not hurt or using the portal upstairs and I'm not about to invite them in! And I'm sure as heck not going to tell Billy there's a pack of werewolves sniffing around the back yard. And cripes...Syd's not here!"

"Of course I am, Acolyte," Syd's voice came from the darkness behind her. She felt his hands on her hips as he leaned around her to look out the window as well. "What has you so—"

A noise escaped Syd, and Rebecca shivered at its menace.

She turned her head to look at him. "Billy said something about his brother—"

"Rebecca!" Robin hissed in a frightened squeak. She pointed out the window.

Standing in the middle of the back yard was Billy in human form, facing the crowd of six other werewolves all by himself.

"Come on, Acolyte," Syd said. "It's time you learned what 'neutral ground' is supposed to mean."

He grabbed her by the arm and pulled her away from the window.

Billy, now in wolf form, faced another wolf. This one was gray-furred and much larger, and in far better condition. Compared to him, Billy didn't look like he could win a fight with a wet paper bag. The other wolves looked ready to join their gray friend, but were holding back as though waiting for the brewing fight to really start.

A shot broke up the evening calm, startling the snarling, circling wolves.

Billy and the others turned at the sound.

"Bit, what the hell you think you're doin'?" the wolf that was Billy rumbled, incredulous.

Rebecca stood on the back porch with a rifle gripped in both hands. She was trying to hold the long gun steady, hoping the werewolves couldn't see her shaking. She had fired into the air this time, but she lowered the barrel slowly, promising that the next shot would hit somewhere a lot more painful.

Just as Syd had told her to say, Rebecca yelled, hoping her voice didn't give her complete terror away. "What part of 'neutral ground' don't you understand, Denis?"

Rebecca's heart beat hard against her chest. She felt Robin come up behind her and squeeze her shoulder and it helped her focus her thoughts.

Oh, this is insane! What made her think she could play referee between two really, really big...wolf-man-things?

Rebecca couldn't help but marvel at what she could see of the two creatures in the dark of her back yard. Muscled and lithe, Denis outweighed Billy by at least seventy pounds, and was a good six inches taller than his younger brother.

Billy was going to get pummeled into worse condition than his Mustang.

"And what part of 'disavowed' is hard to fathom?" came Sydney's voice from Rebecca's other side. "That happens to be a member of my clan you're about to attack. I'd think on that very seriously before you make another move."

Something clicked in Rebecca's mind, and she remembered how upset Billy was when he thought she would tell him not to go looking for Ryan. *Billy* is *a member of Syd's clan! But...aren't werewolves and vampires enemies? What's going on?*

Denis snorted and curled his lip at Syd. "Stay out of this, you soulless blood-sucking—"

Whatever was going on, these guys obviously meant to hurt Billy, and if they hurt Billy, Syd was apparently going to do...something...and it wasn't going to be good. Rebecca pulled the bolt back on her rifle like she'd seen her nana do when she'd taught her to shoot tin cans off the back fence, ejecting a silver bullet casing and loading another round. She pointed the rifle at the gray-furred anubi that was Denis.

"The first one was a warning," Rebecca said, her voice steady, light and calm this time. "The second one goes through your heart. Of course, I'm new at this, and it's a bit dark out here. Also, my aim probably really sucks—it's been awhile since target practice. I could miss and hit one of your pack."

Syd looked at one of the werewolves backing Denis in particular. "You hearing this, Johnny?"

"Yeah, Syd, I'm hearing," called one of the man-wolves still across the boundary in the dusty alleyway.

"You unclear about what 'neutral ground' means, too?" Syd asked, his eyes never leaving Denis. "Or you, Jackson? Carl? Gregory? You really want a battle with Clan Cardoza on your heads?"

The three other anubi he named all looked at the ground and mumbled various versions of "No, Master Cardoza."

"Now I don't know a couple of your other boys, Denis, but I do know your sire, and you can be certain he's going to hear about this breach of peace at the house of a Healer."

Denis snorted. "Go ahead. I'm within my rights to challenge my own brother. He's a traitor."

"He's already been judged, and sentenced," Syd replied. "And you're—"

"But he's not dead!" Denis interrupted with a growl. "He was sentenced to death! You can't stop me carrying it out!"

His temper lost to his rage, Denis bolted forward at them, fangs bared, claws outstretched.

"BILLY!" Robin shrieked.

Rebecca, panicked, pulled the trigger on her rifle.

Denis yelped. Rebecca's stomach twisted at the horrific sound of an animal in pain. Blood and fur spilled through the anubi's hand as he cupped his wounded shoulder. Rebecca's own shoulder throbbed, but she held the rifle steady.

Cripes, cripes I just shot a werewolf! Oh God—Rebecca's thoughts raced.

Calm and quiet, Acolyte, even here in your mind, came Syd's voice in her head. *Many things can also hear your thoughts. Keep your emotions in check, and private. Calm yourself and carry on. Finish what you've begun.*

Rebecca swallowed hard and spoke again.

"I'm sorry I had to do that, Denis, but you're still on neutral ground—my ground—and the only one who has any kind of say about life and death on it has a Healer's mark," Rebecca said, her calm voice filled with what she hoped sounded like menace. "Which I don't believe you have."

"What's more, that anubi now bears the surname 'Cardoza'," Syd added. "Thus far you have been indulged in your attempts to harm a member of my clan only at Billy's insistence. However, I cannot as his Master—"

"True anubi have no masters!" Denis growled.

Syd went on as though Denis hadn't spoken. "—stand aside and watch as you attempt to take his life. And, should you succeed, his clan will avenge his death. I, for one, would welcome the opportunity to take your mutt-hide apart one slow piece at a time."

"Rebecca?" Robin asked in a whisper, recovering from her shock. "You shot him! I thought you said you help things that are hurt? Why would you hurt him?"

"Like Syd said...just because we observe neutral ground doesn't mean others respect that," Rebecca replied. "And just because we don't take sides doesn't mean that we don't defend ourselves, or those who need our help. I don't know about you, but I think Billy needs our help."

"Me too," Robin whispered.

Rebecca gestured at Denis with the rifle. "I'd be happy to look at that wound, if you think you can behave yourself," She said.

"She is still in training and could use the experience. She hasn't seen what silver bullets do to an anubi just yet," Syd continued.

Oh, he's got to be kidding, Rebecca thought. *We're in the middle of some kind of—I don't know—war or something here and he wants me to—*

Denis spat on the ground in reply.

Rebecca sighed and shook her head. "All right then." She lowered the rifle to the ground, looked at Billy and nodded.

Billy snarled and lunged at his brother before Denis could comprehend. His fangs bit deep into Denis' neck. Blood spurted from the wound. Denis howled and clawed at his brother, opening long, bloody rents in Billy's brown fur.

"Billy has to handle this," Rebecca said. She turned and put an arm around Robin's shoulders.

146 • DINA JAMES

I just hope he can, Rebecca thought as she looked back at the fight that raged behind them. The dark yard shone with pools of blood, but it was nothing she was worried about. She had interfered as much as she could.

At least she'd evened the odds for Billy somewhat. What had Billy done to be sentenced to death? Why was his own brother out to kill him? She hadn't known the big hairy guy very long, so maybe she was stupid to trust him—and Syd—as much as she did. But Nana trusted them....

Rebecca shook her head and turned away from the fight. Whatever was between Billy and his brother had to work itself out.

⁓

The silence outside was deafening. The other werewolves gone, Rebecca, Robin and Syd sat on the back porch swing, taking in the aftermath of the battle that had gone on for the last half hour. Rebecca felt morbid in a way—like she'd been watching a wrestling match on TV instead of a life-and-death struggle between two Ethereal creatures.

Her eyes found Billy and watched him for a long moment. He was covered in blood, sitting in the middle of the cold, dark lawn, breathing hard. Denis was nowhere to be seen.

"He's hurt," Robin whispered. "Shouldn't we, I don't know, help him or something?"

"He has to ask for help himself," Syd replied. "And I think most of the blood is Denis'."

Robin and Rebecca exchanged a glance and, without a word, Robin crossed the back yard to Billy.

Rebecca watched as her friend offered the anubi a sympathetic smile and laid a gentle hand on his arm.

Billy's large, furred, anubi hand covered Robin's for a moment before Robin returned to the porch.

"Where's Denis?" Rebecca asked.

Syd nodded toward the very back of the yard along the boundary line. "Under the dogwood tree," he replied. "Can't you see him?"

Rebecca squinted against in the darkness, looking to the spot Syd indicated. There she saw the gray anubi, curled into a tight ball leaning back against the trunk of the dogwood tree, his huge furred hands wrapped around his body. Rebecca would have thought he was dead but for the fact that she could see the labored rise and fall of his chest as he struggled to breathe.

"Will he let us heal him?" Rebecca asked.

"I don't know. Again—he has to be the one ask for help," Syd said.

"But...what about the blood?" Robin asked, looking down at the puddles seeping with agonizing slowness into the ground. "Shouldn't we do something?" Her voice caught in her throat.

"It's Ethereal, and already fading," Syd replied in a gentle voice Rebecca hadn't ever heard him use. "Come on. Inside." Syd went into the kitchen, leaving the two girls alone on the porch for a moment.

Robin wiped her eyes and managed a smile at Rebecca.

"If I didn't already have my eye on that furry hunk Billy, Syd would be my first choice for prom," Robin said, sounding like her old self again. "It's after dark, so he could take me, right?"

Rebecca pretended to punch Robin's arm. They giggled and Rebecca knew the worst was over. Robin was ready to be her Helper.

Initiated by a werewolf battle.

Rebecca mentally shrugged. She supposed it was better than being abducted by demons.

They weren't in the house twenty minutes before the kitchen door opened. Standing on the threshold was Billy, still in his natural wolf—and very bloody—form.

The anubi didn't say anything. Rebecca stood up.

A car horn honked outside.

"That's Dad," Robin said, standing up as well. She looked at Billy for a long moment before she spoke again. "You okay?"

Billy nodded, though it was more of a wince.

"Good," Robin said. "Prom isn't until May, so you'll have plenty of time to heal up and look as gorgeous as ever."

Billy started to say something, but then just shook his huge bloody head.

Robin smiled and gave Rebecca a hug.

The car horn honked again.

"Jeeze, Dad. I'm coming," Robin muttered as she pulled away. She looked at Billy again. "I'd hug you too, but you're covered in blood. Next time."

The right side of Billy's mouth twitched and his pointed, furry ears pricked up a little, and Rebecca knew his spirits were lifting.

Robin gave him a nod and left the kitchen with Rebecca, picking up her bag from the foyer. Robin grabbed her jacket.

"You'll take care of him, right?" Robin asked in a whisper.

"Yes, and he can still hear you," Rebecca whispered back, grinning. "Remember? Anubi have great ears."

"He has a great—"

148 • DINA JAMES

"Robin!"

Robin stifled a giggle and shouldered her bag as she left.

Rebecca turned to see Billy climbing the stairs to the enclave, much slower than he usually moved. She sighed and went back into the kitchen and filled the two large kettles to heat water to bring up to the enclave.

Syd had disappeared, no doubt already back up there.

As the water heated, Rebecca tidied up the kitchen, putting away the makings of the hot chocolate she and Robin had made for themselves while they waited for her dad to come. She was just wiping the table when the kitchen door opened again.

In the doorway stood a very bloody gray-furred anubi. Denis refused to look at Rebecca and kept his eyes on the floor.

"If friend ye are and healing ye seek, enter this place and my blessing keep," Rebecca said in a soft voice. "But I already told you that you were welcome. You know that, though, don't you?"

The gray anubi nodded, though it was near imperceptible.

"Look, if you don't want to be up there with him, I can help you down here," she continued when he didn't say anything or come into the kitchen.

"Get your notebook, Acolyte," was all Denis said. "Time for a crash course in anubi."

◆————◆————◆

"You're lucky," Syd said after a cursory inspection of Denis' shoulder. "The bullet's gone clean through. If it hadn't, you would have to dig it out, Acolyte."

Rebecca bit her bottom lip.

"Wouldn't that hurt?"

"It would hurt more to leave it," Syd said. "Silver poisoning is very dangerous. As it is, you still need to see if there are fragments left behind. Your fingers are small enough, though you'll have to widen the entry wound so you can feel for the shards."

Rebecca winced at the instructions and looked at her patient. "Sorry, Denis."

The gray-furred anubi gave her a withering look. "You think one more hole is going to bother me? Look at me, woman!"

"Well, it's not like you didn't deserve it," Rebecca said, scowling at Denis. "You did start it, you know. If you'd just leave your brother alone—"

"Acolyte," Syd said in warning. "It doesn't matter how Denis came by his wounds. You're here to heal him, not judge him. Neutral ground

means a lot more than just 'no fighting here'. This is a place of safety—
from all sorts of things. Denis has the right to be healed without being
subjected to a lecture on how he shouldn't have gotten hurt in the first
place. Don't get involved in the personal affairs of your patients."

"Well said," Denis replied with a glance at Rebecca.

"Why not?" Rebecca asked. "That's part of the healing, isn't it?
Telling him to stay out of trouble?"

"That's entirely different," Syd replied. "What you're doing is
condemning his actions, and that's not something that Healers do. Now,
get the straight razor and the clippers. We'll have to clear the fur around
the area."

Rebecca thought something rude about how she felt more like a
veterinary assistant than any kind of Healer, and was glad anubi couldn't
hear thoughts.

"Not in my lifetime," Denis said. "You're not about to shave me."

Before Rebecca could move, Denis closed his eyes and bit his
bottom lip. A grunt of pain escaped him, and where a large, gray-furred
wolf had been sitting was a black-haired, very naked man.

Rebecca's eyes widened before she looked away. "Could you um..."

"Oh," Denis said. "Sorry. I forget that about human form. I don't
take it all that much."

"Right, thanks," Rebecca said, her face beet-red.

"You can look now," Denis said.

Rebecca looked back at her patient. Denis was still bare-chested,
and had muscles on top of his muscles. His open eyes were a light blue.
He smirked at her. A pair of loose brown boxers covered his lower half.

"There. No hair for you to shave. It's bad enough that you're going
to put stitches in me. Wearing this stupid shape then covering it is worse.
Humans and their modesty."

The hole in his shoulder continued to bleed, and Rebecca remembered herself. She stopped staring at Billy's insanely gorgeous brother
and set to work.

Syd explained the difference between entry and exit wounds,
what injury the bullet itself caused in addition to what harm the silver
wrought inside the wound, and what preparation to apply to heal both
kinds of damage.

"Gross," Rebecca said, wincing as she slid her first and middle
fingers into the bloody hole in Denis' shoulder. The anubi didn't flinch
and Rebecca felt bad about complaining when he wasn't. "Sorry."

"Trying to tickle me, Acolyte?" Denis asked. Rebecca knew he was
trying to sound like her digging around in his injury didn't hurt, but she

could hear the pain in his voice—and feel it in the wound itself. Her fingers burned.

"I can't feel any fragments, Syd," Rebecca said. "It's kind of slippery and my fingers are hot."

Syd nodded. "You're feeling where the silver passed through. If there were fragments, they'd feel like needles when you found them."

"Not feeling any needles," Rebecca said, gritting her teeth as she forced her fingers deeper into the wound.

"I think it's clean," Syd said. "Do the same thing to the back side of the wound just to be sure, then he can change back to his usual form before I show you how to treat and dress a wound like this."

***

"And no changing forms again for at least a mortal month," Rebecca said to Denis with a stern glare. "Follow the instructions for the herbs I gave you and have your pack Healer keep a close eye on that wound. It isn't likely to fester, but you never know. I'm not sure how old those bullets were, but I know they were pretty old."

"Silver content of them was low," Denis replied in a sullen growl.

"Still enough to poison an anubi," Syd said, eyeing him. "After today, I'd think you'd want to stay out of the enclave as much as possible."

"Won't be coming back," Denis said, looking at his brother though his words were for Rebecca. Denis turned to her before speaking again. "Hope you learned your lesson."

"Hope you learned yours," Rebecca replied.

Denis laughed. "My gratitude, Acolyte."

He stood, studied her for a long moment, seeming to debate something with himself, then sat back down. He reached and put a large, furred hand on her shoulder and gave it a hard squeeze before he glared at Syd.

"Listen, bloodsucker," he began. "You're not doing a very good job of keeping her power under wraps. You can feel this little one's light shining between and across every realm. It's not difficult to figure out that something's going on, and it's making a whole lot of beings nervous. Let me take her back to the den. She'll be safe there, among the anubi. We'll protect her until she comes into her own."

"No," Syd said, his tone leaving no room for debate. "She already has an anubi to protect her, in addition to me."

Denis snorted. "You and him? At least with us, there's a chance she *wouldn't* die."

"I said no," Syd said, taking a step toward Rebecca and glaring at the anubi. "She stays with me. With us."

"Remember you said that when Billy's dead, you're a crispy critter and this little girl is in the hands of asses badder than yours." Denis stood. "There are already reports of Healers missing from their enclaves. Council declaration or no, war has begun, and unless you get her under control, there's nothing but heartache and misery coming your way. All of you."

Billy and Syd exchanged a glance.

Denis turned to Billy and considered him a moment before he spoke. "Brother, you're dead to me."

Then he disappeared from the enclave.

Rebecca was stunned.

"Did he...does he mean...?" she started to ask.

"Yeah, Bit...that's what he means," Billy said. His dark brown anubi eyes glittered, and Rebecca wasn't sure if he was relieved or hurt.

"I know it's probably none of my business, but since you are living here now, I'd like to know what you did to—you know—"

"Piss my brother off and earn myself a death mark?" Billy finished for her.

"Well...yeah," she said. "I mean...is this going to be a regular thing? Random werewolf fights in the back yard?"

A rumbling came from Billy's chest and she knew he was laughing a little.

"Nah," he said. "We're done, Denis and me. You heard him. He's the only one got a grudge anyway. Pissed I survived the death part is all. Pissed at me for what I done to deserve it."

"What was that?"

"Rescuing a damsel in distress. Told you I wasn't much for it, but—"

The anubi wiped his furry arm across his eyes and Rebecca could see that he stifled the urge to stretch, lest he tear the stitches she had put in him yet again. He sighed.

"Don't know about you, Bit, but I could certainly use a bite to eat."

CHAPTER THIRTEEN

Rebecca realized her eyes were open. It was still very dark in her room, and a glance at the red numbers of her alarm clock informed her that it was four o'clock in the morning. Her brow furrowed. She hadn't been asleep all that long.

She worked her jaw a few times. It hurt and so did her head. She must have been clenching her teeth. She only did that when she was nervous or upset.

Syd had told her to try not to worry or be upset, but after the werewolf fight he'd avoided her the rest of the evening. She wondered if it had anything to do with that...weird moment in the enclave when Denis wanted to take her to the Anubin den to keep her safe. How was she supposed to not worry when Syd said he would be here to protect her and he wasn't?

And why was she worried about him anyway? Shouldn't she be worrying more about what Denis' had said? About the demons plotting to somehow kidnap her before her birthday tomorrow?

So why was she more worried about Syd than anything else?

She'd been tired and had gone to her room to read, and didn't remember falling asleep. Why was she awake now?

Her neck itched, and she reached up automatically to scratch it. Warmth met her fingers and she gasped as she pulled them away from her skin. Rebecca reached for her lamp and snapped on the light.

Her fingers looked fine. Her neck tingled more, and she reached tentatively to touch it again.

Her birthmark, she realized, as she felt the difference in temperature. The itchy spot was definitely warmer than the skin around it.

The large, star-like Healer's mark.

Something like a gentle breeze brushed her skin, and Rebecca shivered. Was someone whispering? She closed her eyes and strained to hear, wishing for a moment that she had Billy's anubi hearing. Maybe it was just the wind outside.

The sound came again and the mark on Rebecca's neck seemed to grow warmer. She looked to the ceiling and waited for another moment, wondering if it was only her imagination.

When she heard the whispering a third time, louder than before, she knew it wasn't her mind playing tricks on her or the night breeze through the bare-branched trees.

The enclave was calling, beckoning to her.

"Okay, I'm coming," Rebecca whispered into the dark, and she reached for the candle holder and box of matches Syd had told her to keep by her bed. Rebecca had wanted to substitute a flashlight but Syd had said that Ethereals preferred candlelight as artificial light was harsh on sensitive eyes.

The sound of whispered voices came again, low and soothing. Rebecca tried hard to make out what they were saying and couldn't.

Getting out of bed, she looked down at herself and shook her head. She'd fallen asleep in her clothes. Oh, well. At least it kept her from having to get dressed. Candle in hand, she shivered and left the bedroom.

Wow, the house was creepy at night. She'd never been up in the middle of the night alone before, in the dark. Not that she was afraid of the dark. At least, that's what she told herself. Rebecca couldn't keep a shiver from running down her spine. She went back to her room and found her robe and slippers before she went upstairs. It was cold!

Entering the enclave, Rebecca looked around. The candle at Ryan's bedside was out. The only light came from the one in Rebecca's hand.

"Hello?" she called.

Nothing answered her.

Well, as long as she was up here, she could relight the bedside candle and check on Ryan. Syd had told her that vampires were weakest just before dawn when they went to rest and just after sundown when they woke. Poor Ryan.

Ow! Her Healer's mark stung, like someone had stabbed her in the neck with a needle. She clapped a hand over it and scratched it in an attempt to soothe the pain.

Replacing the burned-out candle with a new one, Rebecca struck a match and lit the wick.

Her breath caught in her throat as she realized Ryan's bed was empty.

"I'm here," said a voice from the end of the room. "Don't start screaming or anything."

Rebecca breathed again, recognizing it.

Ryan stood before the long mirror portal to the Otherworlds.

"What are you doing?" Rebecca asked, trying hard to make sure her voice was calm, though she heard it shake. "You shouldn't be up."

"What are *you* doing?" Ryan replied with a question of his own. "If anyone should be in bed, it's you."

He turned back to the mirror.

"Ouch!" Rebecca yelped as the lit match she still held burned down to her fingers. She dropped it and it went out.

Ryan laughed and shook his head. "Now you see why my lighter is lucky," he said, amused. "Speaking of, where is my lucky lighter? And my jacket?"

"Lighter is in the pocket of the jacket, which is hung up in the coat closet downstairs," Rebecca said, coming to stand beside him. She looked past him to the mirror. "What are you looking at?"

"Just...seeing if it's true," Ryan said, gesturing to the reflection that showed only her and not him.

Rebecca slid an arm around his bare waist. The mirror showed her alone, standing with her arm crooked around nothing but air.

"It is, sorry," she whispered.

"I know that," Ryan replied with a snort. "Unlike you, I don't need a candle to see in the dark. I just wanted to see if it was true. The thing about not having a reflection. Now how am I supposed to see how good I look in my lucky jacket?"

"Is everything you own lucky?" Rebecca asked as she looked up at him.

"Pretty much," Ryan said. "At least, everything that's mine."

"Come on," Rebecca said. She gave his waist a little tug. "Let's get you back to bed."

"I feel fine," Ryan said as he shook her off.

"Well, you don't look fine," Rebecca countered. She scowled at him.

"I'm tired of bed!" Ryan said, scowling back at her. "Leave me alone!"

He took a step away from her and stumbled. Rebecca caught him before he fell. Ryan groaned.

This time Rebecca didn't give him a choice. She slid a firm arm around his waist again and half-dragged him back to the bed.

Ryan all but collapsed on it, and it was a struggle for Rebecca to get him in something of a comfortable position.

She gasped when she pulled the blankets back.

Blood.

Dark patches stained the pillowcase where Ryan's head had lain. The sheets and blankets too were dotted with dark red blotches. She looked up and saw a fine sheen of bloody sweat had broken out on Ryan's forehead, and his eyes were so dark they were almost black. She settled him in the bed and immediately took off her robe and began rolling up her sleeve as she sat down beside him.

"No," Ryan moaned, grabbing at her wrist. He clenched her arm hard, his inhuman grip making her wince in pain. His nails dug deep into her skin. "Listen."

"I...I'm listening, Ryan," Rebecca said, making sure to use his name. Syd had said that names helped, and sometimes it was the only thing a creature would respond to, or hear.

"Listen," Ryan said again, his iron grip on her arm tightening even more. "You have to hear."

Rebecca tried to loosen Ryan's hold on her arm. "Ryan, you're hurting me! Let go!"

"I want to go," Ryan babbled. "Home. I want to go home."

"Yes," Rebecca agreed, prying at Ryan's fingers with her own. "Yes, I know. We'll get you well, then you can go home, Ryan."

"No," Ryan said again. "No, you don't know. I can hear you thinking. You don't know."

The wounded boy rolled his head from side to side as if trying to get something to leave his mind.

Syd had said that sometimes a turning didn't go well. Was Ryan slipping into the insanity that came when new vampires couldn't cope with what they had become?

Ryan suddenly let go of her wrist and sat bolt upright, grabbing her shoulders. Rebecca screamed.

"You have to be careful," Ryan demanded. "He's been watching. Waiting for you. Stay away from mirrors. They see through mirrors. See your soul. He's watching you! He'll get you through the mirror like he did the others..."

Who? Who was? Rebecca thought. *What mirror? Does he mean the portal?*

It's not difficult to figure out that something's going on, and it's making a whole lot of beings nervous, Rebecca remembered Denis saying. *There are already reports of Healers missing from their enclaves. War has begun, and unless you get her under control, there's nothing but heartache and misery coming your way.*

What was Ryan talking about? Who was watching?

"Ryan, you're scaring me," Rebecca said, much calmer than she felt.

"Promise me," Ryan said, ignoring her words. "You promise me."

"Promise you...what? What do you need me to promise, Ryan?"

Ryan shook his head and fell back on the bed as convulsions overtook him.

This time, Rebecca knew what to do.

She didn't panic. Grabbing her nana's old healing case, Rebecca found the tincture her nana had made especially for Ryan's bite and seized the waistband of his pajama bottoms. The liquid hadn't been working fantastically well, but it was better than nothing. It was all she had until she could figure something else out.

Rebecca gasped as she saw his wound smoking and hissing. She ripped the cork from the bottle and dumped most of the bottle into the festering blackness that was Ryan's hellhound bite.

What is going on? Why is it getting worse?

Ryan groaned and writhed in pain. Rebecca laid her wrist over his mouth in an effort to calm him, and Ryan instinctively bit down hard. She yelped as his fangs pierced her wrist. Instead of pulling away, Rebecca forced her wrist even harder against his fangs, pushing him firm against the bed.

With her other hand, Rebecca pinched the sides of the hellhound bite closed and leaned into her elbow along Ryan's thigh. The wound hissed and bubbled more as the potion she'd poured into it couldn't find much of an escape and tried to do its work.

Rebecca whimpered and closed her eyes against the pain.

Almost immediately, the image of chains and spiked bars assaulted her. The same over-rotten stench she'd been aware of last time invaded her nostrils, making her retch.

This time, she could hear someone—more than one person—screaming.

Nearby there was sobbing. The sound of panicked, hysterical crying echoed off the thick stone walls.

"Hello?" Rebecca called. "Who's there? Can anyone hear me? I hear you..."

Nothing replied to her.

She was so focused on keeping her eyes closed and the picture clear in her mind that she didn't feel it when Ryan's thrashing stopped.

His fangs disengaged from her wrist, taking the images behind her eyes with them.

Oh, cripes. Did he die? Oh, please...don't let him die...

But she didn't smell anything, and Ryan's body was still there. Rebecca breathed again.

"Mind getting off me?" she heard Ryan say in a weak voice. "Your elbow is really starting to dig into my leg."

Rebecca lifted herself up. Ryan groaned, and Rebecca smacked his stomach.

"You scared me!"

"Sorry!" Ryan defended, holding his hands over his face.

Rebecca swatted him again anyway, sighing through gritted teeth. "Oh, hold still and let me have a good look."

She grabbed the candle in the holder off the night-table and brought it close to his leg, trying hard to see.

"Hey, bite me again," Rebecca murmured, thrusting her bleeding wrist back toward Ryan's mouth.

"What—?" he began.

"Just do it!" Rebecca ordered.

Ryan shook his head and brought her wrist to his mouth. She didn't flinch this time as his fangs slid into the punctures they'd just made.

"Mmm?" Ryan made the noise a question.

"Drink," Rebecca said, keeping her eyes on his wound.

"Mmm." He rolled his eyes and did as he was told.

Rebecca's vision changed, just as it had before. She saw Ryan's wound clearly in the dark, and suddenly the candle was too bright. She moved it and studied the hellhound bite carefully.

Glowing, pulsing flecks of black and gold wriggled inside the wound, but something bright green—Rebecca could only guess that it was the potion she'd just poured into it—made the black and gold flecks go out as it touched them.

"Mmm?"

She was tempted to close her eyes again, just to see if she could see—or hear—anything more from whatever she'd seen.

But Syd wasn't there to keep her safe, and Rebecca didn't want to chance doing something she didn't understand without him there.

"Good," Rebecca said, pulling back a little. "You can quit now."

"What'd you do?" Ryan asked as he lifted his mouth from Rebecca's wrist.

"Nearly every time I've fed you, I've seen things," Rebecca said, shaking her head. "And last time, when I opened my eyes before you finished, I could see in the dark as though it were daylight. I thought maybe if I looked at your bite while you were doing that, I might see why it's not healing."

"See anything useful?"

Rebecca shook her head. "Bits of hellhound drool and the medicine I just dumped in there. It's working, sort of. Other than that, not a thing. It's so frustrating!"

She deliberately avoided telling him about the...other things she could see when he bit her. She didn't want to sound crazy, and something

158 • DINA JAMES

inside her told her not to mention it to him. She shrugged and looked down at the inside of her wrist.

"Now that you're awake, do you think you could eat more?"

"What?"

Rebecca held out her bleeding wrist again.

"Eat more," she repeated. "You look horrible. This should at least make you feel better."

"What are you doing?" Ryan asked, edging a little further away from her.

Rebecca frowned at him. "You need to eat, and it's not like I can bring you a plate of bacon and eggs."

"You're not...I won't..." he stammered, looking very afraid again.

"You will too, and you have been," Rebecca said, gentle but firm. "You're a vampire now, and you're still badly hurt. You can't hunt yet. That's why you're here, Stereotype. You need healing and guess what? I'm a Healer."

"Yeah, but..." Ryan eyed her wrist, unsure.

"Come on," Rebecca said. "You need your strength, and for the moment, I'm all there is. Don't get all snobby on me like Marla Thompson. She wouldn't take my blood if I were the last human on the planet. Now, come on. I know you need this."

"Yeah, but I don't want to drink your blood, Rebecca," Ryan said with a scowl.

"Yeah, well, I don't want you to either. I mean, how do you think *I* feel? I know guys are only supposed to be interested in one thing, but it's a little creepy when it's your blood. Still, it's what I do and what you need, so, get to it, would you? I can tell by your eyes that you're practically starving. You're over the worst, so I don't think you're not going to go all crazy on me."

She gave her arm a meaningful shake. "It's okay, really. You're not going to hurt me," she coaxed.

Ryan took her hand, unsure, and brought her wrist to his mouth. He looked to Rebecca and, at her nod, closed his eyes and bit down again.

She, too, closed her eyes and tried hard not to flinch for his sake. If he thought it hurt her, he might stop feeding, and not take her blood again. He needed to eat, and she needed to help him.

What's more, she *wanted* to help him. So what if it hurt a little?

She opened her eyes and caught him studying her face. She smiled for him, hoping it looked like a smile and not a grimace.

He winked at her and her smile broadened. Rebecca blushed and turned her head, hoping he hadn't seen that he'd flustered her.

"Not too much, now," Rebecca cautioned after a long minute. "You're still turning, and too much is just as bad as not enough according to Syd."

Ryan continued feeding from her for another moment or two, then lifted his mouth and let go of her hand. He tilted his head back, and Rebecca saw red glistening along his white fangs.

He closed his mouth and swallowed a few times.

"It's...it's not as bad as I thought it would be," Ryan said after a moment.

"Gee, thanks. I'm glad my blood meets your standards," Rebecca said with a giggle. "Now, could you finish?"

Ryan looked at her, confused. "What?"

Rebecca held out her bleeding wrist again. "You're the vampire," she said. "Don't you just *know* how to do this? Why am I the one teaching you how to suck blood?"

"Because he is a fledgling, and untrained, just as you are," Syd said, placing his hands on her shoulders as he appeared behind her in silence. "Allow me."

Syd brought her bleeding wrist to his mouth and, looking pointedly at Ryan, ran his tongue along the wound Ryan had made. The punctures sealed shut, and Syd licked them again, removing any stain of blood or trace that she'd been injured.

"Thanks," Rebecca said, looking up at Syd. His blue eyes glowed and pulsed in a gentle rhythm that reminded Rebecca of a heartbeat.

Syd released her wrist, letting it fall to her side without care. "The young fledgling has fed well, I see. Well done, Acolyte."

"I'd take that as a compliment if you didn't sound like you were making fun of me," Rebecca replied, hesitant now as she rolled her sleeve down again.

Why is he acting like...? Why is he so different when we're alone?

"Perhaps you are overly sensitive, as you're accustomed to being mocked," Syd replied as she stood up. "Or so Ryan tells me."

Rebecca just looked at Ryan.

"What? We talk," Ryan defended. "You've come up on occasion."

"Why? Have you guys been spying on me or something?"

"Yes." Syd raised an eyebrow and smirked down at her.

"No," Ryan said at the same time.

Rebecca caught Ryan glaring at Syd.

"Why can't I see?" Ryan asked. "I mean...like normal?"

"It's the light," Sydney answered. "And you no longer have human eyes. Come nightfall, or in darkness, it will be different."

160 • DINA JAMES

Syd gestured with his hand and the candles in the enclave went out. The room fell into instant darkness.

"You see?"

"Cool," Rebecca heard Ryan murmur. "Wow...hey this is neat! Is it always like this? Your hair looks like fire, Hot Stuff, and your eyes—"

The candles illuminated again, making Ryan squint against the sudden harsh light.

Rebecca glared at Syd. "We want him to feel better, not worse." She really wanted to be angry with him, but just looking at him made her stomach all jittery.

"My apologies," Syd said, though he didn't sound at all sorry.

"Well, I'm going to go back to bed," Rebecca said as she got to her feet. She pointed a stern finger at Ryan. "You stay put. No matter how you might feel now, you're not healed yet."

Ryan lay down again. "I'm not going anywhere. I feel like you say I look."

"Hey, you don't look as bad as you have been," Rebecca teased back. "This is an actual improvement."

She reached under Ryan's chin, cupping it as she tilted his head up toward her. He closed his eyes.

"Look at me," Rebecca ordered in her calm Healer's voice.

Ryan opened his eyes, and Rebecca studied them intently, making careful notes in her mind about their shade.

"You still hungry?" Rebecca asked.

Ryan shook his head a little, careful not to disturb her gentle hand beneath his jaw.

"How do you feel?"

"Awful bright in here," Ryan murmured, closing his eyes again. "And I'm real tired. More tired than I ever been in my life."

"You probably will be for a while longer," Rebecca replied. "You've been through a hard time, but you're safe here, so you just rest."

Rebecca moved her hand and laid the back of it against his cheek. Ryan opened his eyes again and looked at her, but didn't say anything.

He pulled away when Rebecca brought her hand to his forehead.

"I'm not going to hurt you," she assured him, confused. "I just want to see—"

"I'm tired," Ryan said again, interrupting her. "Quit poking at me."

His tone carried a trace of viciousness, and it scared her. She remembered what Syd said about newly turned vampires being unpredictable and unable to help themselves. She took a step back, flinching as Syd's hands caught her upper arms and held her steady.

His grip wasn't warm this time. It was tight and painful, and made Rebecca wince.

"He won't harm you," Syd said, glaring at Ryan over Rebecca's shoulder.

"*He* might not," Rebecca said. She turned her head to look up at him. "But *you* are."

Syd's grasp relaxed instantly. "Forgive me," he whispered.

"It's all right," Rebecca whispered back. "I know you guys are strong. Stay with him?"

Sydney nodded in reply but didn't look at her. Rebecca smiled at Ryan and blew out a few of the lit candles on her way out, to make the room more comfortable for him.

Rebecca woke up refreshed and strangely energized. She was used to getting up early for school and to help Nana get ready for the day, and it was strange to wake up and have to do neither. There had been some days when she would have beyond welcomed the chance to sleep in, but again she'd slept better than she had in weeks. Months. Maybe years. She just couldn't stay in bed a moment longer, even though the clock beside her bed read 7:37AM.

Her stomach growled. She went into the kitchen and shook her head at the mess Billy had made before she set about making a couple pieces of toast. The untoasted bread reminded her of something and she set another piece aside before popping the other two in the toaster. She poured herself a glass of milk, then took a small pint of cream out of the fridge and poured a few tablespoons into a shallow saucer. As her own bread toasted, Rebecca took the other piece of bread and the cream out to the back porch and set it on the top step.

"Brr!" she said to herself as she went quickly back inside to the warm kitchen. It was *cold* out there! If they didn't hurry, the bread and cream might freeze before the faeries got it. That is, if any still lived around the house. Rebecca could remember Nana leaving out the traditional offering of bread and cream out on the back porch, but she'd thought it had been for the neighborhood strays or something. Now she knew what her nana had really been doing, and what she had been so adamant about being done each morning before Rebecca left for school. She'd been thanking the garden fae for looking after the plants and trees around their house.

Rebecca had yet to see one of the Wee Folk, as the book had called them, but Billy assured her they were there. As she put the cream away

162 • DINA JAMES

in the fridge, a large brown form filled the kitchen doorway.

"Reminds me," Billy rumbled. "Need to get more cream. Coffee too. Sugar. Bread. Whiskey—"

"Whiskey?" Rebecca interrupted. "Faerie beer not strong enough for you?"

Billy gave her a surprised look. "Can't make a decent cup of coffee without whiskey, Bit."

"I manage fine without it," she replied, though she tried hard not to smile.

Billy grinned at her. "You're a little human, and drink weak coffee. Anything else you want while I'm out gettin' stuff? Figure since I live here now, we're gonna need supplies. What kind of ice cream you like?"

Rebecca just looked at him. "I can't think about ice cream before dawn."

"Why not?" Billy asked. "Oh, right...you're mortal. You got that 'time of day' thing going on. Weird beings, humans. Oh, well. I'll get a bunch of different kinds. You're bound to like at least one. It's ice cream!"

Billy enveloped her in a huge hug and kissed the top of her head before he left the house.

Rebecca stood there for a long moment, stunned.

A werewolf had just kissed the top of her head and given her a hug.

Either she was going crazy, or Billy had eaten something that didn't agree with him.

Before she could think too much on it, the mark on her neck tingled and she felt the now-familiar tug below her breastbone. Voices whispered in Rebecca's ear. She sighed.

The enclave was calling to her. Something needed help, and she knew it wasn't Ryan.

CHAPTER FOURTEEN

She still didn't feel ready to face whatever was waiting for her on her own, but after taking care of Ryan by herself just last night, how could she refuse? She took a deep breath, went up the stairs, and entered the enclave.

A quick glance around showed Ryan asleep—his open eyes still unnerved her. Syd was gone—no surprise there this early in the day. It was just after dawn, and he needed rest too. As she was learning to do, Rebecca put her own thoughts and concerns aside and made herself focus on what Billy called "what needed doin'." It took Rebecca's eyes a moment to adjust to the light of the single candle near Ryan's bed, but still she couldn't see anything waiting for her.

"Hello?" Rebecca said in her gentlest Healer's voice, hoping she wouldn't wake Ryan. "Does someone need help in here?"

"You are indeed still blind, if you cannot see what is right in front of you," she heard a very faint voice say.

"Uh...where?" Rebecca peered into the darkness where she thought the voice came from.

"Could you not shout? We can hear perfectly well," the little voice answered. "Look to the candle!"

"Sorry," Rebecca said in the softest whisper she could manage.

Then she saw them. Two tiny specks of bright white light that danced around the candle. No wonder she hadn't seen them at first glance. They could easily have been mistaken for dust particles or sparks rising from the flickering candle.

How am I supposed to heal a light? And what could possibly hurt—

As though they could hear her thoughts—she really needed to learn to shield them, but it was so hard to do, let alone *remember* to do—Rebecca's eyes widened as she watched the pinpricks of light become two tiny creatures standing at the base of the candleholder. They were no bigger than her hand, and one was waving its arms and grinning up at her.

She smiled back. She knew these creatures from one of Nana's old books she'd thumbed through. So this was what came to the back porch for the grained bread and cream Nana had insisted Rebecca put out every morning, even on her "bad days." The ones who made the ale Billy so loved.

Garden faeries.

With slow, careful steps, Rebecca approached the table on which the candle sat. She crouched down so she was at eye level with the two small creatures. Their beautiful wings were thin and iridescent, nearly touching their ankles. They reminded Rebecca of the wings of a dragonfly.

Though the one fairy was still smiling and waving, his companion did not share his enthusiasm. Rebecca could see why right away—one of its wings was bent backwards, almost to the point of tearing.

That looked like it hurt a lot.

"My brother fell foul of your labyrinthine, my lady," the smiling faerie said. He tried to look sympathetic, but he had a pleased twinkle in his eye.

Rebecca had no idea what he was talking about. Her labyrinthine? What was that? And why did he call it "hers?" She didn't have...whatever he was talking about. But that didn't matter. She put the questions she had away in the back of her mind to either look up or ask her nana later.

"I see," Rebecca said. "May I know the name of the injured?"

He hesitated. Rebecca had learned that garden fae observed politeness and protocol before anything else, and didn't give their names to anyone without significant need. Still, she would need a name in order to try and help.

"You may, Acolyte," a second small voice said before his brother could answer. "I am Cort."

Cort looked to be in considerable pain, but somehow Rebecca knew he was trying hard not to show it.

"All right, Cort," Rebecca said. "Let's get you something for your pain."

"Nay, my lady. It's nothing I can't bear."

"If you don't need me to help you, why did you come here?" Rebecca asked, raising an eyebrow at the little being.

Cort shook his head and looked at his companion. "My brother has watched you make your offering in the mornings—"

The other faerie cleared his throat. Rebecca hid a smile and lowered her eyes as she saw the other's cheeks darken.

She knew she couldn't help Cort without his permission and she told him so.

"Aye, then. As you say," Cort replied with a sigh, shaking his head.

Rebecca found her nana's suitcase and looked through it for one of the glass vials it contained. She opened it and shook out a minute portion of dried skullcap. She crushed the leaf to tiny bits between her thumb and forefinger and separated a faerie-sized dose of the herb out. She held it out to the injured faerie with instructions to chew and swallow it.

Cort wrinkled his nose but took the herb and did as she said. He grimaced at the bitter taste but managed to get it down.

"Yeah, it's pretty awful," Rebecca sympathized. She turned to Cort's brother. "You know, if you wanted to meet me so badly, you could have just shown yourself. You didn't have to wait until your brother got hurt."

The faerie blushed even more.

"Oh, but—" Rebecca hesitated a moment as something about faerie protocol entered her mind, and she remembered what Syd had said about keeping up with the speed at which her suppressed knowledge would surface. "Your kind can't just introduce themselves, can they?" *That was it!* "I'm supposed to ask if I may have the honor of your name. Will you honor me with it?"

The faerie hesitated again, and Cort made a noise like a growl and kicked his brother. "I am suffering for your fancy!"

"I am Inth, Acolyte," the fae managed in a rush.

"You are an *idiot*," Cort grumbled.

"That wing looks pretty damaged," Rebecca said to Cort. "It's very kind of you to endure everything just so your brother could meet me."

The acknowledgement had the effect Rebecca hoped it would. Cort couldn't help but smile at being called "kind."

"It was nothing, Acolyte," Cort replied, as brave as he could.

"How are you feeling? Is the pain still there?"

"Not nearly as much before," Cort said, though he didn't sound very sure. "The wing does not ache anymore."

"Good. The medicine is working," Rebecca moved toward him, slow and careful. "Now, Cort, I need to touch you. May I have your permission?"

"Aye," Cort replied, swaying a bit on his feet. "As the Acolyte needs. I take no offense."

"My gratitude," Rebecca said again.

She reached toward the small being and touched his wing, careful and delicate, willing her hands not to shake, though she was very nervous. This was the first healing she'd attempted by herself, and for a second she wondered if she shouldn't wait for Syd to return, at least to supervise, but waiting for Syd could take minutes or hours, and Cort was in pain.

166 • DINA JAMES

Besides, Rebecca thought, *I need to learn fast and can't wait around for someone to hold my hand. The knowledge is there. I just have to...*

The wing was as light as tissue paper. When she moved it a little, it seemed to change color. Rainbows of watercolored light, like the spectrum of a crystal, played around the dark room as the faerie wing caught the glow of the candle.

She knew she could read wounds and see things with a touch, and she concentrated on the injury beneath her fingers. Rebecca learned that Cort's wing was only bent, not broken. Yes, the damage had indeed been caused by a...cat? Was "labyrinthine" their name for "housecat?" She remembered when Mishka went through her phase of leaving dead mice and headless birds at the foot of Nana's chair. *Gross.*

All thoughts of running to Syd for help fled as the knowledge of what to do spread through her in a flood of tingles.

Rebecca cupped the tiny being in her palms and spread her fingers around Cort's back. She closed her eyes and, with slow precision, rotated her hands until the fingers of one of her hands pointed skyward, while the other pointed toward the earth.

"How warm," Cort murmured. "My gratitude, Acolyte. That was... unexpected."

She smiled and removed her hands, looking down at them in wonder. For a moment they'd generated a strange kind of heat, and now they were cooling as if she were a toaster that had been unplugged. It seemed vampires weren't the only ones whose power she could replenish. Cort would need all his strength in order to finish healing on his own.

She went to the chest of drawers near the bed and gathered the supplies she needed. "Now, I'm going to tape your wing flat against your back so it will heal straight, Cort. Inth, please don't let him remove the splint for one whole human day."

Rebecca marveled to herself at how she just knew that a faerie's healing time differed a great deal from a human's. *Just knowing* stuff was both scary and kind of fun. Freaky but cool. One human day should be enough to heal Cort's bent wing.

She turned to Inth. "You'll take care of him, won't you?"

Inth nodded, though Cort gave him a dark scowl and muttered something Rebecca couldn't hear.

"Cort, I'll also want you to put a cold compress on your head at home for at least a couple of mortal hours."

"A compress? Why?" the faerie asked, sounding indignant. "My head is fine!"

"You didn't tell me you were knocked unconscious," Rebecca

said, giving Cort a sharp look. "Faeries can suffer from concussion just like everyone else. You took a nasty blow to the head, and it's going to swell. I hereby order you to one full mortal day of rest, beginning right when you get home. And you'll go straight home from here, gentlefae. Understand?"

"I cannot! I am a guardian of the Queen! I must return to my duties!" Cort protested.

"You are a wounded fae, and I'm your Healer," Rebecca said. "You'll do what I tell you to and your Queen knows that perfectly well."

"Perhaps so, but that doesn't mean the Queen won't be upset with me," Cort grumbled. "Nor the Captain of the Guard." He glared at his brother. "I hope you are pleased!"

Rebecca smiled to herself because she could hear the fondness in Cort's voice.

Rebecca had just closed the drawer that held the supplies she'd used when she heard Ryan moan. She went to him without hesitation and sat down on the bed at his side. She touched the side of his face and Rebecca took in the confused look on his face—he could see her, but didn't recognize her.

She was very familiar with that particular expression.

"Hey," she called softly. "It's okay. You're safe."

"No," Ryan managed through clenched teeth. He began to convulse. "They're...coming..."

Rebecca didn't have time to ask what he meant—or who—before Ryan's thrashing escalated.

She leaned over him, keeping him from falling out of the bed. His eyes were so dark they were almost black. Rebecca forced herself not to panic as she let go of Ryan's thrashing body just enough to begin rolling up her pajama sleeve.

"No," Ryan moaned, grabbing at her wrist. "Listen."

"Ryan, let go!"

"Listen," Ryan said again, his iron grip on her arm tightening even more. "You can't—"

"Can't what?" Rebecca said, trying to pull away, though she knew even in his weakened state that Ryan was ten times stronger than she was.

Ryan babbled. "—can't fight them. Neutral ground. Don't let them..."

The dark-haired boy suddenly grabbed her shoulders. Rebecca couldn't stifle her short scream.

168 • DINA JAMES

"You have to be careful," Ryan demanded.

"I'll be careful, Ryan," Rebecca said, much calmer than she felt. "You have to let me go, though."

Ryan fell back on the bed as convulsions shook him.

This time Rebecca threw her own body over his, using all of her weight to pin him down. She felt something hot against her hip and looked down. She gasped as saw Ryan's bite wound smoking slightly and hissing beneath the waistband of his pajama bottoms.

With one hand, Rebecca jerked the material down and then fumbled in the drawer of the bedside table that held the candle until she found the tincture for Ryan's hellhound bite wound.

She ripped the cork from the bottle and dumped the contents into the festering blackness that was Ryan's hellhound bite. Rebecca brought her wrist to his mouth and Ryan bit down on it.

She reached down and pressed her hand hard against the seeping wound. The injury hissed and smoked as it had done the last time she'd poured the potion into it.

Rebecca was so focused on keeping Ryan's wound closed that she didn't realize it when Ryan's thrashing stopped beneath her until he spoke.

"Hey," she heard Ryan say in a weak voice. He turned his head toward her and gave her a slight grin when she looked at him. He looked down toward his exposed wound. His underwear was still in place, but it was clear Rebecca had all but ripped his pajama bottoms off. "Moving kinda fast here, aren't we?"

Rebecca blushed and reached to pull his pajama bottoms back up. Ryan groaned and his eyes went blank, though they remained open.

"That you'll quite literally throw yourself into your healing is encouraging, Acolyte," Syd's voice came from behind her.

She could hear the amusement in his tone.

"Though I would very much appreciate it if you'd...remove yourself from atop my thrall," he continued. "He is still healing, after all."

"Shouldn't you be resting, or hibernating, or whatever it is your kind does during the day?" Rebecca asked as she slowly moved from the bed and began to straighten the bedclothes. She was glad Nana hadn't been there to see her in a bed tearing the pants off some guy she barely knew while she climbed on top of him. Rebecca might be nearly seventeen, but she'd never even kissed a boy.

She could totally understand now what Syd meant when he said that a lot of new Healers took things that weren't meant...like that...the wrong way.

"The demons have indeed begun kidnapping Healers."

"Why?" Rebecca asked, trembling. "I thought...that one at school... when he tried to pull me through the mirror...said I had to go willingly, or something. If that's true, why...how did they get these other Healers to go with them? What do they want them for?"

"I don't know," Syd replied, shaking his head. "I truly haven't any idea. I'm just as confused as you are. The only thing I do know is that they will, most certainly, attempt to come for you again. We can't worry now about why. All we can do is keep you safe until your power can manifest in its entirety."

"They're kidnapping Healers much older than me, whose power has already done that. I don't know why you think my birthday is going to make me any safer," Rebecca replied.

"It will," Syd said. "I promise you, it will. Now try not to worry, remember. Peace and calm."

Rebecca told him about being able to see Ryan's wound when he bit her, and asked him about it.

"I can only guess that you were seeing through Ryan's eyes some-how," Syd replied. "For that is a very close description of how a vampire sees."

She bit her bottom lip and looked around the room, nervous, and then reached down to brush Ryan's dark hair away from his face. She gasped as her hand came away wet, and she could see the dark liquid shining against her hand.

Syd shook his head. "He should have stopped shedding by now. This does not bode well for his recovery."

"Shouldn't we...I don't know..." Rebecca looked at Syd, worried. "Call his mom, or something? He wasn't in school today, and obviously didn't go home last night. What if the police are looking for him?"

Sydney laughed, and Rebecca could tell he was laughing at her.

"What?" she demanded with a scowl.

"Acolyte, quiet and calm, remember," Syd chided. "Also remember to be respectful."

She felt like Syd should try and remember that, too.

"What's so funny about calling his mom? She's probably worried about him."

"No," Sydney replied in a whisper.

"Or the school? Won't someone come looking for him?"

"No one is going to come looking for him. No one will even notice he's gone."

"He's human," Rebecca protested. "I mean...well...he was. He has a mother, and teachers, and—"

"No one," Sydney said again, meeting Rebecca's eyes with a dark glare for a fraction of a moment. "It's how he...became one of us in the first place. His mother won't even notice his absence. Not for quite some time. And when she does, she will not notify the authorities, or even bother to look for him. She is...most unconcerned with anything other than obtaining her next drink."

She looked to the boy on the bed for a moment before she dared to meet Syd's metallic-blue eyes, despite knowing she wasn't supposed to. Something in his tone compelled her to. "What about his dad?"

"Ryan spoke of him only once," Sydney replied. "And that was to say that his father abandoned both him and his mother when Ryan was barely walking. He's never known his father."

Rebecca continued to look into Sydney's eyes, saying nothing.

"They will not bother, either," he said in reply to a question she didn't ask but he knew she wanted the answer to. "Ryan is well-known for his disappearances. The school will attempt to contact his mother, and his mother will tell them to mind their own business. As I said... no one will bother looking for him. No one cares where he is or isn't."

"Except you," Rebecca said with soft smile.

She couldn't help it. She kept her eyes on his, marveling at how amazing they were. She felt as though she were falling into them, being pulled somewhere by them. She couldn't look away, even if she'd wanted to. She didn't even think it was possible to do that.

The world outside the room vanished. Nothing existed but her and her desire to stay right here, and do whatever Syd asked of her. She wished he would ask her to do something, just so she could hear him speak, but then she'd have to leave where she was to obey him, and she didn't want to do that. Ever.

She just wanted to stay right here.

Then that strange, sudden warmth coursed through her limbs and she jumped back, blinking several times as she stared at him. She blushed, deep and pink, very embarrassed. She knew better than to look into the eyes of a Master vampire. She'd been told several times. Warned more than once. It wasn't very nice of Syd to hold her entranced like that.

"Stop it," she said, though it didn't sound very much like she wanted him to. "That's not fair."

"I...I wasn't holding you, Acolyte," Sydney stammered as he looked away and shook his head. "You...you were holding me."

He looked shocked at the realization. He looked back at Rebecca, studying her.

"Do that again," Sydney commanded.

"Do what?" Rebecca asked, confused.

"You were *holding* me," Sydney replied.

"I was not!" Rebecca said, shaking her head. "I mean, I didn't mean to...um...offend you, or anything. I just...you looked...upset..."

Sydney reached for her arm. Clasping her wrist firmly, Sydney brought her hand up. He pressed the palm of his own against hers and closed his eyes with a sharp breath.

"Now, think of something you want to know," he murmured. "A question you wish answered."

"Okay," Rebecca replied. She closed her eyes and did what he said.

A wry smile came to Syd's lips. "Be serious!"

Rebecca giggled and tried again.

"No, no. Think of something else," he said aloud. "Something I should know. I don't know who is going to win the next presidential election. It hasn't happened yet."

Rebecca took a deep breath. Syd said she'd see a lot of strange things. This was certainly strange.

The boy on the bed gave her an idea.

How did you get to know Ryan? she asked in her mind.

"He saw Billy's car at the fairgrounds with the keys inside and attempted to steal it," Syd replied in a low murmur. "Billy caught him, and instead of tearing him to pieces, Billy got to know the boy, then brought him to me. He'd never brought me a human before, and I wondered why he did so then—"

Sydney jerked his hand back as though he'd been burned. He looked at Rebecca, incredulous, and pulled away further as he eyed her.

"Such...such a thing has never been done to me," Sydney said in an awed tone.

Rebecca shrugged. "Nana's books say that reading is a useful ability and that wounds aren't the only thing Healers are capable of reading. You can get into *my* head. What's so scary about me being able to get into yours when I try?"

"This wasn't 'reading'," Sydney replied with a scowl. "You were in my thoughts, seeing what I knew! Compelling me to answer!"

"And that's a big deal why, exactly?" Rebecca asked, shaking her head as she went and sat on the bed. She dabbed at Ryan's forehead with a fresh damp cloth. "You keep saying I've got all this power, and have this Seer ability. Maybe it's got something to do with that." Rebecca looked at Syd with an impish grin. "Maybe I'm the most powerful Healer ever!"

Syd didn't smile at her teasing. He just continued to stare at her, his shock clear upon his face. When he spoke, it wasn't with amusement,

172 • DINA JAMES

only awe. "Maybe you are."

He was silent for a long moment, then reached down and brushed her hair away from the Healer's mark on her neck.

"What—" she began.

"Hush," he said, and offered his hand to her.

Unsure, Rebecca set the cloth aside and took his hand. Syd helped her stand and led her around the framed curtain that separated Ryan's bed from the rest of the enclave.

"Would you consent to replenish me, Most Powerful Healer Ever?" he asked.

Rebecca swallowed hard. His eyes weren't dark, but neither were they as bright as she'd seen, nor were they pulsing like a heartbeat as they normally did. He didn't really need feeding. He was perfectly fine. Still, he had asked, and it wasn't in Rebecca to refuse.

In fact, something in her leapt and filled her with a warm wanting. *Yes, please*, it said. *Yes.*

Rebecca just nodded, not trusting herself to speak.

"My gratitude to thee," Syd replied, and bent his head low. "Even now, though not of age, you quite literally radiate power. Even just standing here beside you is somewhat soothing, though I admit it merely makes me hunger all the more."

Rebecca just stood there, trembling and unsure. She'd said he could take her blood. Why wasn't he doing it? And why was she so nervous? She'd fed him before.

Yes, but those times it was your idea, she reminded herself. *Now he's asking.*

"Yes, I've asked, and you've consented, but I'll make it even easier for you. Do you, Acolyte, offer to restore my power through your own life's force of your own free will? Now, you say 'Yes, I do.' That is, if you are indeed giving your consent."

"Yes, I do," Rebecca said, though her voice shook a little.

Sydney reached for her hand. Instead of bringing her wrist to his lips as she'd done earlier for Ryan, Sydney brought her hand to rest on his shoulder, as though they were about to begin a dance. She marveled for a moment at how tall he was.

He reached with his other hand and brushed her hair back from her neck again. He smiled and looked into her eyes.

"I won't hurt you," he whispered.

Rebecca nodded, unable to take her eyes away from his. They were compelling, almost luminous. They seemed to glow from inside. It was quite beautiful the way the deep blue outside gave way to the lighter blue glow in the middle.

Sydney pulled her close to him and brought her other arm up around his neck. He returned his arms to her waist. "Willing prey is always more rewarding. Resistance erodes the life-force, and you have so much to give. Thank you for sharing it with me."

His words faded away as he lowered his mouth to her neck. As his lips touched her skin, she squirmed a bit, uncomfortable with his closeness and his very obvious longing. She had to remind herself that she'd agreed to this, that he needed this. He'd helped her nana. But what if he were lying to her? What if he'd had her get rid of Nana just so he'd have her alone, to—

Her stiffness and feeble attempt to pull away from him seemed to force Syd to focus again.

"Shh," he soothed. "You are not a kill. You are a Healer. You are not a common human. Still your mind. Quiet your thoughts. You would know if I were lying to you. So many, so very many, Acolyte, would simply take this from you violently—force your consent with pain or torture. So few take pleasure in it. Let me savor this. Let me enjoy. Savor it yourself, and learn. That's what you want, isn't it? To learn...?"

Rebecca nodded in mute agreement, not even caring what he'd said about killing. She shivered and closed her eyes, fighting the sluggish warmth that made her arms heavy and legs feel like they were going to go out from under her any moment.

"Promise me I will not regret it," she mumbled as she felt herself relax into his hold.

He smiled at her and somehow she knew that the formal request for assurance came far too late in the asking. She had already consented. He would have to teach her about that, too. Later. She was frightened and confused enough, and she could feel that he really was desperately hungry. He probably couldn't stop now even if he wanted to.

"Upon my honor, my lady," he assured her with a strangled whisper in spite of his overwhelming need. Then he fell silent as his fangs pierced her throat, just over the mark on her neck.

She gasped, and was surprised that there was no pain as there had been when Ryan's had done the same thing to her wrist.

He is a fledgling, and inexperienced, she heard Syd say in her mind. *It doesn't have to hurt. It certainly doesn't have to hurt you, Acolyte.*

What was with that? He called Nana "Lady Healer." Was it kind of the same thing? Or was he still making fun of her?

Even if she'd been able to speak, she didn't have to ask the questions aloud. She knew he would hear her thinking.

It is the term one uses with an untrained Healer, Syd replied in her mind.

Now hush, and relax. Enjoy.

Oh, it was enjoyable. Oh, man, was it enjoyable. Rebecca hadn't ever felt anything like it. On and on it went. It was warm, light, exhausting and invigorating all at the same time.

Her arms tightened about his neck and she gave herself completely over to him. His arms did the same about her waist, taking her weight as her legs ceased to support her.

Liquid fire coursed through her. For one insane moment she was filled with panic at the onslaught. Syd trembled against her.

She felt his hold on her tighten a bit more as an unfamiliar feeling washed over her. Then Syd lifted his head, disengaging his fangs. His tongue parted his lips and he licked the wound. She could feel the two punctures he'd made closed in an instant, leaving clear, unblemished skin behind. He did it again, taking any remaining trace of blood or power with him, then rested his head on her shoulder.

"My gratitude," he murmured, soft and formal. "You are...unbelievable..."

Rebecca could hardly keep her eyes open. His soft voice was compelling and so wonderful to listen to. She smiled. How nice it felt to be appreciated for something. Anything. She noticed his blue eyes were again bright and glowing, almost pulsating in time with her beating heart.

"Anytime," she managed to mumble.

"Power such as yours is bound to attract all manner of unwanted attention," she heard him say. "All manner of evil things from the dark depths of the Otherworlds. Damn it, I will not have it! I knew, but I didn't realize..." He looked down at her. "I'll have to teach you to better conceal your power. What I've just taken from you isn't nearly enough to obscure how much you still harbor within you. One of many more things I have to teach you..."

Rebecca could have listened to his voice forever, but powerful or no, she didn't have the ability to keep her eyes open a moment longer, and fell asleep in his arms.

CHAPTER FIFTEEN

After a long, much-needed shower, Rebecca went into the kitchen.

There was a huge brown beast standing at the counter, drinking coffee straight from the pot.

"Gross, Billy!"

"What?" He wiped his furry chin on the back of his hand.

"Get a mug!" Rebecca said, pointing to the cabinet near his head.

Billy snorted. "Those things don't hold more than a mouthful for me, Bit, and I ain't gonna stand here and pour myself ten drinks when one will do just fine! Besides, cups are for humans!"

"Then get a bowl or something instead of drinking right out of the pot. You could at least act like a civilized being." Rebecca crossed her arms over her chest.

"I ain't no 'civilized being'! But since it bugs you so much, look! I'll wash it!"

Billy rinsed the coffee pot under the sink and made a big show about wiping off the rim where his lips had been.

The phone rang.

Rebecca rolled her eyes at him as she answered it. "Hello?"

"Hello, little dove."

"Nana! How are you?"

"Fine, fine," her grandmother said. "Having a grand time here. It's nice to see Gretchen and our other friends. We're finally getting together for a real bridge game tonight. Enough about me. How are you?"

"I'm good," Rebecca said. She wished she could take the phone in the other room, but Billy's anubi ears would still hear what she was saying. "I...um...haven't been back to school. Syd doesn't think it's a good idea until Monday."

"I don't like the idea of not being there for your birthday tomorrow," Nana said. "But..."

Nana trailed off and Rebecca wondered if there wasn't someone

176 • Dina James

else in the room.

"Rebecca," Nana went on, her tone very serious. "I want you to listen to Syd and do just what he tells you. He'll keep you safe. Is Billy still there?"

"Uh-huh," Rebecca confirmed. "I...um...I kind of asked him to stay. Like, for good."

"Rebecca! You asked an anubi to den in your own home?!"

Nana had to be alone. She wouldn't talk about anubi if she weren't.

"Yeah," Rebecca replied, cringing inside. "Was that...wrong? Is it bad?"

"Not entirely," Nana said. "It's just, well...they have rules about sharing personal dwellings, and...and Billy has a sordid history. His brother—"

"Denis, I know," Rebecca interrupted. "We've met."

"I see," Nana said.

Rebecca could tell she wasn't happy about that.

"And you're all right? Billy?"

"We're all fine," Rebecca assured her grandmother quickly. "It's just..."

"What?"

"I um...I can't really say..."

Because Billy's standing right next to me, she thought. *And it's stupid, anyway.*

"You're not...you're not starting to...have feelings for Sydney," Nana said in a quiet tone. "Are you?"

"No!" Rebecca protested immediately. "No, Nana! Ew! I mean... well..."

"Oh, Rebecca," Nana said.

Rebecca could almost see her shaking her head.

"It's not like that!" Rebecca protested again. "It's just...weird, that's all."

"Listen to me very carefully, Rebecca Charlotte," Nana said in a stern voice. "Syd is your mentor. Your instructor and your protector. He's there only to do those things, and that is all. Whatever else might be going on, however you think you might feel around him—it's not real, understand?"

"I understand," Rebecca said.

"Rebecca, I mean it," Nana said. There was a strange urgency in her voice. "Do not look him in the eye. Ever. And I know that's what you've been doing, or you wouldn't be talking this way. Feeling something you shouldn't be. I know he's been coming to you for—"

Nana cut herself off, as though she had started to say something and realized she shouldn't.

Rebecca's stomach clenched with a horrible feeling.

"Coming to me for what, Nana?" Rebecca asked. "What did you and Syd talk about, before you left?"

Nana didn't reply right away.

"Nana?"

"You're very powerful, Rebecca," Nana said, so soft that Rebecca had to strain to hear. "Syd is only doing what he has to."

"What he has to, or what you asked him to?" Rebecca forced herself to ask.

Nana didn't reply, and Rebecca knew that Syd taking her blood had been her grandmother's idea.

"Why?"

"To keep your power somewhat in check long enough so that you can't be found before your birthday," her grandmother replied. "He's doing what he can to hide you. He's the only one who can, but even with both him and Ryan there—"

"Well he's not doing a very good job, according to Denis!" Rebecca interrupted, hurt. "No matter how much he takes from me! Damn it, Nana! Why didn't anyone tell me?"

"Don't swear, Rebecca! We're just trying to protect you," Nana offered. "We thought that if you knew, you wouldn't consent to it. You wouldn't want to be a burden, or trouble anyone. It was better this way."

It was true. Nana was right. Had she known that Syd was taking her blood only to keep her power in check, she'd have resisted.

"But...but he needed me..."

Rebecca hadn't realized she'd spoken aloud until her nana replied.

"I'm sure he did. Ryan is taking a great deal out of him, and he's been ensuring the talisman he gave me is still in working order, not to mention he has a clan to see to and other protections he's arranged. He's needed replenishment, Rebecca. He just didn't have to take it from you. It was thought that perhaps he should add to Ryan's drain on your power, to keep you safe."

"I understand," Rebecca said, thought it still hurt to think about.

She felt used. And lied to. Deceived.

At least Marla Thompson did mean things to her face and not behind her back. This felt a lot worse than anything Marla had ever done.

"I'll be home on Monday, little dove, and we'll talk more then, all right?"

"All right, Nana," Rebecca made herself say, and hope she sounded normal when she really just wanted to burst into tears. "Have a good bridge game. See you Monday."

"I love you, Rebecca."

"Love you too, Nana."

Rebecca hung up the phone, feeling like someone had punched her in the stomach.

"Ain't nothin' to eat in this house," Billy grumbled as he pulled his head out of the fridge. "Going out to get some grub. Want anything?"

Rebecca shook her head.

She didn't think she could eat now. Or ever again.

Rebecca waited until the sun started to set to go up and see Ryan and change the sheets on his bed. She told herself that it was out of politeness—sunset was when he should be awake and she wouldn't have to wake him to remake the bed—but really it was because she didn't want to chance seeing Syd.

She didn't think she was ready to see him, knowing what she knew now. Normally the day seemed to drag by as she waited for the sunset. Today it seemed to come all too quick.

That, and she really didn't want to feed Ryan, and see horrible things. The images had been getting worse—stronger—and she didn't want to feel any worse than she did now.

She understood now, Syd's absences. She knew he was a Master and had a clan to see to, but she'd never suspected he was going to...to *collude* with her grandmother. Sure, Nana's talisman needed to be checked on and refilled if needed, but Syd had made it sound like what he'd given her was all Nana needed.

Syd had told her not to worry about Nana's safety. Not to worry about anything, because stress and anxiety just made her a bigger target.

Rebecca snorted. More like "undid all his hard work" or something.

And what was all that about not leaving her unprotected? He and Billy were gone practically all the time!

Rebecca shook her head and sighed. There was no getting around it. She had to go up and see Ryan. She could feel his hunger tugging at her. She went to the downstairs linen closet to pull out a clean set of sheets.

"He's fine," she heard Syd say.

Rebecca turned to see him standing behind her. Everything she'd come up with during the day to say to Syd left her mind. Her stomach did a funny little flip at the sight of his blond hair, but she squelched it and told herself to stop being stupid.

"Oh, hi," Rebecca replied as she turned back to the linen closet.

ALL WOUNDS • 179

"'Oh, hi,'" Syd repeated. "What kind of greeting is that? Is something wrong?"

Rebecca shook her head. She didn't trust herself to speak at the moment. She didn't know whether she was more angry or hurt. She selected a set of clean sheets and turned back to face him, clutching the bedding to her chest.

"Oh, come now," Syd replied. "I've done you the courtesy of not hearing your thoughts for myself. Do me the courtesy of sharing them with me."

He reached to touch her face and ran his thumb along her cheek in a gentle caress, like a boyfriend—or a lover—might.

Rebecca flinched back.

Syd raised a brow at her. "What is it?"

"Nothing that would matter to you," Rebecca replied. She made to push past him. She wasn't ready to talk about it just yet.

His strong hand on her upper arm stopped her. "Do not force me to look for myself," he warned. "I asked you a question, and I expect an answer."

"Like it matters!" Rebecca flared as she jerked her arm away from him.

"It does matter!" Syd retorted. "Tell me what's upset you."

"Why? Worried that my little *upset* will interfere with the plan that you and Nana made to keep me safe?" Rebecca demanded, hating herself for the tears forming in her eyes. She'd had all day to think about this conversation, and it wasn't going at all like it had in her head. "You know, the one where you take my blood to keep my power under control until my birthday so no more demons would find and attack me?"

"We couldn't have another attack like the one that happened to you at school," Syd replied. "We had to do something."

"You told me that by letting you feed from me that I...I was helping you!" Rebecca said, wiping her eyes before her tears could fall. She did not want to cry in front of Syd. "By letting you...consenting to...I thought I was replenishing the power that Ryan was taking from you—that you'd used to help Nana. Not that you were just doing it to keep me off some demonic radar!"

"We didn't want to add to your fear," Sydney replied. "It was better to let you believe you were helping me than that we needed a way to keep your power hidden. It was easier. You believed you were helping, consented of your own free will, and most importantly, were not afraid. If it had been a chore or you believed you had to do so to preserve your safety, you would have been tense and anxious—something we're trying to avoid. It was better all around if you thought it was your idea and did it of your own free will, and you *were* helping me. Just not as you expected."

"I see," Rebecca replied. She still couldn't figure out if she was more hurt or angry. "You used me! And you think I'm supposed to be okay with that because you made me think it was my idea? Oh, please! I might be an idiot, but I'm not stupid, despite what you think!"

She bit her bottom lip and shook her head. She made to leave again.

Again, Syd stopped her.

"You're being unreasonable," he said. "It was necessary. My apologies that you had to find out like this, and that..."

"That...?" Rebecca prompted, shaking him off again.

"That my actions have caused you to misunderstand me," Syd said. "I did warn you. The apprentice often misunderstands the closeness and intensity of the relationship with her teacher."

So it was all a misunderstanding, was it? It was her fault for feeling something when he was the one that had caused her to?

"Flatter yourself much?" Rebecca managed as she turned away again to hide her tears from him.

"Stop it," Syd said. "It has nothing to do with flattering myself. These things happen. You were warned. Even if it were possible for your kind and mine to have the kind of relationship you see happen in films, it still would not be so between you and I. You are a human. A Healer. And I am a Master vampire."

Rebecca hated the amused pity in his voice. She almost expected him to start laughing at her. He may as well go ahead. Everyone else did, and at least she'd done something to deserve *him* laughing at her.

"What are you truly upset about? How does this knowledge change our relationship? By letting me drain you a little every day, you're kept safe from further demon attacks. You're doing what you can to save yourself! This is what we all want. We all need you to stay safe, to reach your birthday and allow your power to manifest in its entirety. Soon after that, you won't need me anymore. You'll be powerful enough to look after yourself. Teach yourself. I should think you'd look forward to that."

"Yeah," Rebecca replied with a sniff. "Yeah, that'll be great."

"It's actually beneficial that this came up," Syd said. "What Ryan and I have been taking from you isn't enough to keep you hidden any longer. I'm going to have to take a great deal more this evening."

Rebecca wouldn't—couldn't—look at him, even when he pushed at her arm to turn her toward him.

"Look at me, damn you, and stop sulking like a child!" he demanded.

Rebecca shook her head. She dropped the sheets she held and hid her face in her hands.

"As you wish," Syd said after a long moment. "I said I would not leave you unprotected, and if you will not consent to me taking your blood, I cannot help you. If you don't allow me to take your blood—and with it what power I can—they will find you and there will be nothing I or anyone else can do about it. Just your tears this moment are making you more of a target, no matter the strength of your power right now."

She took a deep breath and closed her eyes. She lifted her head. "Do what you have to," she said. "Just...just get it over with."

She pushed her hair away from the mark on her neck and bent her head to the side, exposing her throat to him.

"Your wrist will suffice, as you cannot even bring yourself to look at me."

Did he sound...hurt?

No. She was just a duty to him, that's all. "Wherever."

She just stood there, tears escaping her closed eyes, her neck bared for him.

"Oh, Healer. Why are you putting yourself through this?"

Rebecca refused to answer him. He wouldn't understand anyway.

At least she'd finally managed to shield her thoughts. She could feel him, pushing against the mental block she'd erected in her mind. All it had taken for her to master the lesson was a thought she didn't want him to see, and she certainly didn't want him knowing what she was really thinking at the moment. What she'd really thought.

How much what he'd said truly hurt.

"I see," Syd said. "Would you like me to entrance you? It might feel better if—"

"No," Rebecca said, shaking her head. "Just do it."

She felt his blond hair brush her cheek as he bent his head low. She felt his fangs pierce her neck.

And it felt like fire.

Rebecca's already closed eyes squeezed shut even tighter as she fought not to squirm away from him. Her arms went around his neck and she clung to him to keep from dropping to the ground as her knees buckled from the sheer agony coursing through her limbs.

Pain wasn't anywhere close to an accurate description of what Syd was doing to her insides. She understood now why Regular people died from vampire bites—they'd want to, if this is what it was like. She felt as though her insides were being ripped apart by a thousand tiny knives.

Nothing she'd ever experienced in her life had felt like this.

Syd spared her no gentleness. She could feel everything. Her skin suddenly felt as though she'd been sunburned then rubbed with coarse sandpaper.

She was determined that she would not cry out, or beg him to stop, no matter how much it hurt. She understood now, what he meant when she said she was food to his kind. She certainly felt like just that—as though she was being consumed bite by small, agonizing bite from the inside out.

For the briefest of instants, Rebecca wondered if Syd wasn't being deliberately cruel just to punish her for her anger with him.

Her anger with him. Her hurt. Her fear.

Her blood must taste horrid to him.

Just when she was on the verge of screaming and begging him to stop, she thought she heard Syd moan. She almost asked him if he was in pain. Maybe he was taking her pain into himself? She felt his hand tighten on her neck. His fingers tangled in the hair at the base of her head and Rebecca's mind went blank.

The only thing she felt was warmth and safety, like the Syd she knew.

She tried her best to keep her mind empty and not think about anything as she waited for him to finish with her. The pain had gone, but it still seemed like a very long time until he pulled away from her.

"My gratitude, Acolyte," he managed, though his voice was barely above a whisper.

Though she hated herself for it and pleaded with herself not to do it, she looked up and met his eyes.

Is that...really nothing to you? I'm *nothing to you?* she asked in her mind as she pulled her hair forward to cover her neck.

Syd reached and brushed her hair back from her mark again.

Don't be absurd. Wait until your birthday. Wait and see what you're going to become. What you feel now will be nothing compared to that, and you'll forget all about me. You'll see.

Then his hand cupped the back of her neck and he pulled her toward him. Rebecca thought to panic for only a moment before she felt his lips upon her throat, and his tongue seal the wound he'd made.

Of course that was all he was doing. She hadn't felt him do it before he'd pulled away. She hated herself for thinking that he might have been about to kiss her. Of course he wasn't. He was just doing what he had to. Making sure she wasn't going to bleed all over the place after he'd done what he could to help hide her power. Besides, there was that "she" he and Billy had vaguely mentioned now and then. Of course he'd have someone. Someone...like him.

She closed her eyes. Rebecca felt completely stupid and pushed herself away from him. Ryan needed her.

Without a word, Syd vanished from the hallway, leaving her alone in the darkness.

"Happy birthday!" Ryan said as she entered the enclave.

Rebecca closed the enclave door behind her. "Thanks, but my birthday isn't until tomorrow. You're looking good! I think this night feeding thing agrees with you."

"Mornings never were my thing," Ryan said. "What's wrong? You look upset. Come here."

He motioned her to come and sit on the bed. She did and he grinned at her.

"Nothing's wrong. Why would you think that?" Rebecca asked as she tried to hide the fact that she'd just spent the last hour in her room crying over Syd's callousness and disappearance.

She couldn't help but notice Ryan's fangs when he smiled, and that his eyes were blue but not as bright as they could be. He really needed to be fed, despite the things she saw behind her eyes when she fed him. That didn't happen with Syd, and Rebecca could only figure it had something to do with Ryan's hellhound bite. Whatever the reason, he still needed her.

Unlike Syd.

She started to roll up the sleeve of her sweatshirt.

"Wait," Ryan said, putting his hand over her wrist. "Here."

He set a small white box tied with a yellow ribbon in her hand. She looked up at him.

"What—?"

"Just open it," he instructed, still grinning. "Never mind I'm a bit early. Let's call it 'prompt'!"

"You? Prompt? Nairhoft would die," Rebecca said with a giggle.

"Which is, of course, an excellent reason to do it," he replied. "Go on. Open it."

Rebecca eyed him and removed the ribbon before she lifted the lid. She smiled even more, shaking her head as Ryan's old, silver lighter caught the light of the bedside candle and glinted up at her.

His lucky lighter.

The same one he'd used to light his stolen cigarette the day she'd had her first detention.

The day she first learned she was a Healer.

Rebecca took the lighter out of the box and flipped open the cover. She flicked it to life and smiled as the flame ignited, then snapped it shut

184 • DINA JAMES

with a flick of her wrist as she'd seen him do the day they met.

"Thanks, Stereotype. I'll treasure it."

"I was going to give you my lucky pencil, but I figure I can still use that. Kind of hard to smoke when you don't breathe anymore," Ryan teased. "Always said I'd die before I quit. And they say *smoking* kills."

"You didn't have to give me anything," Rebecca said, shaking her head at him. "You could have used it to light candles and stuff. I mean, it's still a lighter."

"Yeah, but why should I keep that when I can do this?"

He opened his hand and a bright plume of blue-black flame appeared in his palm. Rebecca gasped.

"I asked Syd about it," Ryan said. "He thinks it has something to do with being bitten by a hellhound just before being turned. It's not something—uh—it's not usual for...my kind. Some of the Masters like Syd can do it, but it takes a lot out of them, and isn't a usual thing. Especially for newbies like me."

"Maybe you're special," Rebecca said.

"Yeah, and you're a delinquent." Ryan laughed and the flame in his hand vanished. Rebecca smiled at him.

"I can't imagine how hard this all must be for you," she said as she reached for his hand. "It really is like you died, even though you haven't. You can't go back to your old life—school...your mom...whatever you did after school—and that's got to be hard."

Ryan rolled his brighter blue eyes.

"Even for you, Stereotype," Rebecca went on. "I know you act all tough, like nothing bothers you, like you're not going to miss anything you used to do—"

"I'm not."

"—but you are. I know you don't think anyone will miss you, either, but they will."

"Who?" Ryan asked, curling his lip at her. "Mom? Like she'll even notice I'm gone."

"The other day, you said you wanted to go home."

"I don't remember what I said the other day. I was more than a little out of it, and I wasn't really sure being a vampire was the thing for me. Sure it's cool from the outside, when you're not one of them and you see what they can do. Actually being one is a lot different than I thought. But you know what?" Ryan smiled at her again. "Today I'm fine. Today I'm all right with it, and I'm going to make a better vampire than I ever did a human."

"Well that won't be too hard," she teased.

"Seriously, Rebecca. My departure from the human world isn't all that tragic. Who's going to miss me? Nairhoft? He'll find some other juvie to pick on. You? You didn't even know I existed until the other day—"

"I knew!" Rebecca interrupted in protest. "If you want to talk about not being noticed except to get picked on, I'm your girl. God, I was *grateful* you left me alone. You're so horrid to everyone! I was scared to death of you, and was happy you *didn't* notice me."

"I noticed! I've been watching you for months—"

Ryan cut himself off. A guilty look crossed his face, as though he hadn't meant to say that much.

"Why?" Rebecca demanded. "For Syd?"

"At first," Ryan admitted, looking uncomfortable. "But later, because I wanted to. I've never known anyone all the cliques pick on. Even the dorks avoid you, and they accept any old reject."

"Gee, thanks," Rebecca said, allowing her hurt to show just a little. She wanted to cry but instead she laughed. To hell with school. She was a Healer. She didn't need anyone at school to accept her for anything. She hung out with werewolves and vampires. She was doing something much more important than picking out the latest fashion or trying to follow the latest trend. Still, it hurt to know that she wasn't just imagining being avoided by everyone. "Glad you think it's neat to be excluded from everything."

"I didn't mean it like that," Ryan said, pulling his hand out from under Rebecca's. "I mean, you're pretty cool. Cooler than anyone else at that school. And I'm real glad no one else sees it because that means I really *am* special."

"I'm not...cool," Rebecca said with a nervous laugh.

"Sure you are. Who else has something as awesome as this?" He brushed her hair back from her neck, exposing her Healer's mark. "People might tease you about it, but I have to tell you, I think it's sexy as hell."

He buried his face against her neck but she pulled away, laughing and shocked.

They sat in silence for a few minutes, Ryan recovering from his admission and Rebecca from her embarrassment.

She composed herself and cleared her throat. She was a mature Healer, not a giggly schoolgirl with a crush embarrassed about a birthmark anymore. "How are you feeling? Hungry?"

"I like to think of it as 'thirsty'," he replied. "And yeah, I could use a drink."

Rebecca smiled and set the box he'd given her aside on the bedside table before she pushed up her sleeve and held it out to him.

Ryan took her hand and pulled her closer to him as he sat up. His hand moved up her arm to her neck. He leaned in as though he wanted to get a closer look at the Healer's mark he claimed to find attractive.

His lips pressed against hers.

Rebecca's eyes flew open wide in surprise. She held very still, unsure what to do. She'd never kissed a boy before.

Did she even want him kissing her?

She decided that she did. It wasn't bad. It was actually kind of nice.

Rebecca shut her eyes and leaned forward a little, hoping she was doing it right and kissing him back.

She tried hard not to think about the fact that Ryan was a vampire now and not a "boy."

The kiss was over almost as soon as it began, and Rebecca barely had time to open her eyes before Ryan spoke.

"Happy birthday, Rebecca."

He leaned close again and sank his fangs into her exposed neck.

"Oh!" Rebecca couldn't help but gasp. She closed her eyes again and tilted her head a little.

The darkness behind her eyes blazed in an instant with flickering light. A young woman struggled against the hold of a tall, gray-skinned being.

A demon.

It laughed and reached to snare the girl's head by the hair and jerk it back.

"ROBIN!" Rebecca heard herself yell.

"REBECCA!" she heard Robin scream. "REBECCA, HELP! HELP ME! THEY'RE GOING TO—"

Robin's scream was suddenly cut off by a vicious backhand from another demon. Robin's body went limp in the grasp of the demon that held her.

"No!" Rebecca screamed into the vision. "Don't hurt her!"

"If you want to save your friend, go to a mirror," a demonic voice growled outside the scope of Rebecca's vision. "Find one inside a mortal hour, or she, and the others, will die. You for them, Acolyte. We grow weary of waiting."

Ryan's fangs disengaged from her neck and the connection broke. He began to convulse.

Rebecca jumped from the bed and watched him thrash and moan.

Ryan. He'd been bitten by a hellhound. Every time he bit *her*, *she* saw demons.

Saw Hell.

The demons had possession of Ryan.

Rebecca swallowed hard and brought her hands to her mouth, horrified. His thrashing...convulsing...shedding... They weren't because he was still turning into a vampire, like she and Syd thought. He'd finished that days ago, before the—

Her eyes widened in deeper realization.

Before the demons had attacked the enclave and taken him hostage.

Ryan had been healing then. Had stop shedding, had turned completely. Then he'd worsened.

Why hadn't she seen it before? His wound then...his hellhound bite. It had worsened, and it wasn't healing.

Had they...done something to him? What? How?

Ryan sat up. Beads of bloody sweat dripped down his face. He grinned at Rebecca as he got up.

She took a step back. "Ryan, stay away from me," she pleaded, holding her arms in front of her.

He didn't seem to hear. "They're waiting for you," Ryan said. "You're the guest of honor. Isn't that nice, Hot Stuff? You're finally popular!"

"You don't know what you're saying!" Rebecca cried. "They've... done something to you! You're not Ryan!"

"Of course I am," Ryan replied as he took another step toward her. "How about another kiss?"

Rebecca looked around in desperation. A bright yellow object on the chest of drawers next to her caught her eye.

Ryan's lucky pencil.

She grabbed it and held it tight in her hand, her thumb on the eraser end. "Stay away from me! SYD!"

Ryan laughed. "He can't hear you. Even if he could, what makes you think he'd come to your rescue? You're food to him. You think he'd rescue a burger?"

"BILLY! BILLY, HELP ME!"

Ryan laughed again. "Filling his stomach means more to Billy than you do."

Rebecca took another step back and realized Ryan was herding her toward the mirror portal at the end of the room.

She felt the wall hard against her back.

Before she could blink, Ryan had her pinned hard against it. He smiled. Her blood still coated his fangs.

"What're you going to do, little Rebecca?" Ryan taunted. "And do you really think it matters to us? This shell has served its purpose. We have no further use for it. Dispose of it if you wish."

We? Shell? Use?!

Ryan grabbed her upper arms, and Rebecca screamed and buried his lucky pencil deep in his chest.

He howled, and for a brief moment his eyes changed, and Rebecca knew it was Ryan behind them.

"Rebecca," the boy she knew panted. "Run."

He moved, but it was slow, and Rebecca could tell it was taking every ounce of effort he had to allow her past him. She wriggled against the wall, out from under his crushing weight and started to run for the enclave door.

She hadn't taken a step before he pulled the pencil from his chest, grabbed her by the arm and threw her across the room.

Rebecca slammed hard into the mirror that served as a portal between worlds. Stars exploded behind her eyes as instant pain shot up her spine.

Before she could get to her feet, gray hands leaped out of the mirror and grabbed her by the throat.

"Consent, or she dies," a demonic voice growled.

Robin!

The hands were clasped so tightly around her neck, Rebecca couldn't speak. She managed a nod, and before it was complete, the enclave before her vanished.

CHAPTER SIXTEEN

Rebecca could hardly draw a breath. She didn't think she could speak.

A huge, gray, winged being with radioactive green eyes loomed before her, its hideous lips twisted into a smirk. Rebecca tried to shrink back as she recognized the demon Billy had called Armaros, but she couldn't move.

"Yes," said Armaros. "You remember me, Acolyte. Welcome to Hell."

The Hell realm. This was the place she'd seen in her mind when Ryan would feed. Where there were other captive Healers.

"Where you will die," the demon said, hearing her thoughts. "An unfortunate side effect of the acceptance and transfer. But we can't have you dying just yet, Acolyte. Oh, no. T'would be a waste of all that glorious power you're about to come into."

He gestured at her and suddenly the air around her was cooler and she could breathe again.

"Robin," Rebecca croaked. "Where's...where's Robin?"

Armaros laughed and changed into Robin for a long moment before taking on his true form once more.

"You should have remembered better our first meeting, Acolyte," he said. "I am truly surprised the same deception worked a second time. I can only blame your naïveté."

Rebecca closed her eyes and felt more stupid than she ever had in her entire life, and with as often as she felt stupid, that was saying something. She'd read about demons. They lied, cheated, deceived, coerced... she should have realized they were possessing Ryan. Using him. That they'd lie to get to her.

But she'd been so blinded by her own emotions that she hadn't noticed. Hadn't cared.

How *stupid* could she be? She'd played right into their hands. Given

190 • DINA JAMES

them exactly what they wanted.

Rebecca saw another of the captive Healers to her right. An older woman, with black hair turning gray, tumbling down from a bun. The woman glanced at Armaros.

"Demon," the woman said, her voice lilting in a French accent. "I don't suppose there's any way to make a deal with you in this matter?"

Armaros shook his head. "No deals. And you will be silent."

The demon made a gesture and the woman clasped her throat.

"No!" Rebecca shouted. "Don't hurt her!"

Armaros laughed. "Why not? She has nearly used up the whole of her life-force. She has but a trickle of her power left in her, but a trickle is better than none at all. We will drain that when we drain yours."

"Why me?" Rebecca asked. "What's so important about me?"

"Silly girl," Armaros said with a chastising click of his tongue. "Don't you know? You're about to be the recipient of power unparalleled. Did you honestly think that wouldn't attract attention?"

"I won't," Rebecca said, shaking her head. "I won't do it."

Armaros laughed again. "Do what?"

"Consent to give you my power."

"Oh, no? What makes you think you have a choice?"

"Free will," Rebecca replied, though her voice shook and she didn't sound as sure as she thought she was. "If I don't want to be a Healer, I don't have to be. Billy told me I don't."

"Never trust an anubi," Armaros replied. "They are brawn, not brains. They know nothing. You're going to come into your power whether you agree to it or not. The only choice you have in is what you do with it. Be grateful, Acolyte! I'm going to relieve you of that burden."

"Uh, I appreciate the offer, but I'd rather stay alive, thanks," Rebecca stammered as she took a step back.

"You mistake my words for a service I will render," Armaros said, and he gestured toward her.

Rebecca was suddenly backed against a hard surface. Bands of wrought iron snaked around her throat, chest, stomach, ankles and wrists.

"They were merely an assurance."

Though she could now breathe, Rebecca certainly couldn't move. She looked around. She was bound against a circular stone slab along with several other women.

Syd! Syd, HELP!

"He cannot hear you, nor has he any idea where you are," Armaros said, sounding very pleased with himself. "Nor can the anubi sense you. This place is shielded and concealed. You are, Acolyte, completely abandoned. There's no one to help you."

"Don't bet on it, Hellspawn."

Syd. Immense relief washed over Rebecca, her skin tingling with instant warmth at the sound of his voice. Whatever happened now, he was here. That strange warmth made her feel as though could face anything with him here.

"How did you...?" Armaros began, then made a gesture.

"Don't bother with your theatrics, Armaros, they get old," Syd said as he was seized from behind by three demons. "I came to make you an offer. Myself for them. A Master vampire is a very tempting drain, isn't it?"

"Compared to the line of Panacea and every Healer in the mortal realm? Hardly," Armaros replied. "How did you find her here?"

"And I'm going to tell you just because you asked," Syd replied with a snort. "I'd tell you to go to Hell, but it seems we're already here."

Armaros gestured again, Syd was suddenly strapped down beside Rebecca, just like she was.

"Two for the cost of one," the demon muttered. "We'll drain you all."

Syd laughed and shook his head. "Good luck draining me without my consent."

"You'll give it, bloodsucker, when her screams become too much for you," Armaros replied in a growl.

"You're the one that will be screaming long before you ever touch her," Syd replied. "Do you think I'm the only one who can find her?"

"Silence," Armaros spat, and he gestured to Syd.

Why hasn't he silenced me as well? And why weren't they...doing anything else? Why were they just milling around, looking at her and one another?

They're waiting for your birthday, she heard Syd in her mind.

She almost smiled, then forced it from her lips just in time. The demons knew Syd could hear her, but they didn't need to know she could speak to him in return.

But that's not until tomorrow, she replied silently.

Time passes differently here. You'll be seventeen in just a few minutes. They're waiting for your power to rise. Once it does so within you, they'll free it and take it for themselves.

Rebecca didn't need to ask how they planned on freeing it. The huge knife Armaros held in his clawed hand was answer enough.

What about you? What are they going to do to you and the others?

Torture us until we plead for mercy and offer our power in exchange for release, Syd replied. *That's consent enough for them.*

Oh, cripes they were in trouble. This was bad.

192 • DINA JAMES

"Uhnn-uh!"

The demons all froze at the sound that escaped Rebecca's lips. Armaros smirked.

"It's begun."

Rebecca looked down at her middle as much as her bonds would allow her and gasped. A dull golden light shone through her clothes.

Something moved inside her, warm and soothing. It called to her, whispering in her mind.

It was wonderful. She wanted to go to it, embrace it, dive into it. It was luxurious.

Now you see. And it's only just begun, said an unfamiliar voice in her mind.

Rebecca glanced at the older Healer beside her and knew it had been she who'd spoken in her mind.

Is this what it's like for you? Is this what you carry inside you? Is this what your power feels like? Is this what I restore to Syd, when he feeds from me? She asked the questions all at once.

Yes. It will grow stronger as well, she heard the woman reply.

She heard Syd again. *Remember my cautions, Acolyte. It will consume you, if you do not bring it to heel. It is your power. Do not let it rule you.*

Rebecca tried to pay attention to Syd's voice and not the feeling inside her growing faster than she could accept.

"Yes," she heard Armaros say. "Let it wash over you, Acolyte. Let it consume you. Accept it."

Rebecca moaned again and closed her eyes. She couldn't blame the demons for wanting this for themselves. Who wouldn't want a feeling like this? It was indescribable. It was as though she'd waited her whole life for this feeling. This was who she was and what she was meant for. It was beyond imagination.

And there were already those who wanted to take it away from her.

But...what would they do with it? Why were they doing this to her, if it would be gone once they took it from her?

She found the presence of mind to ask the question aloud.

"Our kind have rare use for a Healer's abilities," Armaros answered. "But there is always a use for the power that's behind them. Further, taking the power of a Healer denies those abilities to others, namely our enemies."

"So you're going to kill all the Healers, and me, because you don't need the whole of us, but can use some of our parts?"

"Precisely," Armaros said. "Such will also keep those we intend to slaughter from obtaining aid or asylum."

There was something beneath the demon's words. Rebecca stared hard at him and forced her way into his mind.

"But you needed a Healer once," Rebecca said, tilting her head to look at him. "And so did your wife. How are your sons, by the way?"

She turned her head to the other side and looked at the other demons surrounding Armaros. "Are these some of them? You want to have them watch as you kill the daughter of the woman who saved their own mother? Or didn't he tell you he killed my mother?"

"You assume such would make a difference to us," one of the demons replied.

"If demons didn't have feelings, why did it matter to your father if your mother was going to die attempting to give birth to you?" Rebecca asked.

Another bolt of the amazing feeling of her power surged through her and she fell silent with a groan.

She could feel warmth—*fire*—raging within her. It was as though a trillion little drops of water had been thrown upon a hot surface and bubbled and burst, just beneath her skin.

How could one person be overjoyed and petrified at the same time? She understood now why Syd worried this feeling could kill her. It was frightening.

And exhilarating. Oh, she wanted this.

More. Yes, more. Don't leave...

But the feeling ebbed, and when it was over she opened her eyes and looked at Armaros again. She smiled, and knew.

"She didn't live, did she?" Rebecca asked. "My mother...saved your sons, but not your wife, and you've spent all this time since making sure no Healer ever helps anyone else. That's it, isn't it?"

Armaros didn't reply. He looked to the two youngest demons—twin boys—and remained silent. He gestured at Rebecca, and she knew she'd been silenced just like the older woman.

Rebecca felt Syd grasp her hand. While she still had the presence of mind to do so, Rebecca reached for the hand of the woman on the other side of her and clutched it.

"We'll drain the vampire first, just to ensure the Acolyte's cooperation," Armaros said. "We'll do it now, before the acceptance is complete."

The demon moved toward Syd and pressed the large knife he held into his neck.

"NO!" Rebecca shouted.

"She spoke against your bond of silence!" one of the demons behind Armaros whispered in awe. "How is that possible?!"

Armaros ignored the question and looked hard at Rebecca.

"You offer yourself in his place?" Armaros asked, halting his blade.

Rebecca nodded.

NO! Syd shouted in her mind.

I have to, she replied.

Rebecca looked at Armaros and smiled.

Armaros continued to hold his knife to Syd's throat. "A demon knows a lie when he hears one, and you are attempting one of your little human 'bluffs'. That was your only trick, and you think you are clever in using it, or that you have avoided the transfer of his power. I assure you, you have not. However, you have indeed consented."

"Let him go," Rebecca said.

Armaros left Syd's side and glared down at Rebecca. "You agreed that you would take his place—as first to be drained, not that you would take his place entirely. You do not give orders here."

Rebecca closed her eyes as the feeling inside her roared to life again, even stronger than before. Wow, she felt great. This was amazing. This was fun. This must be what it was like to be drunk, or high, or anything else people did that made them feel good. This was beyond fantastic.

"Unnnn-uh!" she groaned again, and her bonds snapped loose.

She heard a collective gasp as she sat up.

The demons standing interspersed between the bound Healers in the stone circle all took steps backward.

She looked up at Armaros and shook her head as she gave him a goofy smile. "I can see inside your head..."

Armaros looked at Rebecca for a long moment before he turned to the others. "She's lost her mind."

"I can see inside your head," Rebecca said again. "You're going to kill us all, no matter what I say, and if I'm going to die, you're not going to get any part of me, no matter what you do."

"When you hear the screams of your colleagues begging you to consent, you'll do it," Armaros said.

"I won't," Rebecca said. "Because I know it won't really be them talking, and they wouldn't really want me to, not even to save themselves. Certainly not to help *you.*"

Armaros scowled and raised his knife above his head. "Then you die now, and so do they."

Rebecca closed her eyes and let her head fall back. Her hands tightened on those of Syd and the woman beside her.

The golden light inside her burst from the hollow of her throat, below her breastbone and from each wrist.

Armaros howled as bands of pure light surrounded him.

Rebecca raised her head and stared at him.

Another whimper of pain infused with terrible pleasure escaped Rebecca as she let go of the hands she held. She brought her palms together and cupped the golden light emanating from her middle.

She slid from the stone altar and brought the harnessed power above her head. She spread her fingers and it arced from them to each woman's bonds, freeing them.

As each Healer slid from their captivity, they ran to gather behind Rebecca. One woman put a hand on Rebecca's shoulder, then another, until each woman was connected to her through the touch of another.

Syd stood beside Rebecca, and she reached to grasp his hand.

Armaros howled again and shook off the light binding him.

Rebecca held up her hand and spread her fingers wide. She knew now what the gesture she'd seen Syd and her nana use so often meant. It was an invocation of power.

Power *she* could now invoke.

"Don't," she commanded. "I thought you'd figured out by now that I'm not your average Healer. I'm not going to let you hurt anyone else."

"And just what do you plan on doing?" Armaros asked.

"I'm not sure what will happen if I tap whatever reserves of power I have standing behind me, in addition to that of a Master vampire. I do know that *we* will still be standing. Not sure about you or your little playground here. Now back off like your little buddies were already smart enough to do," Rebecca replied.

Armaros snarled at her.

"Oh, please. I am so done being afraid, of you or anything else. Now go away before you *really* piss me off. And if you ever, *ever* even think of coming after a Healer again—"

Armaros ignored her and moved faster than anything Rebecca had ever seen.

Before she could ready another concentrated bolt of energy, Rebecca felt the familiar nauseous sensation of being jerked from one place to another.

She blinked rapidly, clearing her vision. It was a familiar room, lit only with a single candle. She and the other captive Healers, as well as Syd, were standing back in the enclave, facing a very large, very angry man-wolf.

CHAPTER SEVENTEEN

Ryan looked even more livid than Billy did. No wonder he always got in trouble, if he looked at any of his teachers the way he was glaring at them.

"What——?" Syd looked from being to being, totally confused.

"Out of the way, ladies," Billy snarled before he shoved the entire group aside with a sweep of his large furry arm. He took the mirror portal into his huge paws. He ripped it from its stand and broke it over his knee like a piece of kindling. He threw the pieces to the floor and growled at them.

Syd eyed the large anubi standing over the pieces of the shattered mirror. "Billy, what do you think you're doing?!"

"Protecting my Little Bit," Billy rumbled. He turned to Rebecca. "You all right?"

Rebecca nodded then looked at Syd. "How did you get us back? I thought they said they'd shielded the..." She couldn't bear to think about the altar she'd been tied to just moments before, let alone name it. "...that place. "

"They did," Syd said. "We were aided from outside." Syd looked at Ryan.

Rebecca gaped at Ryan. He could hardly stand up on his own! How did he manage...? She couldn't help but ask. "But you...how did you...?"

"You have to ask?" Ryan replied, raising an eyebrow. "Those...things used me like a surveillance camera. Works both ways. I could see you the whole time. It took me a while to figure out how to get to you. Besides that, I've been fed on nothing but a Healer's blood since the moment I turned. You honestly think that didn't have an effect? I've had some time to figure out what I can and can't do, and believe me, I'm just as surprised as Syd that it worked."

"What worked?" Rebecca asked, still confused.

"He summoned you to his side," Syd replied for Ryan, looking at him intently. Rebecca could tell he was impressed. "A Master can do such with his thralls. I've never heard of a thrall being able to do such."

"Most thralls aren't fed from a Healer," Ryan said. He looked over at Rebecca. "Maybe I *am* special."

Rebecca laughed and shook her head. "Supervamp."

Ryan's lips twitched in a half-smile. "You were worth it."

Before she could ask what she meant, his eyes rolled back in his head. He swayed forward and fell to the floor in a fit of violent convulsions as he began heaving. He wrapped his arms around his middle, holding his sides as black liquid left his mouth and nose.

"Ryan!" Rebecca broke free from Syd's grasp and ran to her classmate's side.

Or she would have, had a strong hand on her arm stopped her.

"No!" Syd shook his head and grasped her by the shoulders.

Rebecca stared at him, open-mouthed. She struggled against Syd's hold. "What are you doing?! Let me go! Can't you see he needs help?!"

"It's too late," Syd said. He pulled Rebecca closer and held her tight against his chest. "He's used the whole of his power at the cost of his own existence. He sacrificed himself for you. Those are death throes. You can't help him. He'll rip you apart!"

"No!" Rebecca protested. Ryan braced himself against the floor with one hand as he heaved again. Rebecca pulled against Syd's iron grip. "Let me go! I have to do something!"

The older woman Rebecca hadn't noticed beside her took Rebecca's hand. "Sydney is right. There's nothing *to* do, *cher.*"

"Nothin' but leave. Let's get out of here before the stink starts," Billy growled. "Sabine, you're bleeding. Punk's gonna go nutso before he kicks and that's the last thing he needs to smell."

The older woman nodded. She let go of Rebecca's hand and moved toward the anubi.

"The rest of you gals, too, let's go," Billy said, gesturing to the enclave door.

Murmurs and gasps echoed in the small room as the rescued Healers left the enclave with Billy.

Rebecca just watched in open-mouthed horror as they skirted the bed and the convulsing boy on the floor. Didn't anyone besides her care that Ryan was dying?

She resisted Syd as he pulled her toward the enclave door. "I'm not leaving! Let me go! I can help him!"

Syd turned her around in his arms and stared directly into her eyes. "Listen! I said no! I won't let you! My thrall I will lose, and I will mourn, but I can't lose *you*, Rebecca!"

It was the first time he'd ever called her by her name.

Rebecca realized he was looking into her eyes without the compulsion of his Master's power behind them. What did that mean? She'd never heard Syd speak that way.

He was touching her. Touch.

She brought her thoughts into focus and let what he knew sink into her skin. It was then she knew he was afraid.

Of what? Of...?

Rebecca.

No. No, it wasn't like that. He'd said... He just—

She looked to Ryan over her shoulder before she turned back to Syd.

"It's okay," Rebecca said. "You said—you told me—I can't be drained here. I'm in my own enclave—a Healer can't be harmed here. You said..."

"I've said a lot of things. What if I'm wrong?" Syd asked, his eyes narrowing as he reached for her shoulder again. He brought her closer to him, possessive and strong, though Rebecca knew he was using only a fraction of his strength to keep her by his side.

"What if you are?" Rebecca replied. She looked to the Ryan again. "You taught me to do this. You're the one teaching me to *be* what I am. You have to let me help him."

"You're powerful, beyond anyone's reckoning, but even if you could help him, his existence doesn't mean nearly as much to me as yours does," Syd argued, shaking his head.

"His means something to me," Rebecca replied in a gentle whisper. "I can feel him dying right in front of me, and it hurts, Syd. You brought him to me the first time he was about to die, and now you're killing him, every moment you hold me."

Syd looked over Rebecca's shoulder at the form of his dying thrall. He shook his head.

"Rebecca...no..." Syd lowered his Master's gaze to the floor in the ultimate gesture of vampiric submission. "I beg of you. Please...don't do this."

"I have to," she whispered. "He saved me, and you, and...and all of us. I'll be okay. I trust you. I've always trusted you. Trust me now."

Syd didn't reply in words. He simply nodded and let his arms fall, releasing her.

Rebecca stepped away from him and went to Ryan.

The dark-haired boy turned his head toward her, arms clutched tight to his sides. Dark liquid—the blood he'd taken from her and used in place of his own—coated his mouth and chin. Rebecca knew there was nothing of Ryan behind the black eyes that looked at her, but that didn't stop her from taking the dying vampire's shoulders and forcing him to sit back against the bed.

She leaned forward and spoke Ryan's name.

The vampire attacked.

Rebecca opened her eyes and blinked a few times. She was so tired! It felt like she'd...

Like she'd had the life drained out of her. She turned her head and saw Ryan lying beside her on the bed, blue eyes open and staring at the ceiling.

He was still there, and sleeping like a vampire.

"I did it," she murmured, smiling as she closed her eyes again.

"You did indeed," she heard Syd say. "I would never have thought it possible, even for a Healer as powerful as you are."

She felt the bed beside her sink under weight and her hand being taken. Warm lips brushed against her knuckles, and she smiled more.

"My gratitude for the restored life of my thrall."

"You're not going to be like this all the time now, are you?" she asked.

"Like what?"

"You know 'like what'," Rebecca said as she took a deep, deep breath. She could feel her strength returning to her—her blood coursing through her veins, her heart beating against her ribcage, her Healer's mark tingling and pulsing with warmth. "All protective and hovering."

"I assure you, I am not 'hovering'," Syd replied. Rebecca could hear the amusement in his tone. She felt the heavy weight of sleep start to descend upon her.

"Are so. Go 'way. Want to sleep a bit."

"And so you shall."

Rebecca really thought her need to recover would have made getting up in the morning hard, but she woke up feeling absolutely fine. Ready to start the day.

To start her *birth*day. Her seventeenth birthday.

The room was a shade of light gray made by the barely-risen morning sun. She looked up at the ceiling, thinking. She didn't *feel* any different. In fact, all she felt was really good. Not tired, not strange.

Strange. Stranger.

Rebecca shook her head at herself and rolled her eyes. She sighed and was really glad it was the weekend, and she could go back to sleep if she wanted to.

No one should have to go to school on their birthday, she thought and looked over at her bedside clock.

Her brow furrowed. She couldn't read the red digital numbers. There were parts of them visible, and those were fuzzy. Maybe she was tired, after all. It had been a late and scary night last night.

Rebecca blinked a few times and rubbed her eyes before she switched on her lamp and looked at the clock again.

"WAH!" she cried, flinching back from her night-table and the thing—*things*—that were glommed onto the face of her clock.

A chorus of what sounded like giggling greeted her.

"Festive being born!" three little voices sang out.

One of the slug-looking things—the tallest one at about four inches—detached from the clock face and wriggled toward her bed.

Rebecca tried hard not to cringe away even further, but she really hated snakes, and whatever this three-eyed thing was, it looked far too much like a slimy snake for her.

"Is us before others?" it asked, blinking at her.

"W-what?" she stammered.

"Us wants greet the Mistress Healer festive-being-born day before the others! Us is?" the thing asked again.

Rebecca somehow understood what it wanted to know.

"Yes, you...uh...all are the very first to wish me a happy birthday," she said.

The creature beamed and turned back to the others it was with. It said something in a language Rebecca didn't know, and the other beings cheered and waved their...tentacles...or whatever they were.

"Uh, my gratitude," Rebecca managed to stammer. She gave them a big smile.

"Festive, festive-being-born Mistress Healer!" the creature said again. Then it bowed to her and went back to the other slug-snakes. The others bowed as well, and with a wiggle that looked like they were dancing, all disappeared.

Rebecca collapsed back down into her bedcovers, face first into her pillow. Was it always going to be like this? Were little...things—or maybe big things—going to just pop up out of nowhere at her, and then pop back to wherever?

She raised her head again and looked at her slug-snake-free clock.

ALL WOUNDS • 201

There was no way she was going back to sleep after *that* wake-up.

Rebecca left her bedroom and padded down the hall in the pre-dawn light. She smiled at the sight in the living room. Sleeping Healers of every age and ethnicity took up almost the entire space. A large brown furry lump snored in the middle of them.

A warm mug was pressed against her hand.

"Oh!" Rebecca said, startled.

The older Frenchwoman—Sabine, she remembered Billy calling her—smiled at her. "It pleases me that they can sleep," Sabine said. "When I cannot. You, however..."

Rebecca blushed at the awed look the older woman gave her.

"I have never...heard...nor seen... I knew the line of Panacea was the most powerful—descended from the goddess of healing herself. An ancient line, with gifts unknown. But you..."

Sabine said something in French Rebecca didn't understand.

Rebecca rolled her eyes. "Yeah, if I'm so great, why can't I even heal a hellhound bite? Speaking of, I'd better go check on Ryan—"

"He is resting well," Sabine assured her. "Most of us have examined him. Now that he's rid of the demon taint—"

"The what?" Rebecca interrupted.

"He was tainted," Sabine said. Rebecca's confusion must have shown on her face, because the older Healer went on. "His wound. Dark magic was forced into him, and as he had no blood of his own to taint, it consumed yours, and made of him a vessel attached to only you. He was made a puppet of those...monsters that abducted us."

"But he's all right now?" Rebecca asked.

Sabine nodded. "He...you freed him."

"But I didn't do anything!" Rebecca protested.

"Did you or did you not stake him?" Sabine asked.

Rebecca blushed. "Not...not really. He was...he wasn't himself, and I just...reacted."

Sabine smiled. "Your 'reaction' saved his life."

"Still, I should see him," Rebecca said.

"You should," Sabine said.

Rebecca climbed the stairs to the enclave, wondering.

You were worth it.

He had been willing to die to save her. *Had* almost died to save her. He said he'd noticed her. *Hot Stuff.*

Rebecca entered the enclave. A petite dark-skinned woman stood, bowed her head to Rebecca and left Ryan's beside.

"Hey," she greeted her former classmate.

"Hey."

Rebecca couldn't help but smile at Ryan's greeting. He really seemed to be all right. "How do you feel?"

"Good," Ryan replied.

A strange, uncomfortable silence hung between them.

"You must be tired," she said finally.

"A bit," Ryan answered. "I'd really like to get out of here. Go home."

"I could bring up the phone, and you could call your mom," Rebecca offered.

"Not that home," said Ryan. "The lair. That's where I consider 'home'. Have for awhile now. A few years, since I fell in with Syd and the Cardozians."

"Where is Syd?"

"At the lair," Ryan replied.

Rebecca nodded. He'd said she wouldn't need him after she turned seventeen. She just hadn't figured on him being gone the moment after. "Thirsty?"

"A little."

"Feel well enough to eat something?" Rebecca asked, rolling up her pajama sleeve.

Ryan nodded a little.

Rebecca smiled and sat down beside him. He looked so down that she couldn't help but slide her hand up his back and stroke his neck with her fingers, playing with the hair that curled up at its nape.

Ryan laughed a little. "Quit it."

"Sorry," Rebecca said, but she continued for a moment longer, teasing him.

"I didn't hurt you, did I?"

Rebecca knew he was referring to his attack on her. To when she'd staked him. She shook her head. "Uh-uh."

"Good," Ryan said.

Her eyes went to his chest. "I'm glad I didn't hurt you that much," she said.

"Hey. It's my *lucky* pencil."

She giggled and he grinned at her. She held out her wrist.

He rolled his eyes and cupped the back of her neck and pulled her close. He nibbled at the mark on her neck, making her giggle again.

"Stop it!"

"Sorry," Ryan murmured, not sounding sorry at all. "I just really love that mark."

He bit down, and Rebecca closed her eyes.

No pain.

All she felt this time was warmth, like she had the first time. She felt exceptionally wonderful and...what was the word Syd used? Nurturing.

It didn't hurt at all. This was more like what Syd did, only it was warmer. Lighter. Where what Syd did was—she didn't know how to think of them, other than "formal," Ryan's bite was kind of...*friendly*, if that made any kind of sense at all.

It was certainly nicer than any other time she'd fed him. Ryan seemed to be getting the hang of it.

The best part of it was that she didn't see horrible things behind her eyes.

She was only partly aware that he'd finished when she felt him seal the wound he'd made.

He rested his head on her shoulder. Rebecca couldn't help but stroke his neck with her fingers again.

Ryan laughed a little. His voice was muffled by her shirt.

She tried to pull back to look at him and realized his own arms were tight around her waist. He was hugging her—holding her close.

Syd did the same thing when he drank from her neck. It didn't mean anything.

Ryan seemed to realize how tightly he was holding her and relaxed, letting her pull away as he sat back.

"Thanks," he said.

Rebecca nodded, and reached to pull her hair back over her neck to hide her mark.

She smiled and stopped herself. She wasn't ashamed of it anymore.

"I know you probably don't want anything to do with mirrors for a good long while, but you really should have a look at your eyes," Ryan said.

"Why?" Rebecca asked with a nervous giggle. "What's wrong with my eyes?"

"Nothing," Ryan said. "They're just...different. Brighter. No one who doesn't know you would notice."

"Well, you'd notice then, wouldn't you? Stalker," Rebecca teased.

"Seriously! They're...more than one color now. Gold on the inside, like it's taken over the blue partway, but still blue on the outside. The gold looks kind of like a star. Almost like the mark on your neck."

"Really?" Rebecca asked. "Great. Something else that makes me look strange."

"Hey," Ryan said and reached for the back of her neck again. He brought his forehead to hers and rested his head there. "You don't let anyone say anything to you about anything, especially anyone at that school.

204 • DINA JAMES

Bunch of losers there who don't know anything about anything real or important. You don't have anything to be ashamed of, you hear me?"

Rebecca nodded a little. Ryan's forehead was warm against hers.

"So...when can I go home?"

Rebecca pulled away from him. "Let me go get your jacket."

"Happy birthday, Mistress Healer!" Rebecca heard as she set the faeries' daily offering of bread and cream out on the back porch step.

Rebecca looked up. Inth was fluttering above her head with his brother Cort. They held a banner between them.

"Aw, thank you, guys! I see your wing is working, Cort," Rebecca said, smiling at the older faerie.

Cort grumbled something Rebecca couldn't hear and shook his head.

The two faeries fluttered low and offered her the banner they held. Rebecca opened her hands and they set it in them. Inth gave his brother a sidelong look.

"Idiot," Cort said, and folded his wings so fast Rebecca didn't realize he'd moved until he planted a quick kiss on her cheek. Then he disappeared, leaving Inth by himself.

Inth's brown skin darkened to near-black in embarrassment. He fluttered a moment in front of Rebecca's face before he bowed to her, then lifted his head just enough to kiss Rebecca's nose. Then he, too, disappeared.

Rebecca blushed and stood on the porch, dumbstruck for a moment before she realized her bare feet were freezing.

"My gratitude, gentlefae!" she called before she dashed back into the warm kitchen.

She smiled as she took a closer look at the birthday banner they'd presented her with. It seemed to be made of tiny strands of grass woven tight together and hung from a long twig. Words in a language she couldn't read shimmered in a kind of shiny orange ink against the tight weave of the green grass. When Rebecca touched the lettering, it was cold and hard and didn't come off on her fingers even though it looked sticky and wet.

A faerie birthday card. Who else could say they got one of those for their birthday today? Or any birthday, for that matter!

Rebecca went back down the hall to her bedroom, wanting to put the beautiful thing somewhere safe where she could look at it later.

She bumped into Sabine in the living room.

"Oh, excuse me, sorry!" Rebecca apologized. She smiled up at the older woman. "Look what the faeries made! They were waiting for me this morning and gave it to me."

Rebecca showed the faerie banner to Sabine.

Sabine's eyes widened. "What a thoughtful gift!"

"I can't read this language. Can you?"

Sabine shook her head. "I never learned to read Faerie, though it's beautiful. I do know that that's fae-amber, a hardened tree sap, they used for the letters. You might get one of the fae to translate it for you someday, but I'll bet it says something along the lines of 'happy birthday'. Honestly I'm not sure if garden faeries celebrate their birthdays or even have a word for the day they enter the world. They hatch fully-grown, you know. They must really like you, Rebecca, to have acknowledged today."

"They um...well, two of them...uh...brothers...I helped one...they each gave me a kiss," Rebecca said, blushing furiously. "But it's not like they're real boys or anything—"

Sabine laughed and shook her head. "Faerie kisses for your birthday," Sabine said. "Those are extremely good luck for mortals. I'd say this is going to be a good day for you!"

"The card alone," Rebecca said, awed. "They didn't have to do this. Oh, and um...some little slimy...slug-snakes with three eyes and tentacles were stuck to my clock this morning. They didn't need help or anything. They just wanted to be the first to wish me a happy birthday, which they sort of did...they didn't seem to know very many English words. Then they bowed and left, giggling."

Sabine laughed again. "Arionites. They love to be the first to do something, mostly because they're slow and are most often the last to manage. Their...um...slime, to use your word, is useful to Healers because it helps with skin problems of all kinds. It's also useful in patching the ectoplasm of some of the more adventurous spirits. If you don't have any on hand, you might talk to the Arionite king about obtaining some."

"Slime? I need slime?"

Sabine nodded. "Drool, slime, and some things you really don't want to think about where it comes from. Healers use a great many tools. When you think about it, it makes a kind of sense. We heal all wounds, and sometimes the one thing that will heal a being might be the very thing that injured it in the first place. You might have tried hellhound saliva on Ryan's hellhound bite. Hellhound saliva is extremely cleansing, especially where dark magic is involved, though it's very dangerous to use due to how caustic it is. It's equally dangerous to obtain. It's not as though you can simply ask a hellhound to drool into a bowl for you, even if you had a bowl their drool wouldn't disintegrate. It takes a special container to hold some things, and that's one of them."

"Wow," said Rebecca. "I have a lot to learn. I would never have... thought of something like that."

She looked down at the card in her hands and smiled again. "I'd better put this away and get back up to Ryan. He's ready to go home, and needs his things."

Rebecca leaned against the enclave door, watching Ryan shrug into his lucky black leather jacket.

He straightened his arms and held them out for Rebecca's inspection.

"Well, am I fit for expulsion?"

Rebecca laughed. "Nairhoft has always thought so."

"'Scuze us, Bit," Billy called from the enclave door. "This lot's had enough of my charming company and are ready to head for home."

"Come on in," Rebecca said, beckoning them in with a wave of her hand.

"Shouldn't be no trouble, but I'm goin' with just in case," said Billy as he entered with a group of the rescued Healers. He gestured at the portal. "Never know what might be waitin' on the other side."

Billy had replaced the mirror he'd ripped apart with—of all things—two old car doors. Welded one on top of the other and installed by the anubi himself into the wall, Billy had deliberately taken the glass out of the windows and removed the side mirrors. He wasn't taking any chances with reflective surfaces in the enclave. Rebecca was surprised he hadn't smashed the bathroom mirrors as well.

"Now you don't go nowhere 'til I get back," he continued, giving Rebecca a stern glare. "Promise?"

Rebecca nodded. "Promise."

"Good." He turned to the women behind him. "After you gals," he said, flashing them his lady-killer grin as he opened the car-door portal with its vintage 1970s push-button handle.

The younger Healers looked at one another and suppressed giggles while the older, married women just rolled their eyes. One by one, they disappeared into the wall hidden behind the car door. As the last woman vanished, Billy winked at Rebecca and hopped in after them, slamming the portal-cover behind him.

She laughed. She must be the only enclave to have old car doors for a portal cover. After talking with some of the other Healers, she'd learned a lot about things they did differently, and things they did the same. Rebecca had exchanged e-mail addresses with Sabine and a few of the other Healers. Some of them were even on Facebook and Twitter like...regular people.

Like Regular people, not the Strangers they were. Strangers like her.

Well, maybe not *just* like her. Still, it was nice to have someone to talk to about things, even if they did hold her in some kind of awe or esteem.

That was going to be hard to get used to.

"I'll take that as a yes," Ryan said, and Rebecca blushed as she remembered he was there.

She smiled at him, and didn't know what to say.

Ryan grinned at her and caught her by the back of the neck. He pulled her close and hugged her tight.

Rebecca breathed in the scent of his leather jacket and sighed. She knew he wasn't her boyfriend or anything, but still, it was nice to be hugged by someone other than her nana or Robin.

"Thanks for everything," he said. "I wouldn't be here if it wasn't for you."

"I wouldn't be here if it weren't for you! Thanks for loaning me your pencil," Rebecca replied, blushing.

Ryan laughed and held her away as he looked down at her.

"What?" Rebecca said. "I just realized, I never said 'thank you'!"

"Did too," Ryan countered. "There in detention, when I loaned it to you. Never thought you'd end up saving my life with it. Thanks, Hot Stuff."

She looked up at him, surprised to hear the sincerity in his usually flippant tone. "Um...you're welcome. And...and thank you, for saving mine."

Ryan leaned down and captured her lips for the briefest of moments.

Rebecca blushed again as a feeling that wasn't her Healer's ability tingled through her before he let her go.

"Anytime," he said as he walked to the car door portal. "I promised Syd I wouldn't try shifting until I've had some training. He says I've done enough fancy maneuvers on my own. I guess he's right, and I know how to use one of these things."

"Be careful," Rebecca cautioned, then chastised herself for being stupid. Just because he'd kissed her didn't make him her boyfriend, and that was the kind of thing Marla Thompson said to her latest guy. Rebecca told herself it was just the Healer in her talking.

Ryan didn't seem to notice what she'd said, or thought the same thing. "See ya."

Then he opened the portal cover and disappeared.

CHAPTER EIGHTEEN

"Oh, now that is so unreal!" Billy said with a snort. He threw a piece of popcorn at the TV.

"Hey," Rebecca said, pinching his furry ear in retaliation. "Don't make a mess, or I'll make you vacuum."

Billy scowled and looked up at her. "You and mess. A little dirt won't kill you, you know."

"I mean it, Wolfman," she said. "And I know how much you love the vacuum."

Billy snorted again and turned his attention back to the program. Rebecca smiled and wrapped her arms around Billy's neck and kissed the top of his furry head. Billy growled in contentment, wriggling as he snuggled back against her. Anubi, Nana had told her upon her arrival back home shortly after Ryan left, were social creatures—pack animals—and enjoyed physical contact with those they considered part of their pack. Billy had made it beyond clear that she was "his Little Bit" and didn't like to let her out of his sight, even for necessary things like school. Nana hadn't been exactly thrilled that Rebecca had asked Billy to stay on permanently—something about the rules of anubi dens and pack hierarchy—but she didn't seem to mind the extra help around the house. Besides, Billy wasn't the average anubi, and Rebecca reasoned that the usual rules about dens and such didn't apply to him. Nana hadn't agreed, but didn't negate her. Billy loved his garage den and tinkering with Nana's old Pontiac Bonneville, and for all he ate and made huge messes, the big guy made sure "his girls" were kept warm, safe and fed. With Billy around there was always vast amounts of food and enough wood in the house to keep a nice fire in the fireplace. Rebecca knew Nana wouldn't ever admit it, but her grandmother enjoyed having the werewolf around. Nana could make huge batches of cookies and biscuits and whatever else she wanted and never had to worry about it being too much.

"Look at her! That ain't how you show dominance, you Mortal

mutt! Bit, this is dumb! Why you wanna know how wolves act anyway? You got me! I'll tell you all about how we act!"

"From what I've gathered, you're not real great at acting how you should," Rebecca replied, rolling her eyes. "So if I'm going to learn about animal behavior, Nana said to watch nature programs, so there you go. I'm watching. I can do without the commentary, thank you!"

"I need more popcorn," Billy said, looking at the empty bucket he held. Massive though he might be, Billy was fast and agile, and gone from the living room floor almost before he'd finished his sentence.

Rebecca laughed and shook her head as she turned her attention back to the television.

Or she would have, had her lap not been suddenly invaded by a... thing.

A big thing...bigger than Mishka, with green eyes that studied her with an intensity Mishka never had. Dark stripes like eyeliner ringed its eyes, sweeping in a point back toward its neck. Rebecca held her hands up, careful not to touch it, and sat very, very still.

Whatever it was, it was very light. Rebecca's eyes widened further as the thing pressed its very large paws into her thighs one after the other, like she'd seen Mishka do with Nana. It didn't make any sound, but it closed its eyes and looked extremely content.

"Um, hi," Rebecca said, hesitant as she continued holding her hands up. "Can I help you?"

A soft chuckle came from the dark corner near the old fireplace, and Rebecca looked up to see the blue glow of Syd's eyes there. The tall blond vampire moved from the shadow and smiled at her.

"I wondered if he would take to you," Syd said, amused. "He's very particular about who he likes."

Billy came back with a very full bucket of popcorn in his arms and scowled at the creature occupying Rebecca's lap and hands. "I'm gone two minutes and you're already huggin' some other guy. Hey, Judas. Hey, Syd."

The...thing...on Rebecca's lap glared up at Billy as the werewolf made himself comfortable again, reaching for Rebecca's raised arm to drape around his neck as he sat down. She lowered the other arm, careful to keep it away from the small creature on resting on her legs.

"'Judas'?" Rebecca echoed, looking up at Syd.

"His name. I brought him for Martha," Syd said. "May I?"

He gestured to the couch next to Rebecca.

"Yeah, sure, but Nana already has a cat, and I don't think Mishka will like him," she said, moving her legs a little to make room for Syd to sit down. Judas glared at her movement then closed his eyes again,

210 • DINA JAMES

settling down against Rebecca's thighs.

"Look, Judas, I don't mean to be rude, but um...that's *my* leg you're sitting on, so...if I need to move it...sorry, kitty," Rebecca said.

Syd laughed again. "He may look feline, but I assure you, he's no housecat, and despite the complete contradiction he's displaying at the moment, labyrinthines are known for their extreme aloofness and partiality. See if he'll let you pet him."

"*This* is a *labyrinthine*?" Rebecca said, incredulous. She knew very little about the cat-like creatures, save that they were extremely powerful Ethereal beings and rarely let themselves be seen by anything save their own kind. Yet here was one sitting on her lap like he owned it. One—had it been this one?—had injured Cort the garden faerie. She wondered how Syd managed to know one well enough to have it as a friend. "Wow. And you call him 'Judas'? Why?"

"Because he's a traitor," Syd said, reaching to pet the labyrinthine. Judas opened an eye, offered Syd a baleful look, then got up and moved from Rebecca's legs to her chest.

"Whoa, hey!" Rebecca said as Judas forced her to hold him.

"Hey, that's my hug you're stealing!" Billy protested as Rebecca's arm left his neck to hold the creature. Billy scowled at the labyrinthine. "I don't care what Syd says. You're evil and that's all there is to it."

Judas didn't seem bothered by the insult and settled down in Rebecca's arms.

Rebecca looked taken aback for a moment, then reached to rub the creature's ear.

Judas went limp in her arms. He butted the bottom of her chin with his forehead, pleased.

"Traitor," Syd mumbled in disgust. "As I was saying, I brought him for Martha. He will...assist with power in my stead. That and he gets lonely, though he would never admit it, with me gone all the time. He needs company. I thought that, since Billy is staying here and as I spend a great deal of time here with your training, he might be more comfortable here instead of at the lair."

"I...um...I don't know anything about the care and feeding of labyrinthines," Rebecca admitted.

"Well, then we have tonight's lesson before us, do we not?" Syd replied with a smile. He looked to the television. "That is...after your program. Arctic wolves, are they? Oh, this should fascinate Billy."

The anubi growled. "Watch it or I'll have you for dinner."

"How's Ryan?"

"Well. Hunting," Sydney replied.

"How's he doing with that?" she asked. She was a little hurt that Ryan hadn't at least been to see her in the two weeks since he'd been allowed to leave the enclave. It had made her feel like she wasn't just pretending to be a Healer to see his wound disappear and his health restored.

Was he avoiding her? Because he'd kissed her? And if he was, why did it matter? It's not like he'd ever paid attention to her before he was a vampire. Rebecca supposed she'd just gotten so used to him being upstairs, checking on him and talking with him. She realized she missed that. Missed him.

"Doing well," Sydney replied.

Rebecca remembered that Sydney could hear her thoughts and tried to shield them as he'd been teaching her.

"Tell him I miss him, won't you?" Rebecca asked. "And I wonder how he's doing. If he gets a chance to stop by, that would be cool."

"I shall pass the message on," Syd replied. He looked like he was going to say something else, then changed his mind and disappeared just as suddenly as he'd arrived.

Funny. Rebecca never thought she'd miss him.

But she did.

"This thing itches, and it's too tight," Billy grumbled. He pulled at the tie at his neck for the tenth time, ripping it loose.

"Billy! Leave that alone! Mrs. Reed! Billy's messed up his tie *again!*" Robin said, exasperated.

"For goodness' sake, anubi! You can endure a bloody battle but not handle a few hours wearing a tie?" Nana scolded.

"How'd I get roped into this again?" Billy asked as Nana fixed his tie once more.

"You're making Rebecca feel a little less out of place," Robin reminded him. "With you there, no one is going to notice her, and for once, she'll be happy not to be noticed."

Billy snorted and nodded toward the hallway entrance. "Gonna be hard for people to ignore *that.*"

There Rebecca stood in a strapless gown of blue silk that perfectly matched the predominant shade of her eyes. The bodice gathered under her breasts and was held in place by a jeweled pin set with diamonds and light sapphires. The remainder of the floor-length gown fell from the empire waist in a smooth sheath to the simple blue low-heeled pumps she wore on her feet.

Rebecca held up the hem of her gown so she wouldn't step on it as she walked toward them. "I have no idea how I'm going to stay upright in these shoes. I can barely walk in them, let alone dance in them."

She reached to touch her hair. It felt weird, off her neck, done up in an elegant style that showed off not only her dark Healer's mark, but the teardrop earrings she wore that were identical to the jeweled pin on her gown. A small choker of eight-pointed stars glittered at her neck.

Rebecca smiled and tried not to blush at the open-mouthed stares of the people waiting for her.

"I need to get the camera," Nana said and left the room.

"Same here!" Robin said, and dug into her clutch-purse for her cell phone.

Rebecca cringed. "You guys! It's just a dress!"

"A phenomenal dress!" Robin said. "Look up, Rebecca."

"Ro-oooo!" Rebecca protested. "Put that thing away!"

"Oh please," Robin said. "Get used to it! Everyone's going to be taking pictures of you tonight, so just deal!"

"Maybe you should go without me," Rebecca said, looking horrified as she glanced up at Robin.

"No way," Robin said. "Now smile. You look like a deer in headlights."

Billy snorted his laughter.

Rebecca scowled at him.

"Smile, Rebecca!" Robin prompted again. "Come on. Smile for the camera! Then I'll take one of the gorgeous wolfy-boy!"

Rebecca did smile at that. Robin snapped the photo with her cell phone.

"Now one of you." Robin took Billy's photo as well and scowled as she looked at her phone. "Hey...it's all fuzzy. Hang on, let me get another one."

"Don't bother," Billy said, grinning. "Photos of Ethereals never turn out. Why do you think there ain't no pictures of us nowhere except bad sketches and horror movie props?"

"Good," Robin said with a haughty smile as she put her phone away and threaded her arm through Billy's suited one. "I don't want anyone else taking a good pic of my handsome date."

Billy groaned and shook his head, but Rebecca knew he was pleased.

"Speaking of dates, where's yours? It's getting late, and the limo will be here at seven," said Robin.

"He'll meet us there," Rebecca said. "He's...got some stuff to take care of before he gets there."

"If he looks half as good as you, then I can't wait to see you two together," Robin said with an impish smirk. "And he'd better be there. No way you're walking into that room alone. Guys would be on you in five seconds, so he'd better be there to defend you!"

"Hey! She's got me!" Billy protested.

Robin gave his arm a little shake. "No, *I've* got you, and I'm not letting you go for a second. Hope you know how to dance, Wolfy."

This time Billy grinned, even though he shook his head again.

"Who is that?"

"It's Spot!"

"Seriously?"

"No way! Where?"

"There!"

Rebecca knew her face was beet red as she heard the quiet whispers and a lot of the not-so-quiet comments upon her entry into the winter formal. It was all she could do to put one foot in front of the other. Why Robin had insisted she go first was beyond her. She and Billy were supposed to be there to distract everyone so they wouldn't notice her!

"*Who* is that she's with?"

"You've got to be kidding!"

"*Ryan Dugan?!*"

"You expect her to do any better than *him?*"

"Just ignore them, Hot Stuff," Ryan murmured to her. He had a grin plastered to his face, not caring that he was showing his fangs to everyone in the room. He saw Mr. Nairhoft was one of the chaperones and waved to him.

"Would you stop that?" Rebecca hissed in a whisper. "Everyone is looking at us! They're going to see your...uh...teeth."

Ryan grinned at her and winked. "They'll just think they're fake. Something I did to piss off Nairhoft. Which isn't bad really." He let out a low whistle. "I knew he could move, but check it out." Ryan indicated Robin and Billy with a jerk of his head. "Who knew the wolf had moves like that?"

Sure enough, Robin had Billy out on the floor, dancing to an up-tempo remix of some song from the eighties.

Rebecca was impressed. More so with Robin than Billy's dancing ability.

"Who knew she could dance in those *shoes?* She's wearing the Empire State Building in duplicate! They must make her six feet tall!"

"Billy doesn't seem to mind how tall she is," Ryan said as his arm

214 • DINA JAMES

slid around her waist. "How could he, in that dress. You can totally see she's not wearing anything under it. I'm surprised her tight-ass dad let her out of the house in that."

"He didn't. She changed at my house," Rebecca said with a smirk. She looked up at him. "What? I told you I was just getting started on my delinquency."

"Nice! Now let's scandalize the rest of this crowd with another surprise."

He pulled her close and led her onto the dance floor.

"Did you enjoy the dance?"

Rebecca smiled at the familiar voice that came from the darkest corner of her bedroom.

She let go of the earring she was about to remove and looked at the familiar figure that stood there.

"Not really," she said honestly. "I don't know what I expected. I'm never going to fit in, no matter what I look like or who I'm with."

"That's not so," Syd replied as he crossed the room to her. "You were in your own company. Your Helper, and two Ethereals. You fit in, Rebecca...just not with Regulars. I'm sorry that bothers you."

"It used to," Rebecca said. "But not so much anymore. I used to want to fit in with the crowd, but tonight..." She shook her head.

"Tonight?" Syd prompted in a whisper as he stopped in front of her.

She looked up at him, and into his eyes despite every admonition she'd been given about doing so. "Tonight I only wanted to be here with you."

The words sounded cheesy to say, but it was what she thought, and she knew he would hear them in spite of any attempt of hers to shield them.

Syd lifted his hand and curled his fingers in a slow gesture, and in them manifested a perfect white rose. He took her hand and pulled her to him, enclosing the rose between their joined palms for a moment before he laid it before the mirror she'd been using. "Though I could not accompany you, I am pleased that you went, if only so that I might see you dressed so beautifully."

Rebecca bowed her head to hide her blush. "Thanks to you. Thank you for the gown. And the loan of the jewelry. I wasn't sure...when I'd see you...to give them back."

"They are a gift," he said. "It would honor me if you would keep them."

Rebecca started to protest—the earrings and brooch were diamonds, and antiques! Worth a fortune! It had made her nervous enough to wear them out, but *keep* them?

"Without someone to make them beautiful, they're simply rocks," Syd replied to her unspoken thoughts. "If it makes you feel better, think of them as a late birthday gift. Please...keep them."

"Aren't they...special to you?"

"They are now."

He leaned down and captured her lips, stilling any further thought or words of protest.

This time, Rebecca was sure she wanted to be kissed. Her arms slid around Syd's neck as she returned his kiss, feeling for the first time that evening like herself.

Like she belonged.

"I thought you said...I thought you were...mad at me," Rebecca murmured against his lips.

"Why would you think that?" Syd asked as he rested his forehead against hers.

"You...well...you said that...that there couldn't be anything like this between us, and you haven't exactly been around all that much more than you have to be lately, and have been sending Ryan to do stuff for you, and...and you know that..."

"That you and he...got a little friendly? Yes, I know," Syd said without a trace of accusation. "I know he cares for you much more than you realize. And you care for him."

"But not...not like I...he's not like you," Rebecca said. "I mean...he doesn't make me feel like you do. He never has."

Syd pulled back and studied her for a long moment.

"What?"

"I'm trying to determine your true meaning," he replied. "If you... feel for me because I'm...me, or because I'm a Master."

Rebecca's eyes widened. He *still* thought she liked him because he was...what? Bewitching her, or something? Attracted by his power?

"You're human," Syd replied to her thoughts again. "And easily... influenced."

"Oh," was all Rebecca could manage as her arms fell from around his neck. That hurt to hear, and she didn't know why. Tears burned beneath her eyelids and she fought not to cry. She didn't want to cry in front of Syd.

Then he really would think she was making it all up. Using her tears to show she was serious or something. Rebecca hated it when girls cried

216 • DINA JAMES

to get their way, and didn't want to be one of them, or have him think that's what she was doing.

But damn it, that really hurt to hear him say. That's what he thought, when it had taken her so long to figure out why her stomach tightened at the sight of him? Why her heart beat harder when she heard his voice? Why she always felt safe and comfortable in his arms, like she belonged in them? Why she couldn't wait to get home and stay up all hours learning from him?

Why she saw him every night in her dreams and hated the morning for taking him from her?

"You dream of me?"

Rebecca couldn't reply in words—her throat had closed off, choked with her emotions. She could only nod and hate herself for the tears that escaped her control, and for being so emotional she lost the block in her mind and he'd heard her thoughts.

"Hush," Syd said as he gathered her into his arms.

His compassion only made her cry harder. She slid her arms around his waist and hugged him tight to her as she buried her wet face into his shirt.

"I'm sorry," she whispered when she could speak again. "I know this isn't what you wanted. It's not what I wanted either. I tried. I really did. Not only are you *not* human, you're centuries older than me, you're my teacher, you're a leader of your people. I'm nothing compared to everything you are—"

She felt Syd stiffen in her embrace.

"Don't say that—" he began.

She pulled away to look at him, wiping the moisture from her cheeks as she went on. "There are a hundred reasons this is the stupidest thing I've ever done. I told myself it was just...a dumb feeling. Not real. But it is. If you don't want to be around me, I understand why, but it won't change the way I feel. The way I *really* feel. This isn't some idiot crush like you're a cute guy from school or stupid made-up thing because you're this big important clan leader!"

"I didn't mean that," Syd replied. "It's just...I wanted to be sure. If we're going to acknowledge the...something...between us, we should know what it is, don't you think? I don't want someone interested in me because they're enthralled, or because being what I am makes them feel something that isn't real."

The pained, earnest look on his face clarified his words for her. "You don't have anyone already? I thought...you and Billy have said things about 'her' before. Who is she? I know you must care about her."

Syd nodded. "I do, a great deal. Her name is Aymi, and she's a very special member of my clan. You'll meet her, someday, when you're both ready. She requires some extra care and supervision, but she's not Lady Cardoza. There's no merit in devotion without heart. I could have willing, adoring companions if I wished it. I don't." He reached for her again and wrapped his arms around her, resting his chin atop her head. "I keep thinking back to that night you begged me to let you heal Ryan, in spite of my wishes. You said you trusted me. No one has ever told me they trusted me before. I'm a Master. Trust isn't something I think about having. I just know it's there. I suppose I just...always assumed I had it. Perhaps I confused obedience for trust. To have your trust...I do not know why that frightens me. The thought of losing that, or betraying it in some way... Rebecca, I would never...I would sooner take a stake through the heart and be tied to greet the dawn than do so."

"I know," Rebecca said. She stretched up and kissed him again. He returned it without hesitation. She deliberately met his eyes and held his metallic blue gaze. "Do you honestly think I'd fight with you if I didn't care about you? If I...if I loved you because you were a Master, I'd have done what you said that night, like someone who obeys your every word. It's how I knew what I felt wasn't because you're *what* you are, but because of *who* you are."

He peered down at her and smiled a little. "Forgive me for doubting you? And for doubting my own...inclinations?"

Rebecca giggled and nodded. "As long as you don't expect me to suddenly morph into some adoring girlfriend-type who thinks you're a god, we're good. You already know I'm not real great at that 'obey Syd' thing."

Syd laughed and smiled broader, showing his fangs. "I'm willing to forgive your obstinacy if you're willing to...love me...even though I'm not human, centuries older than you, your teacher, and a leader of my people. Now let us also hope Martha forgives me for...bewitching her granddaughter. And that the Clan forgives me for—"

Her brow furrowed at the faraway look on his face.

"For...?" she prompted when he didn't continue.

"For falling in love with a Healer."

Epilogue

The mark on her neck tingled, waking her up. Voices whispered in Rebecca's ear, adding to her state of awareness.

The enclave was calling to her.

She sat up, switched on her lamp and turned to her night-table. Ryan's lucky lighter fell over. She smiled and used it to light the candle she kept at her bedside. She was about to set the lighter back on the nightstand, then looked at it for a long moment before she tucked it into her pajama shirt's pocket.

The whispering sound came again, reminding her of her purpose. Rebecca got out of bed and switched off her lamp. Taking the candle, she left her room and started down the hallway.

A low growl reached her ears. Rebecca froze.

"Where you think you're goin'?" Billy's sleepy voice asked.

Argh. Rebecca had forgotten Billy was denning in the hallway entrance instead of his garage den this week. With the winter solstice approaching, he said he wanted to keep a close eye on her just in case. Apparently he didn't entirely trust Rebecca's revocation of the oath of neutrality to keep demons out of the house.

It's too late for them to be interested in me now anyway, right? She was already seventeen.

"I heard something," Rebecca whispered.

"Don't hear nothin'," Billy replied with a snort.

Wow, he was grouchy when he woke up.

"Hush!" Rebecca admonished, lifting her candle up a little so she could better see the stairwell. "I need to go up there."

"Not alone you ain't," Billy grumbled as he got to his feet.

"Okay," she whispered with a nod.

Billy snorted again and got down on all-fours, nudging her hip with his shoulder in an Anubin gesture of reluctant acquiescence.

"Thanks, Billy," Rebecca said as she laid a hand on the werewolf's massive head between his ears.

Taking a deep breath, Rebecca held the candle up high, well away from Billy. Together they went upstairs. Rebecca opened the linen closet door and reached in, pushing the knot that swung the shelves back and revealed the entrance to the enclave.

Rebecca cringed as the movement of the shelves seemed to scrape the floor louder than usual. Was it always that loud? Or was it only loud because she didn't want her nana to wake up?

"Wait out here," Rebecca ordered the anubi in a whisper.

"Was going to," Billy growled as quietly as he could. "You be careful."

"I will," she promised.

Billy growled and nodded.

Holding the candle in front of her, Rebecca stepped into the passageway behind the linen closet shelves that led to the Healer's enclave hidden behind it.

Nothing greeted her. It was completely dark inside, but that didn't mean anything. A lot of things needed complete, or nearly complete, darkness. It's why she used candles and not anything brighter.

"Hello?" Rebecca called, remembering to use the low, soothing Healer's voice.

A tingle of fear tightened her insides and she fought to quell a shiver. She was a true Healer now, but would she know what to do?

Rebecca forced herself to think and focus and trust herself. Of course she would know. The knowledge was there, inside her. She just had to let it come to her, and that was hard. It was harder if she fought it or panicked. She took a deep breath and let herself relax, trying to feel what was in the room. What she was needed for.

A faint light caught her attention over by the restored portal. Rebecca held her candle up again and took a careful step toward it. She recognized light like that. Only one being illuminated itself with fire.

A hellhound.

One that size could only be young, and Rebecca couldn't help but smile at the picture that entered her mind. They were adorable when they were young.

Scary, of course, but adorable.

Setting her candle down without a sound, Rebecca lowered herself to her knees and bowed her head. She remembered that respect and deference were extremely important to hellhounds, and Rebecca thought it best not to insult this one, no matter how old it might seem to be.

Though she kept her eyes on the floor in front of her, Rebecca could see the faint, glowing red light move closer. It was hesitant, and Rebecca wondered why.

She waited and didn't say anything. The light dimmed slightly as it approached her, then stopped. Rebecca looked up to see a young, crimson-eyed hellhound, blacker than the darkest night and swathed in flame that didn't scorch its surroundings, holding a bright yellow daffodil in its mouth.

"Hello," Rebecca said in her most gentle voice, smiling at the hellhound puppy.

The slobber-drenched daffodil was deposited on the floor at her knees. Rebecca picked it up.

"Thank you," she said with sincerity as she brought it to her nose. "May I have the honor of your name?"

"They gonna hurt my mama," the thing said, not bothering to answer her question. "And Father."

"Who is?" Rebecca's heart seemed to stop beating for a moment. *Is something attacking the Hell Realm in retaliation for the Healers being kidnapped?*

The poor thing was trying hard not to tremble, and Rebecca could hear the fear in the little one's voice. He was being brave, but she knew he was really scared.

"The ones without souls," he said, his red candle-eyes widening as they dimmed a fraction. "I saw it, in my head. I was sleeping and they came and hurt my mama."

Rebecca bit her bottom lip and thought a moment.

"You were sleeping when you saw this?"

The little hellhound gave a slow nod of his fiery black head, looking less like a tiny black wolf cub with a shark's mouth and more like a scared puppy.

A bad dream. He was telling her he had a bad dream. Hellhounds had dreams? Why not? Dogs did. Anything that slept probably had dreams.

"They hurt Kaia, and Jaia too," the young hellhound continued. "And Porl, he don't run so good as the rest of us."

His littermates, she understood. Rebecca's heart ached for the scared little hellhound who had brought her the traditional Healer's flower in the hopes that she might make his bad dream go away.

Poor little hound. He wasn't hurt on the outside, but he was hurting on the inside. Rebecca did the only thing she could think to do. She held her arms out.

The hellhound puppy came immediately to her and all but jumped into her arms. She hugged him close and stroked the black fur down his back, marveling yet again at how the flames didn't burn her or anything else.

"They won't come," Rebecca soothed. "I know a couple of those 'ones without souls', and I'll tell them not to."

"They won't listen. They'll come and hurt us!" The little thing sniffed and started to cry.

Oh, man. A crying hellhound. Oh, cripes.

"Hey," she said, stroking her hand down his back. Wow, was he soft. She'd never felt anything so soft. "What's your name?"

"I'm Noth," the little hellhound replied. "I'm the oldest."

"That's a nice name," Rebecca soothed. She hugged him closer and rocked with him, slow and gentle, wondering how on earth was she supposed to help a scared, crying hellhound puppy.

She remembered something Nana had told her.

"*Compassion*," Nana had said. "*You'll need that in abundance, because sometimes, that's all you can offer. Sometimes that's all something needs to heal on its own—a safe place to stay and a compassionate hand to hold.*"

A safe place to stay...and this little guy had come to her to make it better. She looked again at the little hellhound, already half-asleep against her neck.

"Want to sleep here with me for a while?" Rebecca asked. "Bad dreams can't come in this room."

The black pup nodded and cuddled tighter against her.

"All right," she said. "If you're sure your mama won't eat me for this. Come on. I'll even stay here with you to make sure no bad dreams try and come here."

The hellhound puppy giggled. "Mama won't eat you! I won't tell," he assured her, already half asleep. "Father said you help hurt things, so you'll help if they hurt us..."

Father? Noth? Is this one of Lord Notharion's babies? A...Nothlet? She remembered what the chief of the Hellguards had said to her.

You and I will have an interesting relationship.

"I sure will," she assured the baby hellhound, and walked out of the enclave.

Billy was still there, waiting. Rebecca held a finger to her lips, warning the anubi to be quiet. She pointed to the hellhound puppy.

"Bad dream," she whispered.

"So?" Billy growled, unsympathetic. "What are you going to do with him?!"

"Stay up here with him while he gets some sleep," Rebecca said. "Look at him! He's so tired. He can't sleep at home."

"Bit, that's a damned hellhound!" Billy argued, scowling. "They guard the Hell realm, and answer to Hellspawn! Want to tangle with demons again? You're asking for it if you don't put that thing back or send him home or something! Get rid of him!"

Rebecca scowled back at the anubi. "He's not a 'thing', he's a baby! Have you already forgotten what it's like not to be able to sleep because you're afraid something might happen now that *you* have a safe place to stay?"

Billy didn't reply to that, but Rebecca could tell by his raised hackles and stiff tail that he wasn't happy about her being so close to a hellhound, no matter how young it was.

"You watch that thing's teeth," Billy growled darkly. "He'll tear your throat out as soon as look at you."

"He will not," Rebecca replied. "He's not like that. Don't ask me how I know. He just needs a safe place to be tonight, and I'm going to help him."

Billy growled again, unhappy, but resigned. "Your hide. Goin' back to sleep. Martha gets up before I see you in the morning, I'll tell her you're up here with the flaming furball."

"Thanks, Billy."

The werewolf snorted and went back downstairs to sleep. Rebecca went back into the enclave and curled up on Ryan's former bed, the hellhound puppy cuddled against her shoulder. She stroked his back and kissed the little hellhound's nose.

He was already asleep and snuffled against her neck as he cuddled closer to her warmth.

She wondered if she was the first human to ever curl up for a nap with a hellhound.

She'd have to ask her nana in the morning.

About the Author

Dina James is an unapologetic geek/gamer girl addicted to writing. She graduated from high school when she was sixteen, holds a college degree in nothing in particular in addition to multiple certifications in various things that captured her interest at the time, is an avid knitter and loves Darth Vader. She lives in Oregon with her husband and a menagerie of pets. She has website at www.dinajames.com which has a far-more-comprehensive biography than this one. It mentions sushi.

Coming Soon from Mundania Press...

Time Heals

A Stranger Things Novel

Dina James

CPSIA information can be obtained at www.ICGtesting.com
Printed in the USA
LVOW101748111111
254490LV00001BA/25/P